HOLLY

HOLLY

A BELLADONNA NOVELLA

ADALYN GRACE

WITH ILLUSTRATIONS BY LOTUSBUBBLE

First published in Great Britain in 2025 by Gollancz
an imprint of The Orion Publishing Group Ltd
Carmelite House, 50 Victoria Embankment
London EC4Y 0DZ

An Hachette UK Company

The authorised representative in the EEA is Hachette Ireland, 8 Castlecourt Centre, Castleknock Road, Castleknock, Dublin 15, D15 XTP3, Republic of Ireland (email: info@hbgi.ie)

1 3 5 7 9 10 8 6 4 2

Copyright © Adalyn Grace 2025

The moral right of Adalyn Grace to be identified as the author of this work has been asserted in accordance with the Copyright, Designs and Patents Act of 1988.

Illustrations copyright © 2025 by Lydia Elaine (@LotusBubble)
Interior art credits: Watercolor window frame landscape © dadyda/Shutterstock.com; holly leaves © Elena_Medvedeva/Shutterstock.com; grunge speckle texture © v_kulieva/Shutterstock.com; watercolor trees © ArtMari/Shutterstock.com; winter background © Natalya Svetlova/Shutterstock.com; snow landscape © Innoria/Shutterstock.com; watercolor sky with snow © Anna.zabella/Shutterstock.com; watercolor mountain landscape © ilustrasiasrori/Shutterstock.com; black wall texture © Ton Photographer/Shutterstock.com; ornament © L Studio Design/Shutterstock.com

Interior design by Jenny Kimura and Neil Swaab

All rights reserved. No part of this publication may be reproduced, stored in a retrieval system, or transmitted in any form or by any means, electronic, mechanical, photocopying, recording, or otherwise, without the prior permission of both the copyright owner and the above publisher of this book.

All the characters in this book are fictitious, and any resemblance to actual persons, living or dead, is purely coincidental.

A CIP catalogue record for this book is
available from the British Library.

ISBN (Hardback) 978 1 399 63276 8
ISBN (Export Trade Paperback) 978 1 399 63277 5
ISBN (eBook) 978 1 399 63279 9
ISBN (Audio) 978 1 399 63280 5

Printed in Italy by L.E.G.O. S.p.A.

www.gollancz.co.uk

In a town that looks like a fairy tale, there lives a girl who believed in this Christmas novella long before I did. This one is for her.

I'm sorry I changed the title, but I hope she loves what's inside.

ONE

Blythe

I T'S SAID THAT THE HOLLY SPRIG HAS LONG been used to ward off evil spirits.

As Blythe Dryden stood with her hands on her hips, assessing the foyer of Wisteria Gardens, she pondered how much of the plant she'd need to decorate with to ensure the most magnificent holiday season. Then she added another bough over the entryway, just for good measure.

It was fortunate that she'd mastered her powers since learning she was the reincarnation of Life, as Blythe could now grow as much holly as it took to repel demons, spirits, or any other mischievous deities that decided to take a sudden interest in her family. She'd shove every bough down their throats if necessary, because this year, they were all going to have a perfect Christmas.

Wisteria had transformed since Aris's return. For years Blythe had missed the magic that once pulsed through the home's very essence. Now, with its owner returned, Wisteria's heart had resumed its proud beating. Giant statues of fantastical beasts loomed near the grand oak doors, welcoming all who entered into a spacious foyer adorned with intricately carved nutcrackers taller than she was, and well-decorated snowmen that never seemed

to melt. The gold-trimmed ceiling showcased a perfect wintry sky, painted with stars and snowflakes.

The hearth burned bright, its flames matching the warm pink glow of strange sconces that lit the room. One of them was shaped like a boar and matched the handle of Blythe's old bedroom from when she'd first arrived at the palace, betrothed to a man she despised. The memory had her smiling as she draped another bough of holly over its tusks, her heels clicking a familiar echo across the marble floors. Withdrawing several paces to admire her work, Blythe startled when she backed into a firm chest. Strong arms slipped around her, embracing her from behind, and Blythe relaxed into the warmth of the familiar touch. Into a comfort that she wished she could bottle up and carry with her forever.

"You've outdone yourself," Aris noted, pulling her closer. She folded into him, tipping her head to the side as he bent to kiss it. Her eyes fluttered shut as he peppered kisses down her neck, and she squealed when he ended one of them with a gentle nip.

"It's not too much?" she asked, forced to finally take stock of her hard work. It was, admittedly, very green. But that was nothing some well-placed ornaments couldn't fix.

"Nothing you do will ever be too much." His lips curled devilishly as they sank down to her bodice.

"Liar." Blythe snorted, slipping her fingers into his blond locks to keep him close. It'd been only four months since her husband had returned to her, and Blythe was still familiarizing herself with this new body of his—broader chested and a few inches taller

than his previous form. His jawline was squarer and more pronounced, his skin a shade darker, and while the changes were just enough to feel jarring, there was enough about Aris that had felt familiar from the moment she'd laid eyes on him. One look and she'd known that the missing piece of her soul had finally made its way home to her.

His eyes were the same, as were the deftness of his clever hands and the way that light always seemed to pull toward him. There were a few *other* differences as well, though certainly none that Blythe could complain about. In fact, she'd probably be continuing to familiarize herself with those differences now, if not for the fact that it was just days before Christmas and their family was in town to celebrate.

Family who did not seem to understand when to make themselves scarce.

"At least there will be no mistaking which holiday we're celebrating," Sylas noted from behind, announcing his arrival with a gentle clearing of his throat. Aris groaned against Blythe's skin, begrudgingly peeling himself away, though he kept one arm slung around her hips.

"A bell, brother," Aris declared. "I shall secure a bell to that cowl of yours before Christmas is through, I swear it."

"I would love to see you try." The cowl in question slipped from his figure alongside his shadows, revealing Death's human form. Sylas was dressed in a dapper black suit with polished boots, and his bone-white hair was tied at the nape of his neck. The only bit of skin he showed was from the collar up, his hands obscured in leather gloves to prevent any unintended harm from his lethal touch.

Taunting seemed to be one of the reaper's

favorite pastimes, and he sported a grin reminiscent of Blythe's father's whenever he had a particularly favorable hand at cards. Sylas crossed the foyer to stand beside his brother, head tipped back to admire the boughs of holly.

He arched a brow at her. "Are you feeling particularly festive this year, dear sister?"

Blythe shot the reaper a sour look, feeling foolish that she'd ever allowed herself to fear this ridiculous man. It'd taken her several months to breathe easy around Sylas after first meeting him, but now, years later, he was a comfort. A strange and curious man with an odd sense of playfulness she rather enjoyed in a brother. It was a nice change of pace, especially considering that the last one had tried to kill her. Twice.

"I'm no fool," she told him. "Our collective luck does not tend to hold up well on

Christmas. We need every bit of good fortune we can get if we're to make it through the holidays unscathed."

"It's only another day," Sylas told her. "You will find no better or worse luck because of it."

Perhaps, but history had Blythe unwilling to take that risk. Upon Aris's return, the two had made the decision to move Wisteria Gardens, which had drawn too much attention to remain safe where it was. They had finally decided on a new town—one right on the outskirts of Brude, a city Blythe had fallen in love with and whose very bones reminded her of falling in love with Aris. And with Elijah fully aware of the truths of his family and what they were, either Sylas or Aris could retrieve him from anywhere for a visit. Now Blythe had her father, a new brother, her dearest cousin, and the love of her life. And with them all, she was determined to make their very

first Christmas together as a true family positively perfect. Or else someone would pay.

For years she'd awaited this moment, remembering the single Christmas that she and Aris had spent together as a pair. It was during the holidays that she'd first realized she loved him. It was then that they had slept together for the first time. For twenty-seven years after that, Blythe's bed had remained cold and her heart was left aching. But this year, all would be perfect. They deserved that much.

He deserved that much, and she didn't want anyone to take this from them.

And speaking of Aris... Blythe disentangled herself from her husband's grasp, voice lowering as she approached Sylas. "How is that *thing* I asked for your help with?" she asked, choosing her words carefully. She could practically feel Aris's curiosity festering.

"I intend to take care of the present very soon," Sylas offered with a smug grin that he turned decidedly toward Aris. "It's quite a good one."

"A present?" Aris echoed. Blythe hadn't expected her husband to look so affronted. "But I don't need anything."

"You are my husband and this is to be our first Christmas together where neither of us is dead or dying," Blythe said with the utmost sternness. "It's a cause for celebration, Aris. Of *course* I'm going to get you something." And for good measure she added, "Sylas has been instructed not to give you so much as a hint, so don't even try."

"I'm very good at keeping my word," Sylas announced proudly, hands folded behind his back. "And secrets, for the most part. Tell me what you got for Blythe and I'll keep yours, too."

"You're as nosy as my wife," Aris admonished, to which Sylas only shrugged.

"As if you aren't?"

"Nosiness is perhaps the one thing this family has in common," Blythe said. "Though, I'm sure to everyone's surprise, I wish to know nothing about my gifts. If you insist on discussing them, you may take your conversation elsewhere." She nudged Aris away.

"It'll be fine. Now get out of here, both of you. I've more decorating to do, and you're in my way." From her bare palm emerged yet more holly, and Sylas laughed.

"Very well," he said. "Join me for a drink, brother?"

"Later, perhaps." Aris was already glancing behind his shoulder, seeming lost in thought. "There's something I must check on first."

"Could that something have to do with finding a present?"

Aris's brows pulled lower. "You are a blight upon humanity."

Sylas only smiled as Aris bent to kiss Blythe quickly on the head before he brushed past his brother, disappearing in a hurry down the hall.

In his absence, Blythe sighed. "Must you always tease him so?"

The reaper smiled. "I'm afraid it's how we show our love."

"Well, your love seems to have put him in a panic."

"He would have been in more of one when we gave him our gift and he realized he forgot to ready one in return. Speaking of which..." Sylas peered out the window to the darkening sky. "It's time I take my leave."

"And you have faith this will work?"

He adjusted his gloves, triple-checking them before setting his hand atop Blythe's head and ruffling her hair. "No. But I intend to try."

Blythe went to swat his hand away, but Sylas was already gone, disappeared into the shadows.

"You really do need a bell," she called after him, smiling as she made her way back across the foyer. There was, after all, much holly left to be hung.

TWO

Aris

Aris Dryden was not a man known for his generosity. He did not often give gifts, as he despised having to constantly outdo himself the next time. Once, he might have thought to whisk Blythe away to some exotic locale, but with Elijah growing older, Aris recognized that family time held more value for his wife than any lavish trip. Moreover, Blythe had changed over the nearly three decades since they'd been

separated. The last thing he wanted was to embarrass himself with a gift that no longer suited her tastes.

She was, of course, still Blythe. Her tongue was just as sharp and she was no less a menace now than she'd been twenty-seven years ago. But time had slipped away from him, and he'd been too distracted getting Wisteria and his new life in order to have considered what he might get her.

It needed to be *spectacular*. A gift that was worthy of the woman who had waited all these years for his return. The wife who, after all this time, had finally made her way back into his life.

What did one even get for a person that special?

He'd have to get her father something, too, of course. Elijah had always been generous with

him, and if Blythe was sharing gifts, then Elijah undoubtedly would be, as well. Then there was his pest of a brother... good God, the list just kept growing. He might as well start referring to himself as Saint Nicholas, as soon he would be expected to come bearing gifts for each of their new neighbors and their children.

Aris dragged his fingers down his face, groaning. It would have been nice to discuss ideas with his brother, but Death's wagging brows and devilish smirk suggested he knew Aris hadn't yet secured a gift for Blythe. He was right, obviously, but Aris would be damned before he let his buffoon of a brother know for sure. Which led Aris to where he was now, pacing the halls in search of the single soul who might be able to help him navigate this conundrum.

He found Signa Farrow in, of all places,

the room he'd gifted to Blythe twenty-seven Christmases prior. It had been a library then, and he'd restored it to that state upon his return. He would have returned to Wisteria sooner, had he been reborn with his memories. Instead, Aris had been born to a family of dressmakers. They were a good family, and he'd lived a relatively normal life as their son for twelve years. Of course, he'd had his quirks—things he wanted would suddenly appear as he thought about them, the light always seeming to follow him in peculiar ways, skin that tended to have a faint glow, and a compulsive need to create that befuddled his family. In an effort to satisfy that need, he'd decided to apprentice under his father, and it was then that Aris had begun to realize the extent of his abilities.

He'd learned more quickly than anyone in the trade and had crafted beautiful suits

and gowns—some of which had even made their way into Blythe's hands, hanging in her armoire when he'd returned to Wisteria. She hadn't known they were his, which meant more to him than she ever could have realized. Even apart, they'd still found ways to be with each other.

Aris had spent seven years running his own shop, though the work was little more than a front as he dove deeper into his powers, realizing that his creative prowess extended well beyond clothing. The first time he'd crafted a tapestry and experienced the life of the fate he wove, Aris believed himself mad or dying. But as the urge to craft another and another struck in a hungry cycle, he realized there was something more to it. A curious magic that only he experienced.

It did not help that he chased his own

memories with every stitch, weaving some nights until his fingers bled and he lost all sense of self, simply because he knew there was something more. He would find himself reminiscing over a laugh from a voice he'd never heard and the sweetness of lips he had never tasted.

For years Aris hunted down those hints of Blythe—those glimpses of his past life—until he remembered who and what he was. He had left his shop to find Blythe that same night and had become lost in her maze of briars not an hour later. It wasn't until he'd stepped back through the doors of Wisteria Gardens with his wife in hand that his soul felt whole again.

Still, the sight had been jarring.

Wisteria's walls had all been painted with murals of Blythe's memories. He'd expected her to abandon the palace, yet there were signs of her everywhere he looked. He'd even been able

to see the phantom progression of her growth into her powers. Several walls had been torn apart with vines that eroded the stone. Certain rooms were made entirely uninhabitable, filled with thorns he never wished to think about. On the outside, though, was a garden well-tended, with flourishing hellebore and wolfsbane. Daisies and roses and flowers so beautiful they seemed as if from a dream. His chest had ached thinking about all he'd missed, though he was glad Blythe was on her way to mastering her powers even without his help.

He supposed he had his brother and sister-in-law to thank for that...

Signa sat beneath a towering Christmas tree strewn with flickering candles and dusted white. Gaudy ornaments covered branches so well decorated that Aris had to squint to see any of the greenery. Her dark hair was tied

haphazardly atop her head as bows and wrapping paper surrounded her. Death's hound lay beside her, one eye half opened. When Gundry spotted Aris, his tail began thumping against the floor, causing Signa to look up.

"Stop where you are," she demanded, her eyes narrowing as she shielded a present from view. "Give me a moment before you spoil the surprise."

It took him a beat to realize that it'd been *his* present Signa was wrapping, and he tried not to look as horrified by that as he felt.

He was lucky there was still several days left until Christmas. Several days to, apparently, find superbly wonderful gifts to shower upon everyone he knew. Which was why he was there, tossing back his tailcoat to take a seat on the floor in front of Signa Farrow once she gave her permission.

"Hello, sister." He wondered whether the day might ever come where he did not feel a faint sense of strangeness around her. How ridiculous his past self had been to believe that she could have been his soulmate. Signa was just so... well, she was odd. He'd tried to believe the quirks charming back when he was pursuing her, but now Aris often wondered whether they'd ever had anything in common. It was unlikely. Signa's curious tendencies made her a suitable fit for his brother, certainly, as Death was every bit as strange as this dark-haired oddity. But for Aris? Had he managed to force Signa into a marriage, all of them would have suffered for it. How fortunate it was that Blythe had intervened.

"Have my cousin's preparations driven you into hiding?" Signa teased, cutting a red ribbon and tying it around a small box.

"More like her insistence on a perfect Christmas." He sighed, scratching Gundry behind the ears. "It's the requirement of gifts that brings me here."

She raised a dark brow. "I'm not giving you yours early."

He wished she would, just so that he could find her one of equal measure. The last thing he wanted was to receive something extraordinary from anyone only to return the favor with some trifle.

Sorting out what gifts to get the others was exceptionally more difficult than he'd anticipated.

"I wouldn't dare ask," he told her before leaning in conspiratorially, hoping that it might draw Signa's interest. Sure enough, she followed his lead and leaned in to listen. "You see, I seem to have found myself with a problem."

She set down her supplies, more eager than he'd expected. "What sort of problem?"

"The sort where I need my sister-in-law's help to acquire the perfect gift for my wife... as well as for my father-in-law and my brother. And you, too, of course. Though I couldn't very well ask your help for that."

"No, you couldn't." She leaned back and tried to continue with her wrapping. Gundry wasn't making it easy on her, flopping onto his back with his bushy gray tail swiping her supplies around like a mop. Aris tried not to laugh at the hound's ridiculousness or encourage him, but the creature reminded him of his fox, Beasty, and the memory stung his heart. Beasty was the only one he'd truly lost. Were he able to do it over again, Aris would have liked the chance to say goodbye.

"I cannot help you with this, Aris," Signa told him. "Gifts are a personal thing, and for

those like us, the possibilities are endless. We want for nothing."

"But surely there must be something we desire? A diamond necklace, perhaps?"

Signa fished out a pair of shears from beneath the hound's tail. "I'm sure she would like a necklace..."

"But?"

"But it's not very personal. Blythe could get herself a diamond necklace any day she wants. She already has several."

He groaned and leaned back, head resting on the hound's exposed belly. "This is impossible."

"That's because you're thinking too hard. Blythe has the only thing she's wanted for decades. She has *you* back at Wisteria, and all of those she cares most about around her. Now, all she wants is an uneventful and merry Christmas."

"An uneventful Christmas," he echoed,

chewing on the words. Surely he could give her that, though he still needed something to *gift* her. "I suspect we can manage that."

"I believe we can," Signa said. "And now that you're here, you might as well help me with the wrapping." She pushed a small pile of empty boxes toward him, stacks of dolls and toys lined up behind them. Aris picked up one of the dolls, inspecting it.

"Why are there so many? Have you and my brother found a way to procreate after all?" he mused. "Should I expect little deathlings running about soon, terrorizing me from the shadows?"

Signa shot him a bland look. "Very funny. The toys are for the children at the hospital."

Ah yes. Blythe had mentioned something about Signa's new employment, but he'd forgotten the specifics.

"How are you enjoying your time there?"

"I do good work," she said, finishing off the next gift box. "Hospitals are full of souls too afraid to pass on."

It was a strange job, but they each had their own. While Death could ferry souls to the other side, it was Signa who helped spirits stuck in the land of the living. It was admirable, he supposed, though he imagined so many dead people would give him nightmares. He'd much rather stick around those still living.

Still, Aris held one of the dolls in hand, his eyes beginning to simmer a fearsome shade of gold. Beneath his fingers the fabric grew brighter, the doll's hair shimmering and its clothes taking on a luxurious hue. Within the span of a second the toy changed from basic to luxurious, and Aris moved on to the next. He made it different from the last, though just as beautiful, and Signa smiled.

"So you *can* be kind."

"Silence, wench." He tossed the doll aside for the next one. "I've a reputation to maintain."

Gundry shuffled behind them, scooting closer to the hearth. Though he looked very much like a large but otherwise perfectly normal hound, Aris knew the truth of what the beast was. He was there the day that his brother had first met Gundry.

His brother, who Aris still very much needed a gift for.

"Would you at least tell me what you got Sylas?" Aris asked, not expecting Signa's cheeks to immediately flush a deep red.

"It's between him and me," she said, and Aris wrinkled his nose, deciding some things were better left unknown. Still, it did give him at least some ideas. All Blythe needed to do was show up in their room wearing only a bow,

and he'd consider it the greatest gift he'd ever received. Unfortunately, he didn't suspect his wife would feel the same.

"You know, I was really hoping you'd be more helpful," he told Signa as he finished the dolls, moving on to tying a red bow on Gundry's collar.

"I'm sorry to be such a disappointing sister. I *am* happy you're back, though."

He was running out of things to fiddle with, and as such was forced to look solely at Signa as he replied. "As am I. You cannot know how much it means to see you all again."

It was strange, who he was becoming. For ages pain had hardened Aris's heart, but these days it was nearly impossible to be angry or bitter. Grumpy, perhaps. He was still quite good at being grumpy. But the rage that had long been burning within him had fizzled out.

How could he be angry when he now had so many reasons to feel joy? These days he felt so much lighter. Contented. *Happy*.

Aris was truly and blissfully happy, and he had this family to thank for it. Which was why finding the perfect gifts meant so much to him. These people had changed his life; it was only fair that he at least made their day special.

He scooted one of Signa's boxes toward himself, his mind sorting through various possibilities. Signa was not one who needed to fill silence with words, and they worked in a steady quiet, packaging and decorating the gift boxes, and stopping only when a sudden crash sounded against the library's bookshelves.

Gundry leapt to his paws beside Aris, who quickly put himself between Signa and the sound. The hound's hackles raised, a low growl rumbling in his throat. He was pointed directly

at the shelves, where several books lay scattered as if by some invisible gust. Aris moved toward them, bending to inspect the novels.

"What on earth..."

"Oh." Signa covered her mouth, muffling her words. "Oh dear."

Aris turned to find that she was not looking at him, but rather over his shoulder, and with great frustration he found that he recognized the look on her face. He'd seen it all those years ago, during the ball at Foxglove, when spirits had terrorized unsuspecting guests.

There was a spirit in this room, and the realization had Aris slumping onto the chaise with a sigh.

So much for an uneventful Christmas.

THREE

SIGNA

SIGNA KNEW THAT, IN THEORY, THERE were not meant to be any spirits in Wisteria Gardens. Death had helped Aris choose this land, perched upon a hill approximately a twenty-minute walk up from the city of Brude. The move had marked the start of Blythe and Aris's new life together. Their new and decidedly *unhaunted* life. And yet how else could

Signa explain the translucent young woman whose face was covered in soot?

Though the spirit had no need for breath, her chest moved as if in heavy wheezes. She had beautiful red hair that was tucked neatly against her scalp, some of the front pieces curled beneath a giant headpiece woven with garland and a pair of thin white antlers. The tops of them had been charred, the very tip of one singed off so that the antlers appeared almost lopsided.

The spirit wore a flouncy powder-pink dress that was shaped like a bell and shortened to her stockinged calves, the color strikingly vibrant. The bodice was cut low and adorned with silver lace and sparkling filigree, and on her feet she wore matching slippers. It seemed a costume of some sort, and a gaudy one at that.

The spirit assessed Signa's every move,

though her attention eventually wandered to Aris. She giggled at the sight of him, smoothing her hair and dress all while Aris lounged on the chaise, oblivious. He had one foot kicked over the opposite knee and was dragging a hand down his face to smother his groan.

"Tell me that what I think is happening is not actually happening," he said.

For the umpteenth time in her life, Signa found herself wishing that the people around her shared in her ability to see spirits. It would have been especially helpful with Aris, considering he might be able to recognize one from his tapestries. Or, at the very least, their peculiar fashions. As it was, even the spirit was growing frustrated with his obliviousness, pouting as she attempted to get his attention.

"If you're thinking that there's a spirit in

here with us, then I'm afraid I cannot assuage your worries. You would be correct." Signa set her hand atop Gundry's head, waiting to see how the hound might respond to their visitor. He was alert, but his hackles continued to lay flat, which was enough for her to take a cautious step toward the spirit.

She stepped backward immediately, eyes wide. *"You can see me?"*

The spirit's voice was higher than expected, and thick with an accent. Over the years, Signa had realized it didn't matter what language a spirit spoke—she'd always be able to understand them. She would have liked to know more about this woman, but one had to be cautious when interacting with a spirit. They may not have *seemed* malicious, but spirits were temperamental creatures. No better than toddlers, really, set off at the drop of a hat. And Signa had

far too many gifts that were in need of wrapping to risk a possession.

"Yes, I can see you," she admitted, keeping a careful distance. "What is your name?"

"My name." The spirit echoed the words several times, though they were never spoken as a question. Rather, it was as if she was testing the words out, uncertain what she thought of them. In the end, the spirit gave no answer, and asked instead, *"Have you seen Jules? He was supposed to be here by now. I have looked for him everywhere."*

"What on this blasted earth is happening?" Aris had tipped his head to watch the scene, squinting in the way people always did when they knew there was a spirit nearby, as if changing the shape of their eyes might somehow allow them to perceive it. Aris was one of the worst offenders, for it seemed there was little he liked less in life than being on the outskirts.

But the only thing he'd accomplish by squinting so hard was a headache.

Signa ignored him. "I'm afraid I don't know a Jules, though I can help you look for him. When did you last see him?"

"Yesterday." The spirit skimmed her fingers over the headpiece. It looked remarkably heavy. *"I saw everyone yesterday."*

Signa very much doubted that but said nothing to correct her. She watched as the spirit paced around the room in her strange headdress and layers of tulle, brow creasing and smoothing as she seemingly searched for this mysterious Jules.

"Yesterday," Signa repeated. "And what did you say your name was?"

The spirit's face screwed tight, then relaxed a second later. Again, she did not answer the question. Likely, Signa thought, because

she didn't remember. Signa had discovered recently that the longer a spirit roamed the earth, the more difficulty they had with their communication. It made her wonder how long the spirit had been here suffering this loop—a few decades, perhaps? It couldn't have been too long given that she was still capable of speech, even if it was a bit nonsensical.

"The door was stuck," muttered the spirit, who was no longer looking at Signa, seeming to grow lost in her thoughts. *"How else was he to get inside when the door was stuck?"* And then the spirit turned sharply toward Signa, whose spine stiffened. *"Have you seen Jules?"*

"Jules?"

Signa nearly jolted at the sound of a male voice behind her. She spun to see a second figure meandering among the bookshelves, dragging his transparent finger down a row of

spines. This one wore a doublet of periwinkle, with white tights that left little of his form to the imagination. His skin had been powdered white, cheeks and lips blushed pink, and he wore a pale blond periwig that curled upward at the edges. The tips of the periwig looked almost like they'd been frosted with snow. *"Might I be Jules?"*

Oh good lord. Signa frowned as the first spirit glided over to this new one, inspecting him. Side by side, they looked as if they'd been magicked out of the same sugary fairy tale. *"No, I do not think you are. You don't look like Jules."*

"Oh," said the man. *"Very well. Then could you tell me who I am?"*

"Stop wasting time standing around! Get to your places, all of you!"

A third spirit? Signa covered her mouth, taking a hopeless seat beside Aris on the arm of the

chaise. This time it was an older woman who stood beside the Christmas tree as she clapped her hands for everyone's attention. She did not wear a strange costume but luxurious silks that matched those worn by the bespectacled man who stood beside her, presumably her husband. He stared up at the tree, appearing entirely disinterested in the situation at hand.

The woman clapped again, then looked pointedly at the first spirit, who flinched beneath her stare. *"Where is Jules?"*

The spirit shrank. *"I don't know... I've been looking for him all day."*

"Then look harder. You cannot go out there without him."

The first spirit gave a quiet whimper, her bottom lip wobbling. But then she zipped away to the shelves, continuing her search. Every now and then she would ask someone about

Jules, and a new voice would crop up. One by one spirits emerged from the shelves and floorboards and ceiling, each one in the most ridiculous attire: tights tufted with fur and antlers for headpieces. Deep green gowns and cheeks as red as holly. Young girls whose pink tulle reminded Signa of fairies. Many had soot covering their skin, and dear God... were those burn marks? On one spirit, it looked as though her tulle had melted into her leg.

Signa gritted her teeth as she looked at Aris, who had his arms folded over his chest.

"Well?" he huffed. "Have you figured out how to get rid of it?"

What a strange loop these spirits were stuck in, each of these people entirely unaware that they were dead. One of the spirits stopped when he noticed the wrapping paper Signa had been using. He stooped to pick up the ribbons

beside it, strewing them through the air. One landed atop Aris's head and he hissed. "Good God! Can you not simply help it to pass on?"

"There is no *it*, Aris." Signa pinched the bridge of her nose, trying to focus her thoughts. "I count at least a dozen spirits from where I sit. I hate to be the one who tells you this, but your home is haunted."

He sat upright, golden fire blazing in his eyes. It was a relief that Aris had calmed over the years; had the anger and pain of thinking he had lost his wife forever continued to fester within him, he could very well have burned the entire world one day.

"My rotten brother helped choose this land," Aris seethed. "If he wasn't already dead, I would kill the fool myself."

It *was* strange that Death had said nothing about the spirits. Had he somehow not noticed

them? Wisteria had been on this land for nearly two weeks already, and Signa had spent at least an hour working in the library before they showed themselves.

"I'll see what he knows," Signa offered, sliding into the seat beside him as Aris impatiently drummed his fingers on the cushion. "But first you must cease your glaring."

He groaned and looked pointedly away from her, jaw tense. Only then was she able to settle into her mind. She thought of Death, lingering on his memory until she felt the bond that existed between them. Mentally she pulled on it, opening her thoughts to his. She knew immediately when he was there listening, able to feel the comforting weight of his presence in the corners of her mind.

Hello, Little Bird, his thoughts whispered to hers. *Finished with your wrapping?*

Not entirely. Signa shared the words with him. *I'm afraid your brother and I are under siege. The library has been overrun by more than a dozen spirits.*

Spirits? he echoed. *How very odd.* His tone, however, did not match his words, for Death didn't sound nearly as surprised as he ought to.

Odd is certainly one word for the situation. She had to squint her eyes shut to focus, already able to feel Aris's stare searing into her skin. He truly was the perfect fit for Blythe—who else could match her nosiness? *Did you not realize there were so many spirits here?*

I never would have let Aris move to land where I felt the presence of hostile spirits.

She had no doubt of that, though she couldn't help but take note of his careful language. *Come here, then. Perhaps we can help some of them pass on before Blythe takes notice.*

The silence in her mind was too drawn out. Too damning. Signa pressed her lips tight, waiting for Death's eventual response: *I'm afraid I cannot join you at the moment.*

Her eyes snapped open. Aris looked away immediately, and Signa bit the inside of her cheek to quell her annoyance. She made her mind hot, hoping Death could feel every ounce of her brewing frustration. *What do you mean you cannot help? Where are you?*

If Death felt her anger, he gave no sign of it. In fact, he seemed distracted. She felt little from him other than a desire to hurry and break free from this connection.

I'm out collecting a gift for my brother. Signa was about to argue when he continued. *It may take me several days to retrieve, but I'll check in with you in the evenings.*

Several days? Signa demanded. *And what*

do you suppose I do about these spirits in the meantime?

Stay in the house, he told her. Was she imagining it, or did he sound amused? *The spirits aren't malicious. As for what to do about them... you are not new to this, Little Bird. I have faith that you can handle this until I return.*

If Aris didn't kill him, Signa would. She snapped their connection shut with a huff.

"What is it? Did Sylas know something?"

"He's off gathering Christmas presents." She kept her tone flat as she pushed up from her seat, smoothing out the wrinkles in her dress. Across the room, Gundry was doing laps around the Christmas tree, tongue lolling as he darted back and forth among the spirits, who were restarting their loop once more.

"Jules? Might I be Jules...?"

Signa tuned the voices out. So long as the

hound was happy, she felt confident that there was at least no immediate danger.

"Death will not be helping us," she told her brother at last, squaring her shoulders as she met his searing golden gaze. "It seems that you and I are on our own."

FOUR

DEATH

DEATH KNEW IT WAS UNFAIR FOR HIM TO find such entertainment in Aris's frustration. His brother was just too easily riled, and the best part was that, in this new form of his, Aris had a vein on his forehead that pulsed whenever he was particularly aggravated. Death had taken a liking to testing it, calculating all the ways in which he might make it most apparent. Unfortunately, he could not be there for a front-row seat to watch Signa and Aris being forced to work together.

As it was, Death roamed the streets of a small village in a different part of the world, far away from Wisteria. It was a quiet town for the most part, with the majority of its townsfolk currently winding down in their homes. A century or so ago, Death had to come here to ferry souls away after a disease had torn its way through most of the country, but things had been uneventful since.

It was a quaint place. The kind where one would walk the streets and see only friendly and familiar faces. There was not a single pretentious gentleman's club nor an overpriced dress shop in sight. Most who made their homes here tended to farmland of some kind, and Death took his time admiring barns full of animals that huddled close together, preserving their warmth. A hound of black and white barked at him as he passed by, herding Death away from its flock.

Had his search not led him to this particular town, Death might never have taken the time for a visit; he and Signa had become something of homebodies, though that wasn't to say he didn't enjoy his travels. Especially during this time of the year, when there was a warmth to the world despite the air's bitter chill. He'd always enjoyed the holidays and the cheer it so often brought out in people, and wished only that they could be so kind and festive all year-round. It was, however, his busiest season—more people died around Christmas than at any other time of the year. Not to mention there were always spirits who mourned their disconnect from the land of the living and lashed out during the holidays.

The spirits back at Wisteria would not

behave quite so erratically. At least, they certainly *seemed* harmless enough, and even if things did go awry, Signa should be able to handle the situation. He'd check in with her every now and again, and would step in if anything became *truly* dangerous, but otherwise Death had a separate mission to complete...

The snow did not yield beneath his black boots as he journeyed through near-empty streets, nor did he feel the dampness of the flurries around his figure. Oil lamps illuminated frosted windows, most of which were filled with small families huddled around a dining table or warming themselves near the hearth. The majority had already put up their Christmas trees—though they wouldn't be fully decorated for several days more, strewn with chestnuts and ornaments and lit in a haze of candlelight.

He smiled to himself as he passed by the windows, the families inside making him miss his own. As much as he enjoyed teasing Aris, what he truly wanted was to spend the holiday with his brother for the first time in centuries. Too many years they had gone about their existence alone, either resenting or being resented by the other. And yet Aris's return was the very reason that Death wandered these snowy streets so far from home. He didn't know exactly where he'd find what he was seeking. He only knew that it was here, hiding on these very streets.

Soon, Death would be home with the others, sipping hot chocolate and participating in the ridiculous games Blythe would surely force them into. But for now, he had a soul to find.

FIVE

Aris

ARIS PRESSED HIS FINGERS TO HIS TEMPLES, attempting to steady the vein that pulsed in his forehead. His eyes were on Gundry, who was looping excited circles around supposed spirits who Aris could pinpoint only by the ribbons they tossed haphazardly in the air. Every time the hound barked, the vein pulsed, and Aris made no attempt to mask his annoyance.

Blast my brother and his meddling. Whatever

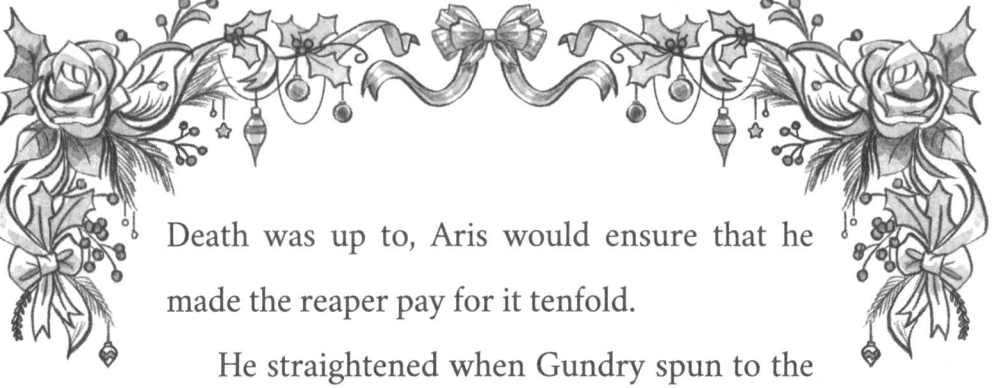

Death was up to, Aris would ensure that he made the reaper pay for it tenfold.

He straightened when Gundry spun to the door, lunging past Aris a second before the handle twisted and Blythe stepped inside.

"What on earth is all of the fuss?" she asked, posing the question to Gundry, whose tongue was frothing as the hound practically bounced on his paws. Blythe stooping down to scratch him behind the ears was the perfect excuse Aris needed for his eyes to flash gold, weaving his threads around the wandering ribbons. He plucked them away from the spirits and fisted them tight.

"Signa and I were wrapping gifts," he said, crossing to stand before his wife with a smile he hoped appeared natural. "I think the hound was growing bored with our monotony."

Blythe hummed under her breath, still

crouched to Gundry's level. "Is that so? Then I suppose it's a good thing I've arrived to rescue you all from such dreadful boredom." She cooed at the hound, petting Gundry with increasing vigor as he rolled onto his back and began kicking his leg.

Aris shoved the ribbons into his trouser pockets so that his hand could rest on the small of her back. "I'm in need of rescuing, am I? And what will you do with me now that I've been saved?" He pulled Blythe to his chest when she straightened, too often forgetting his troubles at the mere sight of her. Intimacy had never been the same without her, no matter who he'd tried to find it with. And now that it had returned as part of his life, he would sooner the world burn than ever give up Blythe again. When he could not be holding her, he preferred to be at her side or in the same room. Once she'd started to get annoyed by his constant coddling, Aris eventually accepted just being in the same house, even if they were floors apart. He did not want to suffocate his new—at least in practice—bride, though he would have loved to whisk her away, just the two of them, for a solid decade at least.

"Oh, don't mind me," Signa called to him, clearing her throat. "Please do continue on as though I am little more than the decor."

Aris rolled his eyes. While he eased back, he did not loosen his hold on Blythe. Instead he whispered to her, "Next year, they will spend the night only on Christmas Eve."

Blythe bumped him on the shoulder, laughing as she pried herself from his grasp and hurried over to her cousin. Aris double-checked that the ribbons were stuffed well into his pocket before he shared a look with Signa,

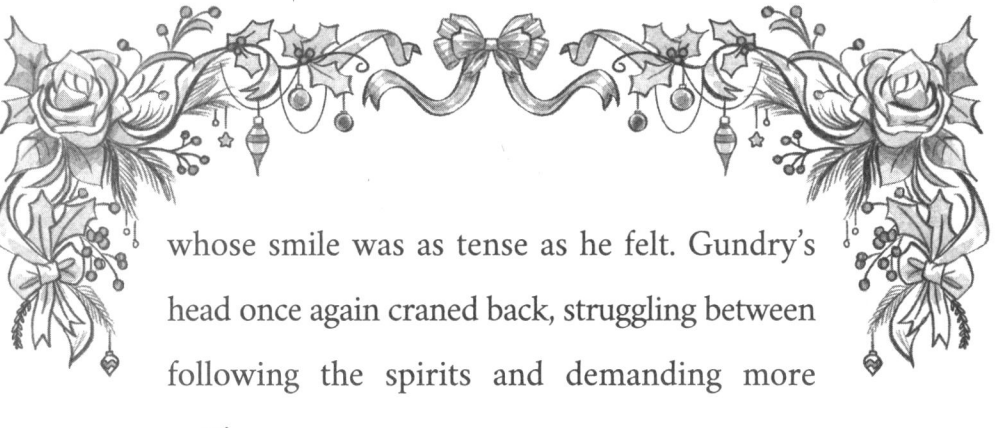

whose smile was as tense as he felt. Gundry's head once again craned back, struggling between following the spirits and demanding more petting.

Not keen to make Blythe aware of their predicament, Aris caught Signa's eye and made a motion toward the door. He didn't quite understand all the rules with spirits or how they operated, but perhaps getting out of this room would be a good first step.

Blythe remained perfectly oblivious, taking hold of Signa's hand and then turning back to fetch Aris's with the other. "For what it's worth, I have something *brilliant* planned for everyone this evening. It's already all set up for us in the parlor."

Aris suddenly found himself wishing he could remain with the spirits, because Blythe had that look about her. Brimming eyes and a

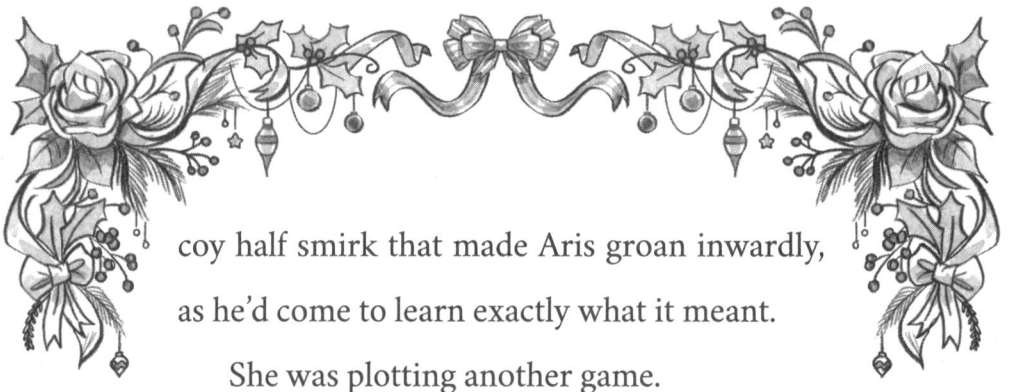

coy half smirk that made Aris groan inwardly, as he'd come to learn exactly what it meant.

She was plotting another game.

Aris didn't know what it was about games that invigorated his wife so, but from their very first croquet match, Aris had learned that there was a monster residing within Blythe. One who awakened only in the face of a new challenge. She was competitive to her core—though he doubted that she'd ever readily admit to it—and soured herself for at least half a day after a particularly bad loss. And yet still she continued to fervently seek out new games that Aris had little choice but to resign himself to playing.

Blythe led them down the stairs to the parlor, which smelled of a wintertime forest. There were twice as many decorations as there had been only an hour prior. Holly hung around every pillar. Two giant wreaths hung on the double doors, filled with cinnamon sticks, pine cones, and dried oranges woven between branches of evergreens. Brilliant red poinsettias filled every corner, and Aris spotted several archways hosting cleverly hidden mistletoe.

"How brilliant you've become," Aris whispered, making a mental note that he, too, would have to step up his creativity for the holidays. If Blythe wanted Wisteria to feel like Christmas incarnate, he was more than happy to oblige.

"*Become?*" Blythe demanded, incredulous. "You've not been paying attention, husband, for I have always been brilliant."

Elijah waited for them in the parlor, seated at a small round table. If one didn't know better, they'd think the man at least ten years younger than his seventy years. There was a cleverness in his eyes, and though he moved a little slower these days, he was in remarkable shape. His blond hair had silvered, and he kept more of his scruff than usual, having grown lazier with his shaving. It was a good look for him. One that attracted attention wherever he went. But while many had tried over the years to get him to change his mind—Blythe included—Elijah had chosen never to court another soul. He'd instead devoted all his time to his remaining family, loving both Blythe and Signa as daughters.

Aris had much to thank Elijah for, as so much of Blythe's well-being after Aris had died was due to her father's support. He'd practically abandoned Thorn Grove until she became well enough to handle being on her own. He was a good man, and one Aris was glad to call his father by marriage. For all their sakes, he hoped that Death would take a very long while to claim Elijah.

Still, the man was not perfect. In fact, Blythe's sense of competition was inherited directly from him, and as the three stepped into the parlor, Elijah's gleaming eyes mirrored his daughter's.

"Behold! Tonight's game!" She swept her hand toward the table, on which sat a large bowl filled with raisins, a bottle of brandy, a pail full of sand, and a set of matches.

Signa took one look at the display and groaned. "Must we play this one? I couldn't manage a single raisin last time."

"That's why we're going to try again. You needn't be so frightened of it." Blythe released their hands to grab hold of the brandy. She poured it onto the raisins, careful to keep all liquid in the bowl. Once that was done she struck a match, setting it to the brandy and grinning as she watched the bowl ignite.

Aris had seen this game before. In many of the lives that he'd lived through the eyes of others, he had even tried his hand at it. His *own* hands, of course, had never dared play. In fact, Aris was quite protective of them, considering how utterly brilliant and creative they were. It would be a shame for the world to lose his skill on account of a silly fire. And yet for Blythe, he supposed he could try at least a round.

"Snapdragon," he said, nodding at the bowl as he settled into the seat beside Blythe. She was already in deep focus, eyes staring unblinking at the fire as she prepared her strategy.

"Precisely. Do you need the rules?"

He didn't. It was a simple enough game: All those participating would take turns trying to fish out raisins from the flames before they were burned. The sand was there out of precaution, meant to douse the fire if things got out of hand.

"Are you certain *this* is what you want to play tonight?" Signa asked, though Elijah and Blythe were both already bent like vultures over the flames, and Aris knew that once his wife had made up her mind, there would be no changing it. Aris tied her hair back with his threads, knowing she'd sooner allow it to singe away than lose this game.

"You first," she taunted her father, who rubbed his hands together as if to warm them up.

"I hope you're not too hungry," he shot back. "I've been playing since long before you were born. You're going to lose."

"Wait, this game has a winner?" In all the times he'd played, Aris had never remembered that part. And yet Blythe and Elijah looked incredulous as they shot him a look.

"Of course it does," Blythe said. "Every

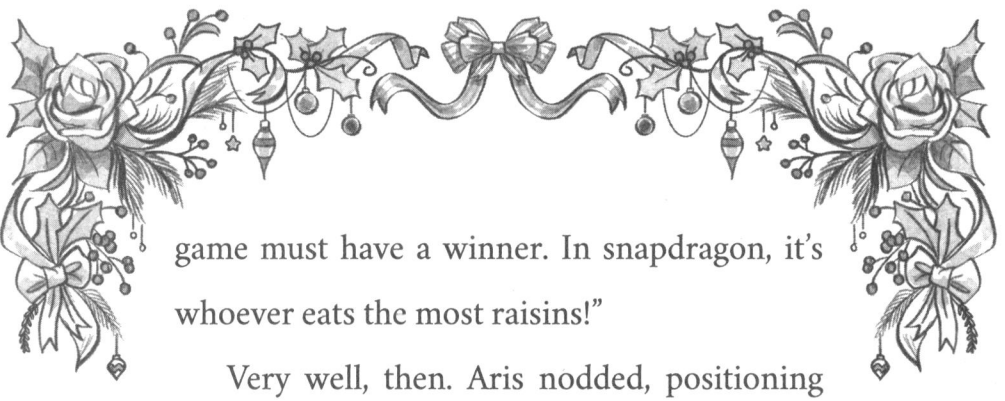

game must have a winner. In snapdragon, it's whoever eats the most raisins!"

Very well, then. Aris nodded, positioning himself over the flames. Surely it couldn't be that hard to win...

"You are no better than they are," Signa grumbled at him as she rolled up her sleeves. Aris didn't bother refuting it. As silly as he found his wife's competitiveness, he knew that he was every bit as bad. In fact, they each brought it out of each other tenfold.

Unlike Blythe, however, Aris had the added distraction of ensuring that his palace did not burn to the ground due to unruly spirits. Still, if he could win *and* manage the spirits, all the better. He smiled at Signa, the warmth of the flames heating his cheeks.

"Let's begin."

SIX

Signa

Signa had lost Aris, the only one who could help her, to a bout of competition. Both he and Blythe were half out of their chairs as they hovered over the bowl, flames illuminating the severity of their faces. Elijah, for his part, was only encouraging the two, seeming to find great amusement in the newlyweds. Perhaps Signa might have, too, had one of the spirits not followed them into the parlor.

It was the young redhead Signa had first spoken with. She seemed to be suffering from great confusion, not abnormal for a spirit withdrawing from her loop for the first time, but concerning nevertheless. Spirits like this were loose cannons, primed to fire at any moment. The spirit seemed most comfortable settled behind Aris, though her face darkened any time he showed affection toward Blythe. Each hostile glance made Signa's stomach tighten. She clenched the edge of her seat, ready to spring to her feet should the need arise.

"Relax, Signa," Blythe chided from across the table, golden threads holding her blond hair back. "The flames won't leap out and burn you. Just sit and watch if you'd like."

Signa could only hope that was true. Especially considering that the spirit's focus seemed to be shifting to the flames. It was mesmerized and no longer moving, which made Signa tense further. A wandering spirit stuck in its loop was fine. But one so consumed by the game that it did not even blink? She had a bad feeling about this.

Elijah managed several raisins before he winced, though Signa expected the sound was fake given that he smirked when Blythe leapt upright.

"How many was that?" she demanded.

"Eleven," Elijah said. "Think you can beat it?"

"Of course I can." She smoothed out her dress, assessing the bowl with a strategic eye before she quickly dipped her hand in and plucked out two raisins at once. She looked quite smug with herself as she popped them into her mouth, repeating the action several more times before she eventually tried to scoop up too many at once. Only then did she jump

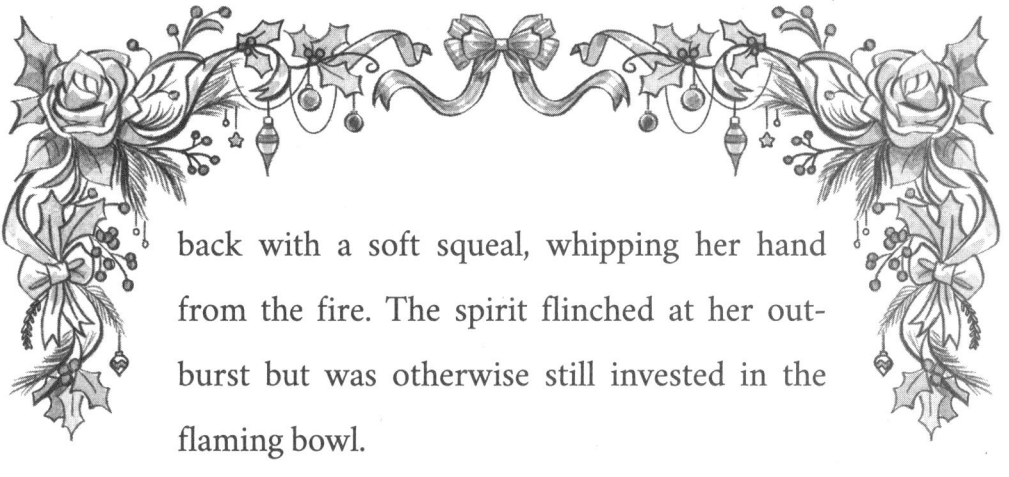

back with a soft squeal, whipping her hand from the fire. The spirit flinched at her outburst but was otherwise still invested in the flaming bowl.

"Thirteen!" Blythe declared, singed but unhurt. Gloating, she twisted toward her husband. "Beat that."

He scooted her to the side. "I intend to." The spirit straightened as Aris positioned himself before the bowl and lowered his hand to the flames. Horror twisted the spirit's face as he did so, her chest rising and falling in hastening gasps as her eyes began to pool with bloodied tears.

"Aris," Signa warned softly, but the man was oblivious. Pushing his sleeve up with one hand, he dipped the other into the bowl with a level of determination typically reserved for matters of far more significance. The spirit leaned in with him, letting out a worried shriek as the flames licked Aris's skin. So shrill was the sound that Signa doubled over in pain, covering her ears.

Even Blythe stilled, the hairs along her arms rising. She shivered, perhaps thinking it only a strange chill. When Aris reached for the flames a third time, blood streaked down the spirit's face. *"Stop it!"* she screamed. *"Oh God, somebody open the door! Jules!"*

The bottle of brandy shattered, shards slicing Elijah's skin. He gasped and drew in his arm while the liquor spilled onto the table, making the flames surge higher.

Aris cursed as the fire singed his hand, whipping it out of the bowl with several colorful choice words and clutching it close to his chest. The spirit was stumbling back, covering her eyes and shaking her head over and over again, as if doing so might somehow banish her

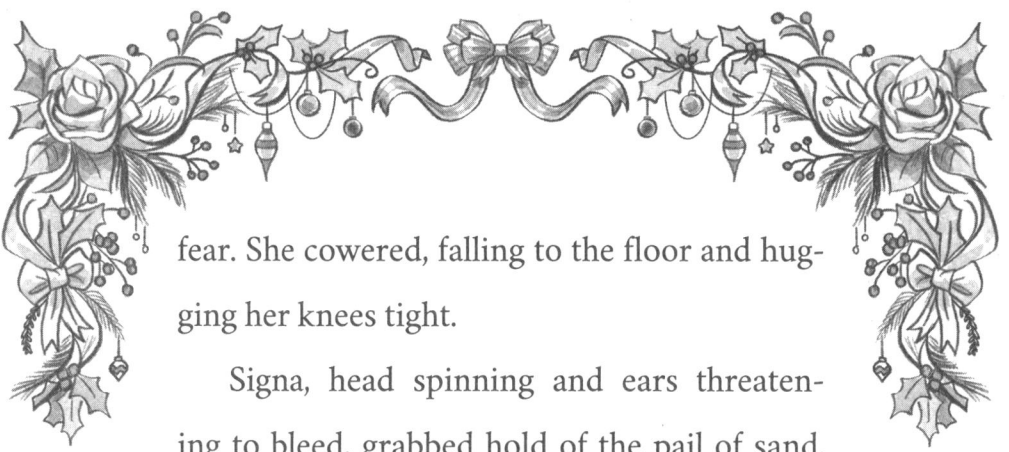

fear. She cowered, falling to the floor and hugging her knees tight.

Signa, head spinning and ears threatening to bleed, grabbed hold of the pail of sand, fighting her nausea long enough to douse the flames. Tendrils of smoke wisped upward from beneath the sandy mound.

Across the table, no louder than a breath, Blythe whispered to Aris, "How many raisins did you get?"

He cast her a withering look, though Blythe paid little mind to it. She was already bent to inspect the hand that Aris nursed. He winced as she set gentle fingers upon it, emitting a beautiful diffused glow as she healed the raw, burnt skin anew. Aris watched in awe all the while.

"Cellular regrowth," Blythe told him proudly. "I imagine it's all very scientific. You can be impressed with me, you know. I

am rather amazing at what I do." She looked around the table next, reaching for her father's hand, damp with brandy. A shard of glass had cut the back of it.

"It's only a scrape," he said, shaking the liquor off his skin. "I can manage."

While Elijah had accepted his children's oddities, he wouldn't allow himself to rely on them for anything more than transportation, which had been enough of a struggle convincing him to accept. Though Blythe didn't look thrilled by his refusal, she nodded all the same. "Is everyone all right?"

Human or otherwise? Signa thought. The spirit was breathing a little easier now that the flames were doused, though she still seemed antsy. Her translucent arms were wrapped around her knees, and she lowered her head between them, perhaps in an attempt to steady

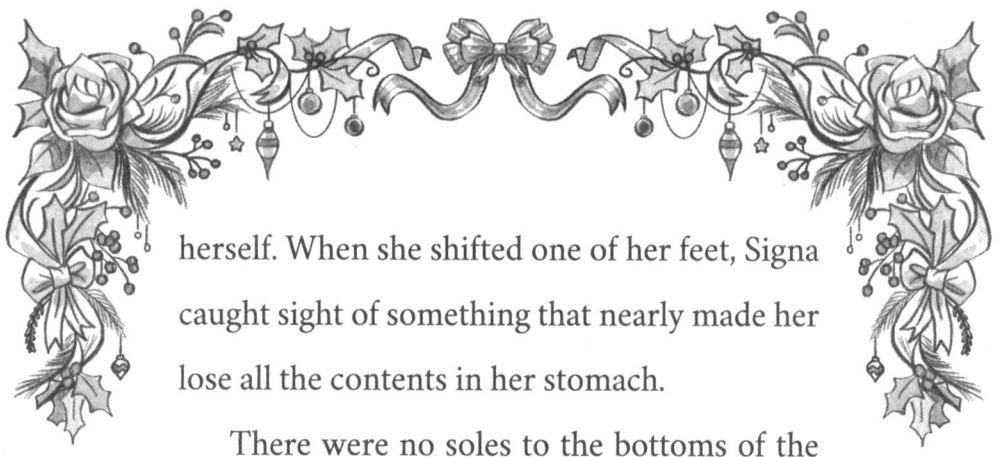

herself. When she shifted one of her feet, Signa caught sight of something that nearly made her lose all the contents in her stomach.

There were no soles to the bottoms of the woman's slippers. More disturbing were the festering holes of burnt flesh where skin should have been.

It was no wonder she'd been so perturbed by the flames. The soot, the scorch marks, the coughing... It was a fire that had killed these spirits, though Signa guessed most had gotten lucky and died by the smoke before the flames consumed them, given that they weren't all burnt to cinders.

It seems that I have no need for you after all, she thought, shooting the words to Death. *I am doing just fine uncovering this mystery on my own.*

His response came a few seconds later, distant and vaguely distracted. *I'm glad to hear it.*

She closed the bond between them, still annoyed. The spirit's reaction wasn't an *answer* to the question of what had transpired on this land years ago, but it was a clue. And one that would lead her closer to learning how to help them.

"What on earth happened?" Blythe asked as she looked over the shards of glass, some of which Elijah was still brushing from his shirt.

"Perhaps one of us knocked it over in our excitement," he suggested, though given the way his eyes skirted across the room to land solely upon Signa, Elijah seemed to already have guessed the true reason behind the accident. Signa nodded once, discreetly. Elijah was no stranger to spirits; he'd been haunted by one on the day they'd first met. He knew their eccentricities far better than either Blythe or Aris, just as he knew there were few coincidences in the world.

"It's no trouble," Signa told him, needing the excuse. "I can clean up the mess." She moved as if to start, but Blythe was beside her not a second later, helping to carefully scoop sand back into its pail.

"I'm the one who forced the game. Let me help—"

"I insist that you let me handle it. You've been working for ages on the palace, and it's the least I can do." Signa didn't mean for the words to come out so aggressively, it was just that the spirit was still in the corner and its cries were getting louder again. Already Signa's head ached with a pain only spirits could cause, and her patience was wearing thin. She looked to Aris, who understood his cue to step in.

He winced, immediately drawing Blythe's attention. He squeezed his hand, face pinched in a look of great pain. Perhaps *too* much pain.

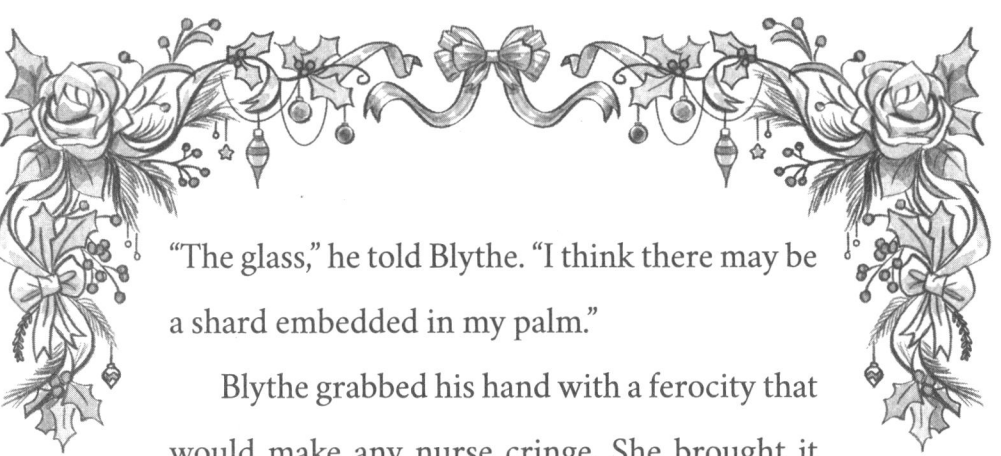

"The glass," he told Blythe. "I think there may be a shard embedded in my palm."

Blythe grabbed his hand with a ferocity that would make any nurse cringe. She brought it to her face, inspecting it. "I don't see anything."

"It's there," he urged, wincing again. "Here, come look in better lighting. Perhaps in the dining room..." Blythe managed only a quick apology over her shoulder before Aris drew her away.

Elijah, however, remained behind. He glanced once to the sand, then to the corner where Signa was trying to keep her eyes from wandering.

"Do I want to know what's actually going on?" he asked.

She scrunched her face. "I doubt it."

"Would you like my help?"

She shook her head, to which Elijah

responded by sighing and squeezing her shoulder on his way out of the parlor.

"Whatever you do, be careful. I'll be in the study if you need me." He was gone a moment later, leaving Signa alone with the distraught spirit. Double-checking that all the others were out of earshot, Signa shut the door and hurried to sit beside the woman, who frowned and curled herself tighter.

"Are you all right?" Signa tried to place her palm on the spirit's back, only for her hand to pass through cold air. Still, the spirit sniffled, seeming to appreciate the gesture.

"That man was burning," she said, dabbing the bloody tears from her cheeks.

"That man's name is Aris, and I promise you that he is quite well. The fire didn't harm him." It was perhaps not her *wisest* idea to engage with the spirit, and yet Signa found herself drawing her own knees up and leaning against the wall. "You've seen fires before, haven't you?"

The spirit's head jerked up so fast that, had it been alive, Signa might have heard its neck snap. She stilled, bracing herself as the spirit's body twitched and flickered out of view and then back a second later, seated across the room.

"There was a fire," whispered the spirit. *"I've been in a fire. There was a fire..."* Her body trembled, then snapped straight again. This time when the spirit looked at Signa, her face was softened with a frown and it looked as though she had never been crying.

"I am looking for Jules," she whispered. *"Have you seen him?"*

Signa had dealt with spirits like this for years, and still she shuddered each time one behaved so erratically. "I know Jules," she said at last, trying a new approach. "Who should I tell him is looking for him?"

The spirit sat straighter, the glow around her suddenly brightened. "*Odette,*" she said, then paused, seeming surprised by the name before excitement overwhelmed her. *"Tell him Odette is looking for him! Let him know to hurry, we cannot begin until he arrives."*

"Very well, Odette. I'll let him know." Signa wasn't quite sure what to *do* with the name, but she was relieved to have it. She was relieved, too, to see the spirit back on her feet, smiling and perfectly oblivious to the fire that had terrified her only moments ago. Smoothing out her tulle skirts and adjusting her headpiece, Odette offered Signa a wave before she gracefully fled the room.

Alone, Signa's heart began to thunder, though it wasn't from fear. Her blood rushed

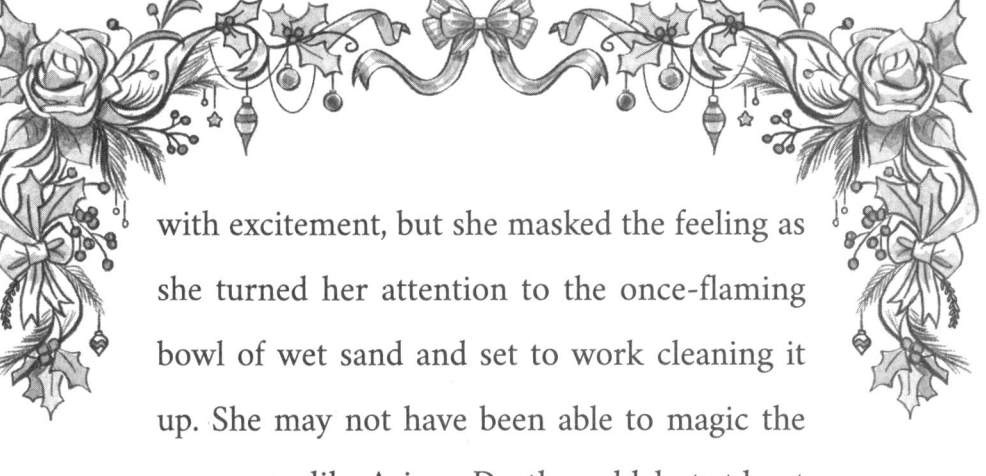

with excitement, but she masked the feeling as she turned her attention to the once-flaming bowl of wet sand and set to work cleaning it up. She may not have been able to magic the mess away like Aris or Death could, but at least something good had come of this night.

All it had taken was a flaming bowl of raisins, and Signa was two clues closer to helping these spirits and getting them out of Wisteria for good.

SEVEN

Signa

"Some help you were," Signa complained as she passed Aris later that evening. Though his skin was healed, Aris was still clutching his arm against his chest pathetically. It seemed he rather enjoyed Blythe's coddling.

Golden eyes flashed down at her, tempered with indignation. "You wanted me to get her out of the room, did you not?"

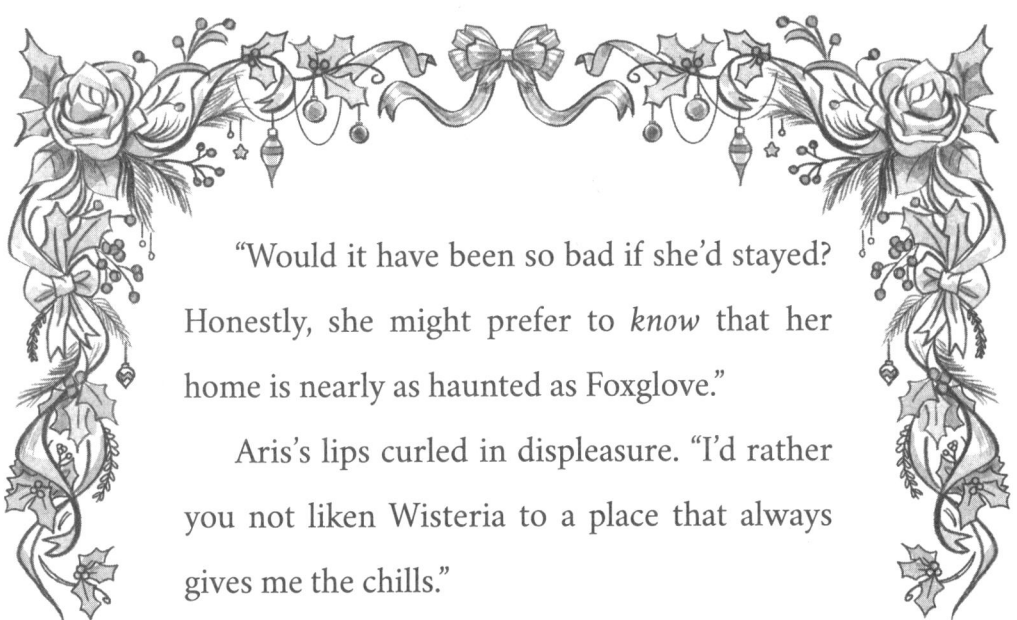

"Would it have been so bad if she'd stayed? Honestly, she might prefer to *know* that her home is nearly as haunted as Foxglove."

Aris's lips curled in displeasure. "I'd rather you not liken Wisteria to a place that always gives me the chills."

"Mind your tongue, Aris. Foxglove is my home." Were there a pillow around, Signa might have thrown it at him.

"My point is that Wisteria isn't like that. Even now, knowing that there are more spirits here than I care to give thought to, I do not walk the halls of Wisteria with my spine prickling. "And look"—he held out his arm for her inspection—"not a single hair is raised."

She pushed his arm back down. Her annoyance aside, Aris had a point. Even with all the spirits, Wisteria did not *feel* haunted. In terms of temperament, it had always been

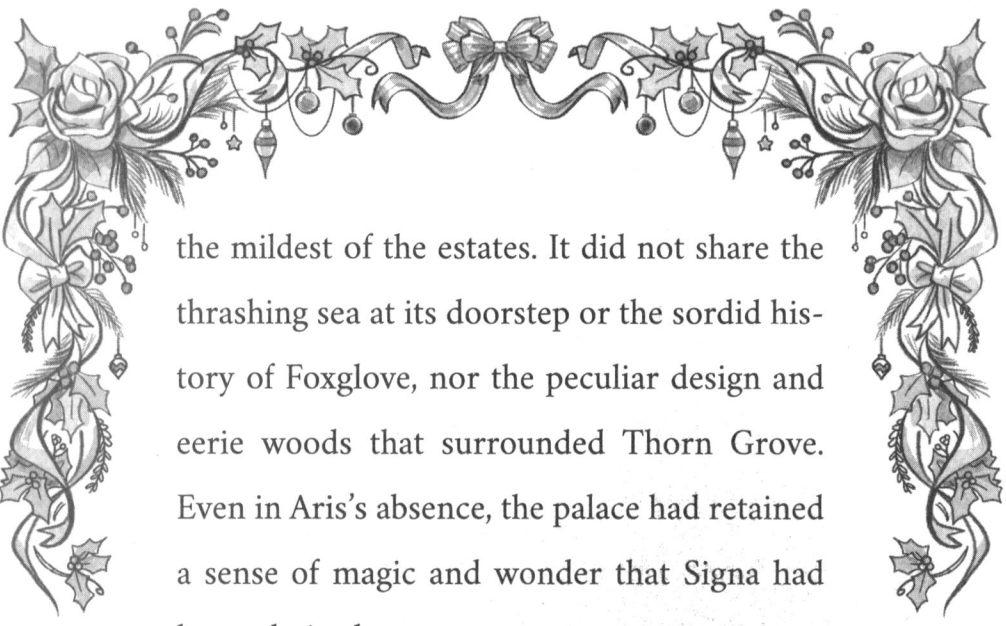

the mildest of the estates. It did not share the thrashing sea at its doorstep or the sordid history of Foxglove, nor the peculiar design and eerie woods that surrounded Thorn Grove. Even in Aris's absence, the palace had retained a sense of magic and wonder that Signa had long admired.

"Should things go poorly for us, I swear that I'll tell Blythe everything," he promised, lowering his arm back to his side. "If you feel strongly about it, we can tell her now, but all I want is for her Christmas to go well. You said yourself that my goal should be to give her the best Christmas possible, did you not?"

"Not exactly in those words—"

"I've no doubt that you had many great holidays while I was gone," Aris pressed, "but I know what it's like to have spent ages of my life waiting for someone I love to return. Even

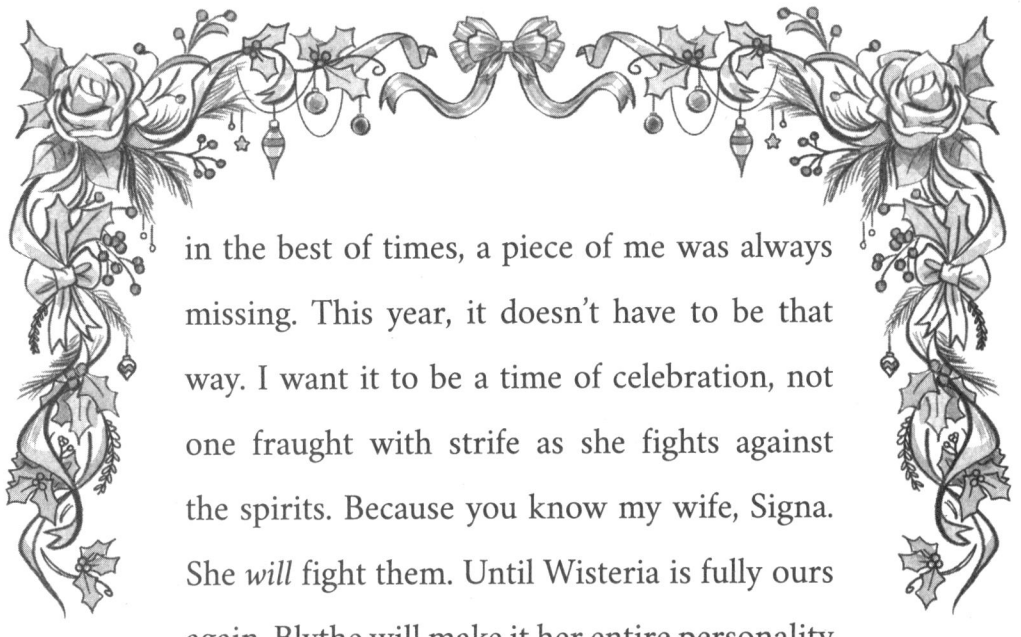

in the best of times, a piece of me was always missing. This year, it doesn't have to be that way. I want it to be a time of celebration, not one fraught with strife as she fights against the spirits. Because you know my wife, Signa. She *will* fight them. Until Wisteria is fully ours again, Blythe will make it her entire personality to be rid of them."

That much was certainly true. While Signa may have grown comfortable living alongside spirits, most people did not share in her sentiment. Blythe included.

"Very well," she relented. "Though if this all turns to folly, it's you who will take the brunt of the blame."

Each of Aris's steps clicked confidently against the marble until he seemed to grow irritated by the sound, a plush scarlet rug appearing beneath his feet. "I accept the risk

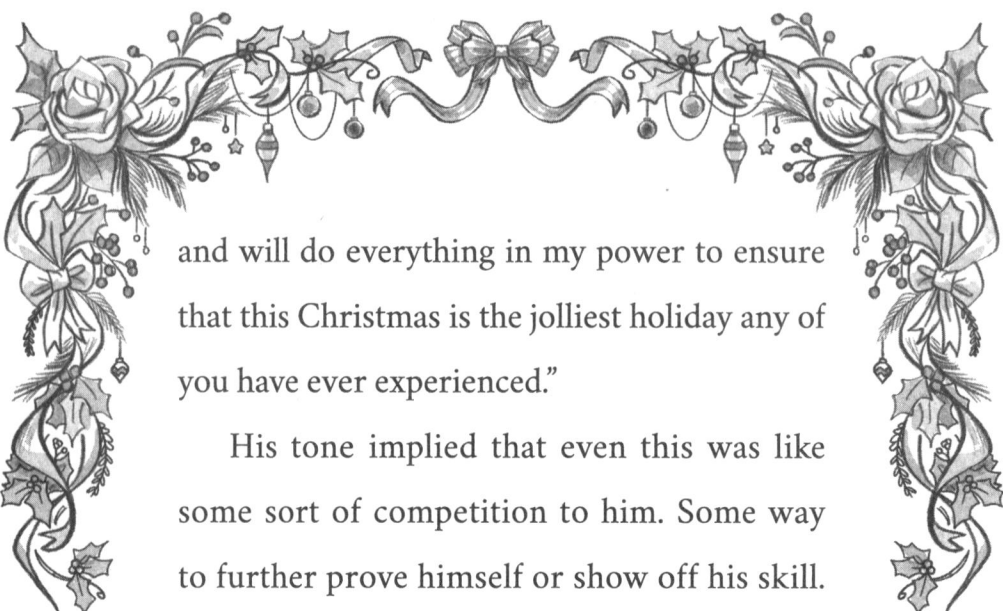

and will do everything in my power to ensure that this Christmas is the jolliest holiday any of you have ever experienced."

His tone implied that even this was like some sort of competition to him. Some way to further prove himself or show off his skill. As much as it made her want to roll her eyes, Signa was glad for it. Aris had not changed even after all these years. If he wanted to make this Christmas a grand occasion just to ensure Blythe's happiness, she would not stop him. Hiding the spirits from her cousin would make her life more difficult, but not impossible.

Beside her, all the light in Wisteria seemed to pull toward Aris, whose skin gleamed like sunlight. Even his eyes were brighter than usual, and in her periphery Signa noticed that the palace was beginning to shift, pillars once

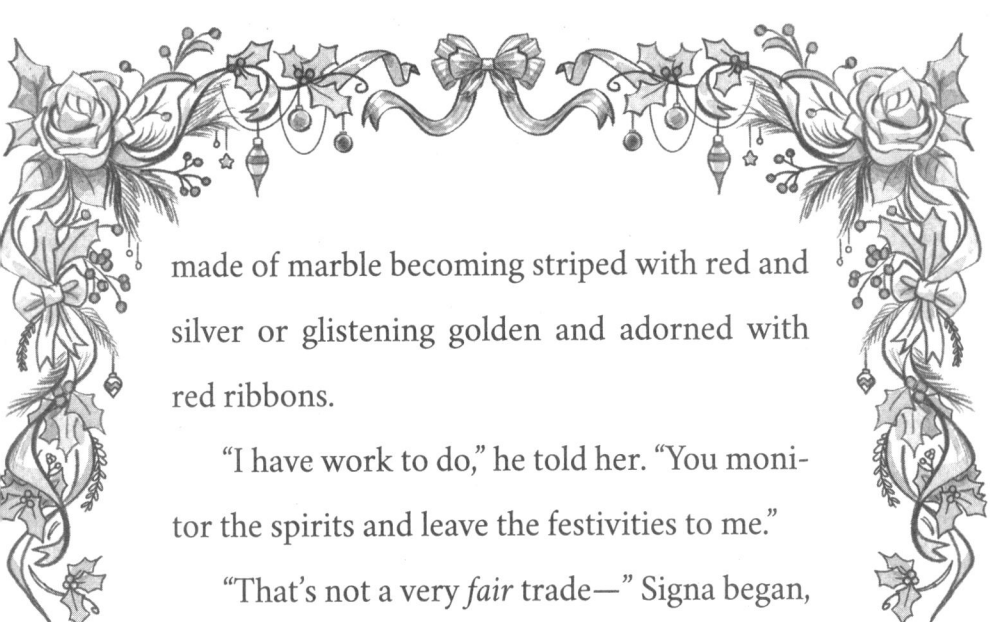

made of marble becoming striped with red and silver or glistening golden and adorned with red ribbons.

"I have work to do," he told her. "You monitor the spirits and leave the festivities to me."

"That's not a very *fair* trade—" Signa began, but Aris was already retreating. Blast him.

She sighed when his figure disappeared down the hall, tipping her head up to the vaulted ceilings to take in his work.

The ceiling was adorned with ever-changing murals and intricate gold filigree. Tonight's mural was of smiling cherubs donning top hats or bonnets dressed with sprigs of holly and mistletoe. They encircled a towering evergreen with ornaments in hand. Snow fell behind them, and though Signa couldn't feel its cold against her skin, glistening flakes glided upon the palace and disappeared without a

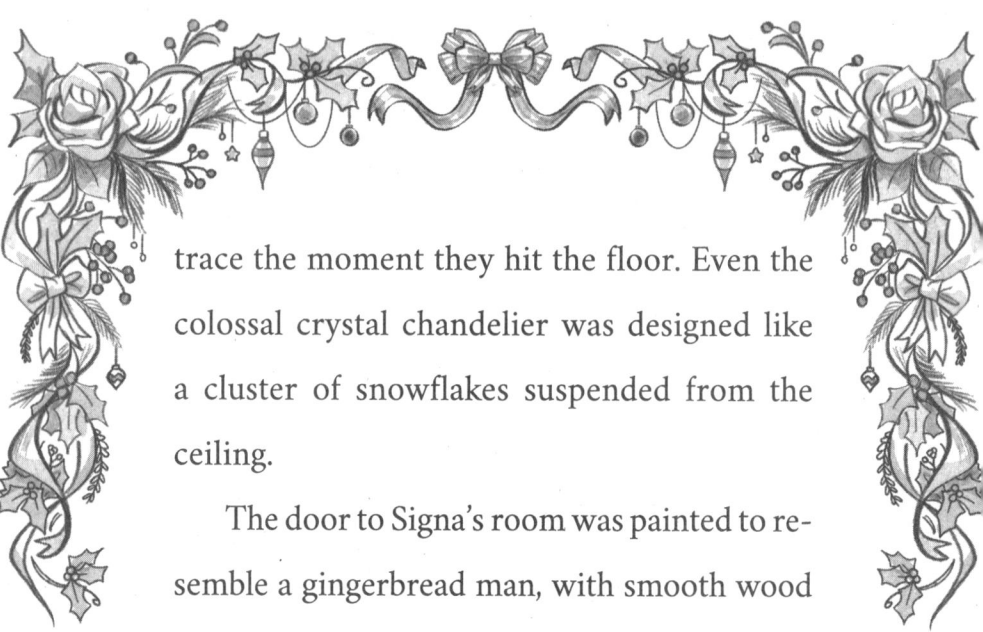

trace the moment they hit the floor. Even the colossal crystal chandelier was designed like a cluster of snowflakes suspended from the ceiling.

The door to Signa's room was painted to resemble a gingerbread man, with smooth wood that smelled of cinnamon and clove. There were frosted buttons down the center and glittering sugarplums for eyes. The knob was striped like a candy cane, and she turned it to enter what was perhaps the coziest space she'd ever seen. A beautiful stone hearth took up the entirety of one wall, decorated with thick garlands. Its amber glow made the wallpaper's golden threads glisten in a way that reminded Signa of a Christmas present. The air even tasted of gingerbread, and by her bed a steaming cup of hot cocoa waited for her alongside a note written in elegant script.

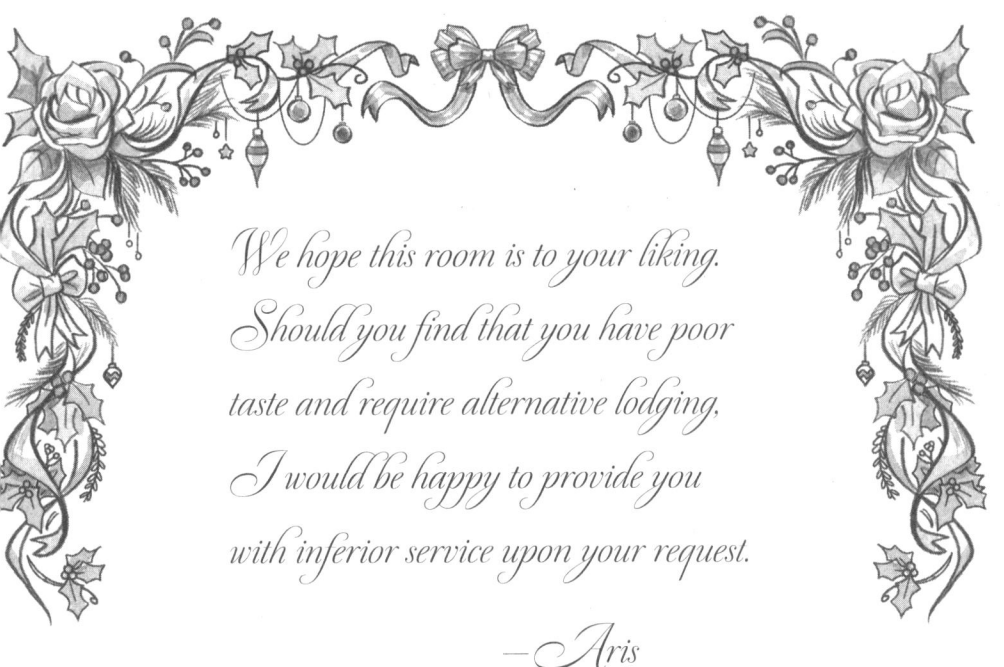

We hope this room is to your liking. Should you find that you have poor taste and require alternative lodging, I would be happy to provide you with inferior service upon your request.

—Aris

Signa snorted as she set the note aside, grabbing her cocoa and taking a long sip, then a hastily followed second one in her surprise.

Dear God, it's glorious.

She'd heard Blythe rave about the hot chocolate before but hadn't expected it would be *this* good. Aris truly did have spectacular—though admittedly sometimes peculiar—taste.

Though... it would have been nice if Death was around to experience it with her.

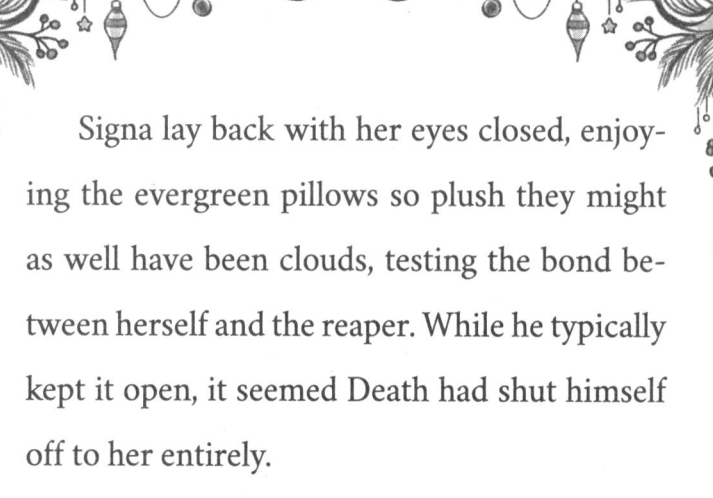

Signa lay back with her eyes closed, enjoying the evergreen pillows so plush they might as well have been clouds, testing the bond between herself and the reaper. While he typically kept it open, it seemed Death had shut himself off to her entirely.

She rolled onto her pillow, scowling. "Just what on earth are you up to?"

She was content to lay there for a while longer, stewing in her thoughts and letting her annoyance fester, but there was no hope. She felt the familiar prickling of her skin and knew there were spirits in the room. Cracking one eye open, she sighed as they filed in one by one, awed by the decor. In their strange attire, they fit in with the theme remarkably well.

Eerily well, in fact. There were several spirits not in excessive tulle or strange wigs and headpieces. Some wore only plain black suits

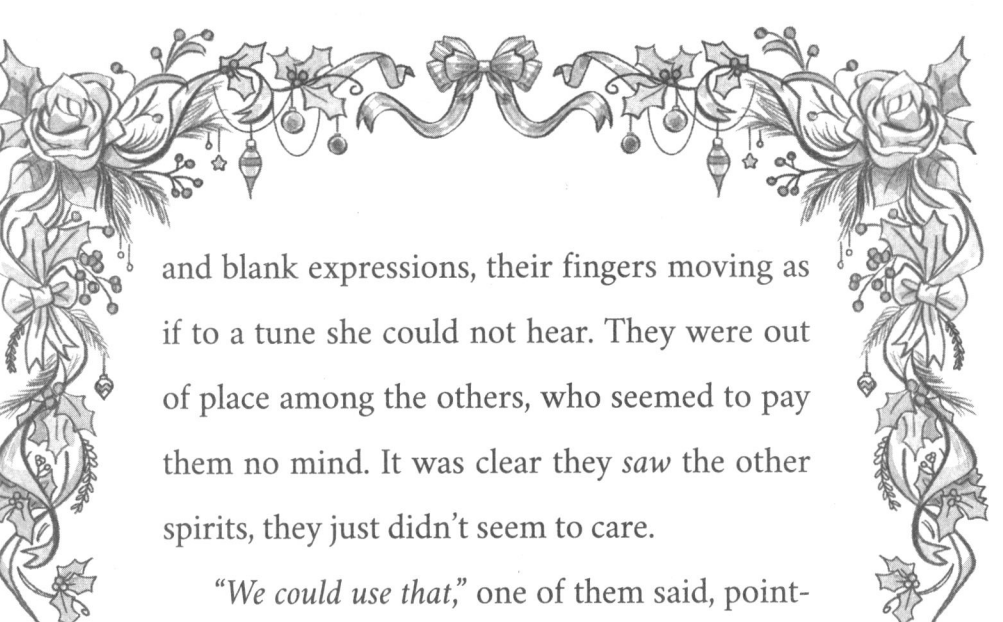

and blank expressions, their fingers moving as if to a tune she could not hear. They were out of place among the others, who seemed to pay them no mind. It was clear they *saw* the other spirits, they just didn't seem to care.

"We could use that," one of them said, pointing to the garland above the hearth.

"The chandelier, too. Did you see it? It would be perfect."

"If it were perfect, it'd be bigger." One of the girls sniffed. *"Large enough to sit on, at least."*

"Not every entrance needs to be grand," said another. It was clear by her face that the first girl disagreed.

The costumed spirits looked from one corner of the room to the next, skimming their fingers over the wallpaper and taking stock of the design. One even tried to take a sip of Signa's cocoa, and Signa had to temper her annoyance

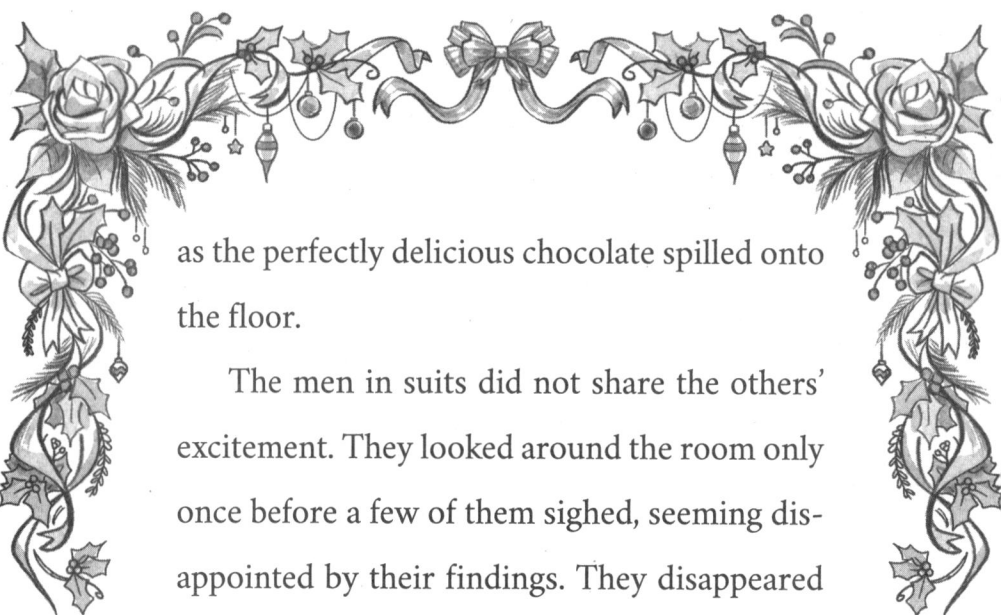

as the perfectly delicious chocolate spilled onto the floor.

The men in suits did not share the others' excitement. They looked around the room only once before a few of them sighed, seeming disappointed by their findings. They disappeared not long after. The others, however, were much more rambunctious.

Three were left in her room—two girls and a young man. All had slender frames and pink cheeks, and they perched contentedly on the edge of Signa's bed.

"If you don't mind," she told them, "I'm going to try to sleep."

They flinched, as if surprised that she'd spoken, then crawled higher up the bed. *"How could you sleep during this?"* one of the girls asked. *"Are you not excited? Heavens, I feel like I'm about to burst from my own skin."*

"Please don't." Signa cringed, kicking out of her boots. She couldn't very well change with the lot of them staring at her like that, and so she only pulled the blankets over her and slammed her eyes shut with great hope. Unfortunately, she could still feel the spirits hovering over her, the hairs along her neck and arms raised in their presence. It didn't help that they were noisy, too, one of them humming some choppy tune.

At this rate, Signa was convinced she might never sleep again. That feeling, however, was admittedly not just because of all the noise and fuss the spirits were making. Rather, it was because they were *there*. Because they were in this house, unable to pass on, and Signa's mind was racing to figure out why. Given how all the spirits had at least a few singe marks on their clothes or bodies, it was clear that a fire had

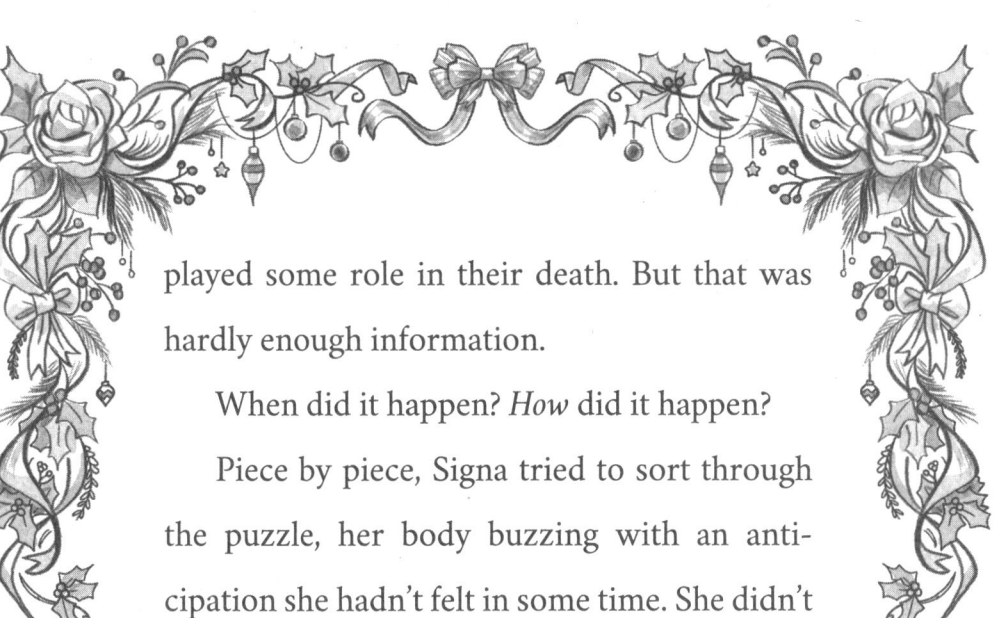

played some role in their death. But that was hardly enough information.

When did it happen? *How* did it happen?

Piece by piece, Signa tried to sort through the puzzle, her body buzzing with an anticipation she hadn't felt in some time. She didn't want to ruin Blythe's or Aris's holiday, nor did she *want* Wisteria to be haunted or anything to happen to the palace... but oh, what a delight it was to be at the forefront of another mystery.

How dull her days had become. For years her life had been turmoil, one upheaval after another. She'd believed that she'd find peace with the stillness at Foxglove, and for a while she had. But too much stillness had made her antsy. She enjoyed her work at the hospital, though those deaths were never part of a grand mystery. Instead, she spent her days consoling frightened or upset spirits whose deaths had

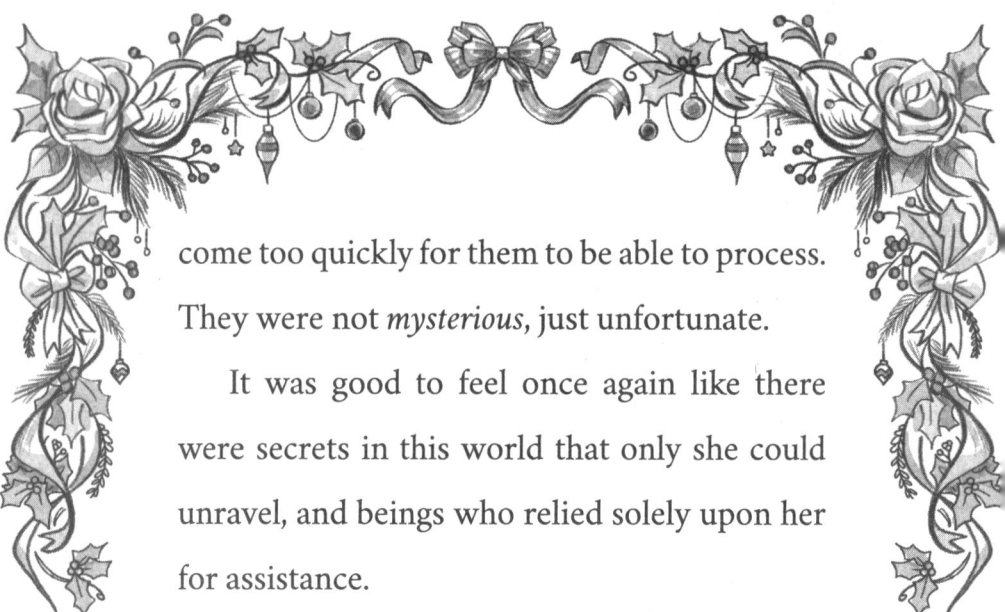

come too quickly for them to be able to process. They were not *mysterious*, just unfortunate.

It was good to feel once again like there were secrets in this world that only she could unravel, and beings who relied solely upon her for assistance.

After all this time, Signa finally had another mystery to solve. And God, was she looking forward to it.

EIGHT

Blythe

It was possible that Blythe might have overdone it with the holly... and perhaps with the other greenery, as well.

While Wisteria *did* smell wonderful, her nose kept dripping and she couldn't go more than two minutes without sniffling. Ever since she came into her powers, Blythe had had two great frustrations—the fact that she could not teleport, and that she was still forced to suffer from allergies. How someone with the power to make life could possibly have such a trivial affliction, she would never understand.

Still, so long as the plants served their purpose by warding off any malevolent spirits, she would happily spend all day with a handkerchief to her nose. Especially if it meant that everyone would have a good holiday.

She did feel a *little* guilty that her first game had gone so awry, though that had always been part of the appeal of snapdragon. Aris and Elijah, at least, had seemed to have a decent time. And considering her immaculate victory, so had Blythe. She'd have to make it up to Signa, however, perhaps by finding a simpler game that they could play the following evening. Somewhere, Blythe had a full list of grand ideas.

But first...

Blythe paused outside the open door of

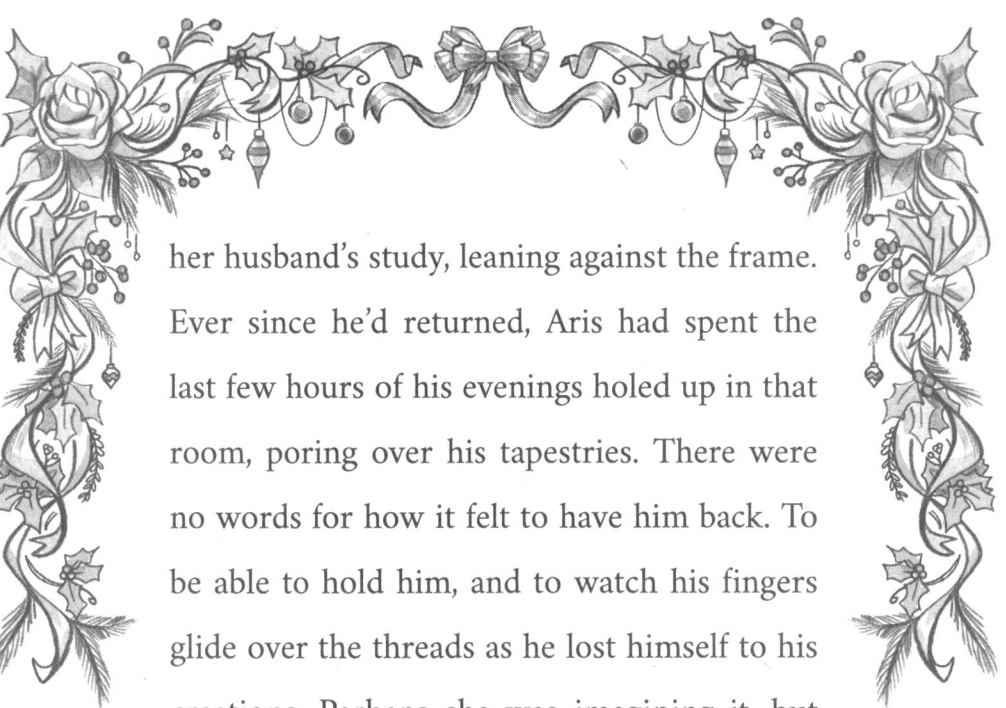

her husband's study, leaning against the frame. Ever since he'd returned, Aris had spent the last few hours of his evenings holed up in that room, poring over his tapestries. There were no words for how it felt to have him back. To be able to hold him, and to watch his fingers glide over the threads as he lost himself to his creations. Perhaps she was imagining it, but it seemed he took more care with them these days, delicate with every stitch.

"Aris," she whispered, waiting until he had finished weaving. It was always clear when he did, as he rested the tapestry on his lap for a short moment after the final stitch, his eyes slowly losing their glazed expression as he came back to himself. Blythe waited until he turned to look at her, then held out her hand. "Come to bed?"

He was across the floor in two heartbeats,

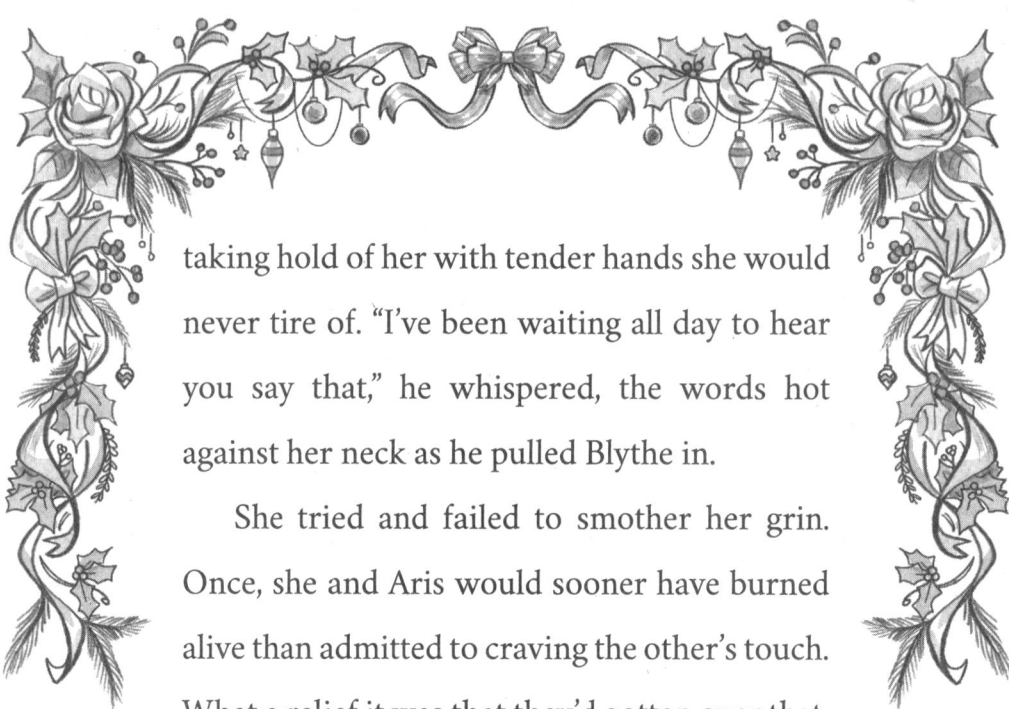

taking hold of her with tender hands she would never tire of. "I've been waiting all day to hear you say that," he whispered, the words hot against her neck as he pulled Blythe in.

She tried and failed to smother her grin. Once, she and Aris would sooner have burned alive than admitted to craving the other's touch. What a relief it was that they'd gotten over that.

She curled her fingers around his, pulling Aris through the decorated halls and down to their bedroom. They'd made a new one to share upon his return, and each day Aris changed something about it. Part of Blythe worried that he was expending too much energy to make Wisteria feel so magical, but if he was growing tired, Aris didn't show it. And, truth be told, returning to the room each evening had quickly become one of Blythe's favorite parts of the day—for a multitude of reasons.

When she opened their door this time, it was to a frosted wonderland. A hearth roared in the corner, its bricks covered by snow that held no chill. The floor, too, was covered in it. Blythe took one step inside, slippers cushioned by powder that did not stick to her soles.

On the wall were crystalline snowflakes that glistened in the flickering candlelight of sconces shaped like wintry beasts—a moose wearing spectacles, wolves, foxes in scarves, even a hound that looked remarkably like Gundry and smoked a pipe with real steam wafting from it.

At the center of the room was a four-poster bed veiled by gossamer. It was piled high with thick blankets and red and silver pillows. Blythe squealed as she hurried over to it, throwing herself onto the heap and curling up.

"It looks like winter exploded in here," she called as she plucked off her slippers and tossed

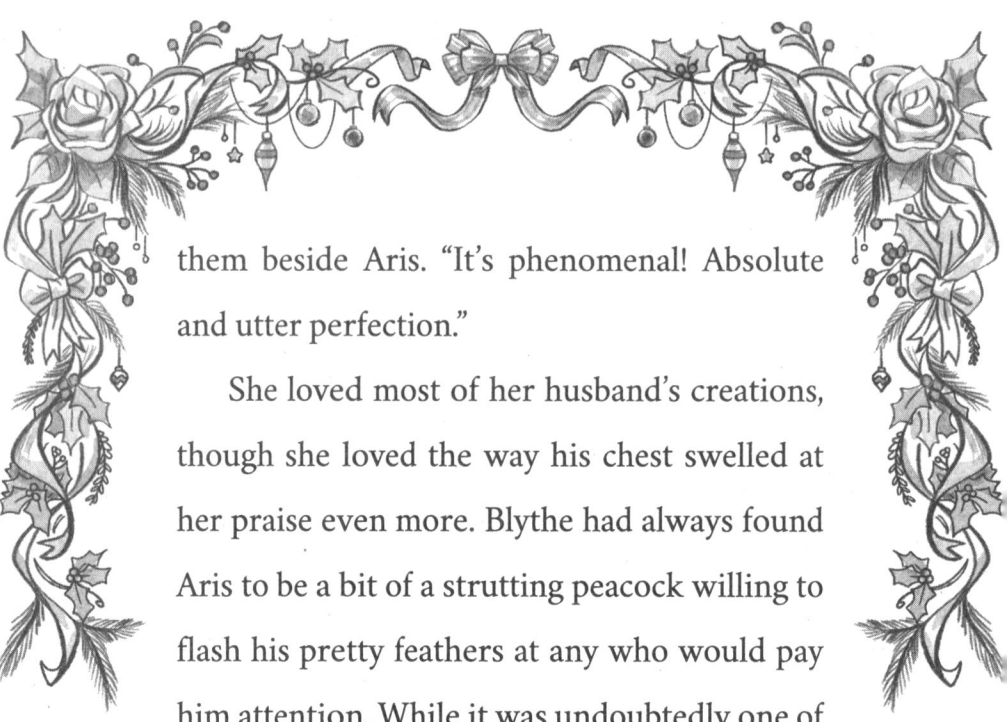

them beside Aris. "It's phenomenal! Absolute and utter perfection."

She loved most of her husband's creations, though she loved the way his chest swelled at her praise even more. Blythe had always found Aris to be a bit of a strutting peacock willing to flash his pretty feathers at any who would pay him attention. While it was undoubtedly one of his more arrogant traits, it was also one of her favorite things about him.

There was, however, a time when he'd been testing out different designs and had arranged their bedroom to look almost like a museum. The floors were sleek and glossy, the lights too bright, and the strange marble busts had felt so lifelike that it'd been unnerving. Blythe had promptly turned and walked out, and did not return until he changed it. He now typically kept the room in some variety of magical

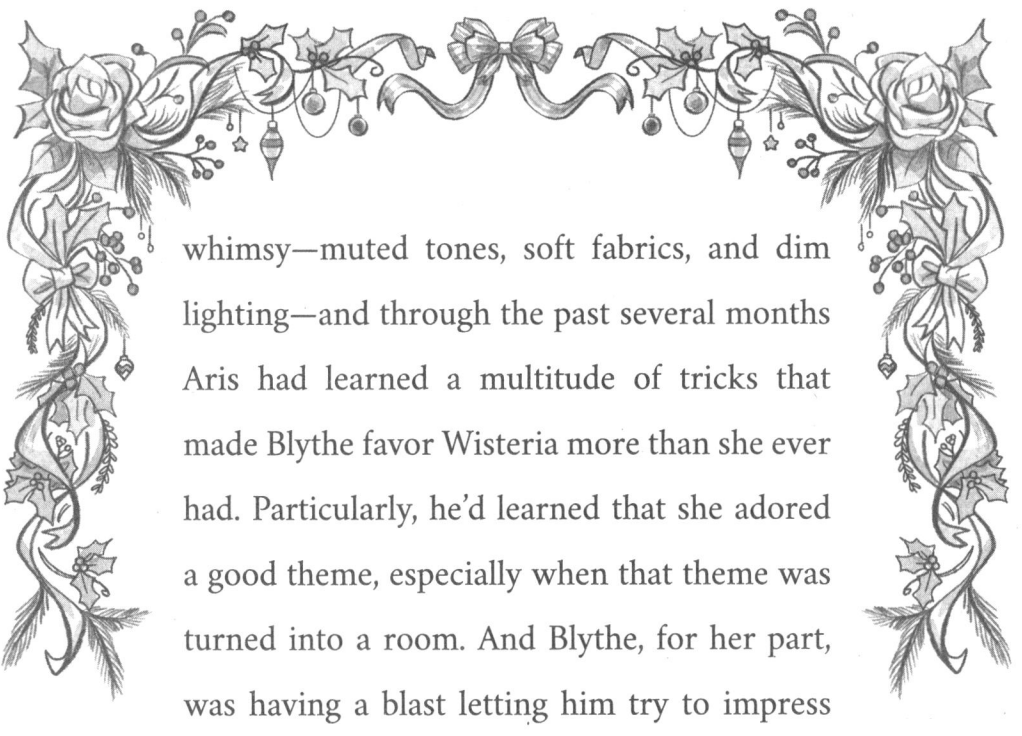

whimsy—muted tones, soft fabrics, and dim lighting—and through the past several months Aris had learned a multitude of tricks that made Blythe favor Wisteria more than she ever had. Particularly, he'd learned that she adored a good theme, especially when that theme was turned into a room. And Blythe, for her part, was having a blast letting him try to impress her.

"Come here," she called to Aris as she snuggled into the bed. It was *just* cold enough to make the fire feel welcome against her skin and for her to warm her toes beneath the blankets without overheating.

"That's not an invitation I need twice." Aris shrugged off his coat, letting threads of gold whisk it away before it could drop to the floor. His belt came next, followed by the loosening of his shirt as he slipped onto the mattress beside

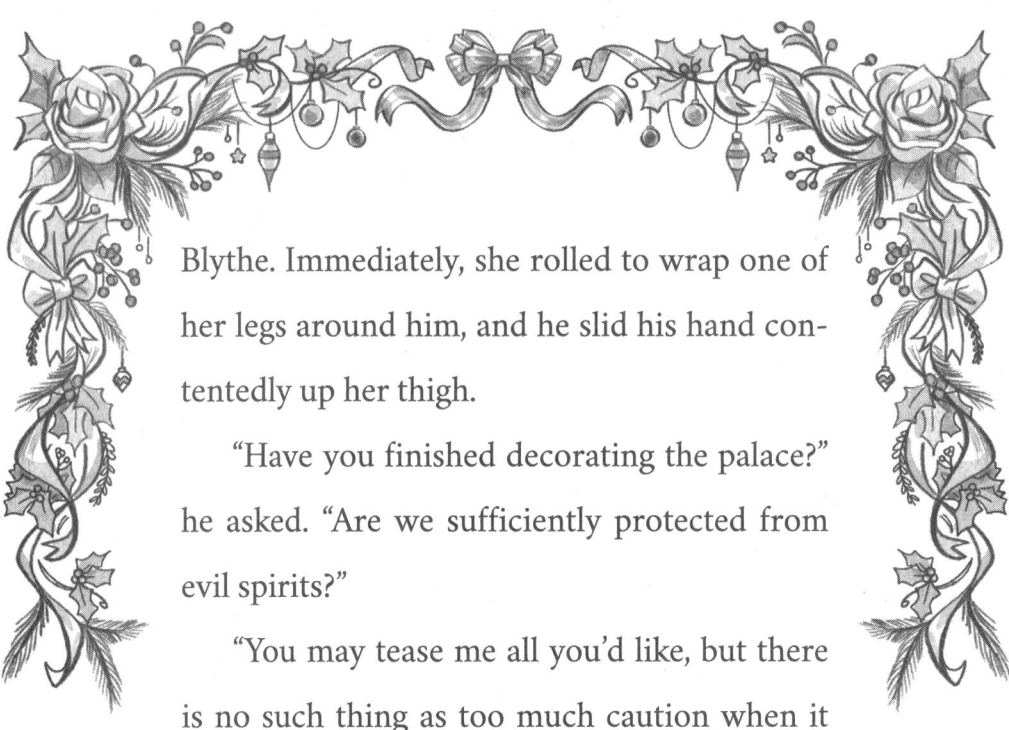

Blythe. Immediately, she rolled to wrap one of her legs around him, and he slid his hand contentedly up her thigh.

"Have you finished decorating the palace?" he asked. "Are we sufficiently protected from evil spirits?"

"You may tease me all you'd like, but there is no such thing as too much caution when it comes to spirits." Blythe sniffled, trying to ignore her protesting sinuses as best she could.

Aris hummed under his breath but did not voice his disagreement. He was too busy sliding his hand higher beneath her skirts, satisfied only when his fingers touched the slice of bare skin above her stockings. Blythe let out a soft breath when he did, relaxing her head against the pillows.

Twenty-seven years she had waited for him. How long would it take to make up for that time?

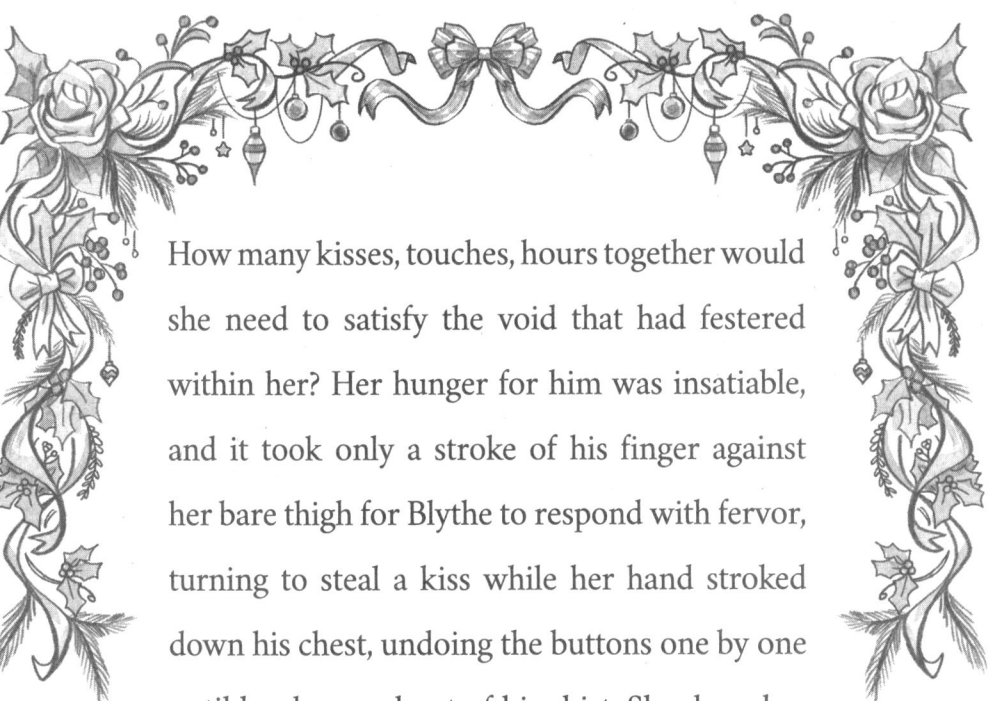

How many kisses, touches, hours together would she need to satisfy the void that had festered within her? Her hunger for him was insatiable, and it took only a stroke of his finger against her bare thigh for Blythe to respond with fervor, turning to steal a kiss while her hand stroked down his chest, undoing the buttons one by one until he shrugged out of his shirt. She drew her fingers down the center of his back, pleased as he shuddered beneath her touch.

Blythe took her time studying each line down his chest and torso. Every dip of his muscles and the strength of his back and arms. He groaned when she kissed the base of his throat, turning to clay beneath her palms, yielding and ready to mold himself however she wanted. When she tipped her neck back he obeyed wholeheartedly, peppering kisses down the length of her body.

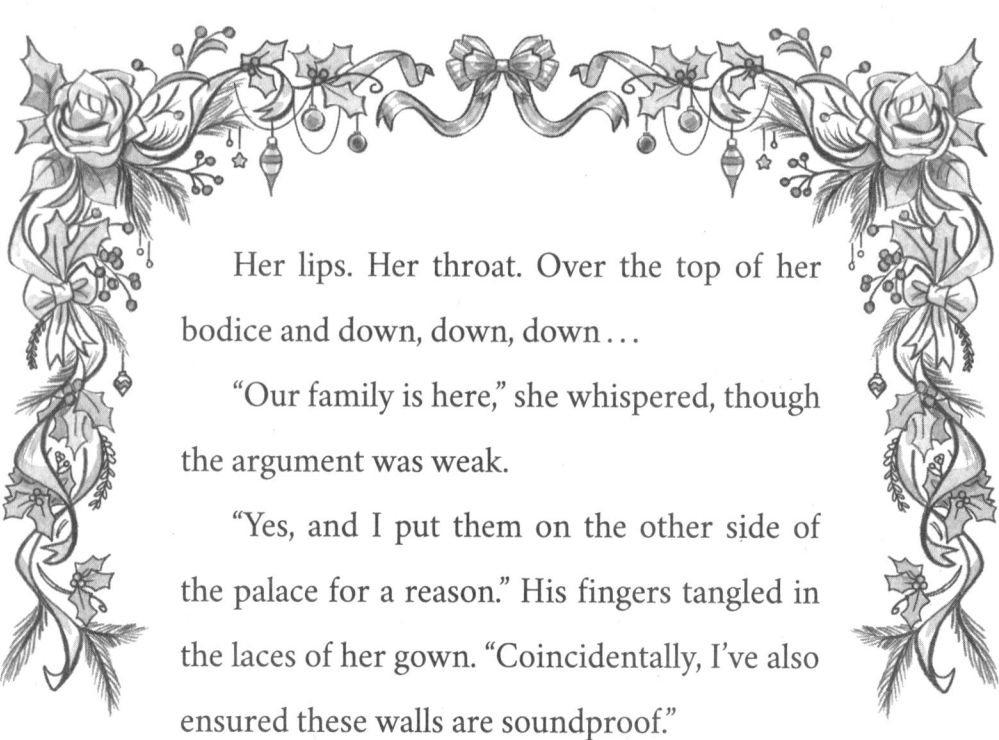

Her lips. Her throat. Over the top of her bodice and down, down, down...

"Our family is here," she whispered, though the argument was weak.

"Yes, and I put them on the other side of the palace for a reason." His fingers tangled in the laces of her gown. "Coincidentally, I've also ensured these walls are soundproof."

"You don't believe in coincidences."

"You're right, Sweetbrier. I do not."

She whimpered as he continued his path downward, kissing the length of her thigh, her calves, the top of her foot as he slid away her stockings, and then back upward again. The room was colder now, and his lips were so warm and welcome against her skin that she shuddered. She curled her fingers into his hair, breath fast with anticipation. But barely an inch from where she most wanted him, Aris went still.

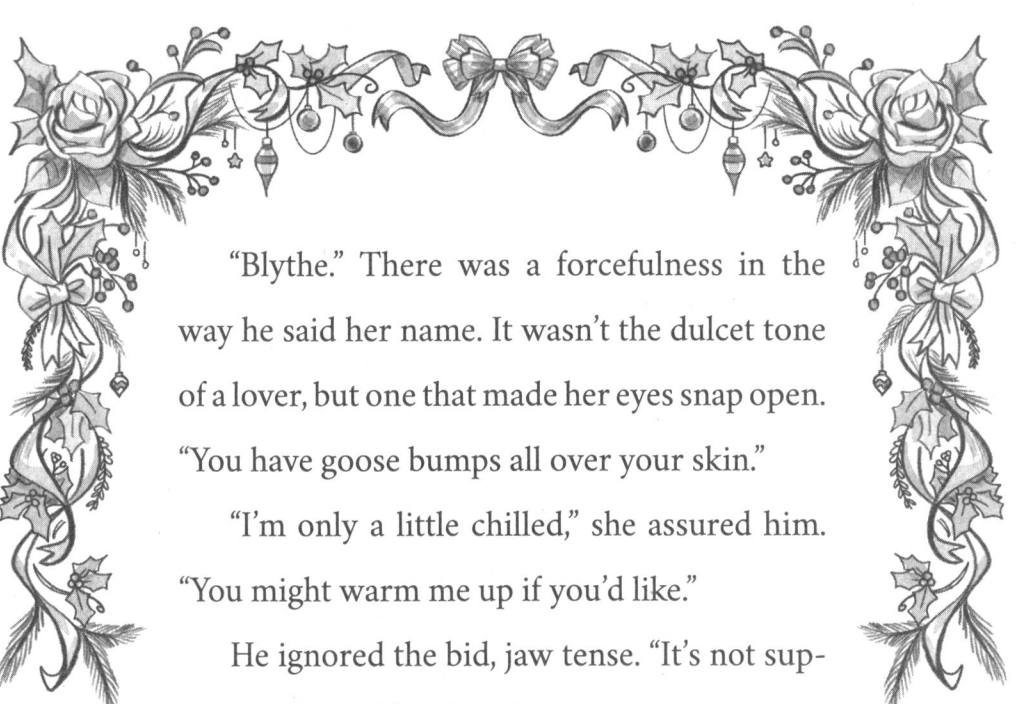

"Blythe." There was a forcefulness in the way he said her name. It wasn't the dulcet tone of a lover, but one that made her eyes snap open. "You have goose bumps all over your skin."

"I'm only a little chilled," she assured him. "You might warm me up if you'd like."

He ignored the bid, jaw tense. "It's not supposed to be cold in here."

Blythe peered around the snow-covered floor. It was chillier than it had been, yes, but the hearth was at least warming the side of her cheek. "I promise that I am quite comfortable," she tried, but Aris was only half listening.

He peeled back, pulling Blythe's skirts back down to cover any exposed skin. There were deep lines creased into his forehead, and the hairs on his arms and the back of his neck were raised. He rubbed them down with great irritation.

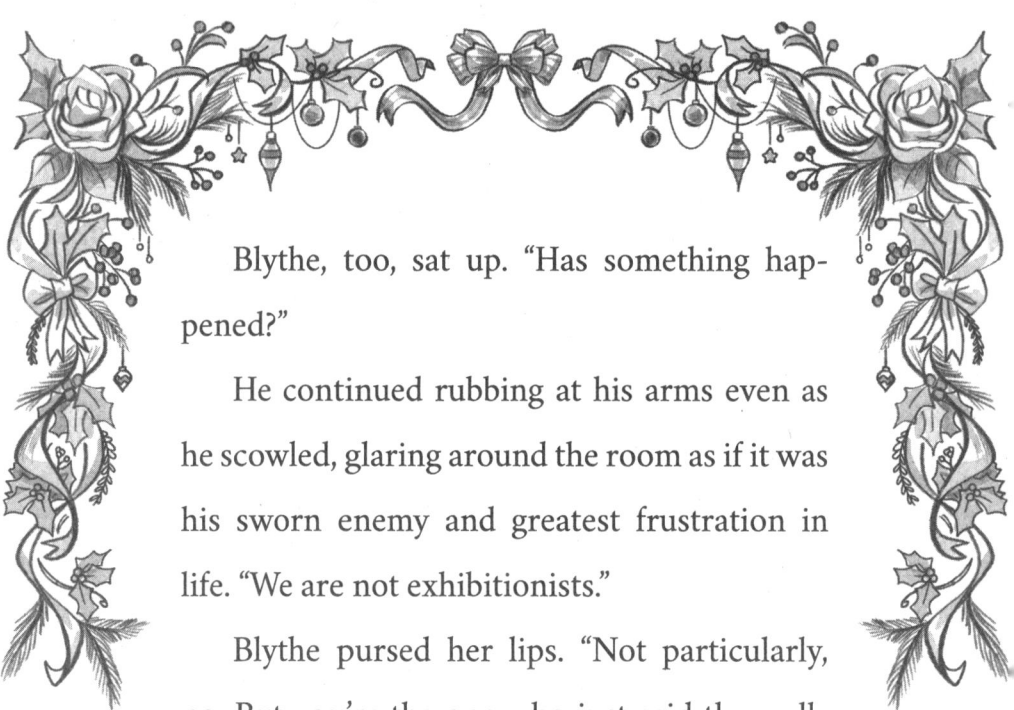

Blythe, too, sat up. "Has something happened?"

He continued rubbing at his arms even as he scowled, glaring around the room as if it was his sworn enemy and greatest frustration in life. "We are not exhibitionists."

Blythe pursed her lips. "Not particularly, no. But you're the one who just said the walls were soundproof."

A quiet grunt was the only acknowledgment that he'd heard her. Aris was too busy gathering up the blankets, tossing one over her thighs, then two more over her chest. There was little that Blythe could do but stare open-mouthed at her husband as he fastened her into a cocoon before settling beside her.

"I do not trust that your family won't find some reason to begin wandering the halls or decide to barge in," he said once he'd finished

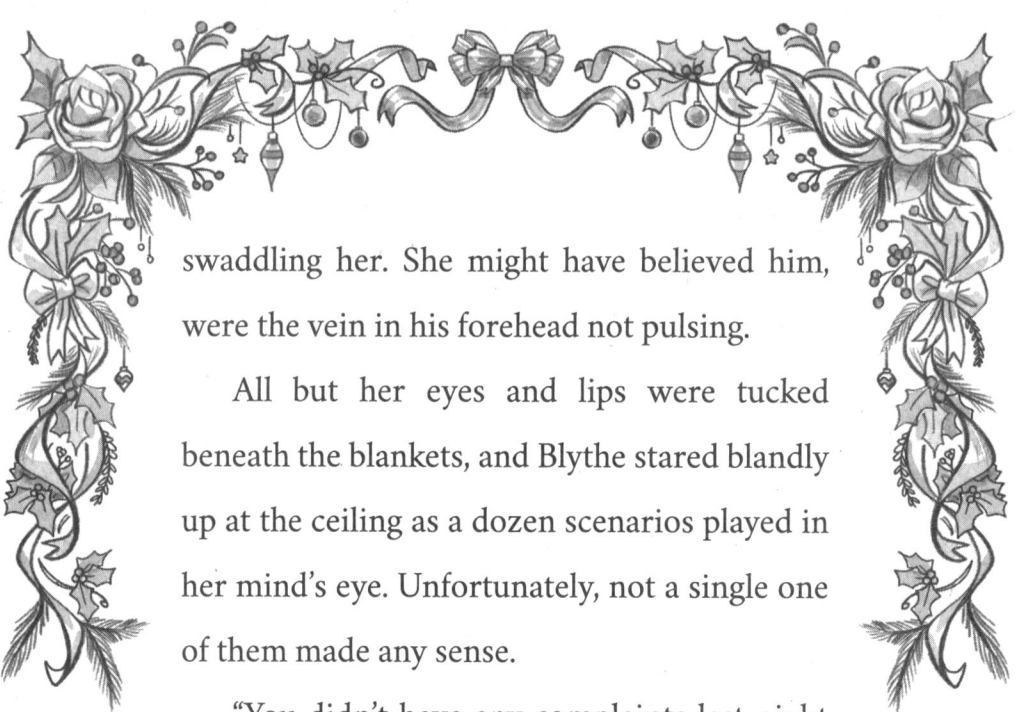

swaddling her. She might have believed him, were the vein in his forehead not pulsing.

All but her eyes and lips were tucked beneath the blankets, and Blythe stared blandly up at the ceiling as a dozen scenarios played in her mind's eye. Unfortunately, not a single one of them made any sense.

"You didn't have any complaints last night when I had you in my mo—" Her words choked off as his threads sealed her lips shut.

"Mind your tongue before someone hears you," he hissed, staring at her for a long beat before the threads unwound themselves.

The moment they did, Blythe shot at him, "You had no complaints about my tongue last night, either."

Aris groaned. Blythe ignored him as she wriggled in her blankets, trying to sit up.

"That clever tongue of yours is one of my

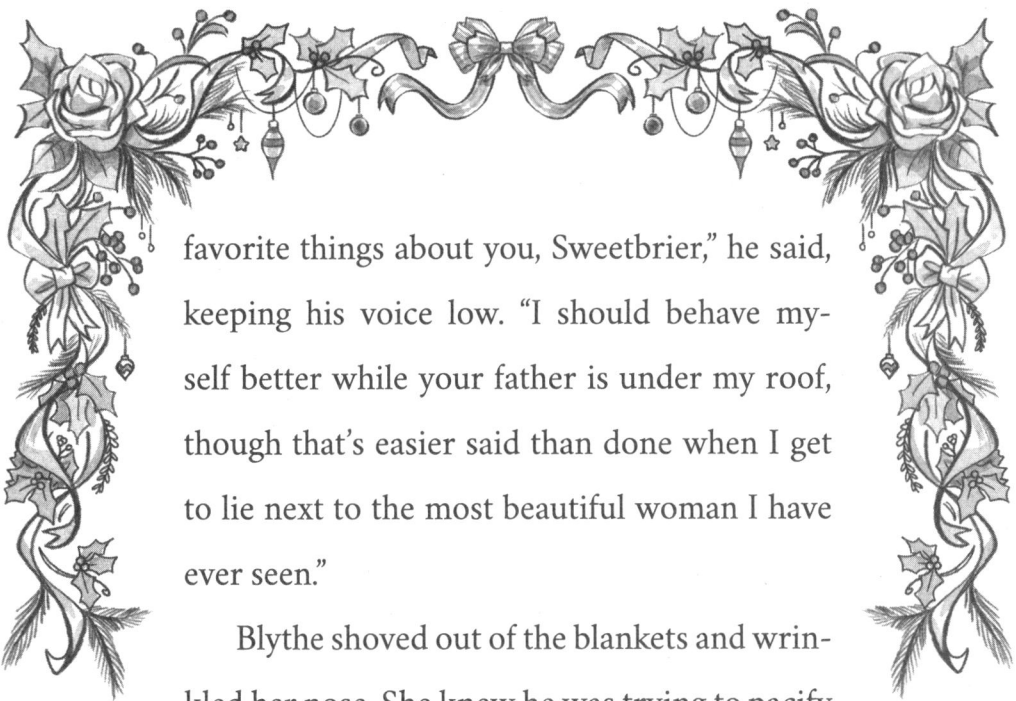

favorite things about you, Sweetbrier," he said, keeping his voice low. "I should behave myself better while your father is under my roof, though that's easier said than done when I get to lie next to the most beautiful woman I have ever seen."

Blythe shoved out of the blankets and wrinkled her nose. She knew he was trying to pacify her, and despised how it was working. She *was* rather fond of compliments.

"Behave however you'd like." She huffed, rolling onto her knees and reaching behind to pull the fastenings of her dress. Aris was there at once, stilling her hand.

"What are you doing?" His horror was enough to make Blythe whip her head around to glare at him over her shoulder.

"What do you *think* I'm doing? If you're not taking this dress off me, I'll do it myself.

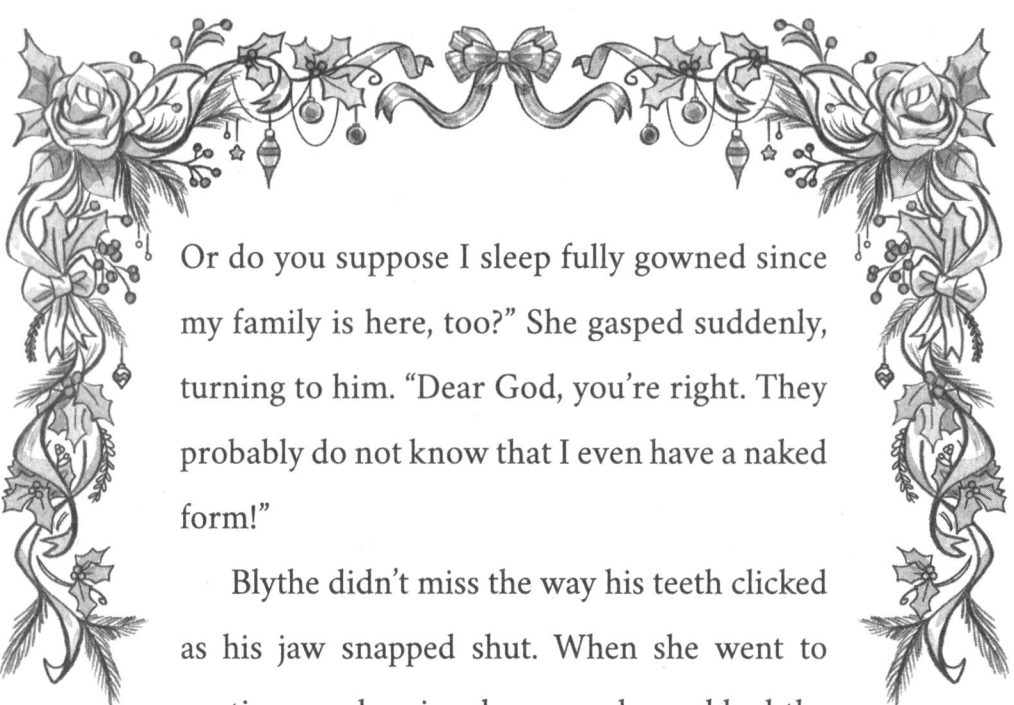

Or do you suppose I sleep fully gowned since my family is here, too?" She gasped suddenly, turning to him. "Dear God, you're right. They probably do not know that I even have a naked form!"

Blythe didn't miss the way his teeth clicked as his jaw snapped shut. When she went to continue undressing, however, he grabbed the skirts of her dress. Beneath his fingertips the fabric began to reweave itself, the silk skirts flattening, the shapely bodice softening into a loose nightgown. By the time he was finished, Blythe was dressed as if to turn in for the night, and she couldn't have been more offended.

"Did you just ruin my dress?"

"I'll fix it in the morning," Aris said, to which Blythe reached behind her to grab hold of a pillow that she promptly threw at his chest.

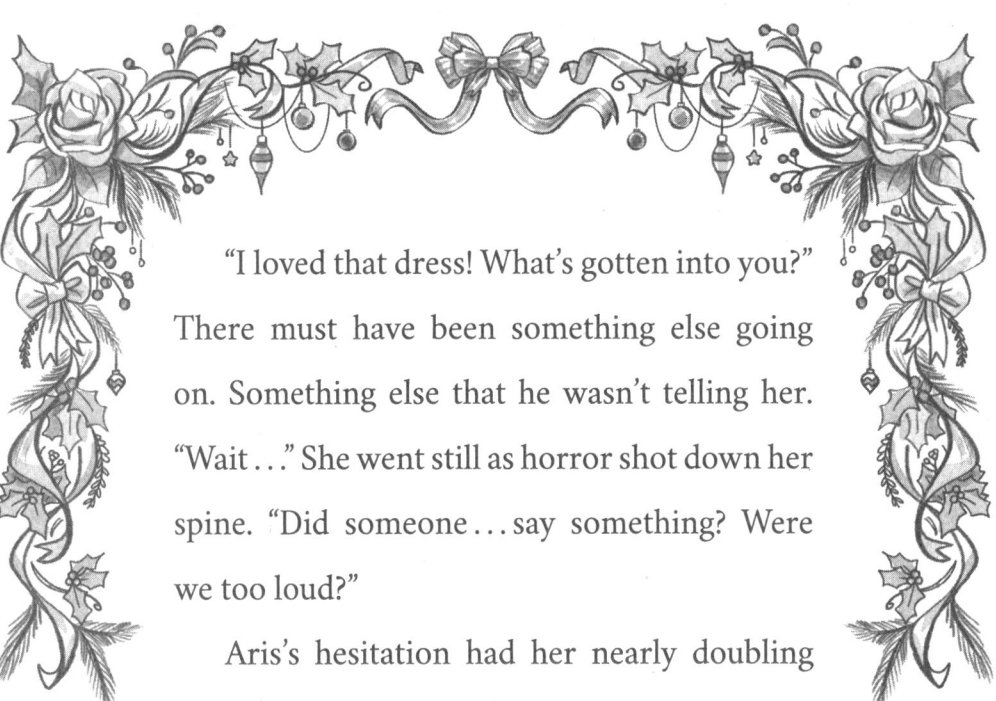

"I loved that dress! What's gotten into you?" There must have been something else going on. Something else that he wasn't telling her. "Wait..." She went still as horror shot down her spine. "Did someone...say something? Were we too loud?"

Aris's hesitation had her nearly doubling over. Blythe wanted to bury herself in the snowy ground and rot there forevermore. She would become one with the earth, never to look upon the faces of those she loved again.

Such plans of rotting, however, were fortunately cast aside when Aris shook his head.

"You really could have answered me more quickly." She sighed, so relieved that she fell back on the mattress. Aris joined her there, hand smoothing down the length of her gown. At first she thought he was doing it to be kind, only to realize that he was once again covering her legs. She kicked at him.

"I'm exhausted, Blythe." He yawned, settling his head on the pillow beside her. "Take pity on me." His golden eyes held hers, and it was as though all the fight melted from her body.

How frustrating it was that he held such power over her. Once, Blythe might have demanded he share whatever it was that he was hiding, but when he leaned in to press the softest kiss to her lips, the last thing she wanted was to stay angry at him. It was Christmastime, after all, and twenty-seven years had softened her resolve.

She laid her head beside him, his face mere inches away. "You'll tell me the reason for your strangeness soon, won't you?"

Aris took a strand of her hair and tucked it gently behind her ear. "Soon enough," he

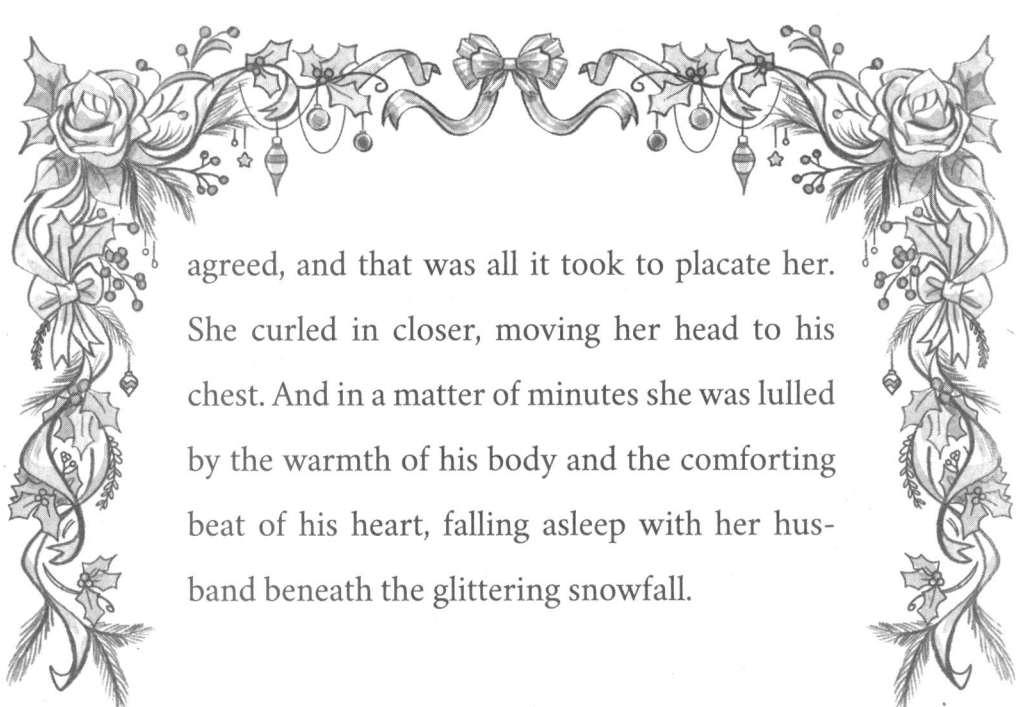

agreed, and that was all it took to placate her. She curled in closer, moving her head to his chest. And in a matter of minutes she was lulled by the warmth of his body and the comforting beat of his heart, falling asleep with her husband beneath the glittering snowfall.

NINE

Signa

Blythe doted on her husband at breakfast, slicing his bacon into tiny pieces, one of which she fed to him. Aris was practically preening from the coddling, and Signa had half a mind to kick him under the table.

"What's wrong with your face?" he asked her between bites of his meal, his voice low and taunting. "Jealousy is unbecoming on you, Signa."

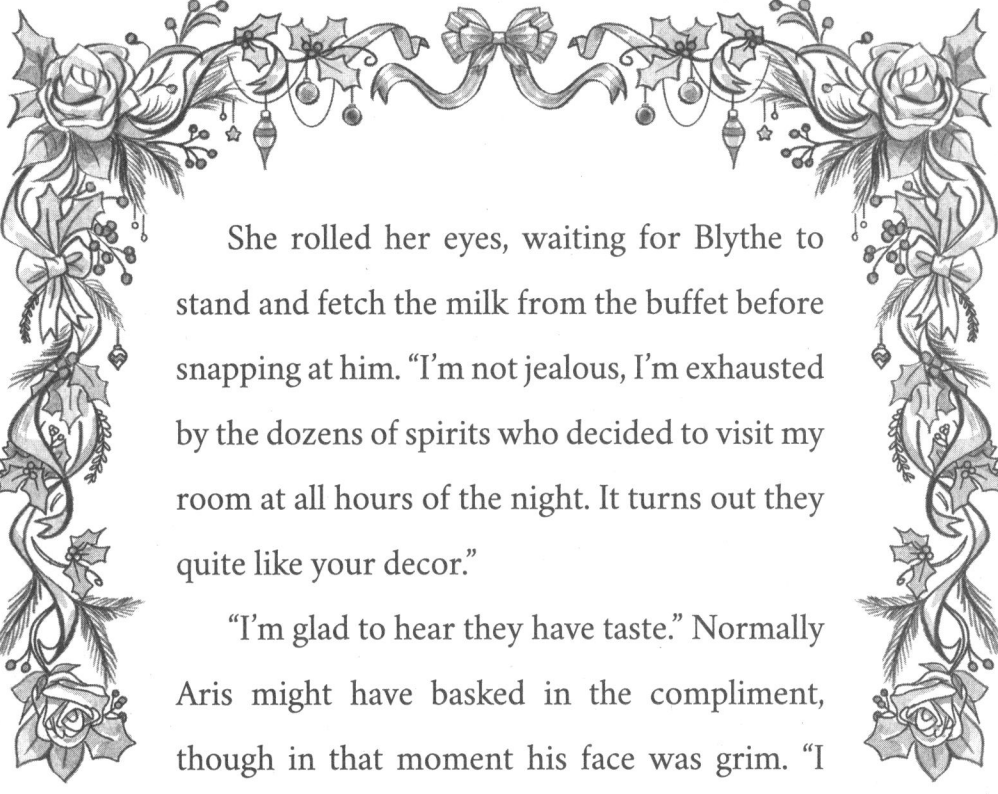

She rolled her eyes, waiting for Blythe to stand and fetch the milk from the buffet before snapping at him. "I'm not jealous, I'm exhausted by the dozens of spirits who decided to visit my room at all hours of the night. It turns out they quite like your decor."

"I'm glad to hear they have taste." Normally Aris might have basked in the compliment, though in that moment his face was grim. "I think they were in our room, too. My skin was crawling all night."

Signa's chest squeezed. It was one thing for *her* to be surrounded by spirits. She, at least, would always know whether they were there and never be forced to wonder whether someone was watching her sleep, eat, bathe, dress...whether they would snap and possess her.

"I assume they did not *see* anything?"

"They're already haunting my home. Do

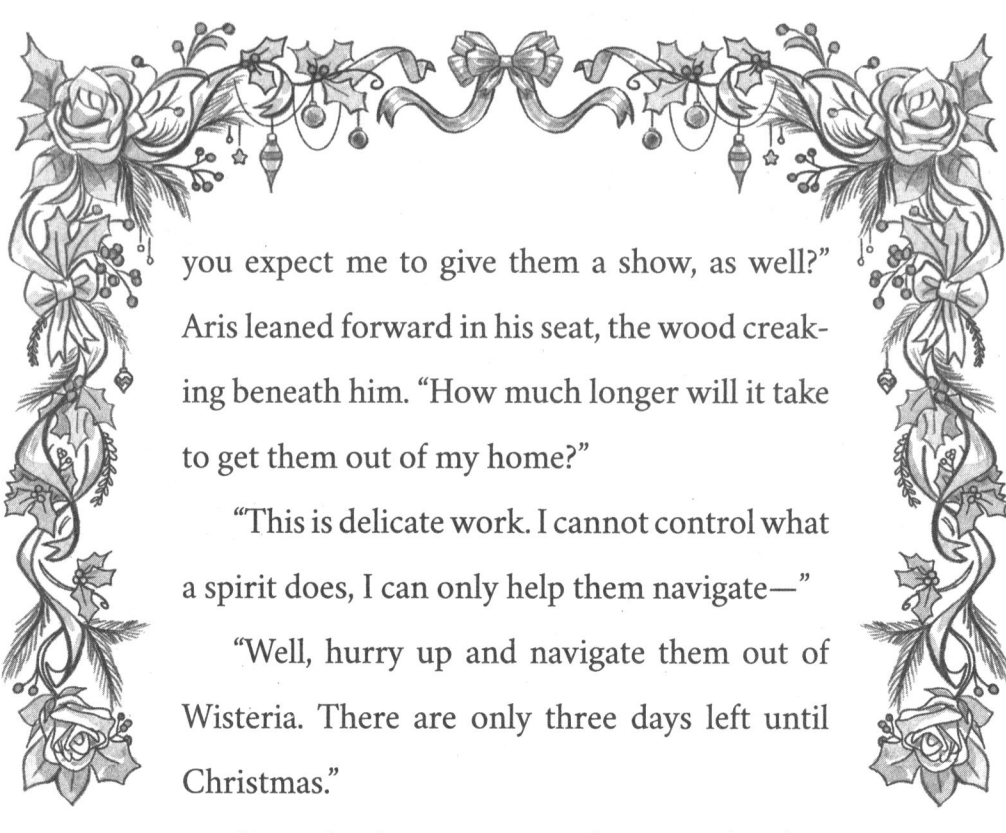

you expect me to give them a show, as well?" Aris leaned forward in his seat, the wood creaking beneath him. "How much longer will it take to get them out of my home?"

"This is delicate work. I cannot control what a spirit does, I can only help them navigate—"

"Well, hurry up and navigate them out of Wisteria. There are only three days left until Christmas."

Signa dug her spoon into her porridge, her eyes bloodshot and her head so heavy that it attempted several times to bob into her breakfast when she forgot to actively hold it up. "I'm working on it."

It was a relief that Elijah spoke up from across the table, noticing Signa's struggle. "Did you not sleep well?" he asked, the question immediately earning Blythe's attention upon her return.

"Was it the bed?" she asked, pouring milk into her porridge. "The room itself? Whatever the issue, Aris can change it to suit your needs."

"I already told her as much with a note," Aris offered. "If she decides she hates fun, I'm more than willing to oblige her poor taste."

Blythe swatted his arm, but Signa only said, "The room was fine. I suppose I was just missing Sylas."

"Ah yes." Elijah hummed. "The man that everyone here can see except for me."

Signa offered him a small smile, though it waned when she heard a teasing voice coaxing the back of her mind.

You're really using me as an excuse, Little Bird?

Signa had been so exhausted that she hadn't realized the reaper was there in her mind, listening. On her next bite, her spoon clanged harder against the bowl. *If you're too busy to come home, then you're too busy to spy on us,* she shot back before promptly ignoring him.

She *did* miss Sylas and had spent a great deal of time considering where he might be and what he could possibly be up to. But the true reason for her exhaustion stood with her in the dining room even then, giggling and dancing without any regard for those who were trying to have a peaceful breakfast. Still, her lie worked, perhaps a little too well. Signa could have sworn that her cousin turned purposefully away at her mention of Death.

"Blythe," Signa said slowly, leaning around Aris to get closer to her cousin. "Do you know where Sylas is?"

"Not precisely, no." She filled her mouth with eggs, refusing to elaborate. Signa wasn't placated so easily.

"But you know what he's doing, don't you?"

Blythe's lips flattened into a grim line. "It's possible that I might have a vague idea. I may or may not have asked for his assistance with an errand."

Signa quirked her brow, but given how much food Blythe continued to shovel into her mouth, it was clear her cousin was intent on avoiding any further answers.

"Then I suppose I will continue to await his return." Signa stood, earning the attention of the spirits as her chair scratched against the floorboards. "I have missions of my own to accomplish today. I'll be leaving Wisteria for a while—"

"*Leaving?*" Aris echoed midbite. He looked as though she'd suggested burning down the palace.

"Only for a few hours, and for work that I

cannot do here." Signa had spent her restless night sorting out a plan, and it had become clearer with each passing hour that if she was going to figure out what had happened to these spirits, she needed to seek information outside the confines of Wisteria. She'd listened to the spirits prattle on and had tried to pry information from them with little success. Now it was time to find out what she could learn from the town itself.

She didn't wait long to leave Wisteria. Signa had already been dressed for town and was out the door a handful of minutes after finishing breakfast, not leaving time for anyone to try to make her stay. She didn't turn back to look at the spirits who followed her, tailing her through the hall and to a front door they dared not venture past. Their eyes darkened as they stared between her and the door as if

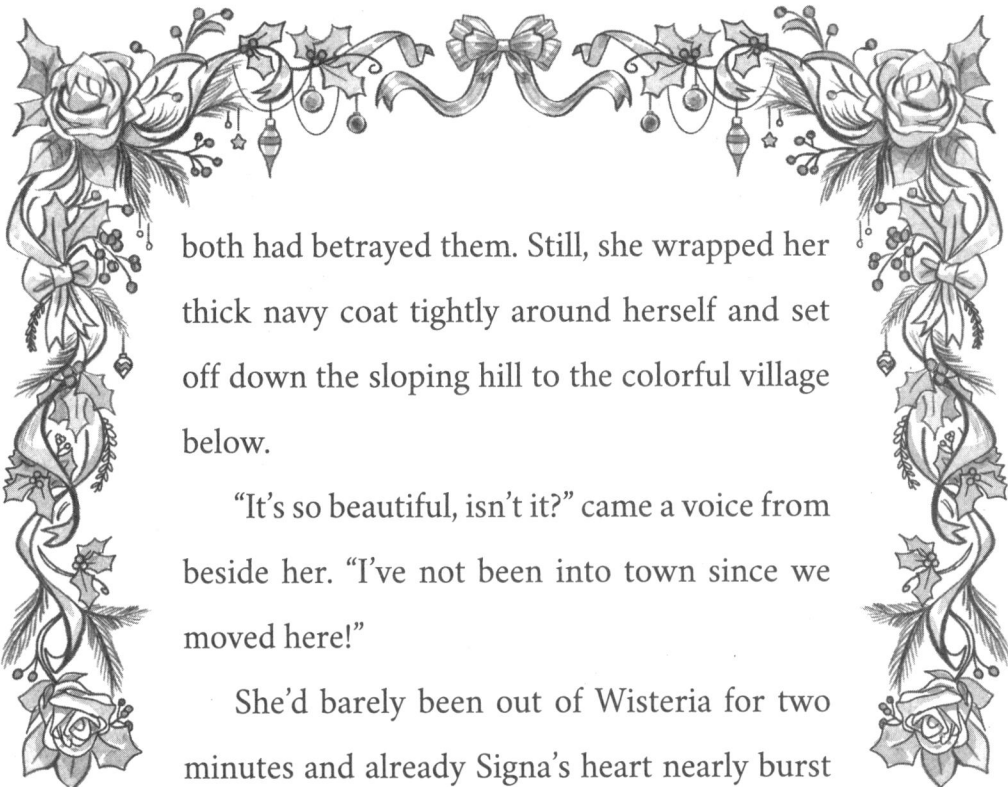

both had betrayed them. Still, she wrapped her thick navy coat tightly around herself and set off down the sloping hill to the colorful village below.

"It's so beautiful, isn't it?" came a voice from beside her. "I've not been into town since we moved here!"

She'd barely been out of Wisteria for two minutes and already Signa's heart nearly burst from her chest at Blythe's sudden appearance. Her cousin was dressed in a cream grown and a blush-pink cloak that matched the shade of her cheeks as the wintertime air nipped at her skin. Aris stood beside her in a striking crimson coat, tendrils of his breath wisping in air that had otherwise been empty only a second prior.

Signa glared at him. "Are you following me?" she asked, annoyed when his face contorted as if *she* were the ridiculous one.

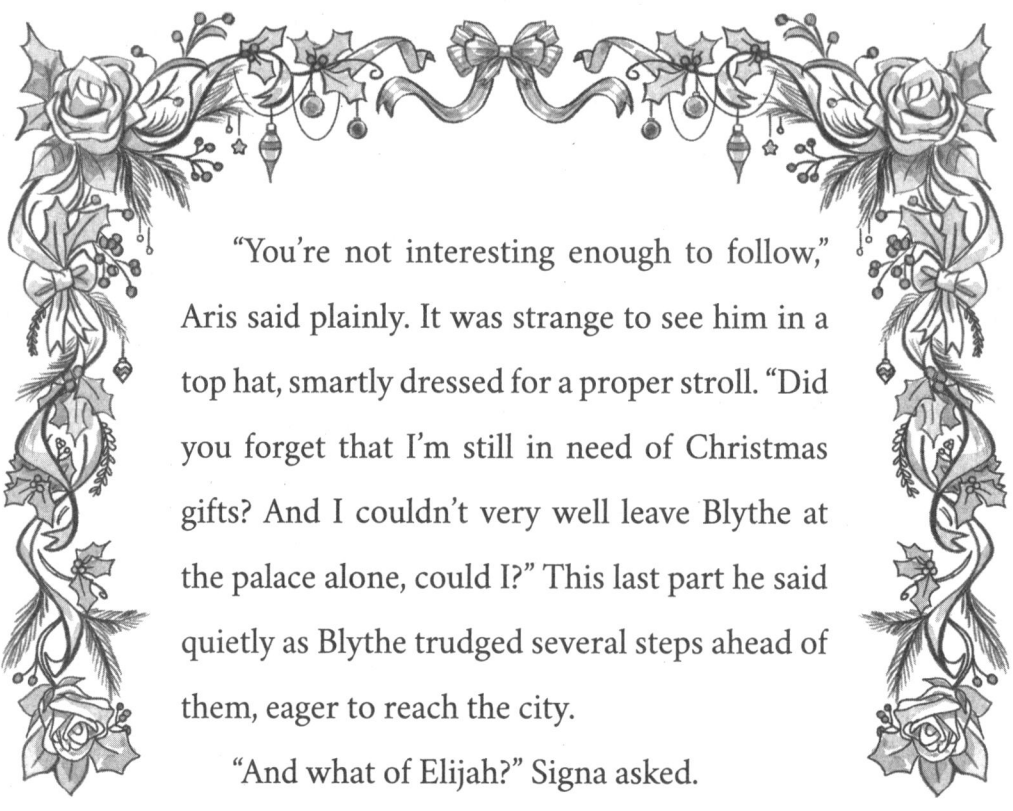

"You're not interesting enough to follow," Aris said plainly. It was strange to see him in a top hat, smartly dressed for a proper stroll. "Did you forget that I'm still in need of Christmas gifts? And I couldn't very well leave Blythe at the palace alone, could I?" This last part he said quietly as Blythe trudged several steps ahead of them, eager to reach the city.

"And what of Elijah?" Signa asked.

"Gundry is keeping him company by the hearth. He says his bones don't care for the snow."

She accepted the excuse, not too worried for his safety. The spirits had been mostly harmless so far, and she doubted that Elijah would do anything that might rile them. Still, she was glad that Gundry was there just in case.

"You are moving slower than snails," her

cousin called back at them. "Make haste, you two!"

Begrudgingly, Signa and Aris picked up their pace, cutting their way down a hill and following a long path that eventually led them to the outskirts of the city.

It was Signa's first time visiting the town that had captured her cousin's heart. Blythe had long talked about the snowy wonderland that was Brude, though she'd refused to visit without Aris. Now that he'd returned, Signa looked forward to seeing the place that had charmed them so thoroughly. Especially when it meant a few hours away from pesky spirits.

Brude was livelier than Signa had expected. Gone were the moss-shrouded Gothic architecture and ardent hills she was familiar with back at Foxglove. In their place were brightly colored buildings with pointed spires that struck

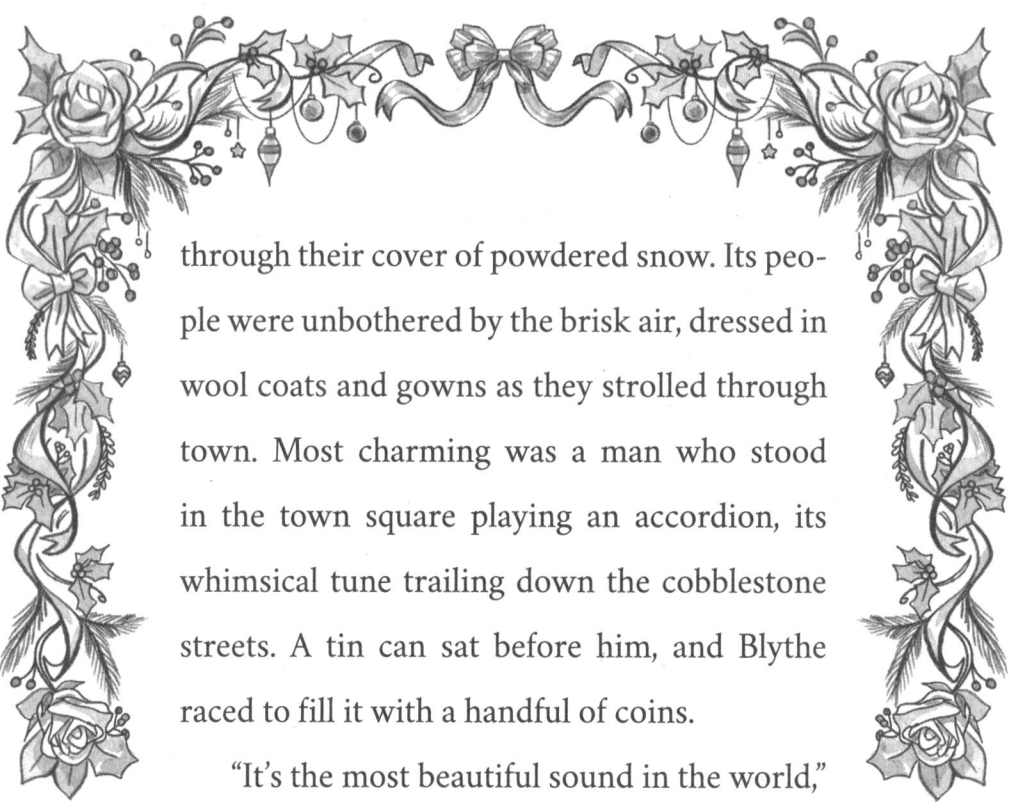

through their cover of powdered snow. Its people were unbothered by the brisk air, dressed in wool coats and gowns as they strolled through town. Most charming was a man who stood in the town square playing an accordion, its whimsical tune trailing down the cobblestone streets. A tin can sat before him, and Blythe raced to fill it with a handful of coins.

"It's the most beautiful sound in the world," she said with a dreamy sigh. "I hope that man never stops playing. Perhaps one day he'll even become a spirit who carries these tunes throughout the village."

"You know it is a poor fate to remain a spirit, don't you? We *want* souls to pass on," Signa reminded her, to which Blythe only pursed her lips, uninterested in having her fantasy swayed.

"Yes, yes. We want them to disappear off to the beautiful and mysterious afterlife. I am well

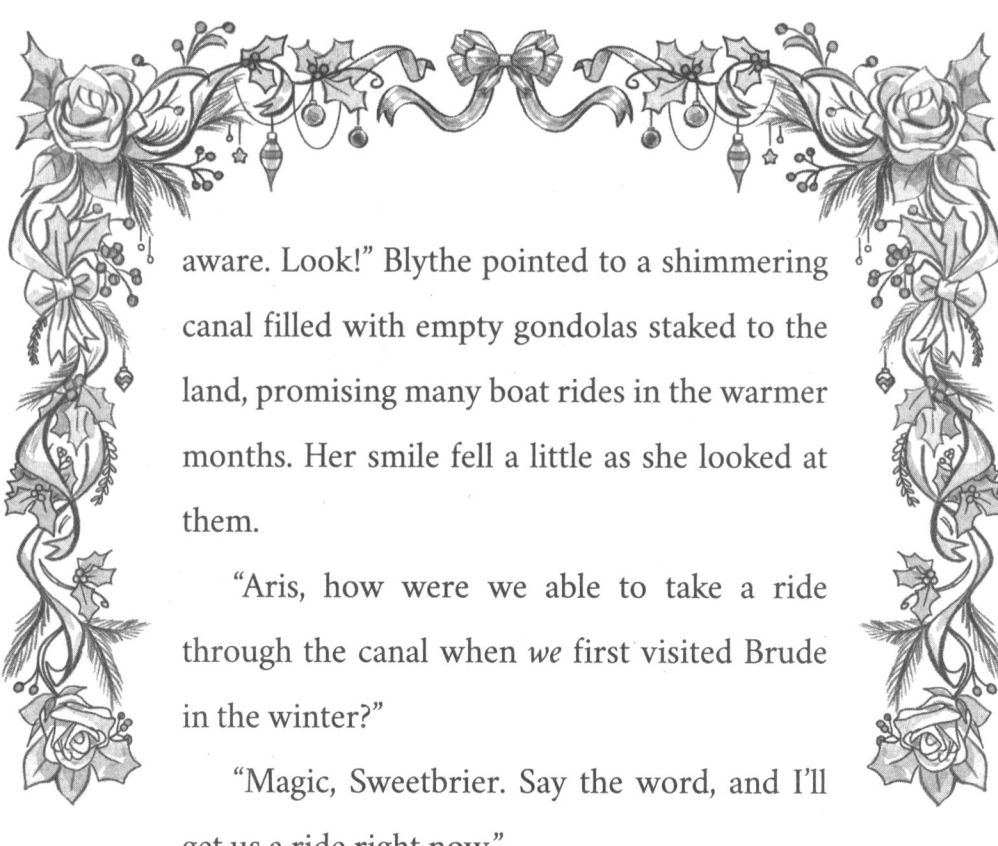

aware. Look!" Blythe pointed to a shimmering canal filled with empty gondolas staked to the land, promising many boat rides in the warmer months. Her smile fell a little as she looked at them.

"Aris, how were we able to take a ride through the canal when *we* first visited Brude in the winter?"

"Magic, Sweetbrier. Say the word, and I'll get us a ride right now."

"That's all right. Signa will simply have to return in the summer." And just like that Blythe was off again, continuing over the canal bridge. Meanwhile, Aris remained beside Signa, his hands folded behind his back and eyes on the water.

"Perhaps I could get her a gondola," he muttered, to which Signa laughed.

"You truly are terrible at this."

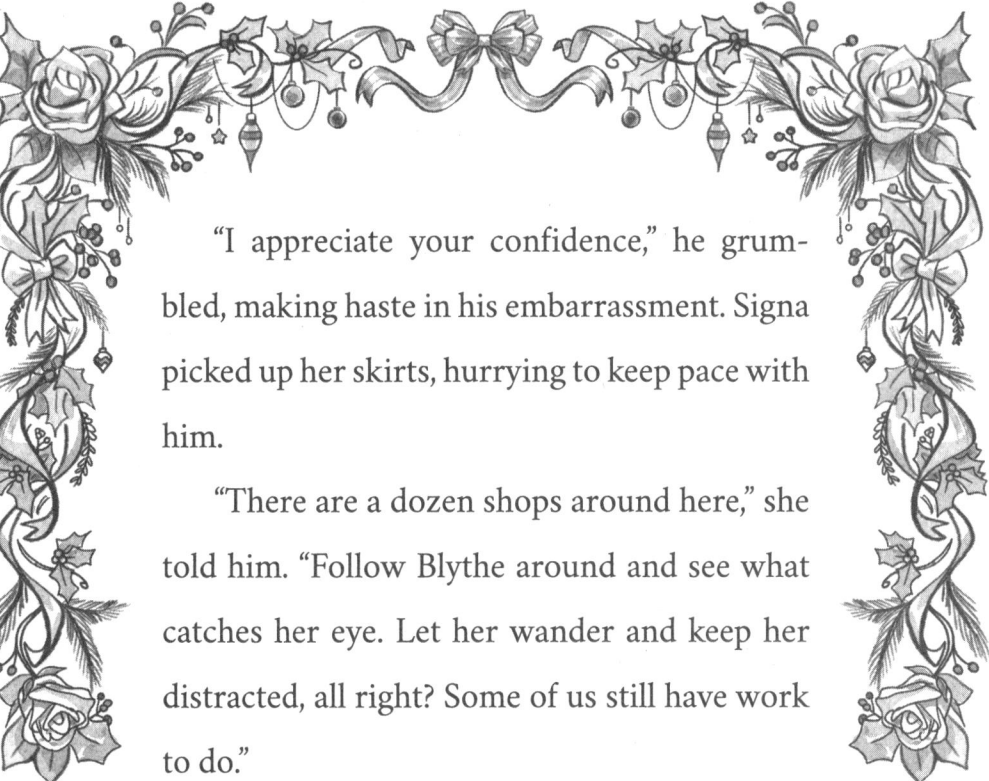

"I appreciate your confidence," he grumbled, making haste in his embarrassment. Signa picked up her skirts, hurrying to keep pace with him.

"There are a dozen shops around here," she told him. "Follow Blythe around and see what catches her eye. Let her wander and keep her distracted, all right? Some of us still have work to do."

"Keeping Blythe distracted is work in itself," he noted, though if the way his shoulders relaxed was any indicator, Aris seemed content with the plan. "But very well. You go learn how to get rid of the spirits, and I'll figure out what to get my wife for Christmas."

"How fair our tasks are," Signa mused, but gave no other complaint as she hurried off in the opposite direction.

The hardest part of solving any mystery

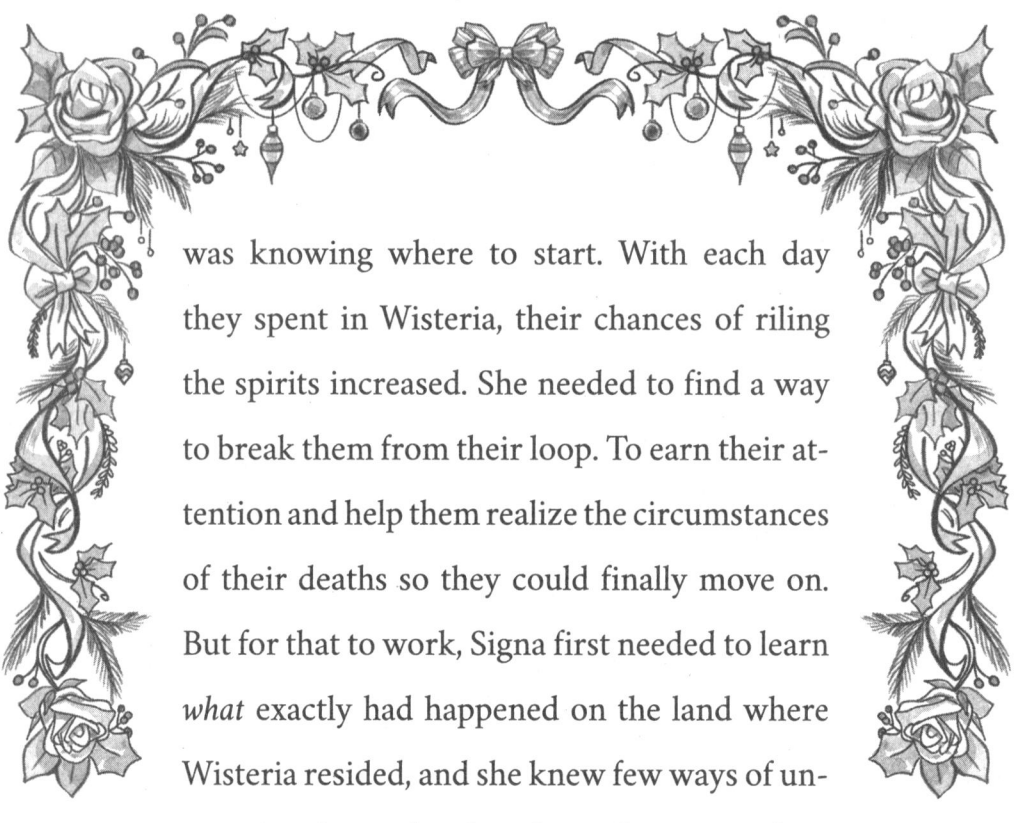

was knowing where to start. With each day they spent in Wisteria, their chances of riling the spirits increased. She needed to find a way to break them from their loop. To earn their attention and help them realize the circumstances of their deaths so they could finally move on. But for that to work, Signa first needed to learn *what* exactly had happened on the land where Wisteria resided, and she knew few ways of uncovering the truth other than asking outright.

Unfortunately, Signa had learned that people did not often take kindly to such forwardness, so she'd need to be clever about this.

As she wandered Brude, it was easy to see why her cousin had been so captivated by the town. Strolling the streets, one would think it a whimsical place unlikely to ever be filled with spirits. And yet Signa saw them everywhere.

Spirits roaming the canals, pale skinned and

blue lipped with soaked hair and clothes plastered to their skin. Curious children who tried to get the attention of everyone they passed, and hollow-eyed women who wandered the streets with their hair unbound and wearing rags for clothes.

Signa could live a million lifetimes, and still there would always be a surplus of spirits who needed her help. They were in every city, whether in a hovel or the most luxurious park, and drawn to her like moths to a flame. Even as she meandered down the cobblestone alleys, tucked into her coat and tactically avoiding their stares, she felt the press of their watchful gaze. Staring. Probing. Sensing that there was more to Signa than met the eye. She did everything in her power to try to avoid them, but they would chase her down to the edge of their limit and be waiting when she returned.

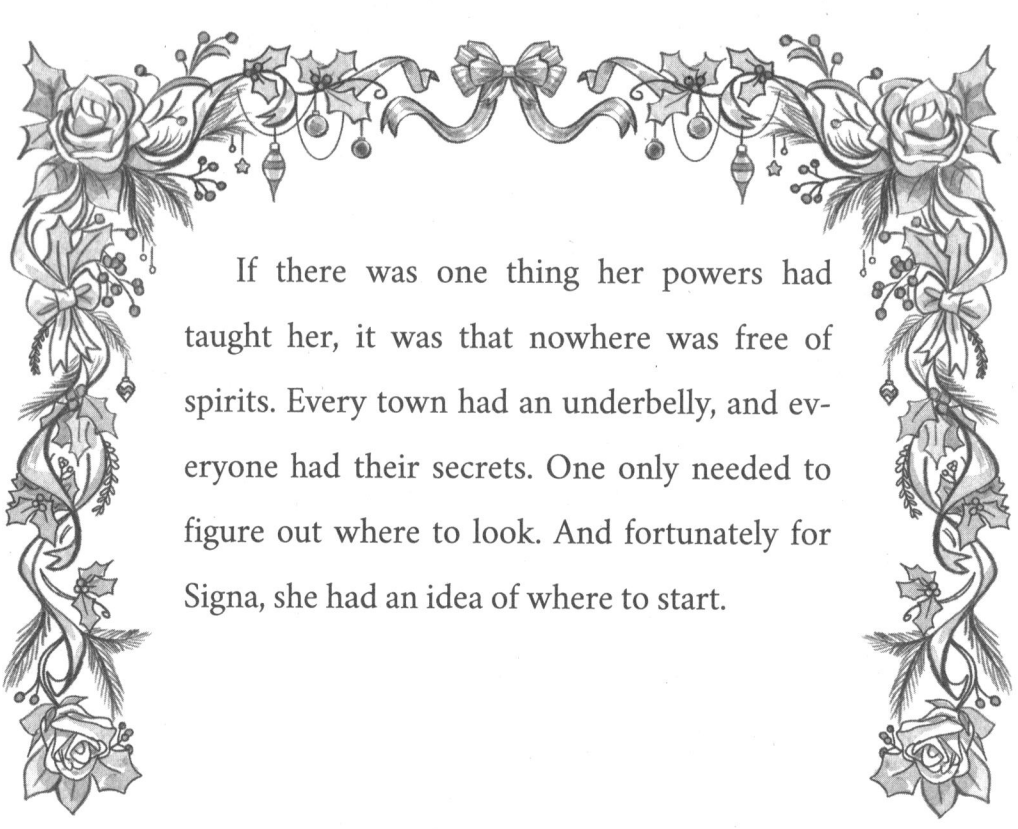

If there was one thing her powers had taught her, it was that nowhere was free of spirits. Every town had an underbelly, and everyone had their secrets. One only needed to figure out where to look. And fortunately for Signa, she had an idea of where to start.

TEN

Blythe

BLYTHE HAD LONG DREAMED OF THE DAY when she and Aris would stroll the streets of Brude once more. When the tune of the accordion would wash over her, and she could drink all the hot chocolate she craved while arm in arm with her husband. How marvelous it was to be back in this town. To make it a part of their daily lives between all the adventures they would one day share. For now, she didn't care

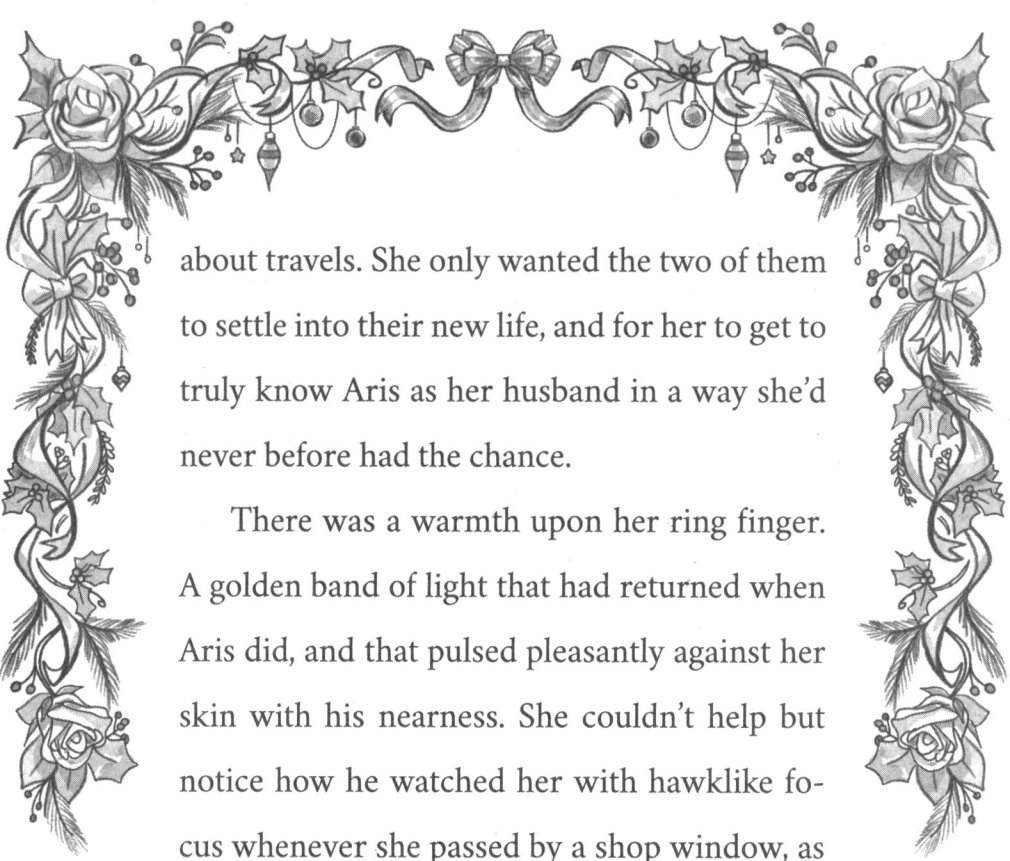

about travels. She only wanted the two of them to settle into their new life, and for her to get to truly know Aris as her husband in a way she'd never before had the chance.

There was a warmth upon her ring finger. A golden band of light that had returned when Aris did, and that pulsed pleasantly against her skin with his nearness. She couldn't help but notice how he watched her with hawklike focus whenever she passed by a shop window, as well as all the whispered secrets he and Signa had shared over the past several days. Blythe knew her husband was on the hunt for a perfect gift, though she wished he wasn't so concerned. She'd loved everything Aris had ever made for her, no matter how small.

Still, she knew her husband, so she knew he would not settle until he found what he believed to be the perfect gift.

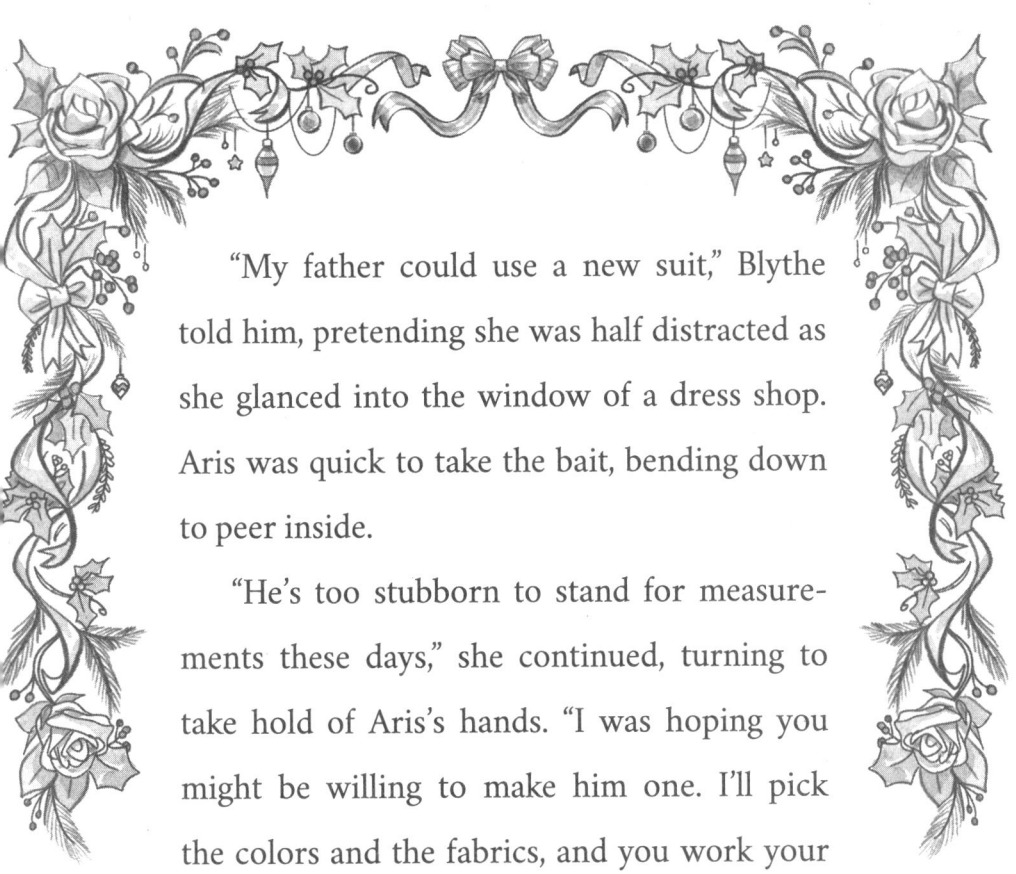

"My father could use a new suit," Blythe told him, pretending she was half distracted as she glanced into the window of a dress shop. Aris was quick to take the bait, bending down to peer inside.

"He's too stubborn to stand for measurements these days," she continued, turning to take hold of Aris's hands. "I was hoping you might be willing to make him one. I'll pick the colors and the fabrics, and you work your magic to make it the perfect fit. It'll be a gift from us both."

He nodded, hands gentle in hers. "Of course. Though I have a gift of my own in mind for him. He was the easiest of you lot to figure out."

Blythe hadn't realized how much those words would mean to her. While it was true that Elijah hadn't always been the father she'd hoped for while growing up, he'd made up for

it a thousand times over throughout the years, and heat pricked Blythe's eyes at the mere suggestion that Aris had been planning something for Elijah entirely of his own accord.

"I'm sure it'll be spectacular," she whispered, keen on not letting him see that her eyes were a touch misty.

"And what about for you?" he asked, drawing her close enough to be just on the edge of scandalous. "Would you like a trip? A new gown?"

"We have all that we need, Aris." She turned in his arms, tipping her head back against his chest. "There's nothing you need to buy. Should you insist on getting me something, let it be a gift you made."

He rested his chin atop her head, and she could feel the gentle pull of his lips as they smiled. "You're not tired of my magic?"

"You, my love, are a fool if you believe that I

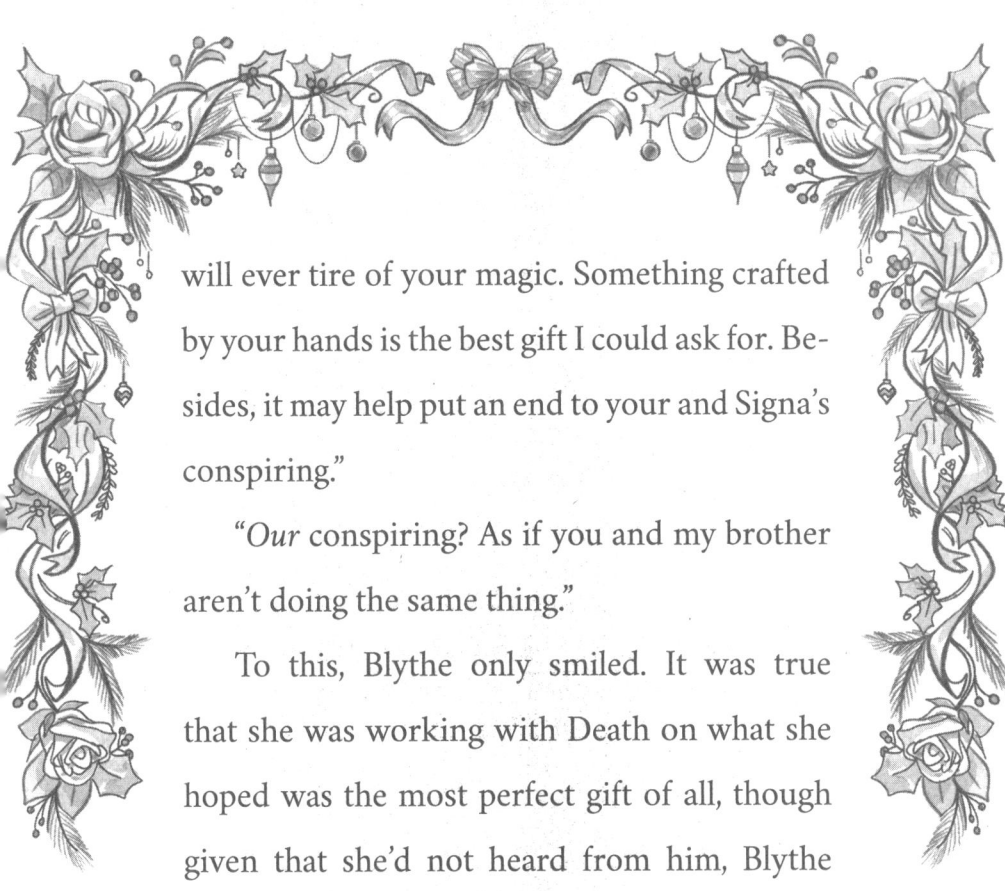

will ever tire of your magic. Something crafted by your hands is the best gift I could ask for. Besides, it may help put an end to your and Signa's conspiring."

"*Our* conspiring? As if you and my brother aren't doing the same thing."

To this, Blythe only smiled. It was true that she was working with Death on what she hoped was the most perfect gift of all, though given that she'd not heard from him, Blythe could only hope that all was well.

"No one needs perfect, Aris. We only need you." It was strange sometimes to remember how new this all was for him. Through his tapestries, Blythe was certain that Aris had lived a million different Christmases, some of them modest, others spectacular. Some full of gifts and family, and others that felt no different from any ordinary day. But Fate himself would

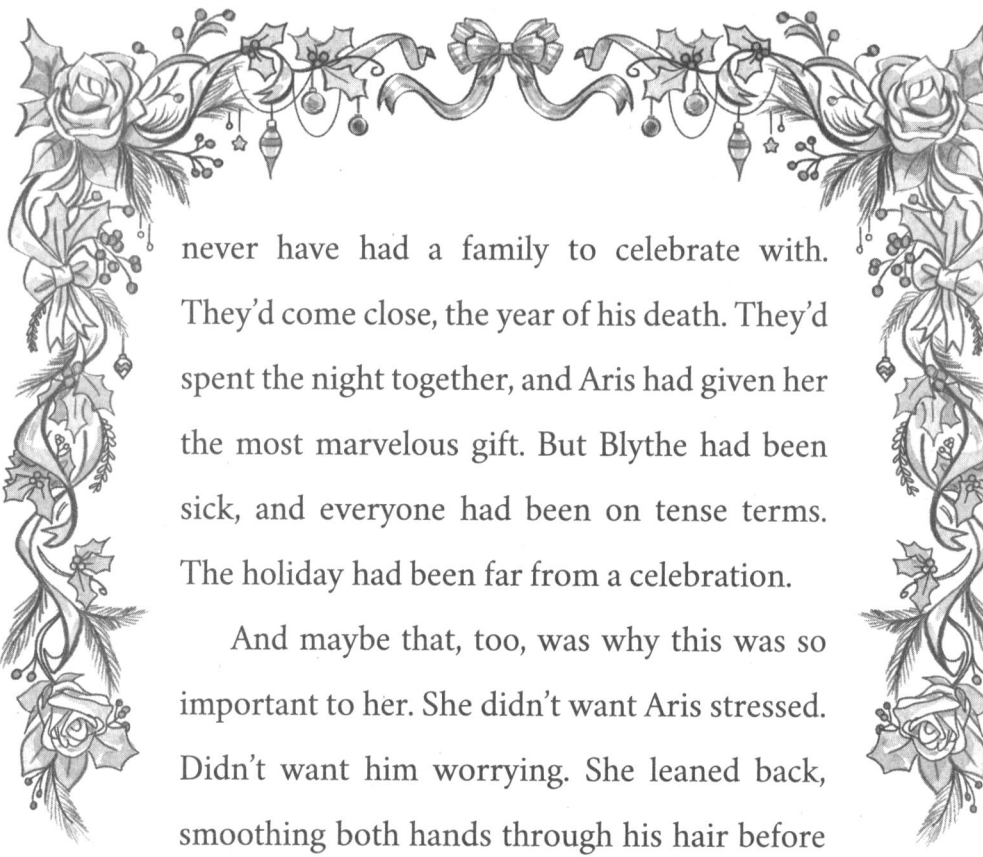

never have had a family to celebrate with. They'd come close, the year of his death. They'd spent the night together, and Aris had given her the most marvelous gift. But Blythe had been sick, and everyone had been on tense terms. The holiday had been far from a celebration.

And maybe that, too, was why this was so important to her. She didn't want Aris stressed. Didn't want him worrying. She leaned back, smoothing both hands through his hair before she cupped either side of his face.

"What I want most is to enjoy our time here. To roll around in the snow and drink the greatest hot chocolate in the world. Return with me later to Wisteria, and let us relax and play games. Let us enjoy the holiday without this unnecessary fuss, all right? No more scheming or agonizing. Just be here, with me."

Though his body softened beneath her

touch, there was a hardened edge in Aris's eye that Blythe worried at. One that told her this request, perhaps, would not be so easy for him.

"We will have the Christmas you dream of," he said, kissing the backs of her knuckles as he took hold of her hand once more. "I swear it. But we need not wait until we return home to have fun."

Blythe squealed as he practically tackled her on the street, grabbing her by the waist and hauling her over his shoulder.

"Aris!" she cried between bursts of laughter. "This is not how you hold a lady!"

"It is when you want to be efficient." He carved a swift path through town, unbothered as Blythe fussed against him. In the end she had no choice but to just hang there on his shoulder, offering a thin smile and a small wave to all who stared at them as they passed.

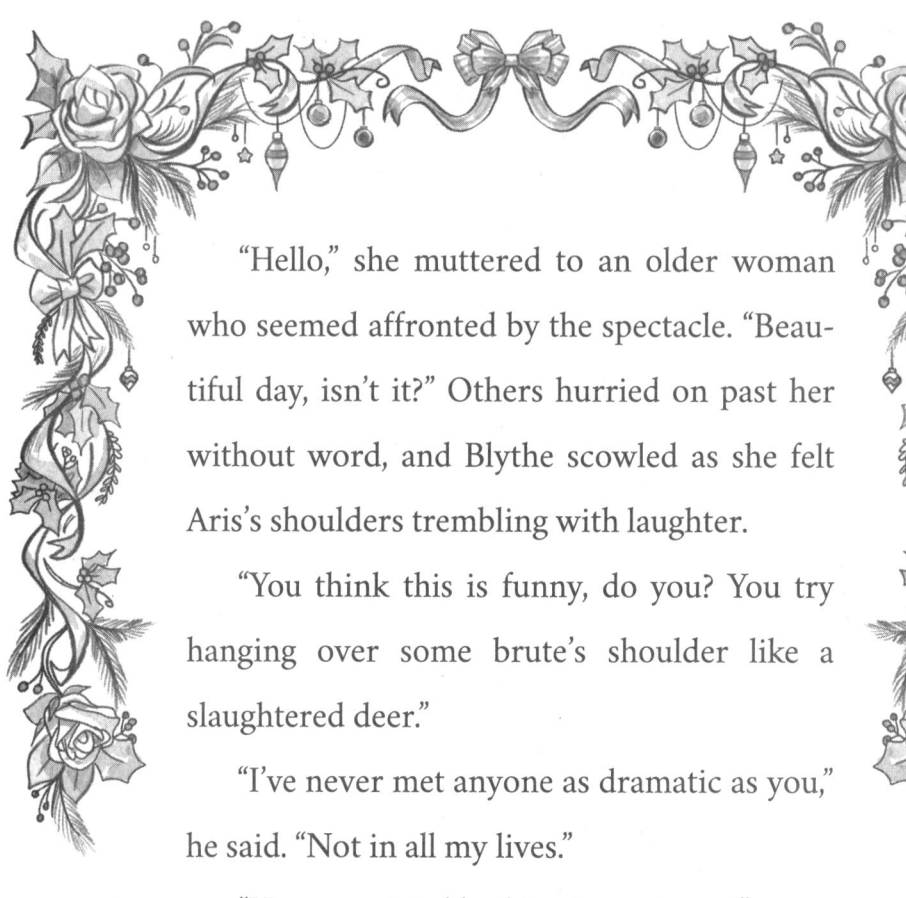

"Hello," she muttered to an older woman who seemed affronted by the spectacle. "Beautiful day, isn't it?" Others hurried on past her without word, and Blythe scowled as she felt Aris's shoulders trembling with laughter.

"You think this is funny, do you? You try hanging over some brute's shoulder like a slaughtered deer."

"I've never met anyone as dramatic as you," he said. "Not in all my lives."

"Have you tried looking in a mirror?"

They were outside town now, back near the woods, and Aris gave her no answer. Instead, he threw her off his shoulder and straight into a mound of powdered snow. She landed on her back, mouth gaping open and her eyes wide in shock as he hovered over her, biting back a smirk.

"You absolute barbarian." She sat upright,

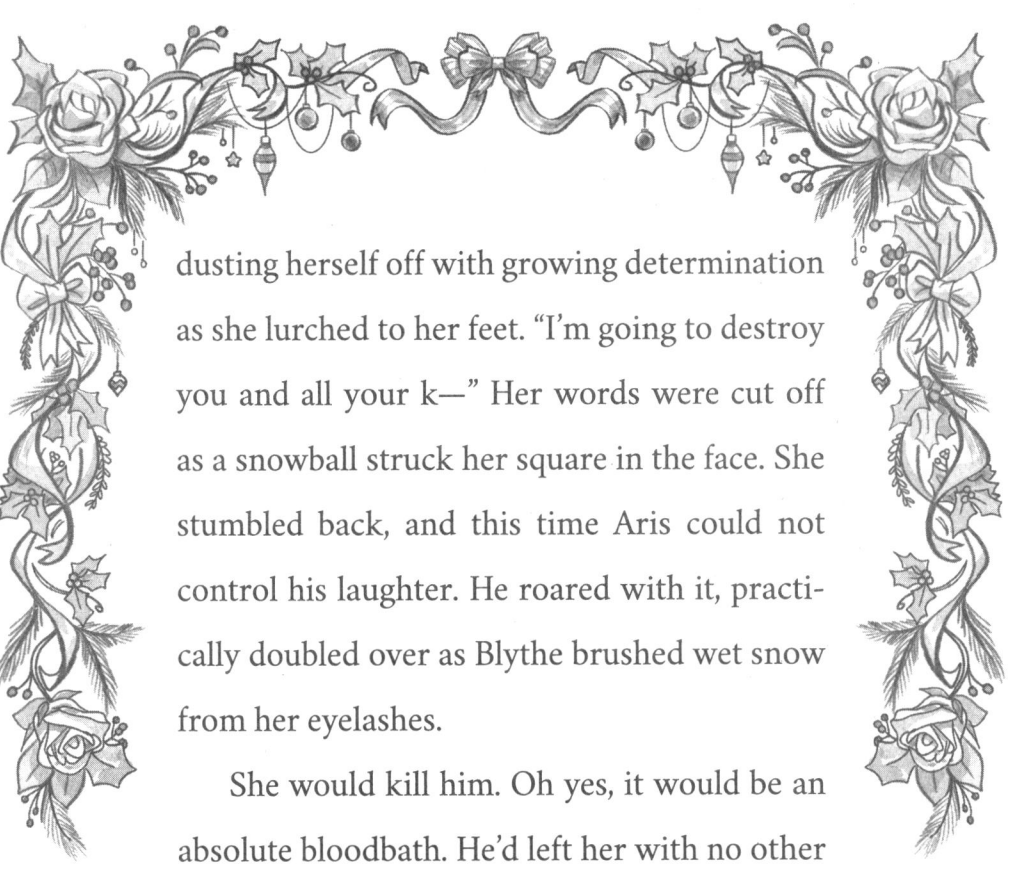

dusting herself off with growing determination as she lurched to her feet. "I'm going to destroy you and all your k—" Her words were cut off as a snowball struck her square in the face. She stumbled back, and this time Aris could not control his laughter. He roared with it, practically doubled over as Blythe brushed wet snow from her eyelashes.

She would kill him. Oh yes, it would be an absolute bloodbath. He'd left her with no other choice.

Aris was already scooping more snow, but Blythe had no intention of playing fairly. The ground rumbled as she called upon the roots beneath Aris's heels, summoning them up to knock him onto his back. He fell into the snow, gasping as Blythe piled a mound and tossed it at him. She didn't bother to properly shape the snow into something easily thrown, but rather continued to rapidly scoop it onto him, as if working to bury her husband. Aris's hair was soaked, blond strands plastered against his scalp and cheeks as he tried to escape the verdant vines that grew from the soil. Only when Aris's eyes darkened to a deep molten gold did Blythe stop, for his threads had woven around her. They forced her hands to turn, and suddenly the snow in her palms was not directed at Aris, but at herself.

She cursed as her traitorous hands hefted armfuls of snow, spluttering as they tossed it up and into her own face.

"Shall we declare a truce?" Aris asked. Blythe had dropped control over the vines in her distraction, and he crossed the ground to stand before her, sporting a smug expression. It'd take a good while until she was truly skilled enough in her magic to go toe-to-toe with

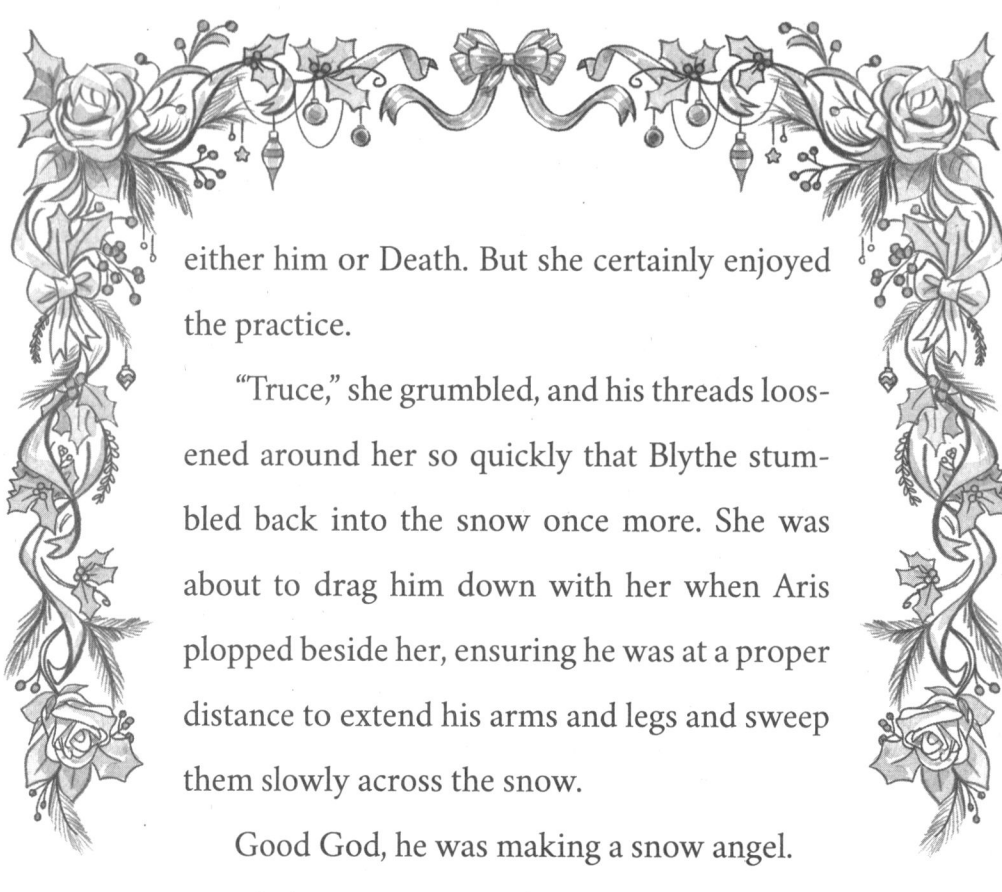

either him or Death. But she certainly enjoyed the practice.

"Truce," she grumbled, and his threads loosened around her so quickly that Blythe stumbled back into the snow once more. She was about to drag him down with her when Aris plopped beside her, ensuring he was at a proper distance to extend his arms and legs and sweep them slowly across the snow.

Good God, he was making a snow angel.

Blythe grinned and followed suit, swiping until she was certain the snow had taken her shape and then carefully standing upright. Aris joined her, taking her hand and guiding them a step back to inspect their work.

Blythe tipped her head as she inspected them. "Yours looks crooked."

"And yours looks tiny and frightening. I didn't know these were meant to be self-portraits."

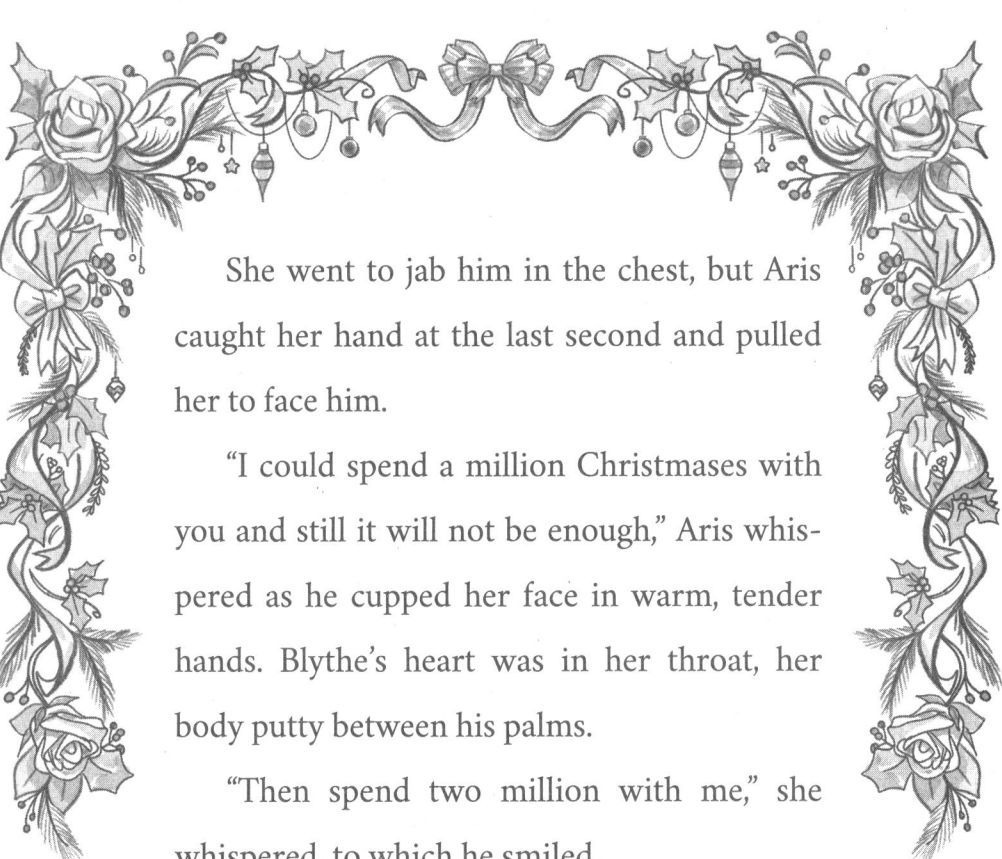

She went to jab him in the chest, but Aris caught her hand at the last second and pulled her to face him.

"I could spend a million Christmases with you and still it will not be enough," Aris whispered as he cupped her face in warm, tender hands. Blythe's heart was in her throat, her body putty between his palms.

"Then spend two million with me," she whispered, to which he smiled.

"Two million." Aris bent to kiss her, and Blythe couldn't imagine herself ever able to feel happier than she did as he whispered against her skin, "Let's start there."

ELEVEN

Signa

Signa enjoyed spending time in cemeteries. In fact, there was a beautiful kirkyard back in Fiore that she would often visit on her strolls. Not because she was macabre, or odd, or whatever people thought to say about her, but because they were one of the quietest places she'd ever found.

It was silly how many people believed cemeteries were haunted. They could be unnerving, yes, when one considered the sheer number of bones and bodies buried beneath the soil, but the best thing about spirits was that they did not cling to those bodies. Rather, they clung to the land in which they had died, and very few people ever truly died *in* a cemetery.

That wasn't to say it never happened. Signa had once seen a man whose skull had been beaten into a tombstone. She'd also seen a spirit who had clearly been buried alive, though that particular situation was one she tried not to think about too often as it reminded her of Percy.

Regardless of what others believed, Signa preferred to think of cemeteries as places to celebrate memories—almost like scrapbooks in the way that so many lives were etched onto stones. Messages for loved ones. Their favorite flowers or pastries delivered so that they'd know they were remembered. That there were

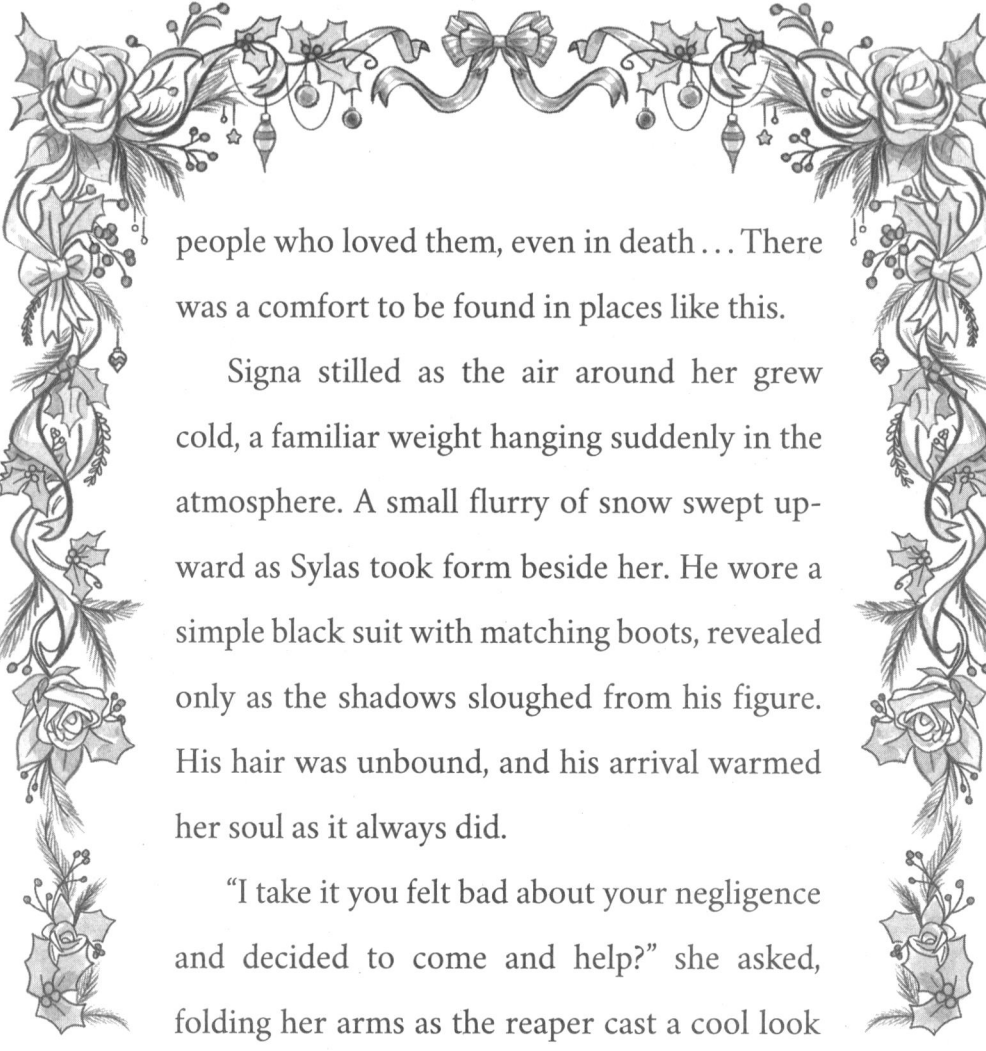

people who loved them, even in death... There was a comfort to be found in places like this.

Signa stilled as the air around her grew cold, a familiar weight hanging suddenly in the atmosphere. A small flurry of snow swept upward as Sylas took form beside her. He wore a simple black suit with matching boots, revealed only as the shadows sloughed from his figure. His hair was unbound, and his arrival warmed her soul as it always did.

"I take it you felt bad about your negligence and decided to come and help?" she asked, folding her arms as the reaper cast a cool look over the cemetery. He watched as a young man crouched nearby, tears in his eyes as his fingers traced a headstone almost reverently.

"I'll never fathom why you enjoy coming to these places." He sighed. "I do not favor heartache."

Signa understood why he found it difficult to watch the mourning, though she disagreed that cemeteries were only for heartache. "Not that you deserve to know, but I'm here to work. There are spirits who need to pass on." Signa plucked a small handful of flowers for good measure. If she was going to be wandering around, it was best to look the part.

Sylas followed as she slipped ahead of him, watching her with great curiosity. "And you intend to help them from a cemetery?"

"I don't have to," she challenged. "We could both return to Wisteria now, if you'd agree to offer your assistance."

"You know I cannot," he said. "The spirits must make their own choice to pass on, and I'm afraid I can't stay for long."

"And why is that? Just where are you running off to, Sylas?"

"It's the holiday season, Little Bird," he whispered. "Things are always busy this month. Do not be angry with me. I would much prefer to be home with you, though your cousin has requested that I help her search for someone."

"For *who*, exactly?"

"She's asked that I not say. It's better that way, in case I cannot find them."

Signa chewed on her lip, still glaring. "And what of the spirits? Why is it that Wisteria is full of them when you helped choose this land?"

Slowly his shadows crept around her waist, luring her toward him. Signa didn't make it easy for him, turning her body into a deadweight. "Perhaps I was lazy in my research."

She scoffed. "Or perhaps you're hiding something."

He hummed under his breath. "You're doing

well with them. But why have you come here of all places?"

It was clear that Sylas had no intention of telling her anything more. She clenched her jaw. Had he taken a page out of Blythe's book with all these games he was playing with her?

"There are dozens of spirits in Wisteria. With that many people having died all together, surely there must be some sign here of what happened."

It was a stretch, but she'd hoped to find a familiar name among the gravestones. *Jules*, or perhaps *Odette*. She didn't know either of their surnames, but she knew a fire had somehow been involved in their deaths.

Sylas's shadows released her, curling on themselves. The reaper, of all people, appeared pleased.

"That's brilliant." His hand slipped into

hers, and before she could roll her eyes, Sylas was pulling her along through the cemetery. "Let's see what we can find, shall we?"

She much preferred having Sylas there with her, but her grumpiness couldn't keep her from uttering a low, "I thought you had somewhere else to be."

"I do, but I missed you." He smiled at her, so disarmingly handsome that Signa felt herself melt. "You said you wanted my help, so I thought I could spare an hour or so."

"Very well." She wrapped her fingers around his, relaxing into the coolness of his touch. "I'm glad you're here."

Brude's cemetery was beautiful. It was not so green as the one back in Fiore, where moss and lichen fought to overtake the tombstones and where every step was crooked and precarious. It was instead bright and pristine, and made even more so by the snow that blanketed the flat ground. Every stone and statue had been meticulously polished to the point that she was convinced no dirt lay beneath this snow. Best of all, just as she'd hoped, there were no spirits to be seen.

But that didn't mean that she was alone.

"These places are always so busy during the holidays," Death noted, watching families bundled in their coats walking with flowers in their hands.

"There's something about this time of year," she said. "It softens our hearts, and makes the absence of those we miss all the more apparent." Signa tried her best to avoid anyone's eyes. It felt wrong to be wandering while there were families crying over tombstones and whispering conversations to the dead. At the end of the day, everyone wanted the same thing—for the spirits of this world to feel loved and cared for. For them to be able to move on to a better and happier existence.

Snow crunched softly beneath Signa's boots as she journeyed deeper into the cemetery, taking her time reading every headstone.

"Look at this one," Sylas said, stopping before a tall headstone. The stone's surface was weathered but still elegant, the inscription framed by a delicate design of ivy and roses etched into the marble. "'In memory of Arthur Pembroke,'" he read aloud, "'who always said, I'll rest when I'm dead.' And so he does." Sylas was grinning by the time he straightened himself. "Perhaps these places aren't so bad after all."

"They certainly have a sense of humor," she said, walking past him and toward a mausoleum near the back corner. It had a statue of an angel holding a trumpet guarding either side of it. It wasn't those alone that gave Signa pause, but the flames carved into the immaculate white stone around them. Hope flooding her chest, Signa entered the building. Inside were more depictions of flames among snowflakes, and several candles left unlit. The dim light made the plaques on the wall so dark that Signa struggled to read them, searching for a familiar name.

Gaspard. Henri. Isabelle. Jeanne. Laurent... She read plaque after plaque until a single familiar name showed up.

ODETTE VAN DER MEER
1682–1705

In memory of a radiant star, whose
light was tragically extinguished
on Christmas Eve.
May you dance forevermore.

The cold seeped through the stone walls as Signa sat waiting in the mausoleum. Snow fell steadily outside, blanketing the cemetery in silence. She'd been there for around six hours so far, watching the steady trickle of visitors through the open door.

Families came and went, laying flowers on graves and bowing their heads in quiet reverence. Some lingered, spending hours among the dead. Others hurried, the cold driving them home. But none ventured inside the mausoleum.

Signa had read every plaque several dozen times, pacing circles and memorizing the names etched in the walls. Her hands had become numb, and she shifted on the bench, the cold biting at her. Winter made the days short, and

already the sunlight was waning. The cemetery would close soon, and though Signa had resolved herself to coming back as many days as it took to find a visitor, the idea was already exhausting her.

She had finally stood to leave when she startled at the sight of a man standing at the threshold holding a beautiful bouquet of poinsettias in his hand.

"Good evening," he whispered, brow furrowed toward his nose. "I didn't expect to find anyone else here."

The man was likely older than Elijah, with a wrinkled face and eyes that crinkled at the corners. He stepped inside to join Signa, setting the flowers beneath Odette's name.

Wariness tightened her gut. Surely it couldn't be this easy.

"I admit that I do not know these people,"

she said softly. She'd gotten better over the years at feigning normalcy around death, and at holding conversations with the living. But still she had to be mindful of her words, especially when there was important information to be found. "But I felt compelled to step inside all the same."

The old man grunted. "Not unusual for the time of year. Many folk from around these parts come and visit during the holidays. Makes for a good ghost story, I suppose. I didn't plan to come here myself, but it seemed a good idea to make sure everyone had some company." He stepped forward, fingers skimming along several of the inscriptions. "It's terrible what they went through."

"I'm afraid I don't know the story," Signa admitted. "I came to see what I might learn, as I have family who live up the hill just outside of town, on the land where I believe these people might have died."

"I didn't realize someone had moved there," he whispered, half distracted as he moved from name to name, dipping his head and taking a moment with each plaque. "It used to be a theater, back before it burned down. For sixty-one years that land has sat empty. People say it's haunted."

"And do you agree?" Signa asked.

His face darkened. "Each night I pray that it's not. I hope that everyone inside the theater went quickly, passing out from the smoke before the flames consumed them."

Something about the way he said it nagged at Signa, prickling the hairs along her neck. She looked again at the man, at the deep wrinkles around his eyes and the sunspots on his hands. He had a lithe body that moved more nimbly than many his age, and there was a sorrow in his eyes and a familiarity that made it clear he wasn't mourning strangers.

"Were you close to any of them?"

The man's gaze skimmed to Odette's plaque, and his jaw tightened. "I was close to all of them. They were my friends, my colleagues... even my first love."

"Jules," Signa said instinctively, unable to filter herself. "Your name is Jules, isn't it?"

He tensed for a moment, then softened again as a sigh passed his lips. "So you do know something about that night."

What were the chances? Signa wondered. How strange it was to have found him so easily.

She had always believed in coincidence. It was Aris and Blythe who had made her less sure of it over time, and far more suspicious of theoretical chance happenings. Still, Signa was here with the man every spirit back at Wisteria sought out. She would not let the opportunity slip by, no matter how curious it was.

"I know they all died, and that a man named Jules was missing that night." Though she put no accusation in her voice, his face hardened all the same.

"Blame me if you'd like. It's nothing I haven't spent a lifetime hearing already."

"I don't blame you." Signa had, of course, been wrong before. But this man didn't strike her as a killer. "I have no reason to blame anyone. I didn't even know those who died."

His shoulders slumped, chest caving in as though he'd been struck. "Well, you *should* blame me. It was my fault the theater caught fire."

She tried to keep her grimace to herself, moving to a nearby bench and motioning for him to join her.

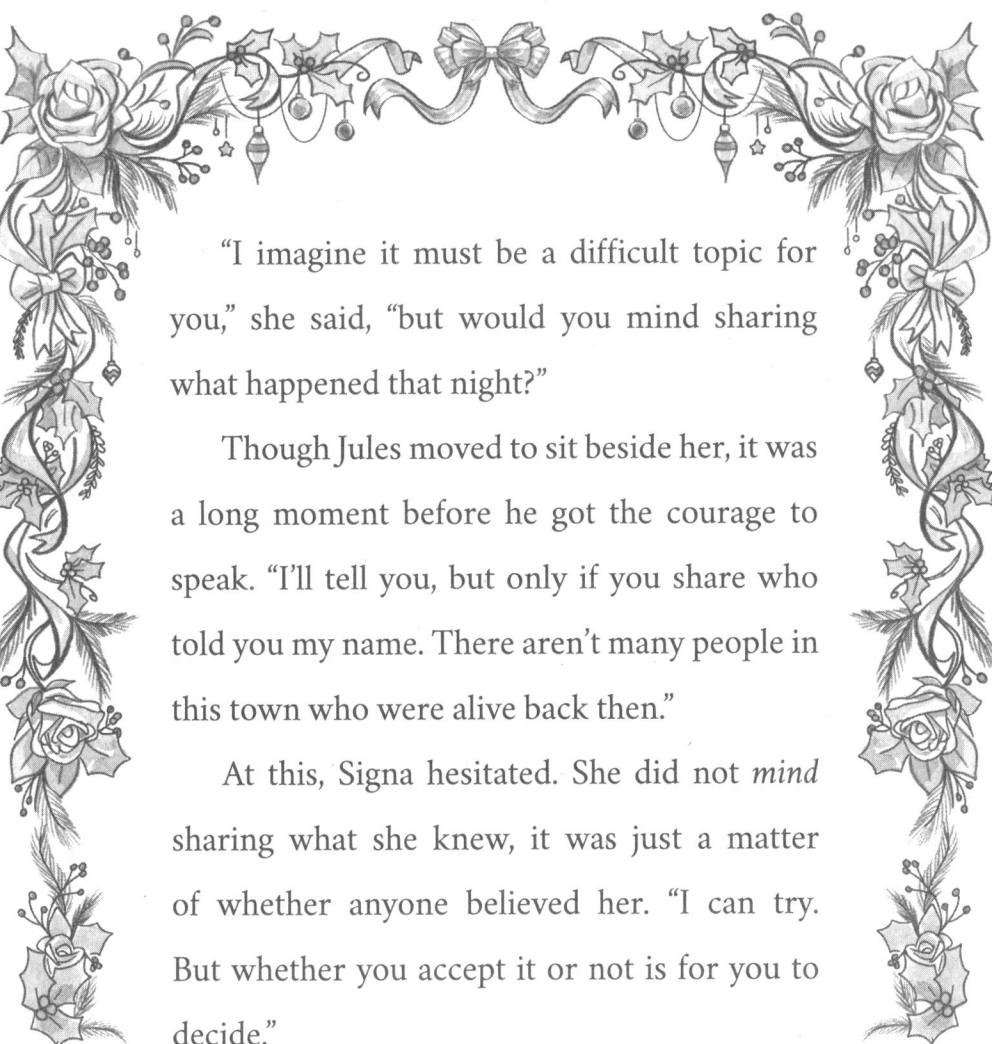

"I imagine it must be a difficult topic for you," she said, "but would you mind sharing what happened that night?"

Though Jules moved to sit beside her, it was a long moment before he got the courage to speak. "I'll tell you, but only if you share who told you my name. There aren't many people in this town who were alive back then."

At this, Signa hesitated. She did not *mind* sharing what she knew, it was just a matter of whether anyone believed her. "I can try. But whether you accept it or not is for you to decide."

"I was a ballet dancer," he told her, "and a good one at that. We were preparing a new show to be performed on Christmas Eve, sixty-one years ago. I had the lead role alongside the most beautiful woman I had ever seen. Her name was Odette Van der Meer, and I fell in love with her the second I first heard her laugh. I was going to ask her to marry me the morning after our performance, on Christmas Day.

"But the evening of the final dress rehearsal I was so nervous. I went outside before the performance to try and relax with my pipe, but the nerves had made my stomach foul, so I threw out the ashes and hurried home to rest before the show. I knew I would be late, but I never thought..." His eyes squinted shut, and the next words came as though he was forcing each one out. "By the time I returned, I was following a path of smoke. I had been too quick putting out my ashes. Sparks had blown toward the theater, starting a fire by the entrance. Not a single other person was able to escape that night. The fire claimed everything, including Odette.

"I told everyone who would listen that it

was my fault, but instead they called it a *tragedy*." Jules kept his gaze on the ground, scuffing his boot across the stone. "Every one of my friends died that night. If I'd not let myself get so nervous... if I'd never left, or had I taken more time to ensure that the ashes were put out... no one had to die."

There were always so many *could haves* with death. So many *should haves, would haves*... Signa hadn't met a single mourning soul who wasn't burdened with regret.

"I'm sorry that you lost them." She took hold of the man's hands, meaning each word. "Have you ever returned to where the fire began?"

"Never. If it's true what people say about the land being haunted, the last thing any spirits will want is to see me. I couldn't dare to show them my face."

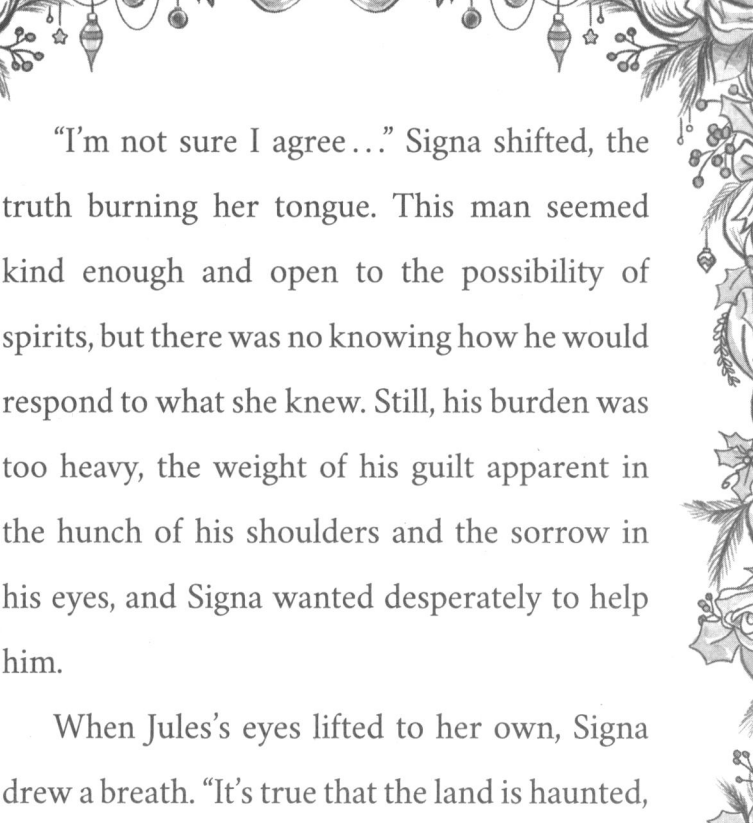

"I'm not sure I agree..." Signa shifted, the truth burning her tongue. This man seemed kind enough and open to the possibility of spirits, but there was no knowing how he would respond to what she knew. Still, his burden was too heavy, the weight of his guilt apparent in the hunch of his shoulders and the sorrow in his eyes, and Signa wanted desperately to help him.

When Jules's eyes lifted to her own, Signa drew a breath. "It's true that the land is haunted, but not in the way you think." She told him of her powers. Of the spirits who wandered the halls, wearing glittering costumes. Even as he stared at her, eyes hollow, she continued to speak of the older woman in charge. Of the way she clapped as the dancers moved about the halls, always eager.

"There's a young woman, too," Signa

whispered at last, unable to stop herself. "One who is searching everywhere for you. She's got beautiful red hair, a pink gown of tulle, and—"

There was a sudden harshness to the man's eyes that caused Signa's words to falter. A darkness settled over him, and Signa recognized the look. She'd seen it a thousand times before, on the faces of too-nosy neighbors who thought her the devil's spawn.

"You are a cruel girl." Jules's finger shook as he brandished it toward her like a weapon.

Signa shot to her feet, panic overwhelming her the very same way it always did whenever she saw such a look. No matter how much older she was or how many times she had experienced similar situations where she acted almost as a medium for the spirits, some fears would forever be ingrained in her.

"I know it sounds like nonsense, but I swear it's all true—" she started, only for her voice to be cut short as the man jerked to his feet. There were tears in his bloodshot eyes.

"Leave this place," he spat. "I don't know what game you're playing, but I will not have you making a mockery of everyone who died!"

Signa wished in that moment that she had more of her cousin's bite, if only to make this man see reason. But experience had long since taught her that there was no use arguing. And so she turned to leave, but not before she offered Jules one last kindness.

"Odette died from the smoke, not the flames. Some of your friends have small burns, but most felt little pain when they passed." She didn't turn back even when she heard him slump against the bench with a sob. Instead,

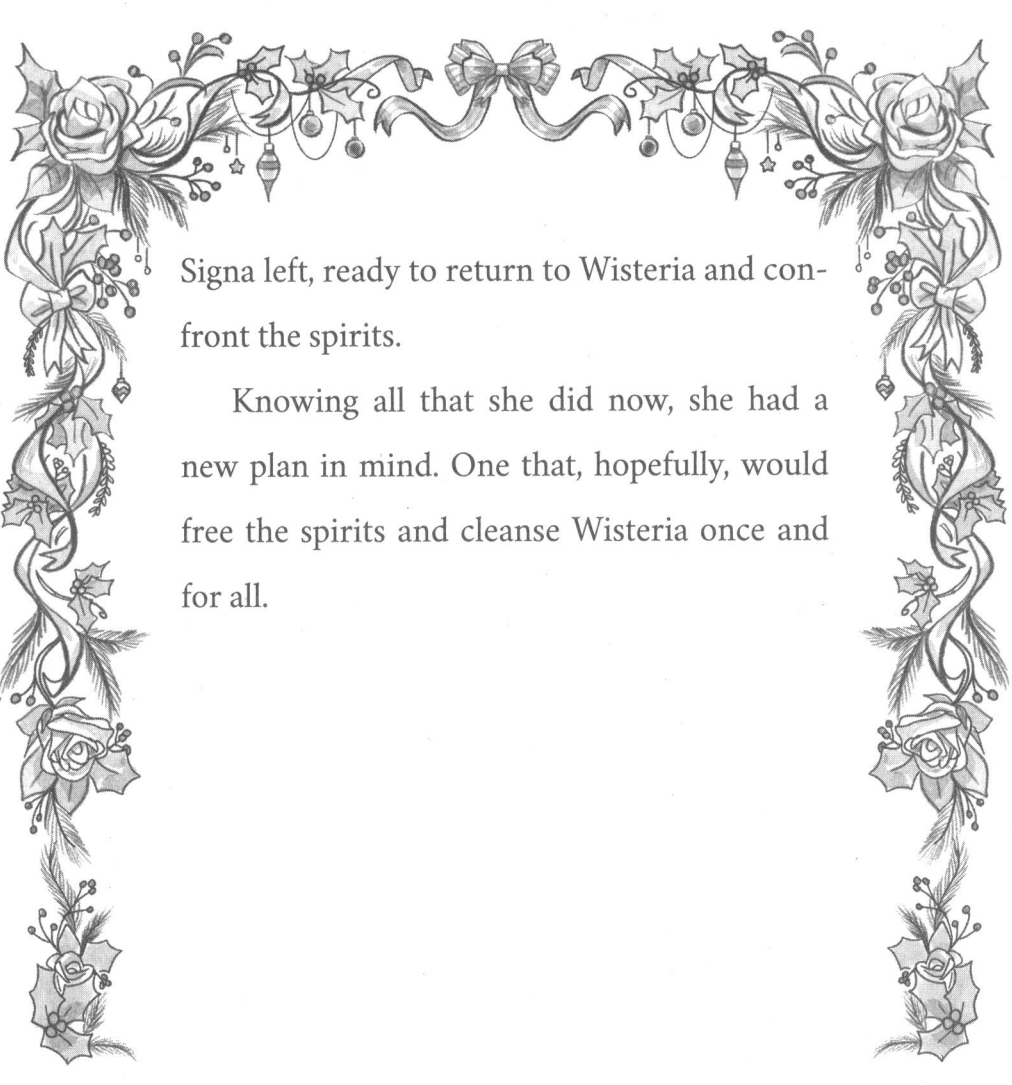

Signa left, ready to return to Wisteria and confront the spirits.

Knowing all that she did now, she had a new plan in mind. One that, hopefully, would free the spirits and cleanse Wisteria once and for all.

TWELVE

SIGNA

ARIS PACED THE HALL OUTSIDE THE library doors the next afternoon, working on building permanent lines between his pinched brows. "Are you certain this will work?" he asked for what was perhaps the fourth time. Signa had lost count.

"My answer isn't going to change, Aris. You can never be certain with spirits."

He was just as thrilled as he'd been the last

several times she'd answered him, which was to say that Aris continued his pacing. Signa brushed her hands down her arms, trying to quell the goose bumps that rose along her skin, a product of his buzzing anxiety.

"Would you please stand still?" Signa snapped when she could take no more of his antics. "It may not be perfect, but at least it's a plan."

His expression turned incredulous. "Surely you don't consider this a *plan*. It's a half-baked idea at best."

He wasn't *wrong*, though Signa cared little for the verbiage. "Do you have any better ideas?"

Aris ceased his pacing long enough to sigh deeply. His foot, however, kept tapping away at the floor. "What happens if this doesn't work? Will we all get possessed?"

Signa drew her bottom lip between her

teeth. "It's unlikely. Possessions are exhausting for spirits, and they tend to be reserved for rare cases—"

"I hope this isn't your way of trying to reassure me."

"It's not as simple as me touching someone's skin and watching them die, Aris. I don't just take a needle and thread and let my powers do all of the work for me. This requires nuance and luck. We need to cater to the spirits' emotions. Their behaviors. To find their triggers and help assuage them."

Aris leaned against the door, oblivious to the noisy spirits who awaited them on the other side. He folded his arms against his chest, watching Signa. "What even are you, anyway?"

"I beg your pardon?"

"What *are* you? I'm Fate, my skulking brother is Death, Blythe is Life . . . but no matter how much I look at your tapestry, I can never seem to figure it out. And so I ask again—what *are* you?"

Signa went still. This wasn't a new conversation, yet her skin grew clammy, and she was immediately on the defensive. This very topic had fueled dozens of conversations with Blythe and Sylas alike, and still there was no decisive answer.

"Not everything that exists can be so definitively labeled," she said, echoing something Sylas had once told her. "I don't know what I'm *called*, exactly, but I know what I can do. I act as a waypoint for unsettled souls. I'm...a bridge of sorts."

"A bridge?" he echoed, staring at her as if she'd grown another head.

"Yes, a bridge. I'm here so that these souls have someone who can understand them. Who can communicate between the worlds of the living and the nonliving and help both spirits and the mourning alike." She stood taller as she said it, as if daring him to rebuke the title she'd given herself. But Aris only shrugged and dropped his arms.

"Very well. Then go be a bridge, yes? Bridge these spirits all the way to the afterlife and out of my home forever."

Signa ignored his dramatics, stepping around her brother-in-law and into the library. Though the spirits had taken to roaming Wisteria Gardens, this room remained their hub. Knowing what she did now, she wondered whether the space had once acted as the theater's backstage, or perhaps the stage itself.

"This place used to be a theater," she told Aris, keeping quiet so as not to remind the spirits of their peril and all that had led them to their purgatory. "They were performers in the ballet. Their outfits make so much sense now."

"Their outfits?" Aris echoed.

Signa grimaced. "They look like they've been magicked straight out of Blythe's old fairy tales. Be thankful that you can't see them."

"Signa, love, I am thankful for that every night." Aris slumped into his usual seat on the chaise, tossing one leg over the other. "Though I *am* a great patron of the arts myself. I love performers—peculiar sorts, but always entertaining."

"That's precisely why we're here, Aris! It's the piece of the puzzle that we've been missing. These spirits are *performers*, and what do performers do?"

"... Perform?"

"Precisely!"

Aris snorted, looking far more comfortable in his seat than someone in a room full of spirits had the right to. "Perform for who? The walls? They have no audience."

"Right again! How is someone meant to perform when they have no one to share their talents with?" Signa crossed the room to fetch a chair that she dragged back to her previous position, situated amid the spirits. In front of her was the older woman who Signa now recognized to be the ballet mistress, continuing to clap and bark orders at the others.

"Excuse me?" Signa made a motion as if to tap her shoulder, though of course she could not make contact. "I'm here to see the performance."

The woman's clapping stilled, a strange look contorting her face. When she finally turned to acknowledge Signa, her voice was softer.

More professional. *"Take your seat, we will begin momentarily."*

"But it was meant to start an hour ago." Signa didn't know exactly *where* she was going with this, nor did she know how much to push to keep the spirit moving along without getting sucked back into her loop.

The woman's eyes grew wide. *"An hour?"* she echoed, following that with a slew of words in a language that Signa couldn't understand. *"Unacceptable! Where is Jules?"*

Signa had to suck in a gasp when Odette appeared from the floorboards with no warning and whined, *"I cannot find him anywhere!"*

This news did not please the mistress, but she clapped her hands again. *"Very well, then you will sit out. The show must go on."* Before Odette could argue, the woman surged forward, black skirts sweeping the floor as she gathered up the rest of the spirits. *"Places, everyone! To your places!"*

The spirits scurried forward while Signa motioned for Aris to take a seat beside her. Signa sat on the edge of her chair, hands clasped together as she prayed this would work. The spirits, to her surprise, had all snapped to attention, standing as straight as toy soldiers. They stood in two lines, one on either side of the room, the women positioning themselves on the very tips of their toes in preparation for their entrance. For an uncomfortably long moment they remained that way with beaming smiles plastered onto their faces. All except for Odette, who paced the length of the shelves behind them, hands fretting and bloodied tears in her eyes. Eventually, though, every smile slipped and the dancers glanced over at their mistress.

"What is it?" Signa asked the woman, earning a groan from Aris that she ignored. "What's the matter?"

The woman whipped to face her, her expression so scalding that Signa felt as if she were being reprimanded. *"Where is the music?"*

"The music?" Signa repeated, sinking back in her chair. "Is...there supposed to be music?"

"Are you daft? This is the ballet, child. We cannot be expected to perform without music."

"What's happening?" Aris asked, doing that annoying squinting thing with his eyes again. "What are they saying?"

"They say they need music," she told him, keeping her voice low but never letting her eyes leave the woman's.

"Of course they do, they're dancers." Aris scoffed as though it were obvious, and Signa threw her arms up and fell back into her chair.

"Forgive my complete and utter idiocy. What a fool I am for not knowing precisely what the spirits would need!"

Aris shrugged. "Not everyone understands artistic integrity."

She rolled her eyes. "Can't you magic them some music?"

"Ah yes, let me pluck the perfect tune out of thin air." He folded his arms. "I can get them *instruments*, yes. Even musicians to play them if necessary, though I imagine they will only perform to a certain score."

Loath as she was to admit it, he was right.

"Have you any musicians?" she asked the mistress, making her very best effort not to glower.

"Of course we have—" She cut off with a frown, searching for them. *"I'm sure they're skulking around here somewhere."*

"Splendid. Aris, come with me." Signa pushed from her seat without waiting to see if he followed, halfway out of the room before she remembered to look back at the stern-faced woman.

"We're going to find your musicians," Signa promised her. "Please, hold your places. I'm sure this won't take long."

Aris followed close on Signa's heels as she hurried down the stairs, making her way into the drawing room. She didn't know how long the spirits would remain even-tempered, and she dared not upset them any further.

It'd been a long while since Signa had played any instrument. Music had never been her forte. Still, she had at least a rudimentary knowledge of the piano, which is why she marched directly to one. As she placed her fingers over the keys, Aris's brows lowered.

"Don't tell me that *you* intend to be their pianist?" he asked.

Signa straightened her shoulders. "If you're not going to be helpful, then you can at least be quiet. Have a seat and leave me to my ideas."

Aris waved a dismissive hand in the air before attempting to do as requested. Given his nature, however, it was physically impossible for him to oblige. Instead, he turned the chair directly toward her and kicked one leg over the other.

"Go on, then," he said. "Let's have a show."

Heavens, how did Blythe deal with this man? Signa wished she had something to throw at him. Preferably something very, very hard. But for the time being she'd just have to put up with her brother and his dreadful personality. She took a seat, hoping she was still capable of playing some light and whimsical tune. Given how long it'd been since she'd sat on a piano bench, however, Signa immediately struck the wrong chord. Her own grimace matched Aris's, but she readjusted her position and tried again with the correct chord, and then the next, slowly but surely.

It was far from her best performance—in fact, it was admittedly rather ghastly, especially if the downward curl of Aris's lips was any indicator—and yet it was accomplishing precisely what she'd hoped. The familiar prickle at the back of her neck told Signa that there were spirits near, watching her. With a quick glance in her peripheral she confirmed that a man in a black suit had wandered into the room, his face contorted as if he'd eaten something dreadfully tart. It continued to twist with each note until the man looked more monster than human, wiry hair sprouting from the sides of his head as he bared his teeth at her. His eyes grew darker as she played, to the point where they were almost entirely black.

Signa had seen plenty of heinous or grotesque spirits in her time, inflicted with horrible wounds or sores that had left them dead. But few people had looked so outright ready to murder her. She had to swallow her scream, the man's face so terrifying that her fingers trembled on the keys. She couldn't look at the spirit directly for fear of what she'd see, nor could she play another note out of worry for how he might react. She could only sit hunched over the piano, chest thundering until the sound of Aris's squeaking chair broke the silence.

"You," he announced, "are one of the worst

pianists I've ever had the misfortune of listening to. I would give up my very magic if you swore to never play again."

Beside him, the spirit made a quiet seething sound that Signa could only assume was his agreement.

"Out of the way," Aris commanded, and Signa nearly tore free from the bench, grateful to have an excuse to put more distance between herself and the spirit who watched her every move with a grimace so wide that it looked as if the entirety of his face had been stretched out.

Blissfully oblivious, Aris stood and adjusted his sleeves before gliding into place at the piano. His spine was perfectly straight and his hands confident as he settled them into position.

And then, music *poured* from beneath his fingertips.

Signa had heard many pianists throughout

her life, but she did not need more than a few notes to know that Aris put every one of them to shame. He moved with an inhuman grace as he finished the whimsical melody she'd been playing and quickly slipped into a new, richer song. It was a familiar Christmas tune, but more beautiful than she'd ever heard it. The song had Signa relaxing against her will, and a cursory glance at the spirit across the room showed that he was easing as well, his grimace smoothing over. His hair, too, lay flat again, and his eyes returned to their normal translucence. Behind him, Signa watched hopefully as two other suited men peered into the room, observing with cautious stares. She'd hoped that the music might lure them, and was relieved to see that she'd been right and would not need to go hunting throughout all of Wisteria to fetch them.

There was, however, one small problem.

"How dare you begin caroling without me?"

Signa heard Blythe's hurried steps echoing from the staircase before her cousin came bounding into the room with a fervor that caused Aris to miss a chord. The vein on his forehead pulsed in his annoyance but smoothed a minute later as he corrected himself and continued. Beside him, the first spirit did the same. He had moved closer to the piano, just inches from the bench.

"No one is caroling," Aris noted, and Signa prayed that he would not stop playing. Not when the spirit was over his shoulder, watching every note. "Your cousin is a terrible musician."

"She's not quite so bad a singer, though," Blythe said cheerily. "We should carol! Oh, it would be so fun!"

Blythe was being gracious with her

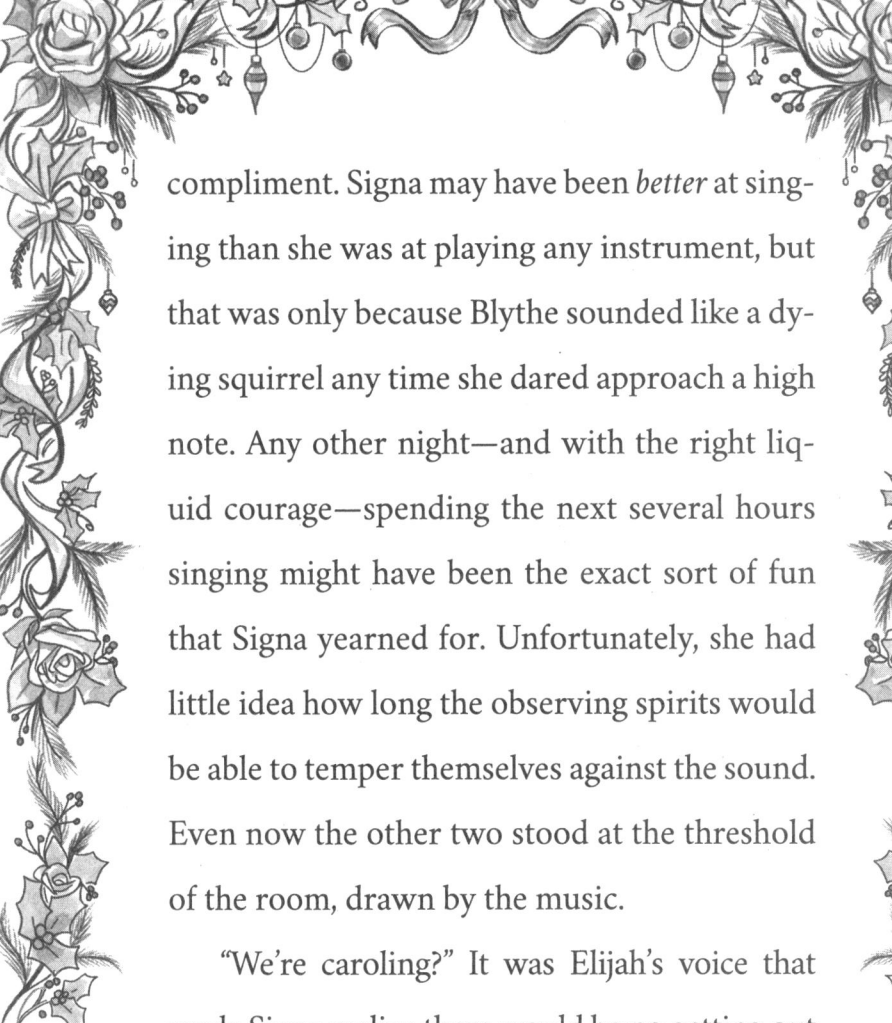

compliment. Signa may have been *better* at singing than she was at playing any instrument, but that was only because Blythe sounded like a dying squirrel any time she dared approach a high note. Any other night—and with the right liquid courage—spending the next several hours singing might have been the exact sort of fun that Signa yearned for. Unfortunately, she had little idea how long the observing spirits would be able to temper themselves against the sound. Even now the other two stood at the threshold of the room, drawn by the music.

"We're caroling?" It was Elijah's voice that made Signa realize there would be no getting out of this situation. He carried a silver tray in his hands, topped with a steaming pot of hot chocolate, four cups, and a plate of warm cookies that looked just the right amount of underbaked, still a touch doughy and precisely how Signa most enjoyed them. Gundry was at his heels, and Signa hoped with everything in her that Blythe wouldn't notice the way the hound kept tipping his head at the spirits, ears perked and tail swishing.

When Elijah set the tray on the table, Signa had an idea. *Blythe's* voice might break glass, but Elijah's was a wonderful, deep baritone full of warmth and clarity. He'd told plenty of stories about showing it off back in the days of his many soirees, claiming it was one of the ways he'd gotten the attention of his late wife.

"Why don't you sing for us first, Elijah?" Signa took a seat on the settee, grabbing Blythe by the sleeve and pulling her cousin down beside her. Before Blythe could complain, Signa poured a cup of cocoa from the pot and set it in her cousin's hand. "You can have the first song."

And perhaps the second and third if I am so lucky...

Blythe, at least, seemed content with this plan, taking hold of her drink and settling into the cushion. She drew her legs up beneath her and cuddled underneath a plush blanket that she "shared" with Signa by sparing her a solid quarter of it. Just enough to cover her legs.

"Very well," Elijah said, clearing his throat as he stepped up toward the piano and across from Aris, who kept flashing Signa curious looks.

Just keep playing, she mouthed to him, giving him an encouraging wave when Blythe wasn't looking. There were three spirits in the room now, the two by the door drawn inside when Elijah began to sing.

"Across the frozen lakes we glide, with dreams of warmth and hearts so wide. The stars above, they hear the sound, of bells that bless the snowy ground..."

The voice that resonated from him was

as smooth and rich as honey. He looked so comfortable there by the piano that even Aris seemed impressed, growing more consumed by the music with each chord. Signa sneaked a glance at her cousin, who watched her husband with such longing even then.

For years, Signa had wanted only for Blythe to find her happiness. There beside her, watching as Blythe held her hot chocolate to her chest and breathed a dreamy sigh, Signa's entire body warmed.

She understood Aris's dedication. Understood why he wanted this to be the most magnificent Christmas for his bride. There wasn't much that Signa and her brother-in-law agreed on, but they would both do anything to ensure Blythe's joy.

"Bravo!" Blythe cheered, setting down her drink so that she could clap.

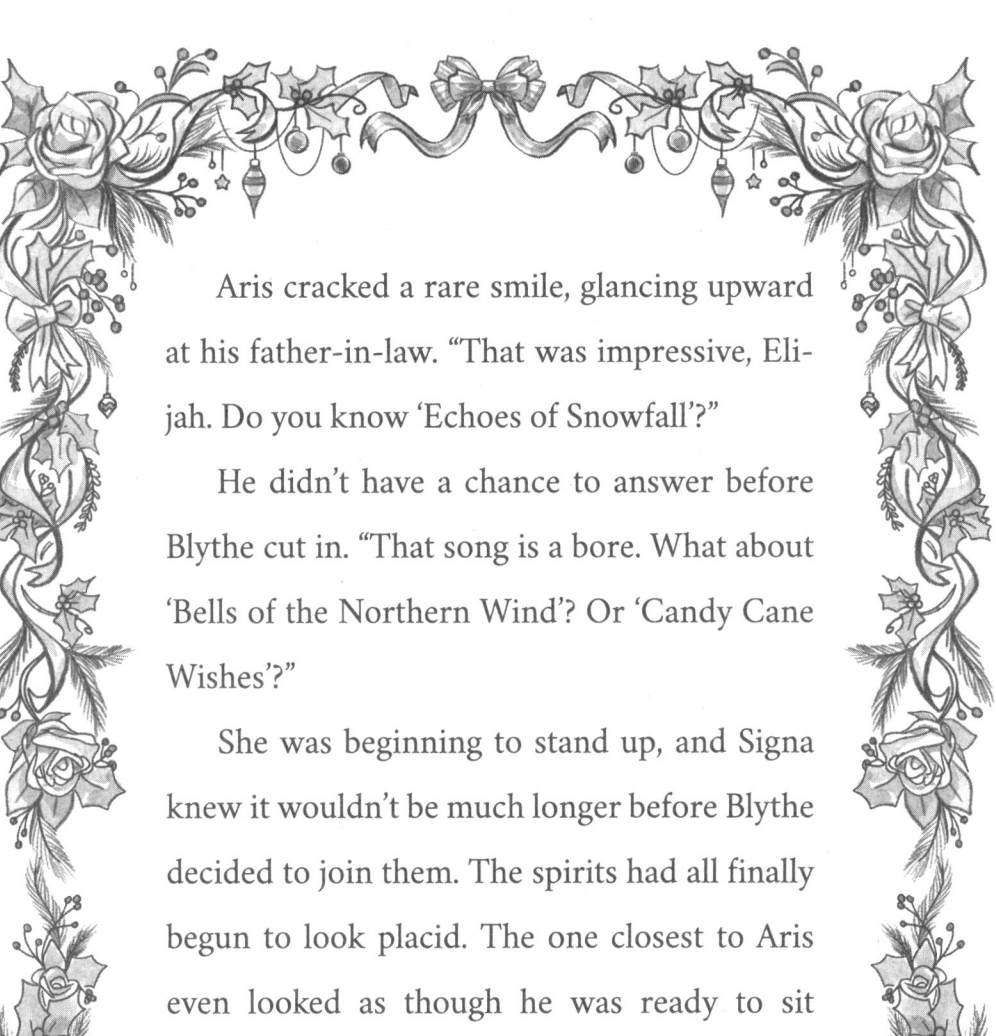

Aris cracked a rare smile, glancing upward at his father-in-law. "That was impressive, Elijah. Do you know 'Echoes of Snowfall'?"

He didn't have a chance to answer before Blythe cut in. "That song is a bore. What about 'Bells of the Northern Wind'? Or 'Candy Cane Wishes'?"

She was beginning to stand up, and Signa knew it wouldn't be much longer before Blythe decided to join them. The spirits had all finally begun to look placid. The one closest to Aris even looked as though he was ready to sit beside him on the bench and begin playing. Signa could already imagine their outcry if Blythe opened her mouth to sing.

It wouldn't be a pretty sight.

"You know, I think you were onto something," Signa said hurriedly. "Caroling does sound like a lovely idea."

Aris's head snapped up so quickly she wondered how he didn't injure his neck.

"Caroling? As in singing outside? In the streets?" *Like a peasant* was the part that Signa assumed Aris wasn't saying aloud, though he may as well have, given his tone.

"As in *performing*." Signa emphasized the word with a thin smile, hoping she might get the message through his thick skull. "You do so love performing, don't you, Aris?"

He opened his mouth to argue, though his eyes went wide just before he shivered violently. The spirit had taken its seat on the opposite edge of the bench, its hand skimming affectionately over the seat.

Aris all but bolted upright.

"Truly a wondrous idea," he was quick to say, the words too sharp. "Caroling is one of my favorite holiday pastimes."

Blythe squinted her eyes at him. "It is? Since when?"

"Since right now." He forced a smile as he crossed the floor to his wife and wound his arm around her. "It's what you wanted, isn't it?"

"Yes, but I never expected you'd *agree*." Blythe was no fool. She knew something was going on, but Signa could practically see her weighing the merit of confronting them or accepting this rare chance at getting Aris out caroling in good spirits. "We should bring caramels!" she added. "I'll fetch a box of them, and, Aris, you can hand them out. Signa, do you want me to grab your coat?"

"I won't be joining you," Signa said, hoping her voice sounded sufficiently distressed. "It sounds like a lovely time, but as I've been sitting here, I'm afraid I've gotten a rather splitting headache."

"Oh no." Blythe's shoulders slumped. She stepped forward, pressing the back of her hand to Signa's forehead. "Do you think you're getting sick?"

"I think I'll be fine after a bit of rest." She hated lying to Blythe, but she had no choice.

"Why don't I stay with you?" Blythe offered. "We can curl up inside and eat cookies by the fire. Maybe play some charades..."

"Dear God, no," Aris spat, though everyone ignored him.

"I'll be fine," Signa urged, hoping her smile was convincing. The spirit at the piano was beginning to let his hands wander too close to the keys for comfort. Another minute, and he'd likely be playing a tune on his own. "Please go and have fun on my behalf. I absolutely insist."

Blythe looked primed to fight her on it, though she relaxed when Aris took hold of her hand, producing a large tin of caramels that he handed to her. "Very well... but do feel better, Signa. Perhaps we can try to continue our games in the evening."

Signa's nose scrunched with her smile. "I look forward to it."

Aris must have sensed her desperation. "I'll have the room ready for you," he whispered before looping his fingers through Blythe's and starting toward the door. Elijah followed at a distance but not before stopping at the threshold to give Signa a stern look.

"Would this whole charade not be easier to manage if you were honest about the situation?"

"It would," she admitted, "but Aris wants her to have the perfect Christmas."

"And you think that's what this is? The two of you running around, trying to distract her? Blythe's perfect Christmas includes you, Signa.

You shouldn't be sitting at home while the rest of us have fun."

Signa pressed her lips together, frowning. Elijah was right. Of course he was. But by the time they returned home from their caroling, she hoped that this entire mess would be over and she'd be able to resume partaking in the festivities.

"I just need a few more hours," she told him. "That's all."

Though he looked far from happy about it, Elijah relented. "Don't do anything risky."

"I won't, I promi—" She cut herself off with a flinch as the spirit pressed down on one of the keys. Elijah gave a long sigh, shaking his head, but he saw himself out of the parlor. The moment the door shut behind them, Signa whirled on the spirits.

One sat on the center of the bench, the

others closing in. Slowly, she stepped forward to join them. Gundry lumbered after her, there if she needed him.

"You miss your music, don't you?" Signa asked.

The spirit trailed his fingers down the keys, a pained look in his eyes.

"It's been ages since I've had a piano," he said. His words were slow and rough, as though he'd not spoken in a very long time. *"I'm not even sure I'd be any good at it these days."*

There was longing in his voice. All the spirits bore the weight of it, their shoulders curved inward and their chests slumped.

"You'll be excellent," she assured him, lowering herself to the edge of the bench and settling her hand beside his. "It's still in you. Time will not have changed that."

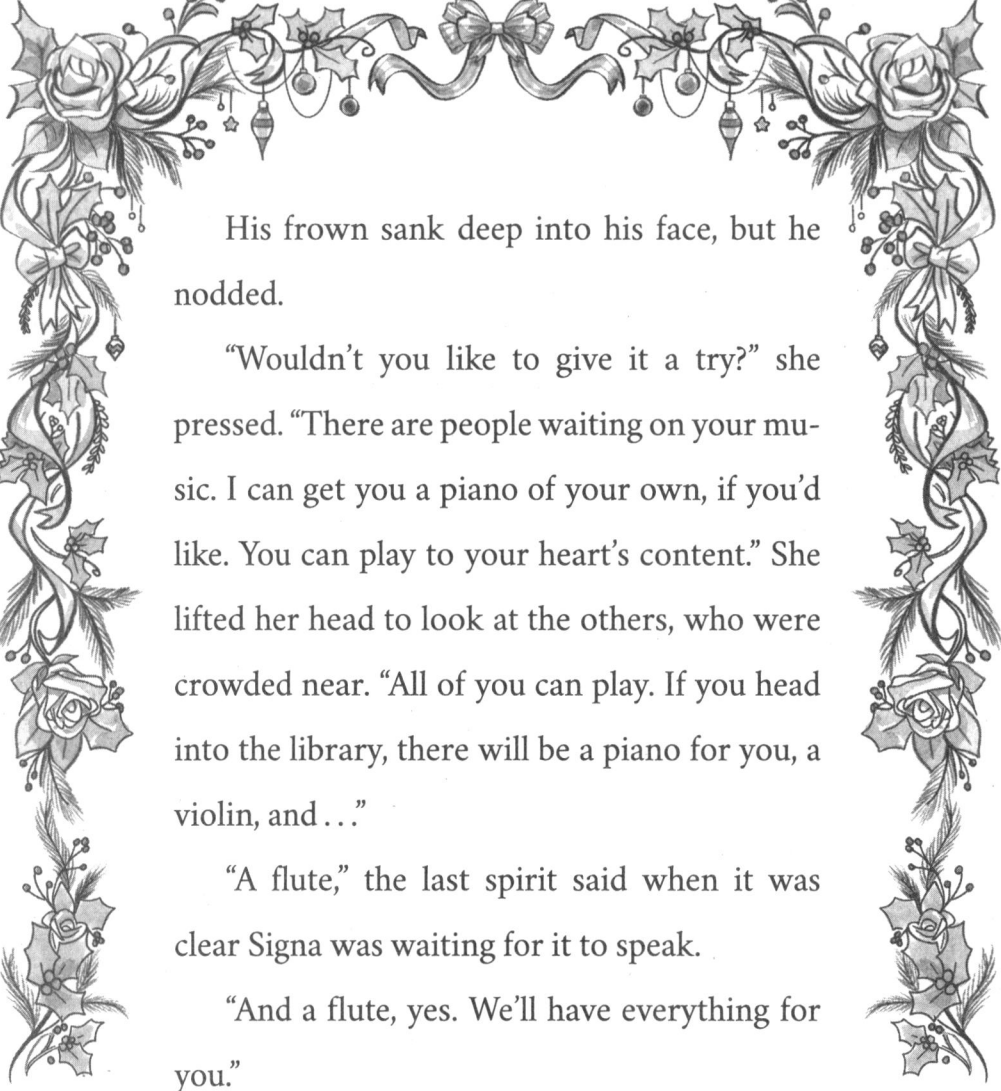

His frown sank deep into his face, but he nodded.

"Wouldn't you like to give it a try?" she pressed. "There are people waiting on your music. I can get you a piano of your own, if you'd like. You can play to your heart's content." She lifted her head to look at the others, who were crowded near. "All of you can play. If you head into the library, there will be a piano for you, a violin, and..."

"A flute," the last spirit said when it was clear Signa was waiting for it to speak.

"And a flute, yes. We'll have everything for you."

The musicians looked among themselves and seemed hopeful as they slipped from the room, disappearing through the walls and making their way up to the library.

Close. She was so close to finally being done with this mess.

Sylas? She spoke his name down their bond, waiting until she felt the comforting stir of his presence listening. *Is there music in the afterlife?*

Yes, Little Bird. His voice was like velvet stroking down her spine. *There is everything.*

Good. It was clear how much these spirits loved their music. Their performing. She couldn't imagine sending them away to exist in a world without it.

Signa stood slowly, stretching out her back. *I'm still annoyed with you, you know.*

I know, Death answered, leaving Signa chewing on the inside of her lip.

Come home. I don't want to spend Christmas without you.

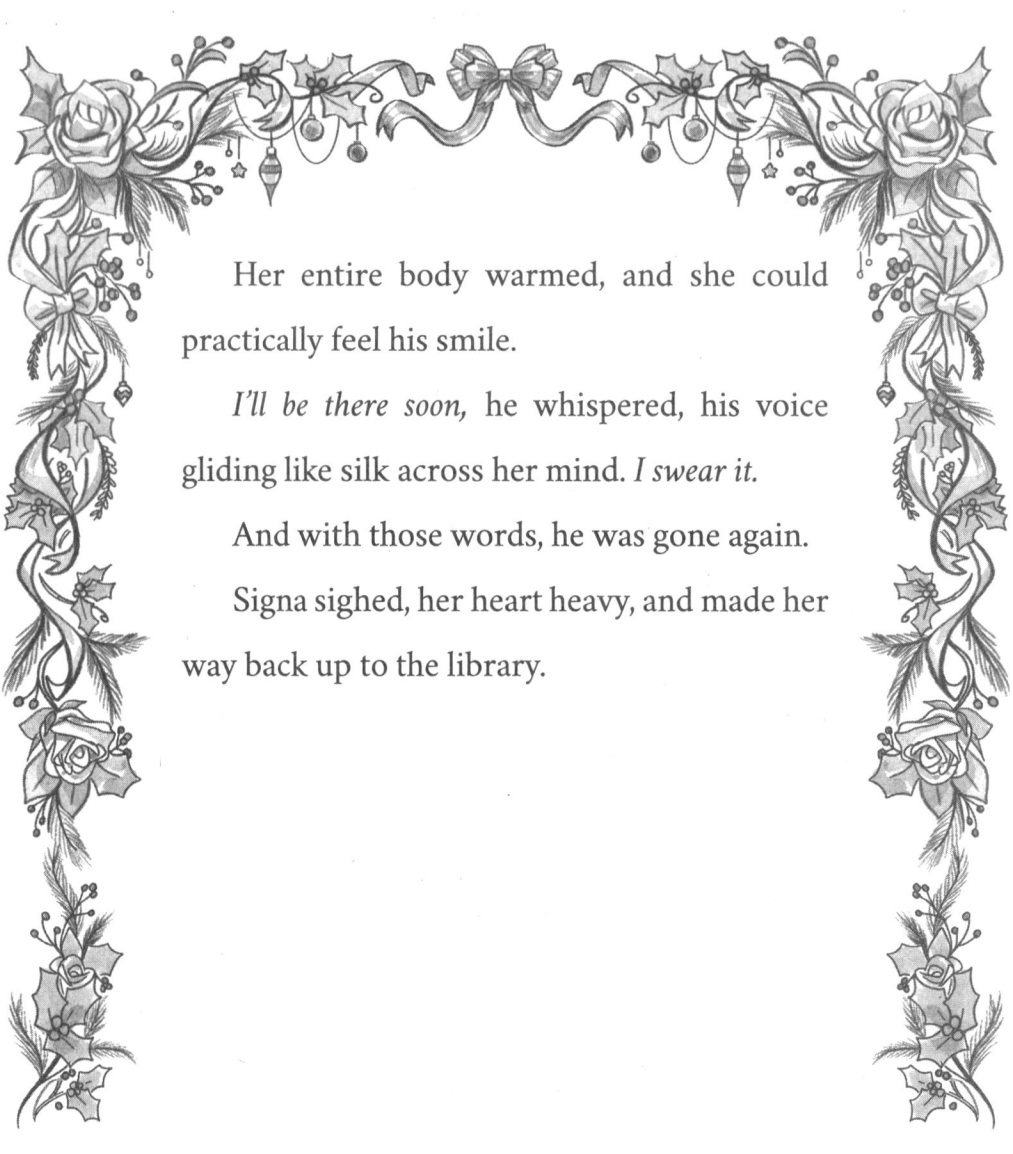

Her entire body warmed, and she could practically feel his smile.

I'll be there soon, he whispered, his voice gliding like silk across her mind. *I swear it.*

And with those words, he was gone again.

Signa sighed, her heart heavy, and made her way back up to the library.

THIRTEEN

DEATH

IT WAS NO SIMPLE VENTURE TO HUNT FOR something when you didn't quite know what, *exactly*, you were hunting for. The job was made even worse when it came at the expense of being away from the woman he loved.

Every part of Death ached to return to Wisteria and check on Signa, though he knew it'd be the wrong choice. He had to trust that she had a handle on the spirits and that he was safe to focus his efforts on his own looming task.

Tired of trudging through the snow, Death had taken a seat outside a quaint tea shop that made him homesick for afternoons with Signa. He leaned back on the bench, disgruntled and admittedly moping, and watched as the townsfolk toddled by with turkeys and ham for their holiday meals. Children ran circles around their parents' heels, and he couldn't help but scowl every time a happy couple wandered by. Sometimes his bitterness got the better of him, and Death would imagine all the ways in which he could make others feel as lonely as he did in that moment. A pox, or perhaps a mysterious wave of deaths that would have people fleeing their cities in terror.

Death wouldn't *actually* do such a horrible thing, of course. But his mind stewed on bleak thoughts whenever his mood was particularly foul. Christmas was but three days away, and still he was wandering around this blasted town, far from his family.

He loved Blythe, truly. They had come a long way in their years of getting to know each other, and Death had unfortunately learned over time that he could be conned into anything if Blythe made it sound important enough. She had quite the penchant for giving orders and maintaining strong opinions about how things should be done, and yet she was little help when it came to actually *completing* a mission. If he hadn't found this particular plan of hers so appealing, he would have returned to Wisteria Gardens long ago, even if it meant foiling his plan with Signa and the spirits.

He'd searched everywhere he could think of, scouring the woods and wandering through the halls of each home in the neighborhood. He'd examined every pointed face and set of beady eyes, and still he felt no closer to finding what he and Blythe sought. His temper was flaring, and it didn't help that people kept *dying*. Even at that moment, he had hundreds of souls hovering near him, circling aimlessly as they awaited ferrying. And these were just the ones who'd found him since sunrise. He ran a hand down the length of his face before dropping his head back against the bench and blowing a long sigh up at the sky.

Why did so many humans have to die around Christmas?

Death stretched his legs out before him, keeping a watchful eye on any living human who might wander too close. As it was, most of the townsfolk avoided him entirely. They may not have been able to *see* the reaper, but almost no one ventured toward a bench where the air grew colder and where their breath grew tighter in their throat. A young man had nearly tried to sit at one point, only for the hairs along his neck to rise. He'd lurched away, rubbing his arms.

And so Death really had no choice but to keep to himself, the snow gliding around him, as he contemplated his next move.

He could try the woods again, though he'd traced every inch of it. It wouldn't hurt to wander through town a few more times, but he'd already checked all the homes.

It was impossible to track something when he didn't even know what form this soul had taken. What he needed was to lure it *to* him.

He let the darkness swarm him, and a second later he was standing in the room that Blythe and his brother shared back at Wisteria.

It was as ridiculously over-the-top as he'd expected, and his eyes adjusted slowly, drawn upward to the dark expanse that loomed above. The ceiling Aris had crafted swirled with faint, shifting colors—green, violet, and the occasional burst of gold—like the northern skies held captive in this quiet space.

The walls were seamless panels of polished black stone, their glossy surfaces catching and stretching the aurora's glow. The reflections twisted into faint trails of light that danced upon the stone like whispers of magic. Above a hearth recessed into one wall were vases filled with clear shards of crystal, frost-covered pine cones, and the occasional bunch of silvered branches. The hearth itself was unlit, but a cold, bluish shimmer lined its edges, a ghost of flames that longed to burn. Facing it was a curved sofa of deep green velvet, the cushions edged with a soft iridescence that caught the colors shifting above.

Death lingered in the center of the room, his

eyes drawn to the bed. The sheets were tucked tight, the covers smooth and unwrinkled. Far too freshly laundered for his purposes.

He crossed instead to Aris's wardrobe, its surface gleaming faintly. When he opened the door, the scent of cedar and wisteria embraced him. Inside, rows of meticulously stitched clothing hung neatly, pressed to perfection. His fingers moved through them, disappointed to find that all belonged to Aris as he was now. There was nothing *old* here, nothing that had what Death was searching for.

He closed the wardrobe and turned toward a smaller one by the window—Blythe's. Inside, her clothes were hung less precisely, soft fabrics in muted tones mingling with scarves that spilled over the edges of their hangers. Death riffled through everything carefully, setting a few pieces aside and continuing to dig for something he recognized until he reached the bottom. There, a pile of folded items rested buried beneath her other things.

Death pulled free a navy coat with its edges lightly frayed, the texture worn under his touch. His breath caught as he stared at it for a long moment, recognizing it as the piece Aris had worn to his and Blythe's wedding all those years ago. She'd kept it tucked away, safe.

It was perfect. Death folded it over his arm, grabbing several of Blythe's nightgowns as well as a few scarves. Then, before anyone could catch him lurking about, Death fled from Wisteria and returned to his bench, where he took a seat, draping Aris's wedding jacket over his lap. Eyes shut, he let his shadows sweep the rest of the garments across the village and the woods surrounding it, brushing them around trees—against oil lamps and the corners of buildings—and back to him.

And as he sat there, all Death could hope was that the scent would work.

He didn't know how long he waited, snow falling around him and his head tipped to the sky, ignoring the press of souls vying for his attention. The oil lamps had been lit, then doused again as the sun rose. The baker in the shop across from him had arrived hours ago, and the rich scent of fresh dough carried on the wind, winding around him. And then, later still, the sun crept into the sky, melting the snow that had made mounds beside him.

It was only thoughts of Signa and her dedication to remaining in that blasted mausoleum that kept him in his seat. The cold couldn't touch him as it did her, and still she'd been willing to wait as long as it took to get what she wanted.

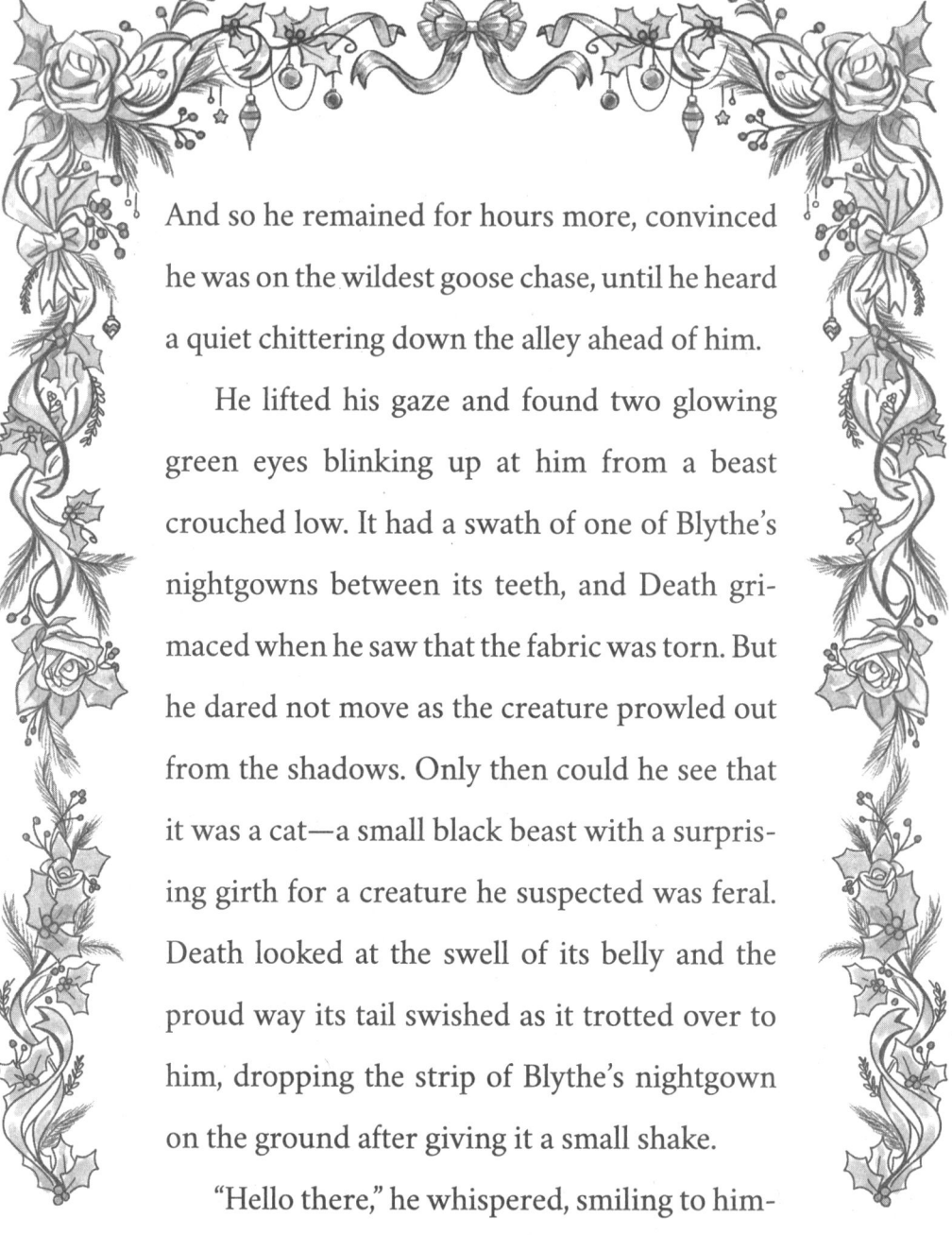

And so he remained for hours more, convinced he was on the wildest goose chase, until he heard a quiet chittering down the alley ahead of him.

He lifted his gaze and found two glowing green eyes blinking up at him from a beast crouched low. It had a swath of one of Blythe's nightgowns between its teeth, and Death grimaced when he saw that the fabric was torn. But he dared not move as the creature prowled out from the shadows. Only then could he see that it was a cat—a small black beast with a surprising girth for a creature he suspected was feral. Death looked at the swell of its belly and the proud way its tail swished as it trotted over to him, dropping the strip of Blythe's nightgown on the ground after giving it a small shake.

"Hello there," he whispered, smiling to himself when the cat chittered in response. He'd always loved animals and the fact that they

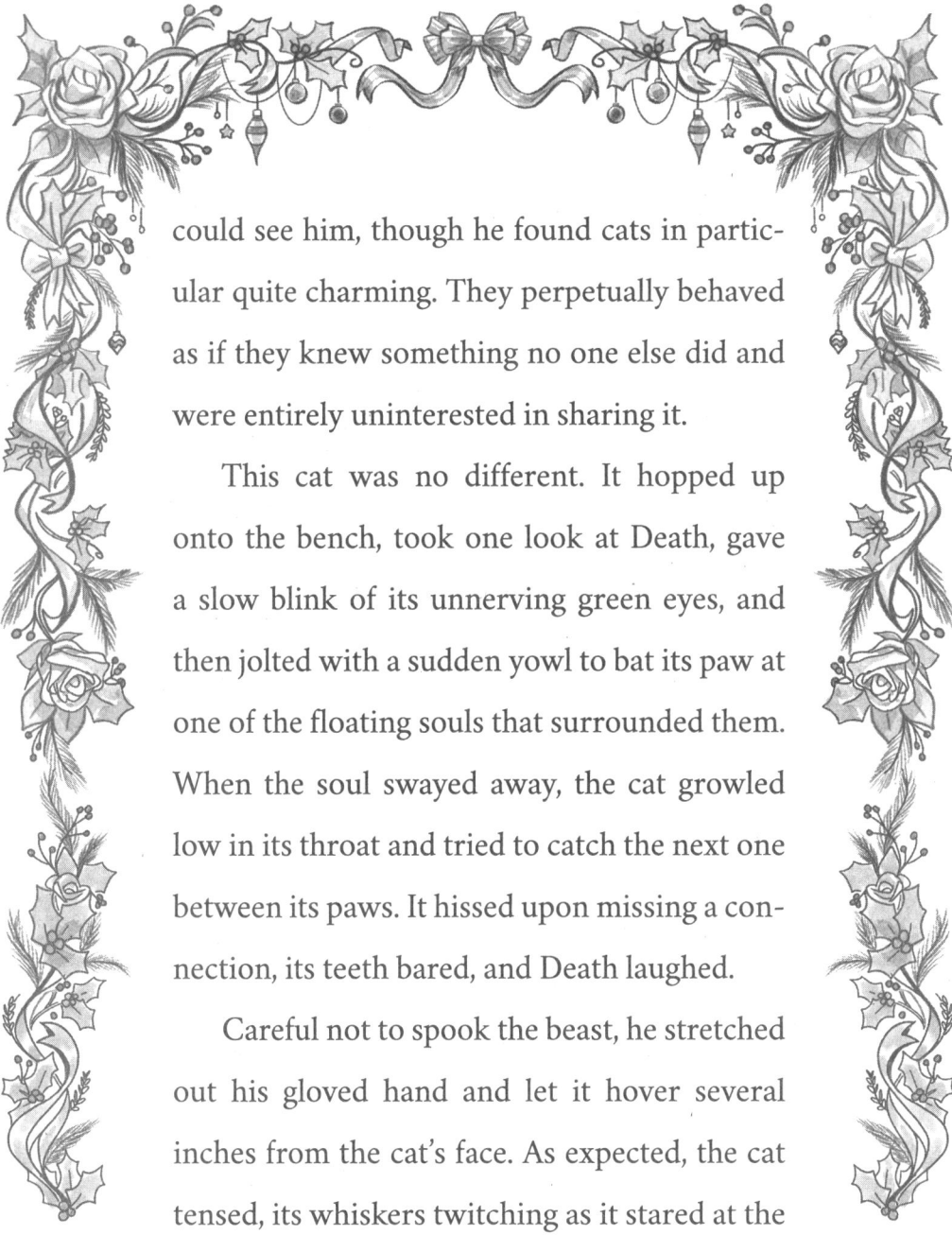

could see him, though he found cats in particular quite charming. They perpetually behaved as if they knew something no one else did and were entirely uninterested in sharing it.

This cat was no different. It hopped up onto the bench, took one look at Death, gave a slow blink of its unnerving green eyes, and then jolted with a sudden yowl to bat its paw at one of the floating souls that surrounded them. When the soul swayed away, the cat growled low in its throat and tried to catch the next one between its paws. It hissed upon missing a connection, its teeth bared, and Death laughed.

Careful not to spook the beast, he stretched out his gloved hand and let it hover several inches from the cat's face. As expected, the cat tensed, its whiskers twitching as it stared at the palm. Then it bent to give the leather a curious sniff, and ducked its head for petting.

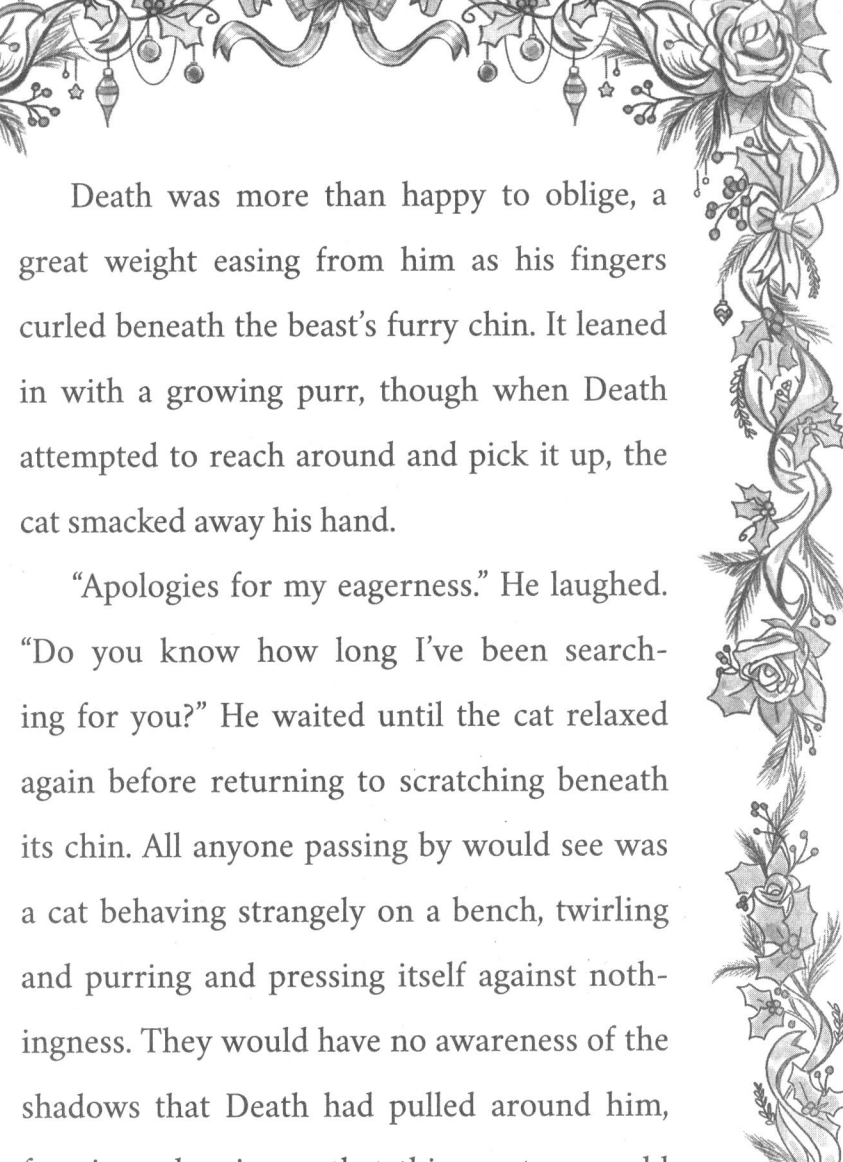

Death was more than happy to oblige, a great weight easing from him as his fingers curled beneath the beast's furry chin. It leaned in with a growing purr, though when Death attempted to reach around and pick it up, the cat smacked away his hand.

"Apologies for my eagerness." He laughed. "Do you know how long I've been searching for you?" He waited until the cat relaxed again before returning to scratching beneath its chin. All anyone passing by would see was a cat behaving strangely on a bench, twirling and purring and pressing itself against nothingness. They would have no awareness of the shadows that Death had pulled around him, forming a barrier so that this creature could not escape him.

Ever so slowly, careful not to give the cat any way to touch his skin, Death worked his hand up its neck. And when the time was right, he grabbed the beast by the scruff.

The cat yowled, scratching at the air. Several people turned to investigate, but Death gave them little chance to witness the situation. His shadows ensnared the beast, and with it tucked in his arms like a screaming child, Death disappeared with a grand smile.

FOURTEEN

Blythe

Blythe wasn't so foolish as to overlook that her husband was hiding something. She *was*, however, clever enough to take advantage of it.

She and Aris walked arm in arm through the streets of Brude, their pace slower to accommodate Elijah, who never allowed Aris to help ease his way with magic.

Elijah was in remarkable shape for his age,

though it was jarring to watch her father grow older through the years. Blythe had gotten so used to everyone in her life remaining precisely the same, at least aesthetically. Elijah was the only full mortal who still existed in her everyday world, and Blythe's chest ached when she thought about the day when he'd finally lay eyes on the reaper he was so curious about and be taken from her.

They hadn't discussed the future or what would happen when he was no longer of this world. Elijah had tried once or twice to broach the conversation, but Blythe hadn't wanted any part of it.

Not yet. Not when she hoped there were still many years left when she could have everyone she loved at her side.

She held tighter to Aris, grateful for his presence and the way his eyes flickered every so often to Elijah, ensuring he was well. Her father

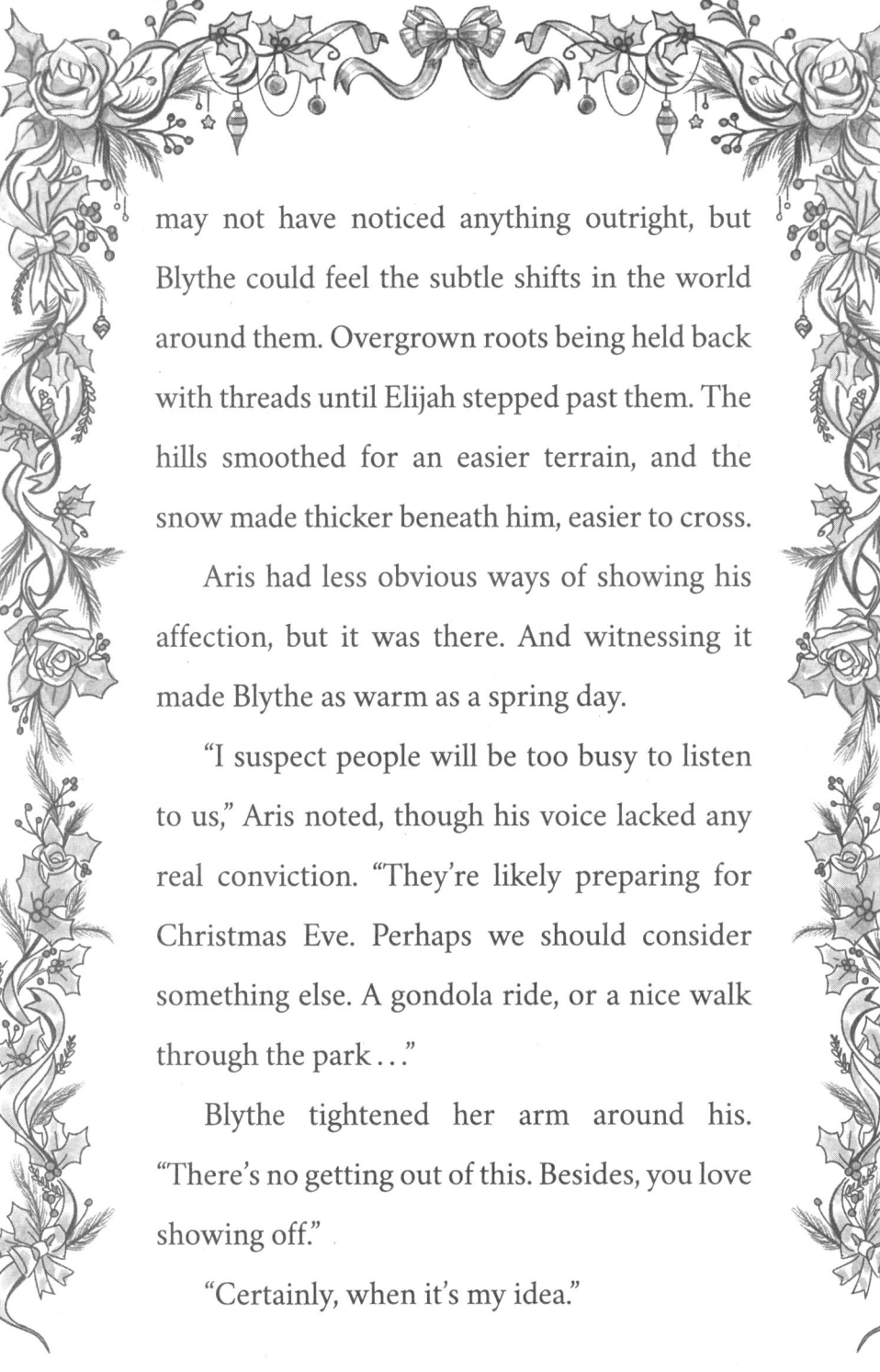

may not have noticed anything outright, but Blythe could feel the subtle shifts in the world around them. Overgrown roots being held back with threads until Elijah stepped past them. The hills smoothed for an easier terrain, and the snow made thicker beneath him, easier to cross.

Aris had less obvious ways of showing his affection, but it was there. And witnessing it made Blythe as warm as a spring day.

"I suspect people will be too busy to listen to us," Aris noted, though his voice lacked any real conviction. "They're likely preparing for Christmas Eve. Perhaps we should consider something else. A gondola ride, or a nice walk through the park..."

Blythe tightened her arm around his. "There's no getting out of this. Besides, you love showing off."

"Certainly, when it's my idea."

Blythe patted his arm gently as she stopped him at the edge of the town square. "Tell you what, you can pick our first song."

Aris let out a theatrical sigh. "Echoes of Snowfall" was his choice, and while he appeared reluctant to sing, one glance at Blythe had him trying his best to appease her. Fortunately, Elijah wasn't about to let his son-in-law have all the fun.

Her father began the song at full volume, not waiting for a crowd but choosing instead to build his own. Elijah, it turned out, did not have a lick of stage fright in him. Blythe had once thought that it was alcohol that gave him the courage to perform so freely, though he'd been sober for several decades now. He took the tin of caramels from Blythe and she joined in, joyously observing more than she was singing as her father shamelessly approached each passerby, brandishing delectable sweets as he sang. Blythe caught several women blushing as they took their treats, and she stifled her grin.

Elijah really ought to have been a performer. There was a glimmer in his eyes as he captivated his audience, his breath blowing tendrils in the frosted air.

Beside him, Aris was starting to find his rhythm. His voice, low at first, grew steadier as he handed out caramels with a flourish that bordered on playful. Blythe could see the tension easing from his shoulders, the corners of his mouth lifting just enough to betray his enjoyment. It wasn't long before he was singing in earnest, Elijah's arm slung around his shoulder as their harmonies carried through the square.

Blythe's own cheeks were flushed, numb from winter's sting. She'd forgotten her gloves, too, and could barely feel her fingertips. Still,

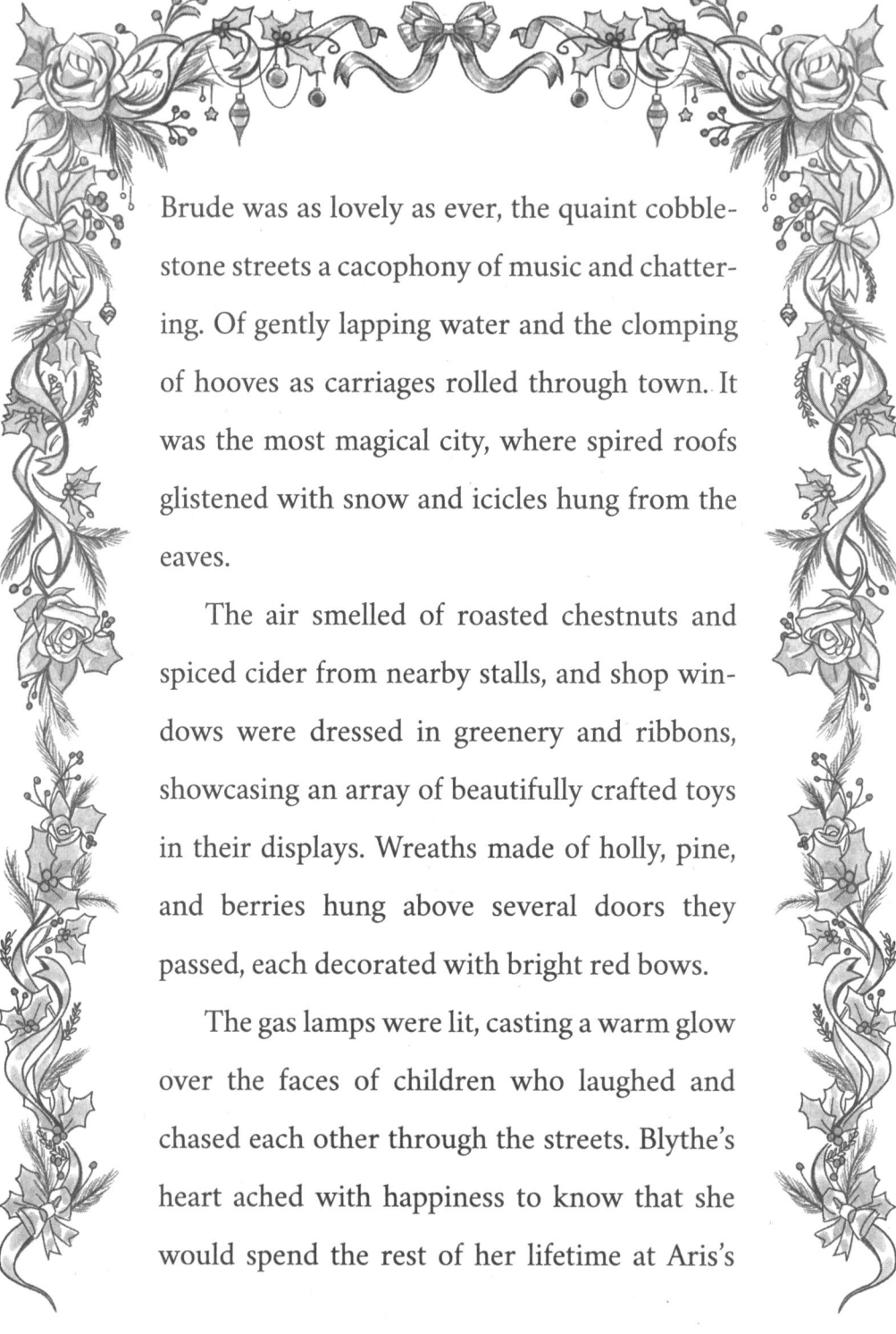

Brude was as lovely as ever, the quaint cobblestone streets a cacophony of music and chattering. Of gently lapping water and the clomping of hooves as carriages rolled through town. It was the most magical city, where spired roofs glistened with snow and icicles hung from the eaves.

The air smelled of roasted chestnuts and spiced cider from nearby stalls, and shop windows were dressed in greenery and ribbons, showcasing an array of beautifully crafted toys in their displays. Wreaths made of holly, pine, and berries hung above several doors they passed, each decorated with bright red bows.

The gas lamps were lit, casting a warm glow over the faces of children who laughed and chased each other through the streets. Blythe's heart ached with happiness to know that she would spend the rest of her lifetime at Aris's

side in a place like this, while also finding more perfect towns that would steal her heart.

Many of the townsfolk had gravitated toward them, welcomed by the spirited men as they joined in the song. Blythe was still moving her mouth to the words, but she'd been swept away by the magic of her home, lost in her own delight.

At least she *was* lost in delight, until she caught sight of a curious shadow flitting across the alleyway opposite Aris. A reflection of the gas lamps on the snow? She couldn't look away, and the longer she stared, the more she realized the shadows were beginning to take the form of a reaper who stood in the alley, wedged between two shops. With the exception of the quick glance he shot at Blythe, Sylas was clearly keeping out of sight.

She hesitated, looking over her shoulder to

ensure no one was watching. Thank goodness it was already so cold, otherwise Aris might have noticed his brother skulking about. As it was, Aris was too distracted, getting louder each and every time Elijah did and filling every child's pocket with caramels.

Meanwhile, Sylas's shadows tugged at the hem of Blythe's dress, then her boots, until she was able to pick up her skirts and dart into the alley. The moment she arrived, Sylas's shadows dripped from him like an abandoned coat, lifting to mask Blythe.

Her brother looked exhausted. The skin beneath his eyes was hollowed, and his cheeks were quite gaunt. His clothes were shredded as well, and he pulled his sleeves down when he caught her staring.

"This beast has a death wish." He glowered. "It keeps trying to scratch me."

Blythe noticed then that there was a cat prowling at his feet and she gasped, glancing behind her to ensure no one could see them.

"You're sure this is the right one?" she asked, her eyes hot.

Sylas drew a step back from the cat, looking torn between touching it and fearing for his own arm. "I believe so, but I figured you would know best."

Heart racing, Blythe bent to try to scoop up the beast. She'd thought it was a house cat considering how plump the creature was, but given how it yowled and scratched at her, it was clear the beast was feral. She had no choice but to stumble back and allow the cat to leap from her arms. Sylas's shadows had it back in their clutches before it could escape, though given the cat's constant protests, curious eyes were already beginning to search for the noise.

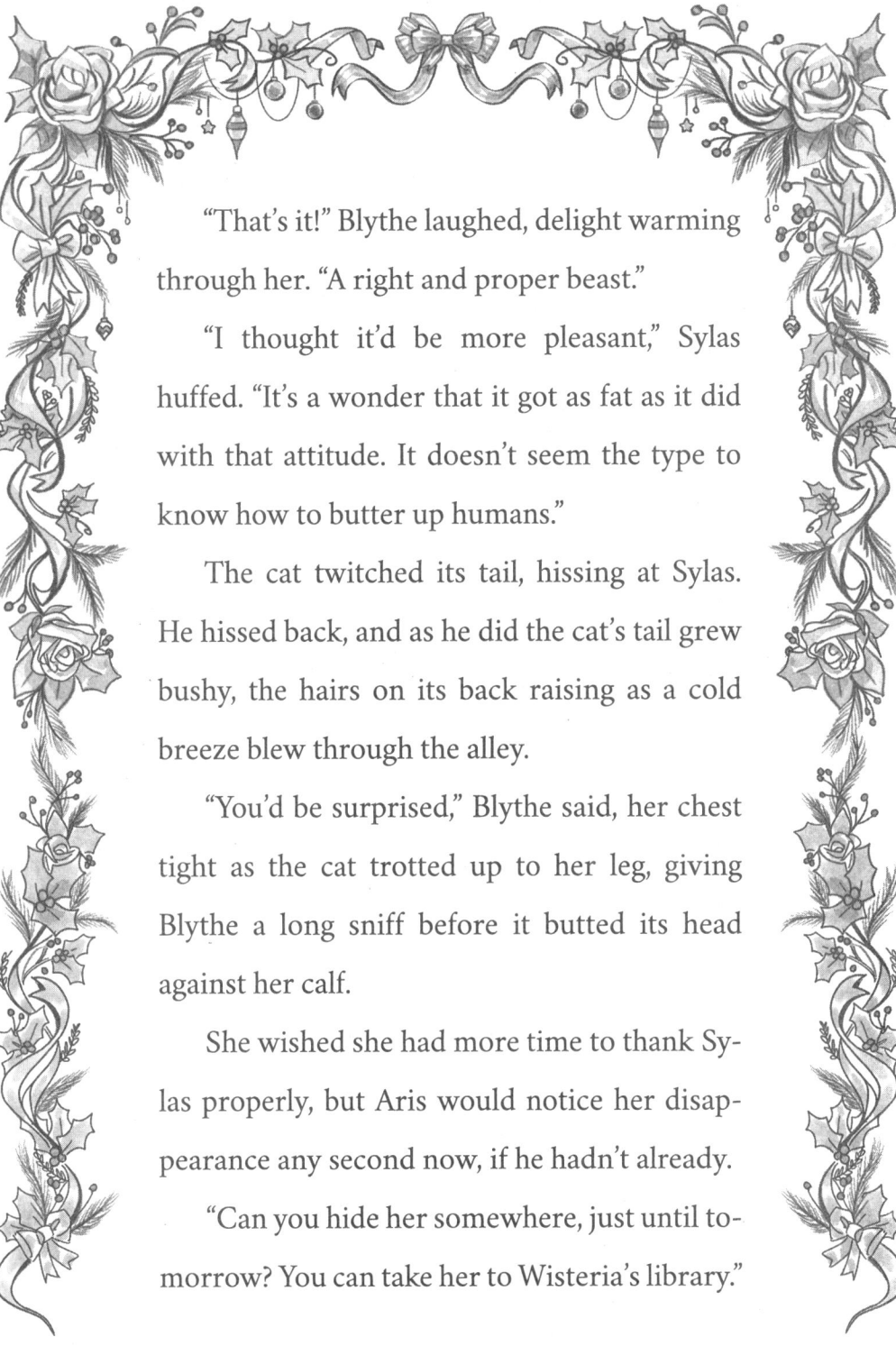

"That's it!" Blythe laughed, delight warming through her. "A right and proper beast."

"I thought it'd be more pleasant," Sylas huffed. "It's a wonder that it got as fat as it did with that attitude. It doesn't seem the type to know how to butter up humans."

The cat twitched its tail, hissing at Sylas. He hissed back, and as he did the cat's tail grew bushy, the hairs on its back raising as a cold breeze blew through the alley.

"You'd be surprised," Blythe said, her chest tight as the cat trotted up to her leg, giving Blythe a long sniff before it butted its head against her calf.

She wished she had more time to thank Sylas properly, but Aris would notice her disappearance any second now, if he hadn't already.

"Can you hide her somewhere, just until tomorrow? You can take her to Wisteria's library."

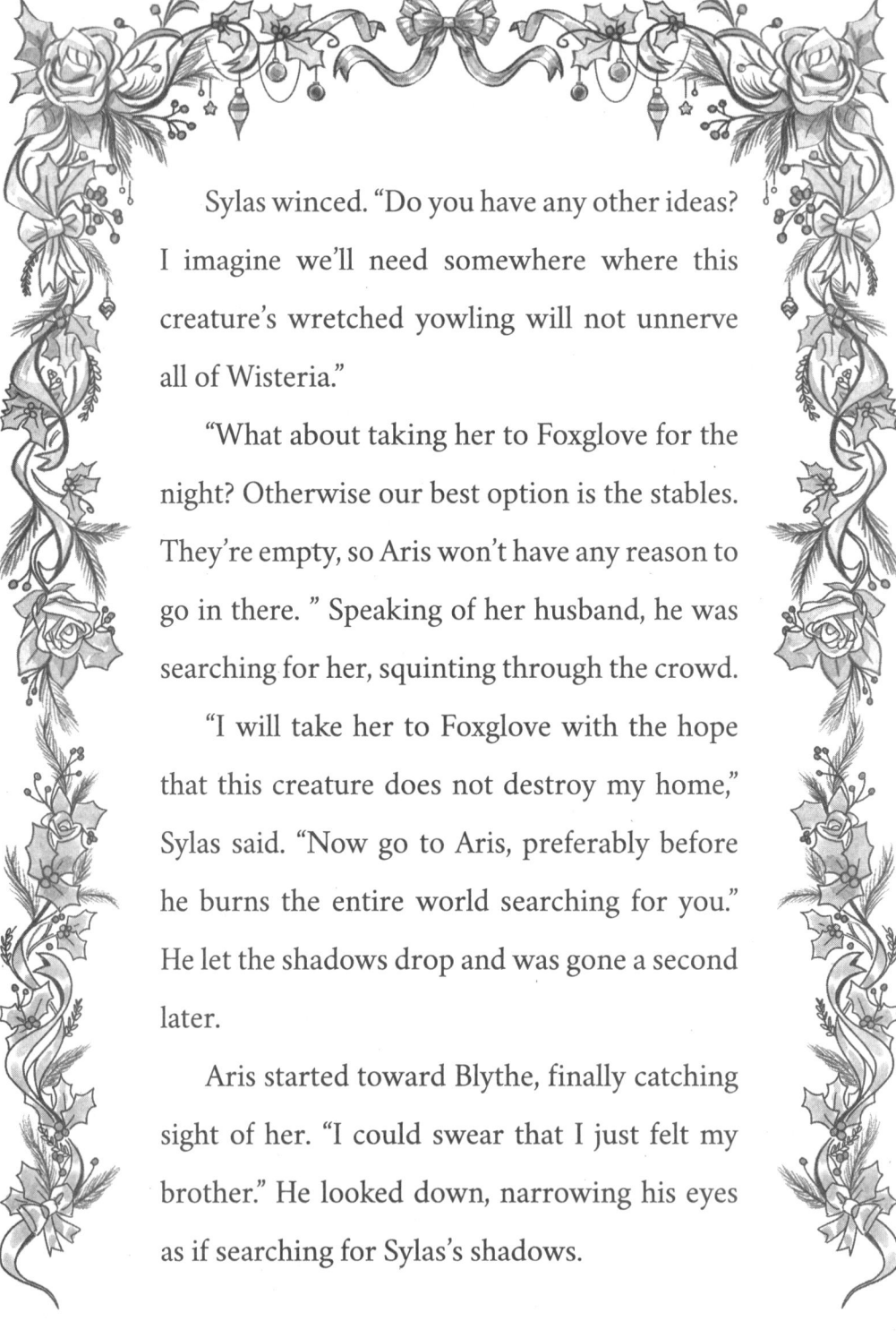

Sylas winced. "Do you have any other ideas? I imagine we'll need somewhere where this creature's wretched yowling will not unnerve all of Wisteria."

"What about taking her to Foxglove for the night? Otherwise our best option is the stables. They're empty, so Aris won't have any reason to go in there. " Speaking of her husband, he was searching for her, squinting through the crowd.

"I will take her to Foxglove with the hope that this creature does not destroy my home," Sylas said. "Now go to Aris, preferably before he burns the entire world searching for you." He let the shadows drop and was gone a second later.

Aris started toward Blythe, finally catching sight of her. "I could swear that I just felt my brother." He looked down, narrowing his eyes as if searching for Sylas's shadows.

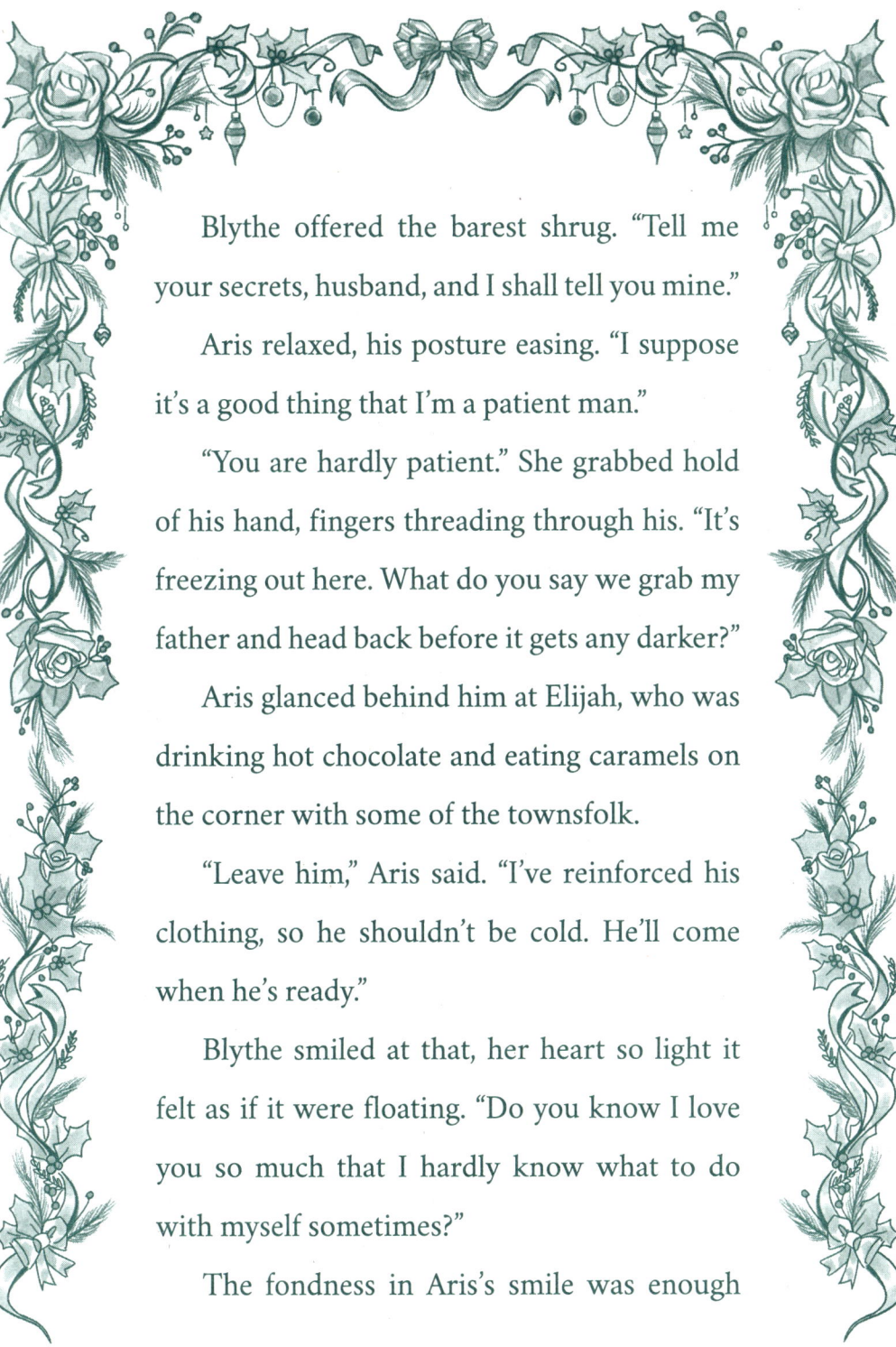

Blythe offered the barest shrug. "Tell me your secrets, husband, and I shall tell you mine."

Aris relaxed, his posture easing. "I suppose it's a good thing that I'm a patient man."

"You are hardly patient." She grabbed hold of his hand, fingers threading through his. "It's freezing out here. What do you say we grab my father and head back before it gets any darker?"

Aris glanced behind him at Elijah, who was drinking hot chocolate and eating caramels on the corner with some of the townsfolk.

"Leave him," Aris said. "I've reinforced his clothing, so he shouldn't be cold. He'll come when he's ready."

Blythe smiled at that, her heart so light it felt as if it were floating. "Do you know I love you so much that I hardly know what to do with myself sometimes?"

The fondness in Aris's smile was enough

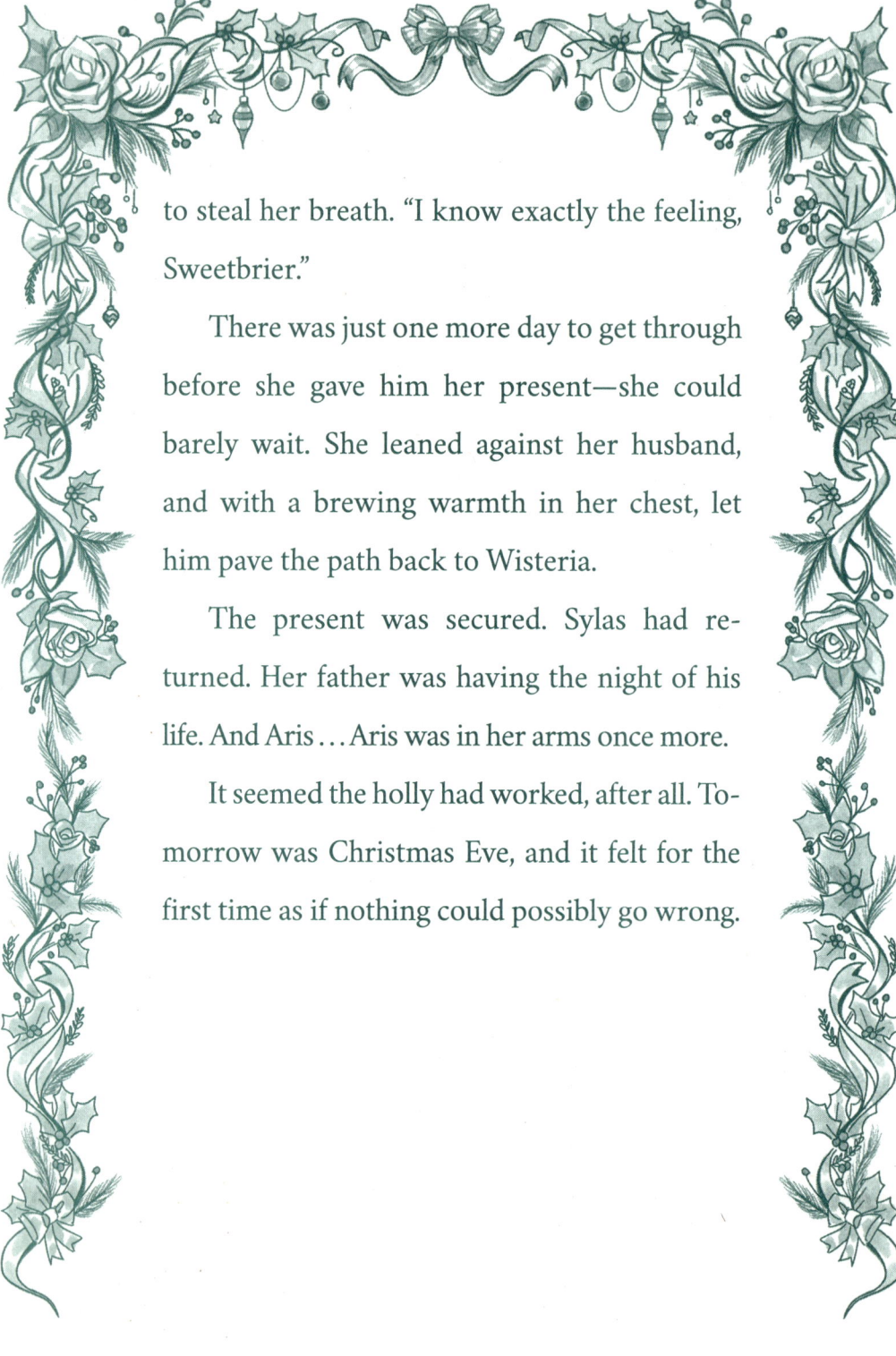

to steal her breath. "I know exactly the feeling, Sweetbrier."

There was just one more day to get through before she gave him her present—she could barely wait. She leaned against her husband, and with a brewing warmth in her chest, let him pave the path back to Wisteria.

The present was secured. Sylas had returned. Her father was having the night of his life. And Aris... Aris was in her arms once more.

It seemed the holly had worked, after all. Tomorrow was Christmas Eve, and it felt for the first time as if nothing could possibly go wrong.

FIFTEEN

Signa

MUSIC THRUMMED THROUGH THE HALLS of Wisteria Gardens.

Signa heard the pleasant trill of a flute before she'd even made it up the stairs and to the library, which Aris had prepared for their arrival. Lined against the wall was every instrument that she could think of, those favored by the spirits already claimed. One of the musicians sat perched on the bench of a piano, his hair smoothed and his expression content. The second had a violin set on their lap as they drew resin across their bow, and the last played a bouncy melody on the flute. They were each already warming up, their bodies looser and faces relaxed.

"I have found your musicians," Signa declared as she approached the ballet mistress, whose sharp face turned toward her appraisingly. Signa's stomach twisted a little—with her long nose and wrinkled skin, the woman reminded her of her late aunt Magda. She wondered briefly whatever had happened to that woman, and whether she'd passed on to the next life yet. It was horrible of her, but Signa rather hoped she hadn't. She would have preferred not to see Magda again in this life or the next.

"*So you have.*" Despite sounding pleased,

the woman's face remained sallow and stern. When she clapped her hands, all the previously chattering spirits glanced up, alert. The tulle of their dresses brushed against one another, their head ornaments jingling as they snapped to focus. The sound made Signa think of sleigh bells, though it was harsher, with a sharp, hollow ring that unsettled her.

The library, so quiet moments before, now buzzed with anticipation. Signa adjusted her stance, unsure whether to stay by the door or find a seat, the energy prickling along her skin.

"*Places,*" the ballet mistress demanded. "*Everyone to their places. Jeanne and Laurent, you will go on for Odette and Jules.*"

A squeal of delight came from one of the spirits in the formation. She was a tiny thing, dressed in a silvery gown with her brown hair slicked back and dusted with tiny silver crystals.

Odette's eyes burned into her back as Jeanne took her place. The others followed behind her, forming two sets of lines as if on either side of a stage. Behind the ballet mistress, Odette sat against the bookshelves, the tulle of her pink skirts flaring around her as she began sobbing into her knees.

Signa's chest tightened. It wouldn't do if she were to help only *some* of the spirits pass on. If Blythe and Aris were to make this their home, she'd need to get them all out.

"Can she not perform?" Signa challenged, motioning to Odette, who sniffled and looked hopefully up at them. "I'd like to see her."

"She cannot go on without a partner." This, it seemed, was not up for discussion. Again the ballet mistress clapped her hands, and this time music swelled around them. Signa had barely stumbled into the nearest chair before the

dancers pressed onto the tips of their toes, plastered their faces with smiles, and began their performance.

The library transformed into a makeshift stage, the spirits moving with an eerie grace that sent a shiver down Signa's spine. She tried to imagine what it might have looked like six decades prior, back when the stage had been real and the costumes festive. As it was, Signa could only faintly make out the shades of their skirts and the shimmering silver threads that tangled around them like cobwebs. The faint glow of candlelight flickered off the jewels and the ornaments sewn into their costumes, casting odd, twisted reflections onto the walls. Even the headpieces became terrifying in the right light, gilded stag horns becoming perilous weapons that made the performers look more like monsters than spirits. There was a gauziness around them that made it feel like the most curious holiday dream—one moment enchanting, the next unnervingly hollow. The dancers twirled so effortlessly that it was easy to forget their feet never quite touched the floor.

Jeanne led the performance, appearing to play the role of an innocent maiden lost in a fantastical, wintry world. She twirled on the very tips of her toes with an ethereal precision that awed Signa, who couldn't look away from such a curious show. Laurent followed, lifting his partner effortlessly into the air while the other dancers circled around them, as if trapping the pair, who seemed to be...struggling to leave? Fighting against them? Or perhaps they were joining the fray.

Odette, too, stared unblinking. She was no longer sobbing, but a palpable fury seemed to fester within her. With every step Jeanne took, Odette's expression darkened. There was no mistaking the tension crackling in the air, or the jealousy that burned behind her eyes.

When the music reached its haunting crescendo, her posture stiffened, hands balling into fists around her skirts. Her ragged gasps were too loud against the soft strains of the piano.

The spirit's glowing, bloodied eyes whirled to Signa, and panic shot down her spine when Odette screamed. So awful was the sound that Signa stumbled to her knees, clapping her palms over her ears. It'd been years since she'd felt such fear. Years since her body was so chilled that not a single bone would move, leaving her paralyzed as the spirits began twisting to and fro. Their bodies flickered once, then twice, and none seemed able to cease their twirling, writhing in a desperate frenzy.

Odette did not move at all, her hollow eyes staring into the ether as her body fizzled in and out of view. Books fell from shelves as the library seemed to tremble beneath the rising chaos. The piano's melody fractured, each jarring note a physical ache that thrummed in Signa's chest. Odette's scream tore through it all, sharper than the music.

Signa? Sylas's voice pressed against her thoughts, sounding every bit as panicked as she felt. *What's happened? Are you safe?*

Her first instinct was to summon the reaper. To tell him that she needed help before one of these spirits possessed her. But no—this was her job. *She* was the bridge between the worlds of the living and the dead; the only one who could truly help these people accept their deaths and pass on. Her job was made far more difficult, of course, when there were over a dozen spirits all suffering simultaneously, but Signa had no choice but to sort this out.

Crouched behind a chair and using it as a shield, she drew a long breath and opened her mind to Sylas. *Don't worry for me, I'm fine*, she told him, then turned her attention to the ballet mistress, whose wrinkled face had stretched and twisted in rage. She was yelling at the spirits in a language that Signa did not understand, but they weren't listening. The music was too loud and their minds too lost. The bookshelves beside them trembled as spirits spun into them, their movements awkward and jerky.

The ballet mistress twisted toward Signa, her eyes consumed by blackness. She was so fast that there was no time to react, flashing out of sight and then beside Signa a second later, spindly hands seizing her by the throat. They drained her not only of breath, but of every ounce of warmth in her body.

Signa swayed on her feet, understanding that the woman meant to possess her but unable to do anything to stop it. The ballet mistress's grip tightened, icy tendrils crawling beneath Signa's skin, freezing her limbs in place. Her vision blurred, darkness crowding the edges as her knees buckled. Gundry was at her heels, snarling and snapping at the spirit who would not stop.

Fortunately, Sylas had not listened.

Gundry's low growl reverberated through the library. Then came a cold that was different from the ballet mistress's icy touch. It was a gentler, familiar cold that seeped from the very shadows themselves and pressed against Signa's skin. She relaxed into the touch, able to breathe again.

He arrived without sound, slipping through the stillness as if he'd been there all along, a quiet force that bent the air around him. Sylas materialized beside them, his presence swallowing the space like a void as his eyes fixed on the ballet mistress, blazing with barely contained fury.

"Release her." It didn't matter how quietly he spoke; his words cut the silence like a blade, sharp and unforgiving.

The spirit hesitated, her grip faltering. In the space of a breath, Sylas had put himself between them, his gloved hand wrapping around Signa's waist as his shadows slipped over them like a shield.

"You're all right," he whispered, thumb brushing against the spot where the woman had gripped her throat as she curled against him. "I'm sorry. I won't let any of them hurt you." There was still an edge to his voice no matter how gently he spoke, like ice cracking beneath a surface.

She tried to form the words—tried to tell him she was all right—but her teeth couldn't cease their chattering.

Around them, the room had erupted into chaos. The ballet mistress's fury radiated like a shock wave, sending the spirits scattering from their makeshift stage. They spun wildly through the library, books flying from their shelves and pages fluttering about while furniture was overturned, crashing violently against the walls. The piano screeched in protest as Signa turned to find the musician's face contorted, his fingers pounding the keys and driving everyone around him into a frenzy.

"This is all my fault," Sylas admitted, half muttering to himself, though there was no chance for Signa to press him for specifics. Gundry had leapt forward, monstrous in size with thick black shadows dripping from his gaping maw. He bared fangs as long as Signa's hand at any spirits who dared approach as Sylas eased her into a chair. She was too numb to move. To speak. To do much of anything but sit there shivering as he extended an open palm, every shadow in the room twisting and pooling together until it formed his scythe.

He brandished it at the spirits, and that's when the front door of Wisteria swung open.

SIXTEEN

Blythe

Aris had the hearth lit and a warm plate of cookies waiting for everyone on the table when they returned. Cups of mulled cider rested on a silver tray, still steaming. Blythe tossed her coat aside, grateful for the warmth that brought feeling back to her cheeks and nose.

She hurried toward the cider, only to notice from the corner of her eye that the parlor was empty.

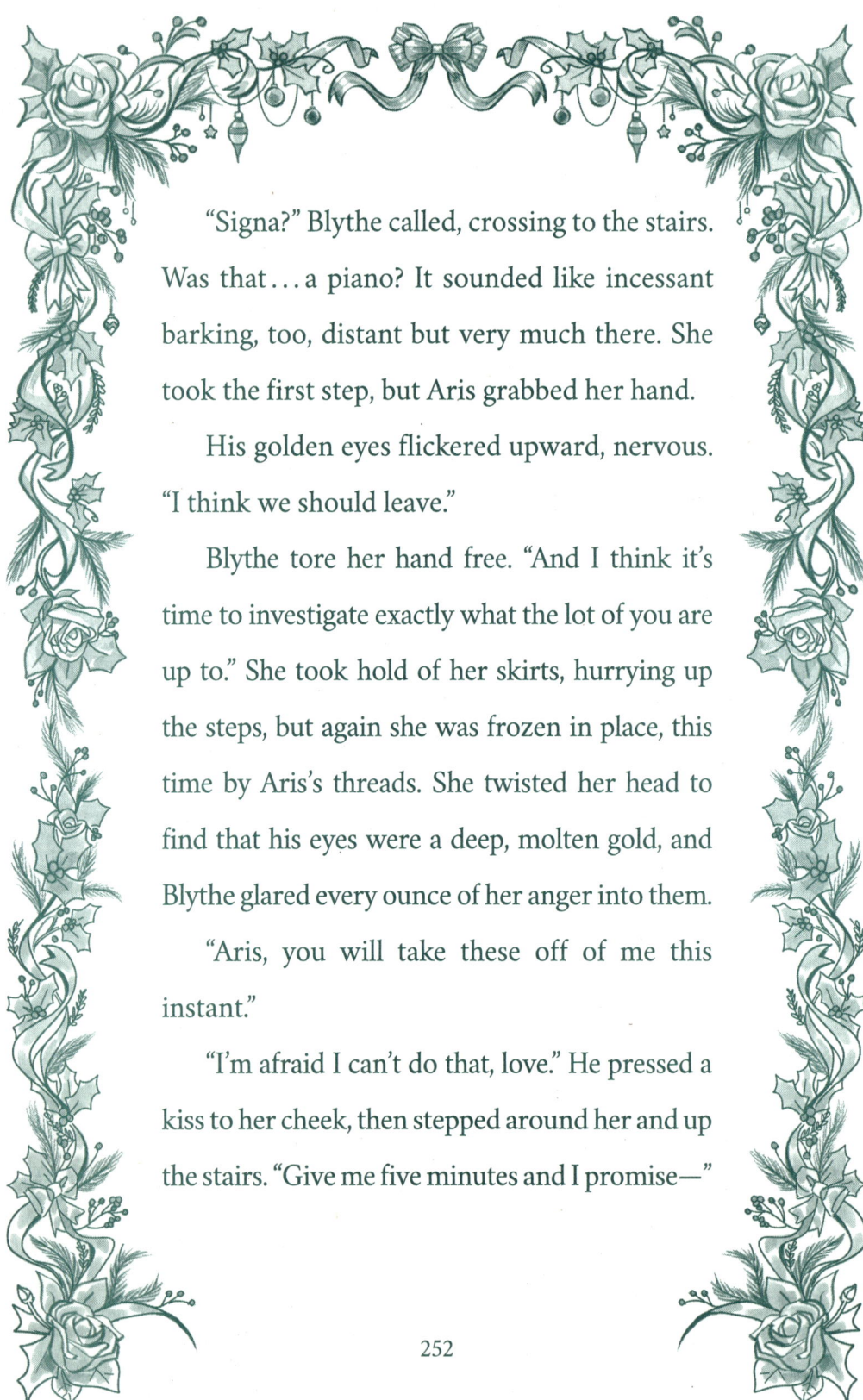

"Signa?" Blythe called, crossing to the stairs. Was that...a piano? It sounded like incessant barking, too, distant but very much there. She took the first step, but Aris grabbed her hand.

His golden eyes flickered upward, nervous. "I think we should leave."

Blythe tore her hand free. "And I think it's time to investigate exactly what the lot of you are up to." She took hold of her skirts, hurrying up the steps, but again she was frozen in place, this time by Aris's threads. She twisted her head to find that his eyes were a deep, molten gold, and Blythe glared every ounce of her anger into them.

"Aris, you will take these off of me this instant."

"I'm afraid I can't do that, love." He pressed a kiss to her cheek, then stepped around her and up the stairs. "Give me five minutes and I promise—"

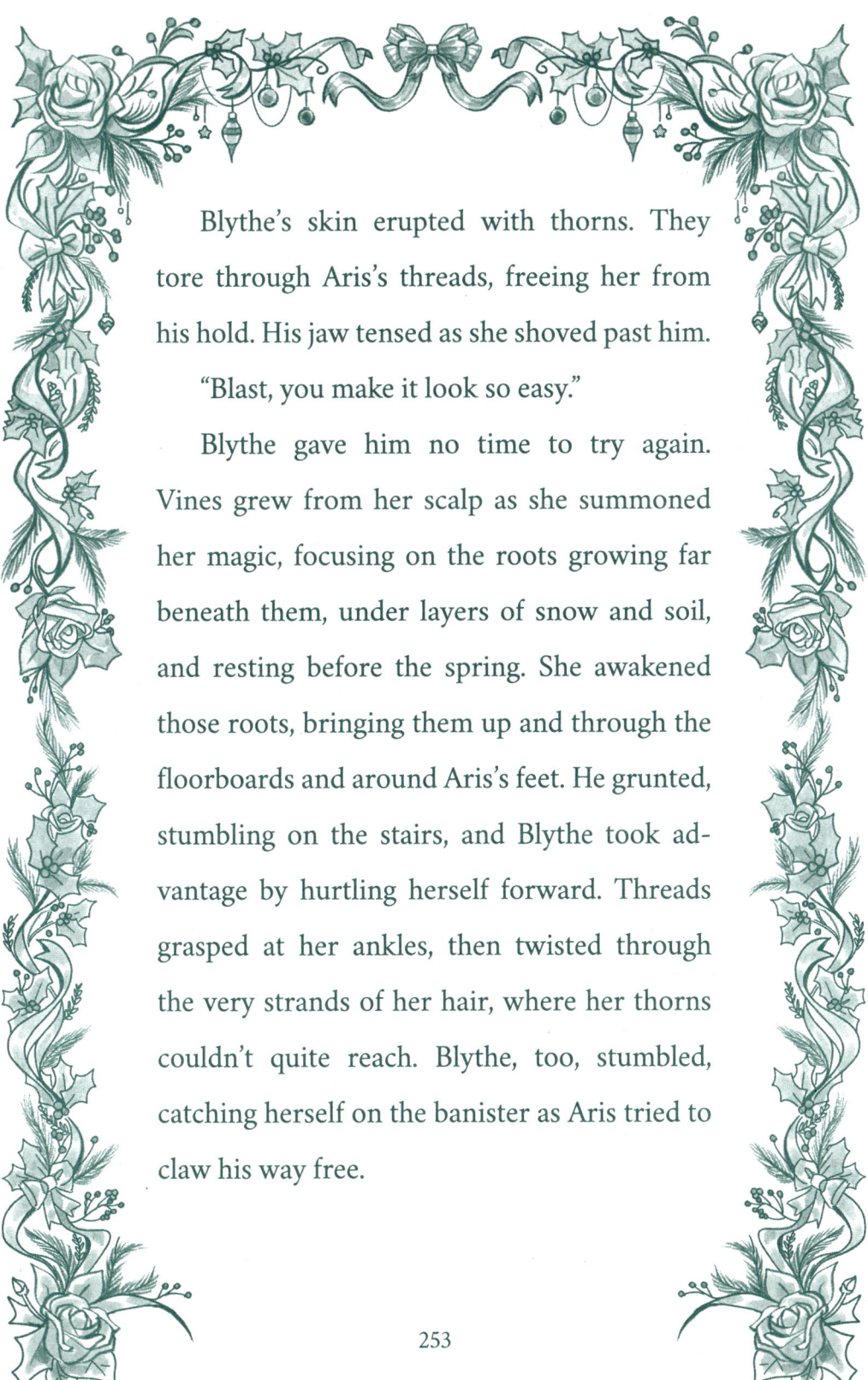

Blythe's skin erupted with thorns. They tore through Aris's threads, freeing her from his hold. His jaw tensed as she shoved past him.

"Blast, you make it look so easy."

Blythe gave him no time to try again. Vines grew from her scalp as she summoned her magic, focusing on the roots growing far beneath them, under layers of snow and soil, and resting before the spring. She awakened those roots, bringing them up and through the floorboards and around Aris's feet. He grunted, stumbling on the stairs, and Blythe took advantage by hurtling herself forward. Threads grasped at her ankles, then twisted through the very strands of her hair, where her thorns couldn't quite reach. Blythe, too, stumbled, catching herself on the banister as Aris tried to claw his way free.

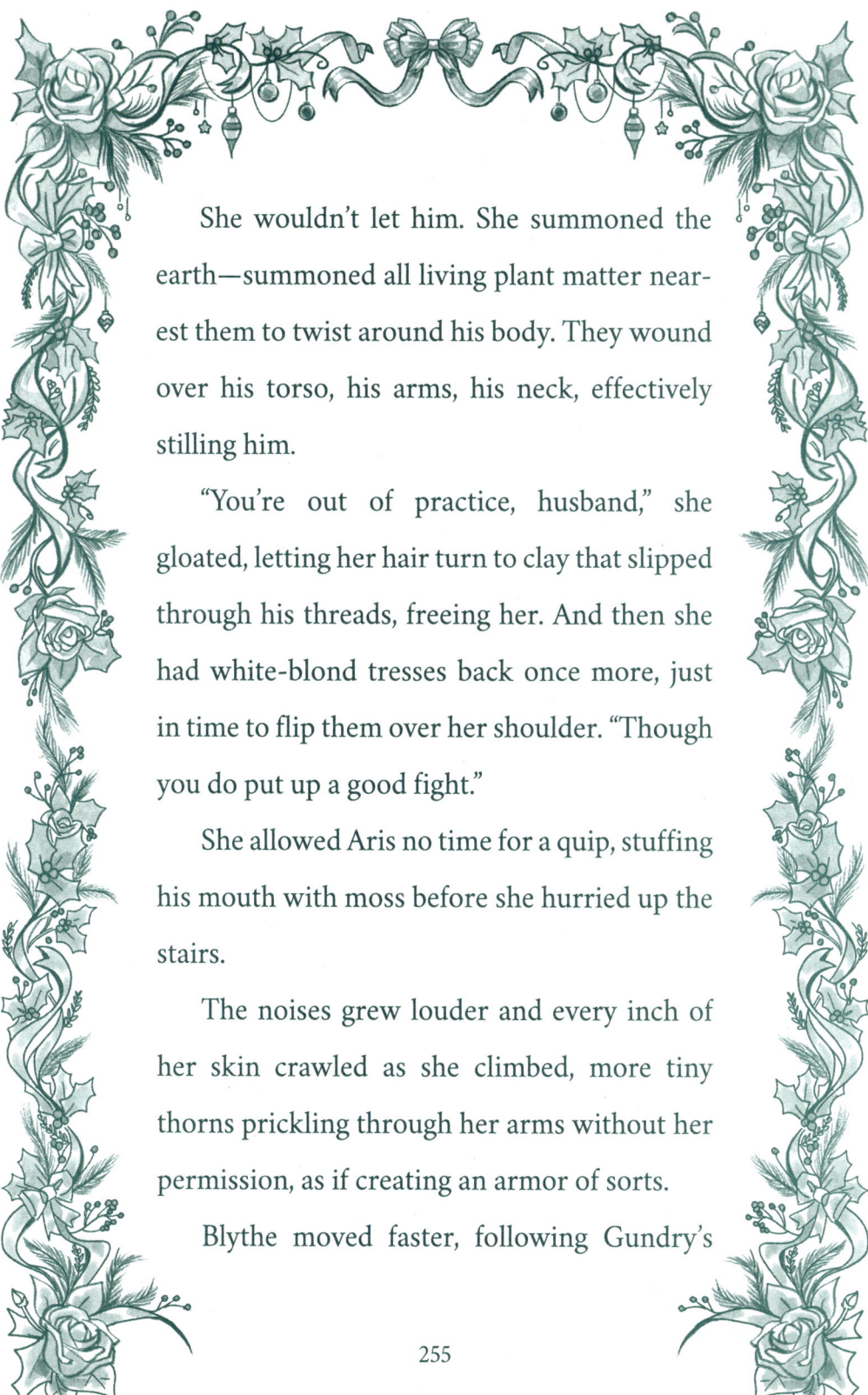

She wouldn't let him. She summoned the earth—summoned all living plant matter nearest them to twist around his body. They wound over his torso, his arms, his neck, effectively stilling him.

"You're out of practice, husband," she gloated, letting her hair turn to clay that slipped through his threads, freeing her. And then she had white-blond tresses back once more, just in time to flip them over her shoulder. "Though you do put up a good fight."

She allowed Aris no time for a quip, stuffing his mouth with moss before she hurried up the stairs.

The noises grew louder and every inch of her skin crawled as she climbed, more tiny thorns prickling through her arms without her permission, as if creating an armor of sorts.

Blythe moved faster, following Gundry's

barking to her library. She reached for the door only to jerk away the second her fingers grazed the handle. It was so cold that it burned.

Behind her, Aris was still stumbling his way up the stairs, spitting out moss and shaking roots from his ankles. He caught his wife's gaze. "Blythe, don't go in there—"

She snorted, those words the very fuel she needed to clench her teeth and force the door open.

Blythe didn't have any idea how to make sense of what was awaiting her inside.

She saw Gundry first, but not in any form that Blythe recognized. He was a monstrous hound several times his normal size, with darkness that dripped from his open maw and paws the size of her head. He was blocking Signa with his body, hackles raised and fangs bared.

His master stood before him, back to the

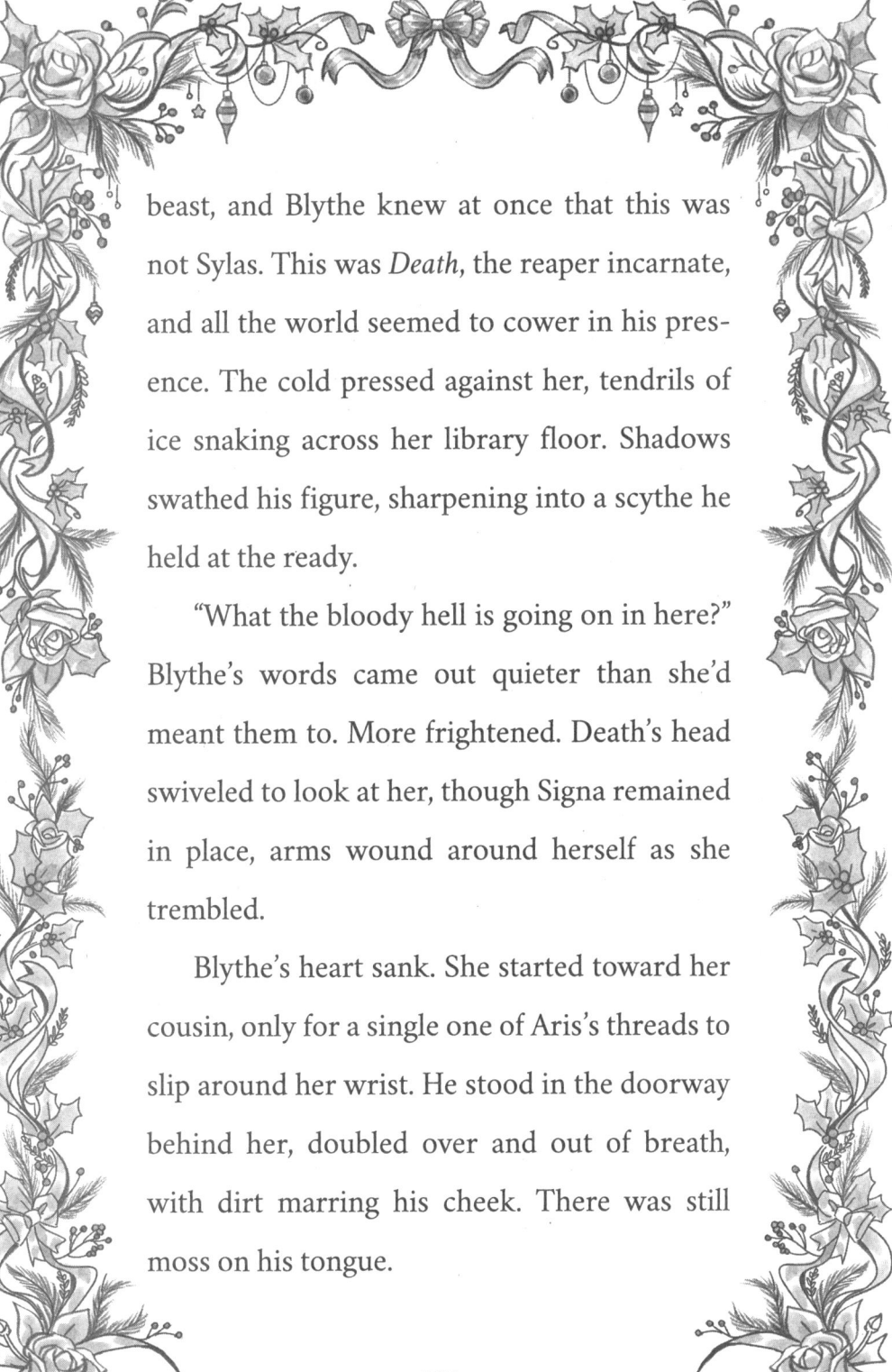

beast, and Blythe knew at once that this was not Sylas. This was *Death*, the reaper incarnate, and all the world seemed to cower in his presence. The cold pressed against her, tendrils of ice snaking across her library floor. Shadows swathed his figure, sharpening into a scythe he held at the ready.

"What the bloody hell is going on in here?" Blythe's words came out quieter than she'd meant them to. More frightened. Death's head swiveled to look at her, though Signa remained in place, arms wound around herself as she trembled.

Blythe's heart sank. She started toward her cousin, only for a single one of Aris's threads to slip around her wrist. He stood in the doorway behind her, doubled over and out of breath, with dirt marring his cheek. There was still moss on his tongue.

"Please," he panted. "It's not safe."

The hairs along her neck stood, and Blythe recognized the feeling as the same one she'd had in her bedroom the night prior. Like there was someone else nearby, watching.

Spirits. There were spirits in Wisteria Gardens.

How strangely Aris had acted last night, though he shouldn't have been able to see them, either. Which could only mean...

"Oh, you devil!" Blythe snarled the words, which now came out much louder than she anticipated, her anger making the thorns rise sharper across her skin. She whirled on Aris. "You absolute buffoon!"

"As fond as I've always been of our verbal sparring, now is not the best time—"

"I can't believe you lied to me!" More vines were taking over Blythe's hair, growing thick from her scalp. "All this time and *that's* what you two have been hiding? That somehow our home has been infested with *spirits*?" The odd behavior. The secretive glances. It all made sense now.

"They're drawn to emotions!" Signa called out. God, why on earth was her cousin *floating*? "Be careful!"

Around her wrists, the gilded threads pulsed warm. "Leave, Blythe," Aris begged. "I can't risk you being hurt again."

"*Me*? You don't want to risk *me* getting hurt?" Each of Blythe's steps shook the ground as she tore her wrist free and stalked farther into the room. As Blythe drew closer, the spirits drew back, watching as vines tore free from the earth and cracked the floorboards. They wound around Signa to offer some measure of warmth. Her cousin's teeth were chattering, her skin a deathly shade of blue. Blythe shot Sylas a glare.

"Did you know about this?"

The reaper sank in on himself, which only made Blythe's anger more profound. She scooted Signa closer toward the hearth, though the temperature had already warmed drastically just with Blythe near.

"Buffoons," she repeated under her breath. "I am surrounded by nothing but buffoons. Aris, stop cowering and get over here."

"I am *not* cowering," he started, though his mouth snapped shut when she shot him a glare that had him crossing the floor toward her in the next second.

"Spirits don't like being near me," Blythe said before he could ask, each word sharp. "Apparently, I *glow*. Which you might have known, had you chosen to tell me about this predicament."

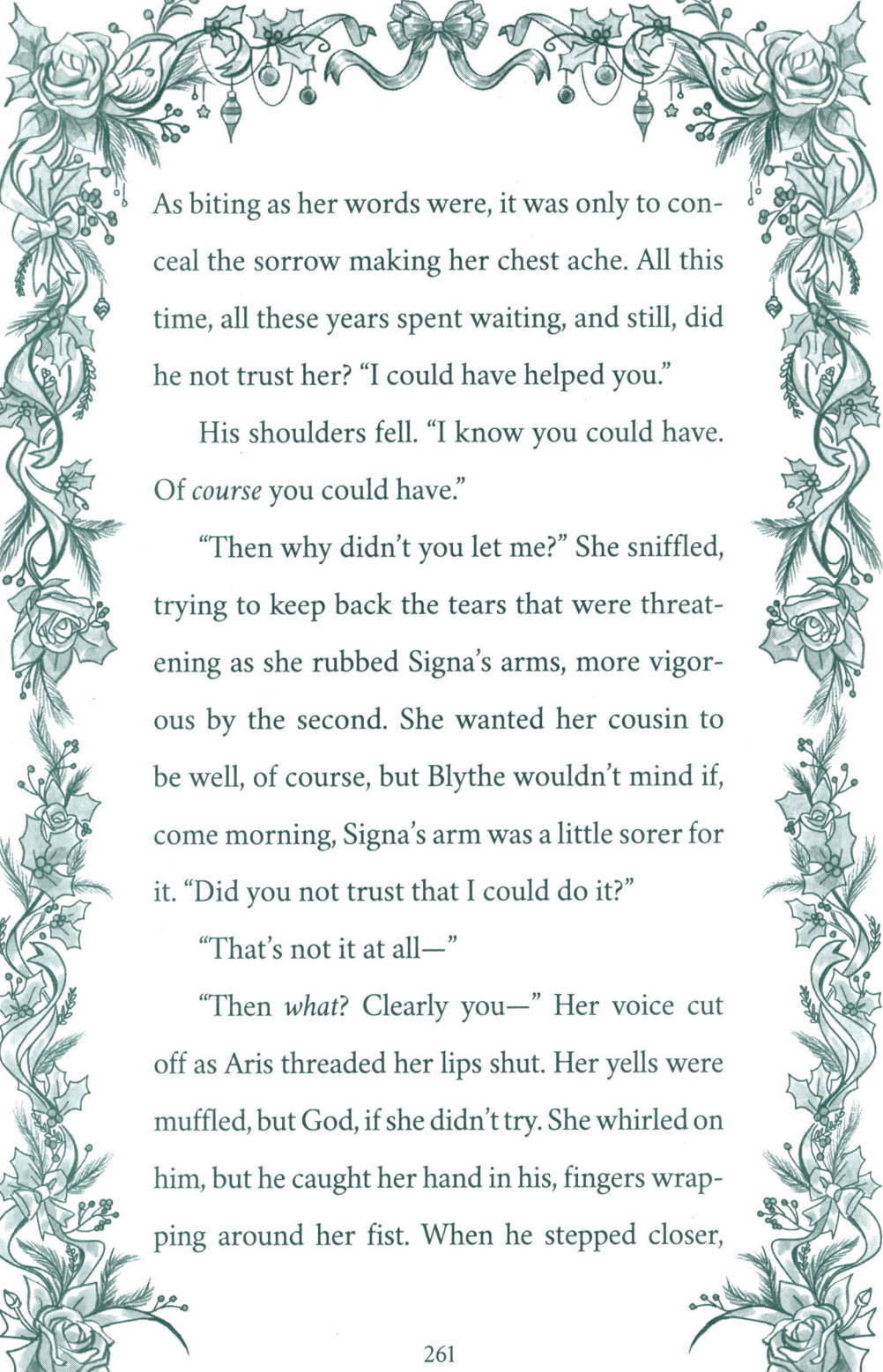

As biting as her words were, it was only to conceal the sorrow making her chest ache. All this time, all these years spent waiting, and still, did he not trust her? "I could have helped you."

His shoulders fell. "I know you could have. Of *course* you could have."

"Then why didn't you let me?" She sniffled, trying to keep back the tears that were threatening as she rubbed Signa's arms, more vigorous by the second. She wanted her cousin to be well, of course, but Blythe wouldn't mind if, come morning, Signa's arm was a little sorer for it. "Did you not trust that I could do it?"

"That's not it at all—"

"Then *what*? Clearly you—" Her voice cut off as Aris threaded her lips shut. Her yells were muffled, but God, if she didn't try. She whirled on him, but he caught her hand in his, fingers wrapping around her fist. When he stepped closer, she could feel the heat of his body against her skin. Not once did he look away, and she fought to hold his stare, too, no matter how smoldering.

"I wanted to give you the perfect Christmas." He held tighter when she tried to pull away, clenching his jaw. "I have never had a proper celebration, Blythe. Not like the kind you deserve. All I wanted was to make it great for you, and for you to not have to worry about something as ridiculous as spirits disturbing our peace. I wanted the holly to matter. For your effort and your hopes to *matter*."

She glared at him, going silent until the threads sealing her lips unraveled.

"Even all these years later and you're still a fool," she told him. "All I wanted was *you*, Aris. A Christmas with you and my family is what makes it perfect. Something like this? Something as ridiculous as spirits? We deal with that *together*, do you understand me? We deal with it before my cousin turns into a freezing and trembling mess."

"I...am not...a mess," Signa muttered weakly, to which Blythe could only sigh. She looked down at her, trying to rein in at least *some* of her fury.

"How many are there?"

"A few...a f-few dozen," Signa said between her chattering teeth. It was, of course, not the answer Blythe preferred. But at least now she knew the truth.

She relaxed, steadying herself enough to withdraw the vines and thorns. "Well, I for one am not about to exist in a house filled with several dozen spirits at *Christmastime*." She scoffed, taking her seat beside Signa. "Tell me everything you know about them."

"It's not much," Signa admitted, dropping her

voice to a whisper. She glanced behind her, likely to ensure that the spirits were keeping their distance, before speaking. "They died in a fire over sixty years ago, during their dress rehearsal. It was an accident—one of their actors got so nervous that he made himself sick. He did a poor job of putting out the ashes of his pipe before he hurried off to rest. But by the time he got back, the entire theater had burned to the ground."

"Oh. Well, that's..." Blythe sucked her bottom lip between her teeth, trying to choose her next words carefully. Unfortunately, she couldn't come up with a single decent thing. "Actually, Signa, that's ludicrous. I swear, do you even hear the things that come out of your mouth? You're telling me there are a dozen—"

"Several dozen."

"—several dozen spirits who were killed because one man was nervous?"

Signa pressed her lips together. "Unfortunately, that's p-precisely what I'm saying. His n-name is J-Jules."

"*Is?* You know him?"

"I ran into him at the cemetery, actually."

Blythe nodded sagely. "Right, because that is perfectly normal." She stared up at the holly she'd strung across the bookshelves. If it was true the plant could ward away evil spirits, it was doing a piss-poor job.

"I think that if the spirits are to pass on, they need to finish their performance," Signa said, speaking easier with each word. Her shivering had died down substantially, and she was able to sit up now. "That's what Aris and I have been trying to help with. First we had to find their music to help them put on a show, and now... I don't even know how to describe it. They started their dance, but it was as if they were becoming angrier with each step. Like they were all expecting something."

"Likely because they were." It was Elijah who spoke, still bundled in his coat as he stared at them from the threshold. Gundry looped circles at his heels, the shadows slinking from him and his bones shortening until he looked like a normal hound once more. He settled at Elijah's feet when the man sat down and rested his chin on her father's boots.

"You said they were performers. If it's true that they've been waiting decades to put on this performance, I imagine they'll want an audience larger than just us."

Blythe grimaced as her cousin squeezed her arm, nearly bursting from her seat.

"I think you're exactly right, all they need is an audience—"

"Perhaps I'm missing something, but have

we forgotten that these people are dead?" Aris asked. A chill passed through the room with his words. Something whizzed by his hair, whipping several strands back, and Aris hissed a breath. Suddenly he was wrangling out of his tunic, letting his threads carry it through the room until it caught onto a form, the shape of a body apparent beneath the fabric. He watched as the spirit flitted away.

"Blasted spirits," Aris seethed, this time at half the volume. "How do you expect to give them an audience when we cannot even see them?"

Blythe looked from her husband's bare chest, then to the tunic-clad spirit flapping around in the air, and she smiled.

"Witness me, family," she said, "for I have the most brilliant plan."

SEVENTEEN

Aris

All things considered, Aris knew he was getting off easy. At least for now, while there was still work to be done.

They sat at the breakfast table early the next morning, rehashing the plan a final time.

"Does everyone understand their role?" Blythe asked. She reminded him of a princess from one of the wintry fairy tales she and Signa liked to read, leaning over the table like they were talking strategy for a war while dressed in a powder-blue velvet gown. He watched her hair sway as she moved, cast over her shoulders in waves and so light a blond now that it was almost white.

Aris knew he should be paying more attention, especially when Blythe was upset with him, but he couldn't stop staring at his wife, eager to be rid of the spirits so he might have her back to himself once and for all.

"It should be easy enough," Elijah agreed, while Signa nodded.

"This just might work." She seemed far more at ease now that Blythe was involved with the planning. Aris tried not to take it personally.

"It'd better," he grumbled. "Otherwise I'm moving our home and we can leave these spirits to twirl away for the rest of their days."

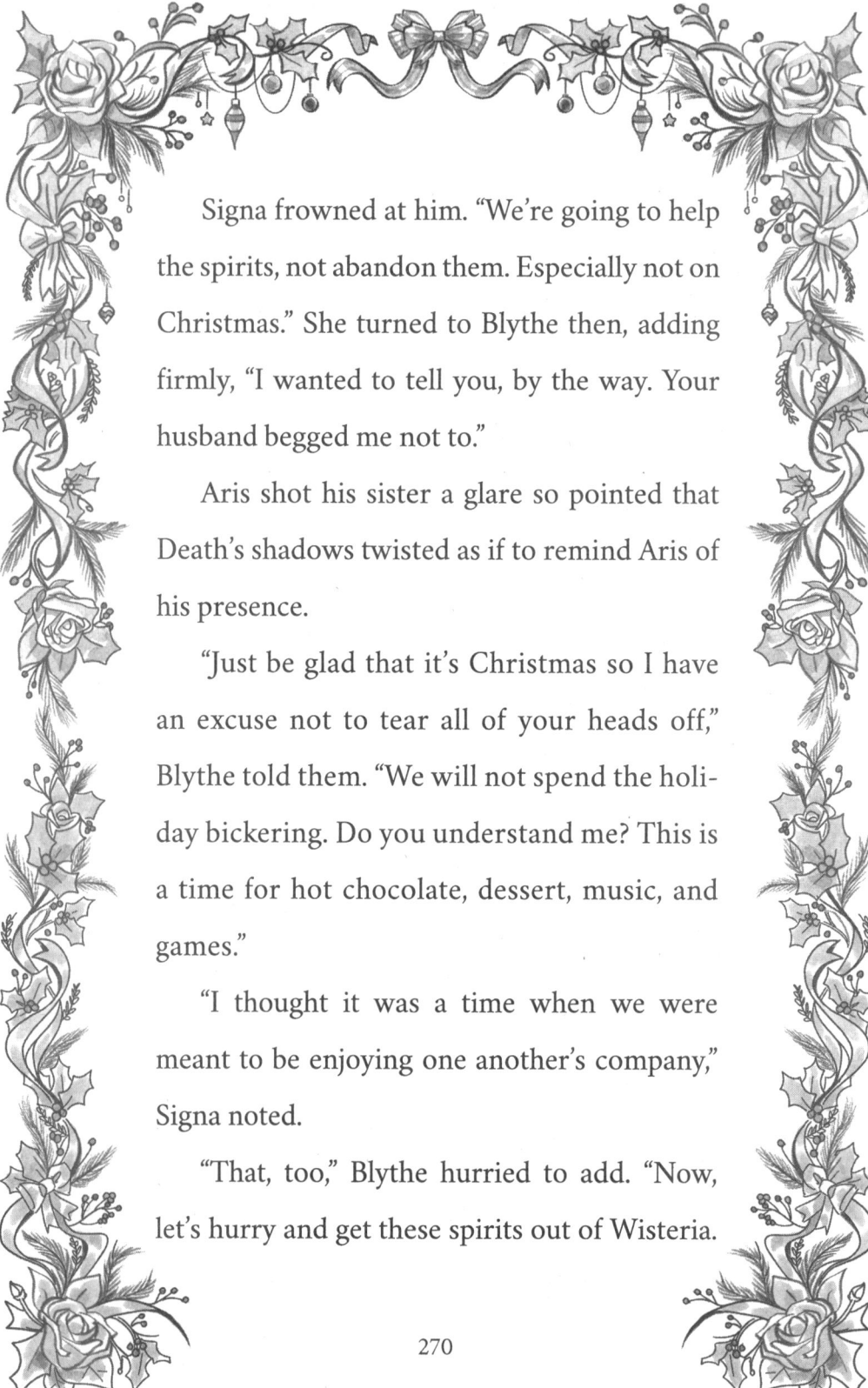

Signa frowned at him. "We're going to help the spirits, not abandon them. Especially not on Christmas." She turned to Blythe then, adding firmly, "I wanted to tell you, by the way. Your husband begged me not to."

Aris shot his sister a glare so pointed that Death's shadows twisted as if to remind Aris of his presence.

"Just be glad that it's Christmas so I have an excuse not to tear all of your heads off," Blythe told them. "We will not spend the holiday bickering. Do you understand me? This is a time for hot chocolate, dessert, music, and games."

"I thought it was a time when we were meant to be enjoying one another's company," Signa noted.

"That, too," Blythe hurried to add. "Now, let's hurry and get these spirits out of Wisteria.

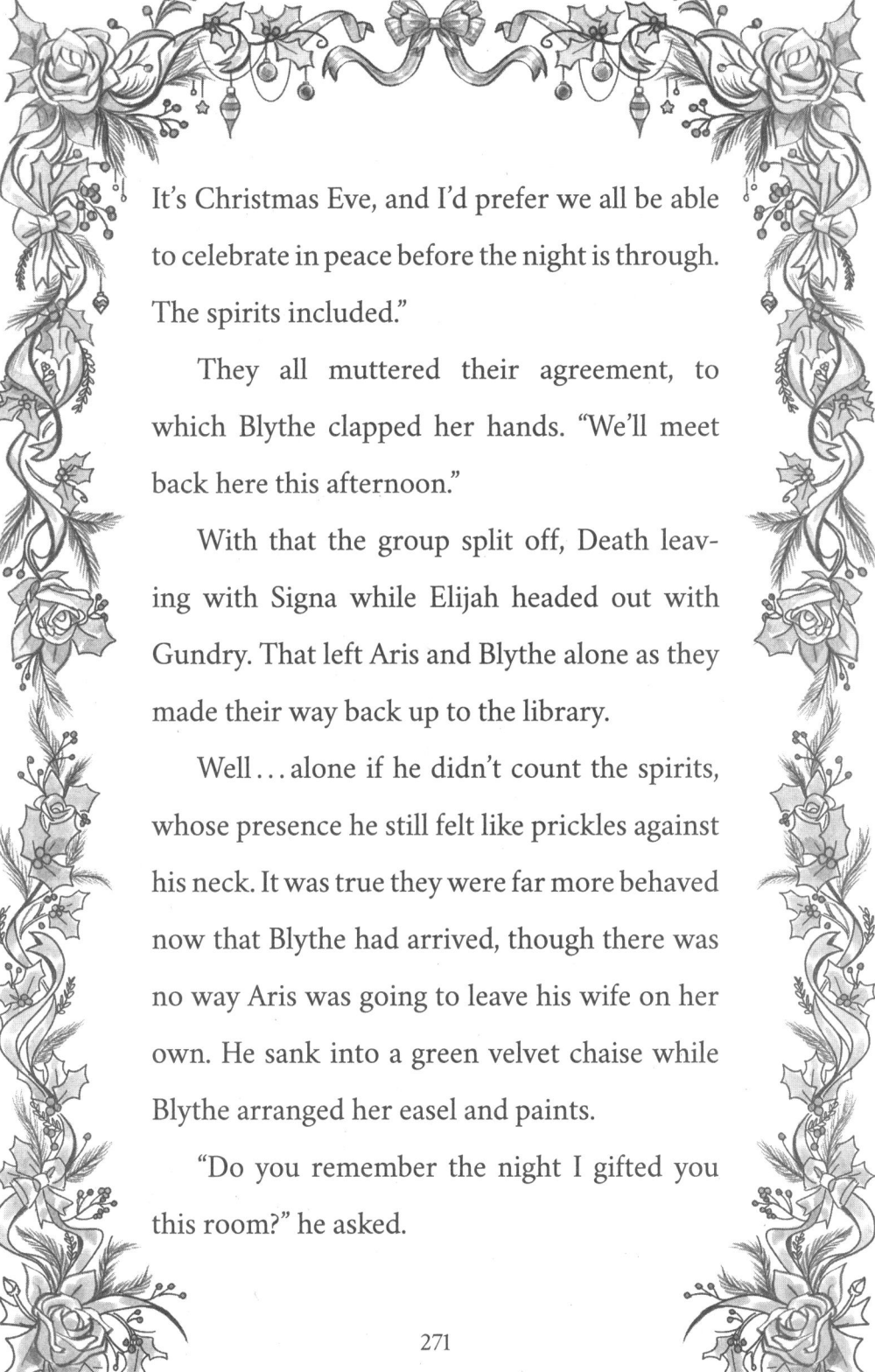

It's Christmas Eve, and I'd prefer we all be able to celebrate in peace before the night is through. The spirits included."

They all muttered their agreement, to which Blythe clapped her hands. "We'll meet back here this afternoon."

With that the group split off, Death leaving with Signa while Elijah headed out with Gundry. That left Aris and Blythe alone as they made their way back up to the library.

Well...alone if he didn't count the spirits, whose presence he still felt like prickles against his neck. It was true they were far more behaved now that Blythe had arrived, though there was no way Aris was going to leave his wife on her own. He sank into a green velvet chaise while Blythe arranged her easel and paints.

"Do you remember the night I gifted you this room?" he asked.

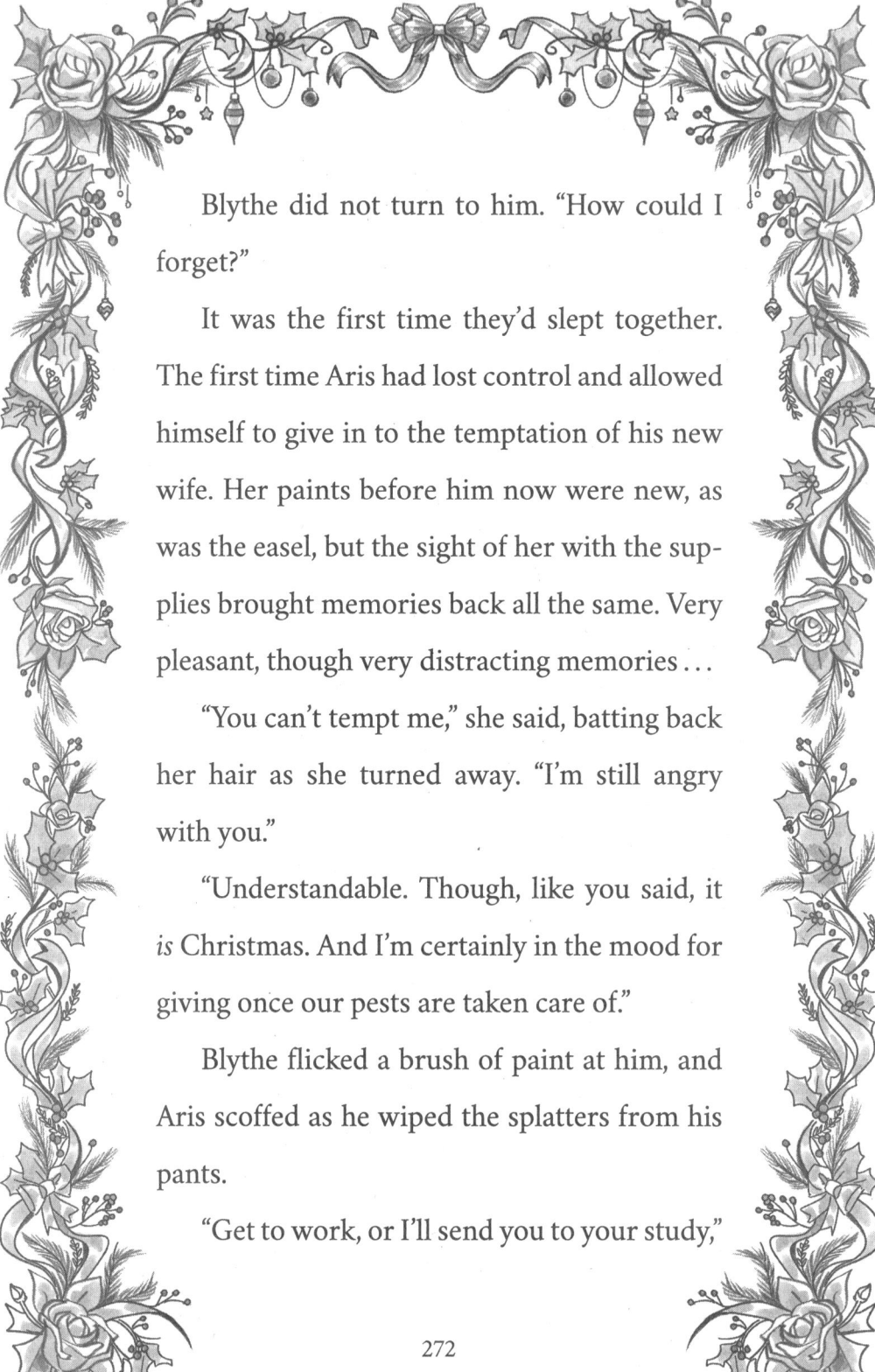

Blythe did not turn to him. "How could I forget?"

It was the first time they'd slept together. The first time Aris had lost control and allowed himself to give in to the temptation of his new wife. Her paints before him now were new, as was the easel, but the sight of her with the supplies brought memories back all the same. Very pleasant, though very distracting memories...

"You can't tempt me," she said, batting back her hair as she turned away. "I'm still angry with you."

"Understandable. Though, like you said, it *is* Christmas. And I'm certainly in the mood for giving once our pests are taken care of."

Blythe flicked a brush of paint at him, and Aris scoffed as he wiped the splatters from his pants.

"Get to work, or I'll send you to your study,"

she demanded, though the words were half-hearted. She wouldn't want to spend the day alone, either. Not when each of them was in a position to show off just how magnificent they were.

For Blythe's part, she set about redesigning the room Aris had gifted her decades ago. It was a magical space, able to adapt to whatever she wanted it to be. All she needed was to create the image on a canvas, and the room could become her wildest dream.

It was an excellent gift, if he said so himself. Which was why coming up with another for her had been so troublesome. He could only hope that she would like her next present just as much.

Blythe set aside the canvas that depicted her library, placed a blank one on the easel in its place, and got to work creating a stage.

Only, the stage was no simple thing. On either side stood polished wooden nutcrackers, their varnish gleaming as they towered at least three times Aris's height. They stood sentinel over what would be the audience, wielding red coats with gleaming buttons and giant candy canes like swords that they pointed at each other over the top of the stage. Dazzling snowflakes hung from the ceiling, and the seat beneath Aris shifted from a chaise to green velvet chairs, plusher than most theaters'. Above the audience was a chandelier draped with ornaments and twinkling icicles, and Aris added a flare of his own, letting the pleasant scent of cinnamon and oranges suffuse in the air. Garlands hung in all the corners, woven with more holly. Not that it'd done Blythe any favors up to this point.

"Impressive," Aris noted, catching sight of

Blythe's smug grin before she pressed her lips together to conceal it.

"Just wait until you see me in a garden. That's where I really shine."

Aris grimaced, still able to taste a faint trace of moss on his tongue. "Yes, I can imagine."

She slid him a sideways look, scowling. "Don't you have your own task you should be working on?"

He did, though he didn't imagine it'd take him long. He held out his hand as Blythe watched him, a glinting needle appearing between two fingers. When he wagged a brow at her, she rolled her eyes.

Aris had made plenty of clothing in his lifetimes. Even more recently, he had dedicated much of his existence to being a dressmaker and learning the trade. However, in that moment he felt rather like the grandmother of a child in a school play, forced to craft ridiculous costumes for them and their friends.

He twirled the needle between his fingers, considering his creation. His talents were greatly wasted on the likes of the spirits haunting his home.

Though if he *had* to make costumes regardless, they might as well be spectacular.

The first thread came as a strike through the air, firm and decisive. He was admittedly more dramatic about it given that his wife was observing, and he had a compulsive need to impress her, but it wasn't until a few more dozen twists of his needle that she'd be able to see the threads crafted by his hand.

The first creation was a gown of gold, long in the back but barely hitting the wearer's hips in the front, where sparkling white tulle flared out. It was one of his simpler designs, ornamented with a headpiece of immaculate bone-white antlers. There really was no rhyme or reason to the costumes he created. He did only what interested him—candy-cane-striped bodices with twinkling skirts, all-white outfits with a subtle frosted sparkle, sugarplum-pink tutus with matching tops... With each pull of his threads he fell more into his work, forgetting at one point that Blythe was watching as he dressed the fabrics in jewels and gemstones until they had just the right amount of sparkle to be dazzling, but not gaudy.

It was always like this when Aris worked. The world fell away as he disappeared into his project, an artist fixated on finishing his latest masterpiece. He had no concept of time. No knowledge of how many costumes he'd made. Aris would have kept going for hours or days more, letting his creativity overtake him, if not for the gentle press of a hand on his shoulder.

"I think you've made enough," Blythe whispered, and all at once Aris felt a snap back to reality. The gown he'd been working on fell limp in his lap, and he breathed out heavily as the weight of reality set upon him.

Scattered around the room were several dozen costumes that had piled up along the chairs and floor. Blythe was leaning awkwardly around one just to reach him, while another fluttered in the air, seemingly claimed by a spirit who twirled about with it.

He was glad to see that they liked it.

Aris let the needle disappear from his hands as he whisked the rest of the garments away by gilded threads that held them in the air like hangers. Then his arm slid around

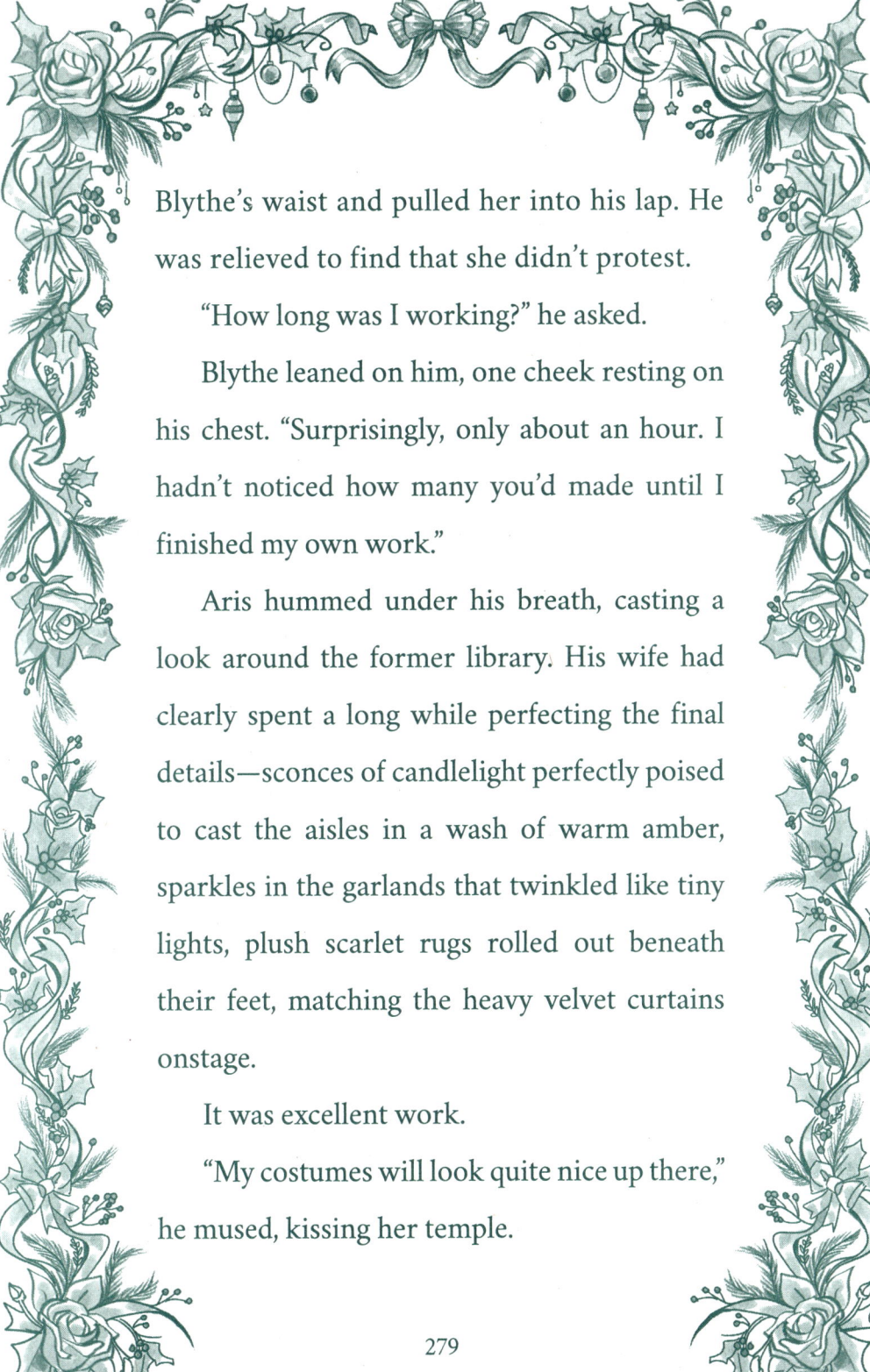

Blythe's waist and pulled her into his lap. He was relieved to find that she didn't protest.

"How long was I working?" he asked.

Blythe leaned on him, one cheek resting on his chest. "Surprisingly, only about an hour. I hadn't noticed how many you'd made until I finished my own work."

Aris hummed under his breath, casting a look around the former library. His wife had clearly spent a long while perfecting the final details—sconces of candlelight perfectly poised to cast the aisles in a wash of warm amber, sparkles in the garlands that twinkled like tiny lights, plush scarlet rugs rolled out beneath their feet, matching the heavy velvet curtains onstage.

It was excellent work.

"My costumes will look quite nice up there," he mused, kissing her temple.

She hummed against his chest, and God, did Aris want to squeeze her. As it was, his arms were around her waist and she was pressed up against his body, but still it was not enough to satisfy the love that felt as though it were bursting out of him. An overflowing chalice that sometimes overwhelmed him, for how could a man like him have been so lucky to end up with a woman like Blythe?

He'd been misguided to keep her out of this, certainly, though it was only because he wanted her to have the world.

"We'll take care of the spirits," he promised. Even now he was aware of their presence, though he had no intention of letting them stop him from enjoying this moment with his wife. "We'll help them pass on, and then we'll feast and drink and have the merriest Christmas either of us has ever seen."

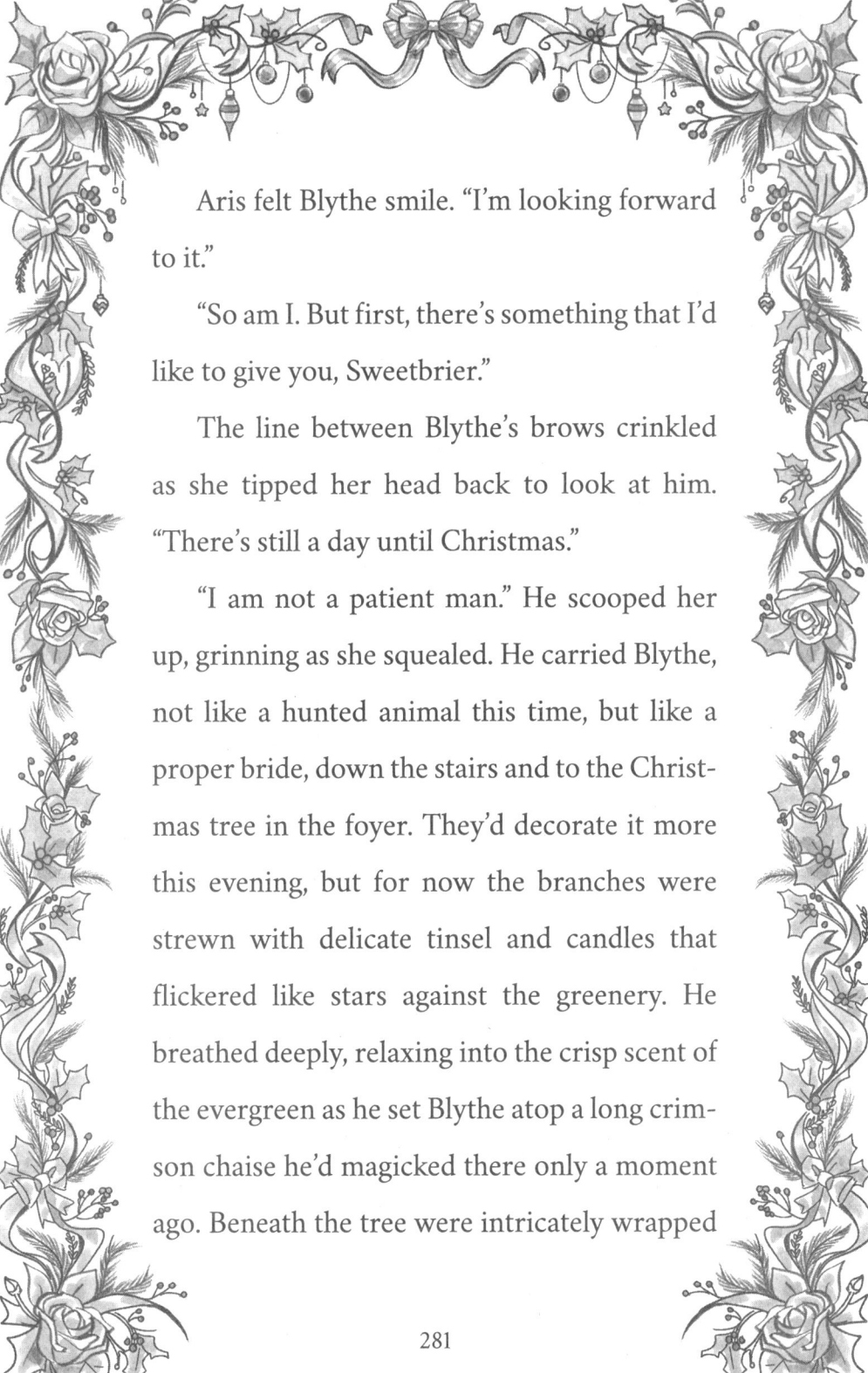

Aris felt Blythe smile. "I'm looking forward to it."

"So am I. But first, there's something that I'd like to give you, Sweetbrier."

The line between Blythe's brows crinkled as she tipped her head back to look at him. "There's still a day until Christmas."

"I am not a patient man." He scooped her up, grinning as she squealed. He carried Blythe, not like a hunted animal this time, but like a proper bride, down the stairs and to the Christmas tree in the foyer. They'd decorate it more this evening, but for now the branches were strewn with delicate tinsel and candles that flickered like stars against the greenery. He breathed deeply, relaxing into the crisp scent of the evergreen as he set Blythe atop a long crimson chaise he'd magicked there only a moment ago. Beneath the tree were intricately wrapped gifts in gilded paper and velvet ribbons that had not been there this morning. He plucked one of them from the floor and set it onto her lap. It was a relatively flat package, though he'd managed to somehow make it beautiful in its wrapping.

Lifting it gently, Blythe arched a brow. "I'm not giving you yours until the morning, you know."

"Yes, yes. That doesn't matter." He waved a hand at her, urging her along. "I don't need the others staring at me when I give this to you."

A grin spread wide over Blythe's face. "Why? Is it *romantic*?" The idea made her laughter all the more devious, while Aris tried very hard not to get nervous. One would think that being as old as the world itself would somehow make him more assured, but when it came to matters of the heart, his was never quite able to stop its blasted fluttering.

"It took me a long while to think of what to gift you," he said as he took a seat beside her. "And if you hate it...I'm sure I can think of something else." He swallowed, knee bouncing as Blythe pried open the crimson paper to reveal the gift that awaited her.

It was a tapestry. Every person had their own—it was the pattern of their life. The threads that bound their fate and told the story of who they were and all they would become. He shivered as her fingers skimmed down the length of this one, turning her eyes up at him with a questioning glance.

He settled his hand atop hers, curling them around the threads. Gently, he brushed her thumb across it. "This is my tapestry. It belongs

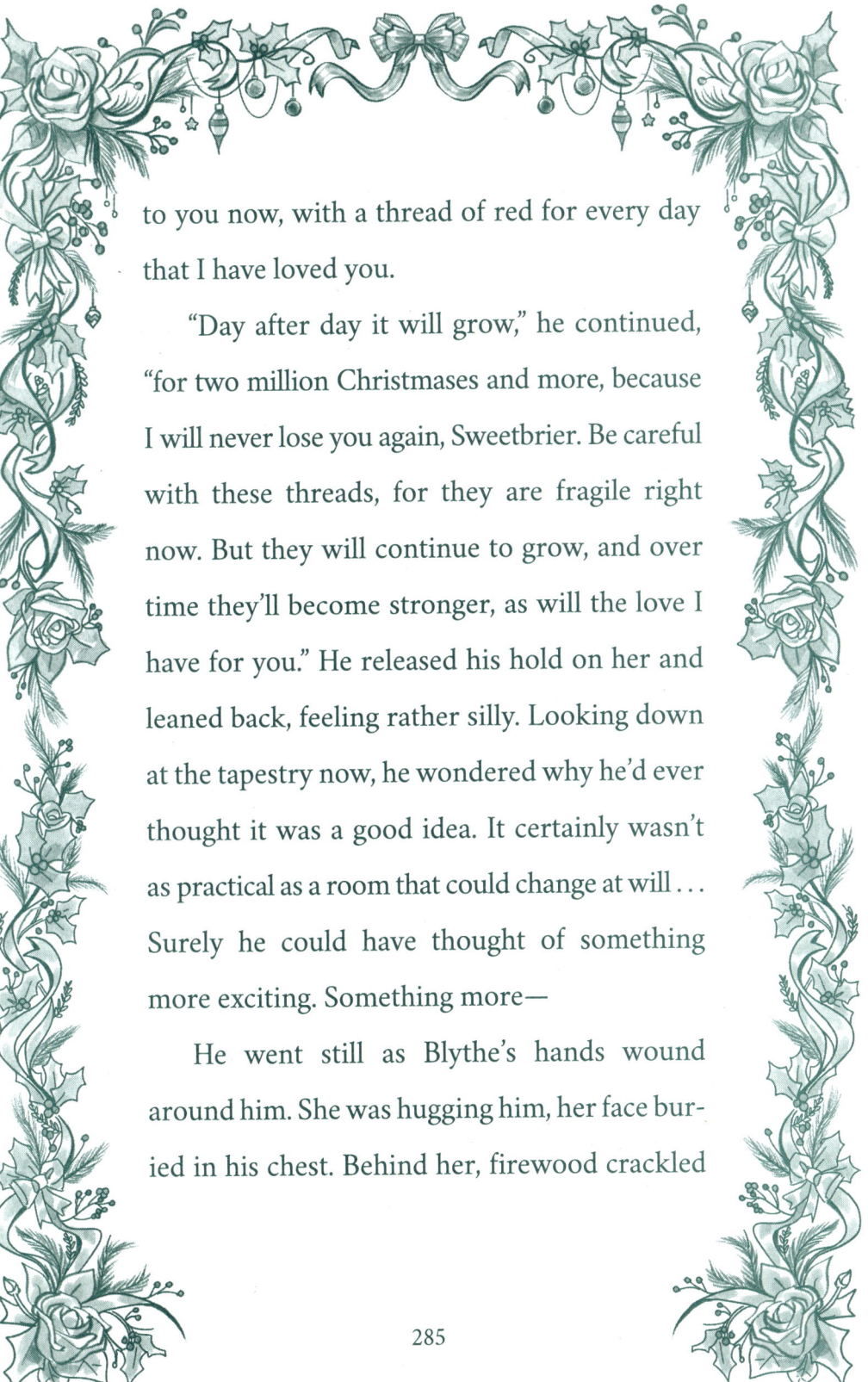

to you now, with a thread of red for every day that I have loved you.

"Day after day it will grow," he continued, "for two million Christmases and more, because I will never lose you again, Sweetbrier. Be careful with these threads, for they are fragile right now. But they will continue to grow, and over time they'll become stronger, as will the love I have for you." He released his hold on her and leaned back, feeling rather silly. Looking down at the tapestry now, he wondered why he'd ever thought it was a good idea. It certainly wasn't as practical as a room that could change at will... Surely he could have thought of something more exciting. Something more—

He went still as Blythe's hands wound around him. She was hugging him, her face buried in his chest. Behind her, firewood crackled

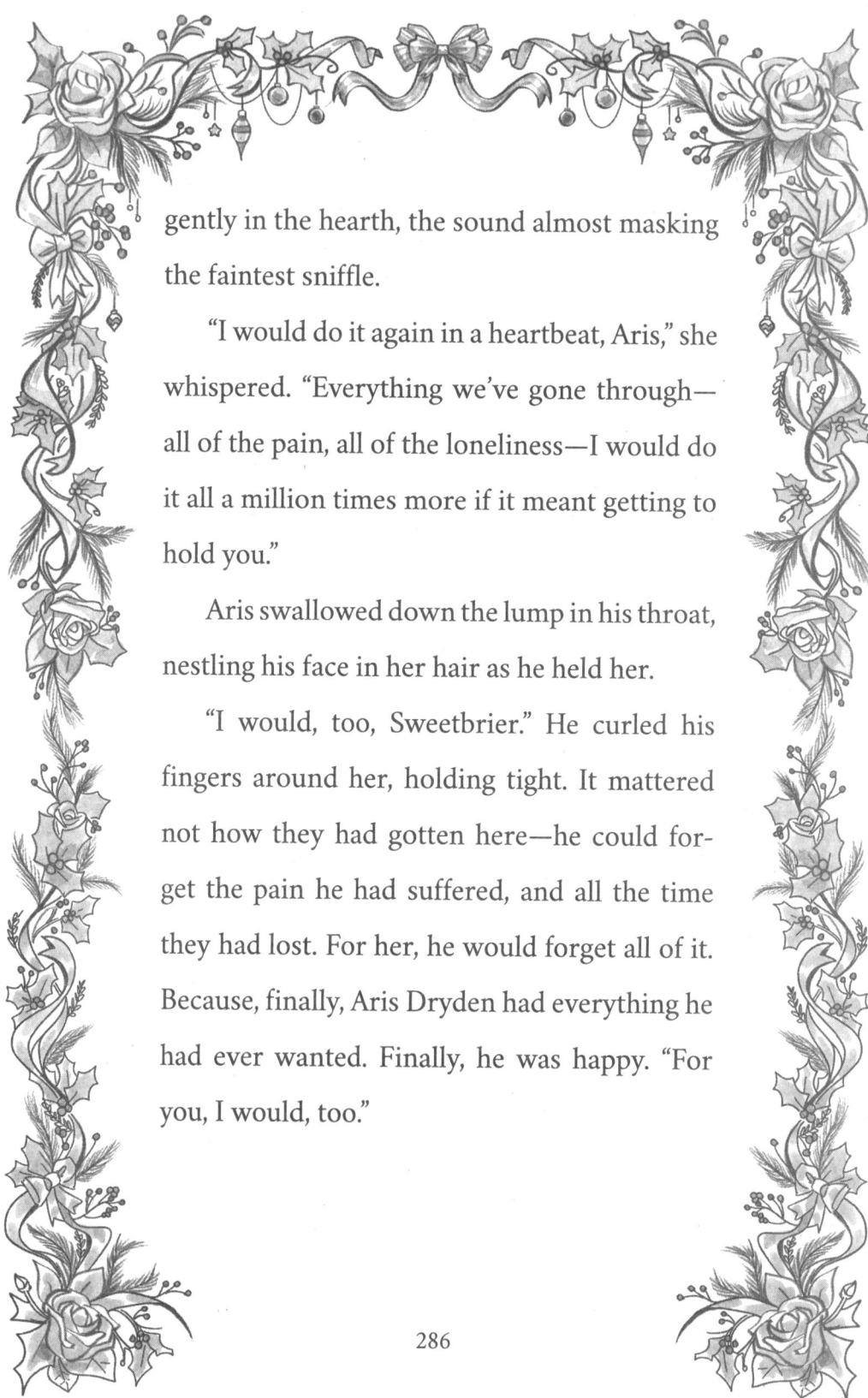

gently in the hearth, the sound almost masking the faintest sniffle.

"I would do it again in a heartbeat, Aris," she whispered. "Everything we've gone through—all of the pain, all of the loneliness—I would do it all a million times more if it meant getting to hold you."

Aris swallowed down the lump in his throat, nestling his face in her hair as he held her.

"I would, too, Sweetbrier." He curled his fingers around her, holding tight. It mattered not how they had gotten here—he could forget the pain he had suffered, and all the time they had lost. For her, he would forget all of it. Because, finally, Aris Dryden had everything he had ever wanted. Finally, he was happy. "For you, I would, too."

EIGHTEEN

Signa

Sylas reminded Signa of a scolded dog as he trudged along beside her, head ducked toward the snow and looking every bit like a hound with its tail tucked between his legs. Even the shadows that trailed him seemed heavier, as if he were dragging them across the ground.

"Aren't you going to say anything?" she asked eventually, despising the growing silence that loomed between them. Sylas glanced up, dark gray eyes watching her.

"I wasn't sure you'd want me to."

Signa snorted. "Letting you stay quiet would be like letting you get away with something."

His sigh, gentle though it was, caused a rustle in the trees around them, and blast it if Signa wasn't drawn to that. She watched Sylas from the corner of her eye as they made their way to town, smitten even in her annoyance by the power he carried. By the strength of his shoulders and the broadness of his chest. By hair so white it rivaled the moon itself...

"I want to know whether you guided your brother to these spirits on purpose," she said, collecting herself. "Was it a prank? Were you having a go at him?"

"It had nothing to do with that," he insisted. "I *did* know they were there, but Aris and Blythe both liked the property, and the spirits seemed harmless enough—"

"Harmless?" she demanded. "No spirit is ever *harmless*. You and I know that better than anyone." It wasn't like Sylas to be so foolhardy. "What were you thinking?"

"I was *thinking* that your mind has been bored lately, Signa." He raked his fingers through his hair, tugging gently at the ends. "I admit I did not consider all angles as well as I should have, but I've watched you puttering around the manor, starting one book only to toss it aside for another. You seemed in need of something to occupy your time, and I sought to give that to you."

She stopped walking, turning to face him with her cheeks flushed. Signa hadn't expected that he'd notice such a thing. "You guided us to these spirits on purpose?"

"I lined up all the pieces for you," he

whispered. "This town had all the clues you needed to figure out what happened. I knew you'd manage to solve it and help those spirits."

Her mind raced as she picked apart the last several days at Wisteria. "I expected to spend days waiting for someone to show up to the mausoleum, but Jules came so quickly..." Signa looked at the reaper, trying to claim his stare. "Was that your doing?"

He watched his boots as he walked, scuffing them along the snow. "I didn't want you waiting that long when it was so cold out. All of this was meant to be my gift to you. A mystery that only you could solve, with people who needed your help. But I realize it was foolish to put Aris and Blythe at risk."

Signa nodded, but kept silent as she contemplated. It surprised her to realize just how well Sylas knew her. The timing was horrendously off, yes, but he was right that she'd been bored, feeling that something was missing from her life. She realized now how perfectly this new mystery had been occupying that once-empty space.

And so Signa laughed, her head falling back against the morning sky as the sound poured out of her. Tears of laughter swelled in her eyes, and she brushed them hurriedly away.

Sylas's head jerked to her, but he had no chance to question Signa before she stretched onto her toes and kissed him.

"You are a fool," she noted between his lips, though even then she laughed again. "Just like your brother. Never, ever do this again. Do you understand me? If we're ever to solve another mystery, we must do it together."

The reaper's shadows wound instinctively around her, one arm resting on Signa's waist and the other on the back of her neck, cradling her to him. "I've learned my lesson. It was a regretful decision, especially while I was off traveling."

"What *have* you been doing, anyway?" she pressed. "Just where have you been if not at Wisteria? Was that part of your ploy, as well?"

"It wouldn't have been as rewarding for you if I simply handed you a solved mystery," he noted. "But no, at least not entirely. Blythe sent me on another task."

Signa cocked a brow. "What task, exactly?"

"You'll find out tomorrow... though try not to be too upset with me if our home is worse for wear because of this. It's currently locked away in my study while I'm gone."

"*It?* You really chose to complicate Christmas, didn't you?" It was alarming the things that his smile did to her, even after all these years. It pulsed through her, striking Signa to her core until her knees felt weak and her belly hot.

She was glad to have him with her and said as much with a lingering kiss that Sylas had no hesitation returning. His arms still rested firmly around her, and soon Signa was allowing herself to be backed farther into the woods, suddenly pressed against a tree as his lips sank to her jaw. Her neck. Her collarbone, devouring her with a fervent hunger.

"Did you miss me, Little Bird?" he teased, skimming lower still.

As much as others may have complained, there were certainly merits to having Sylas unable to be seen by most people. Over the years it had enabled them to get away with a plethora of things they shouldn't have, and it seemed that Sylas was eager to add another tally to that list.

He lowered himself to his knees, shadows slipping under her skirts and brushing up the

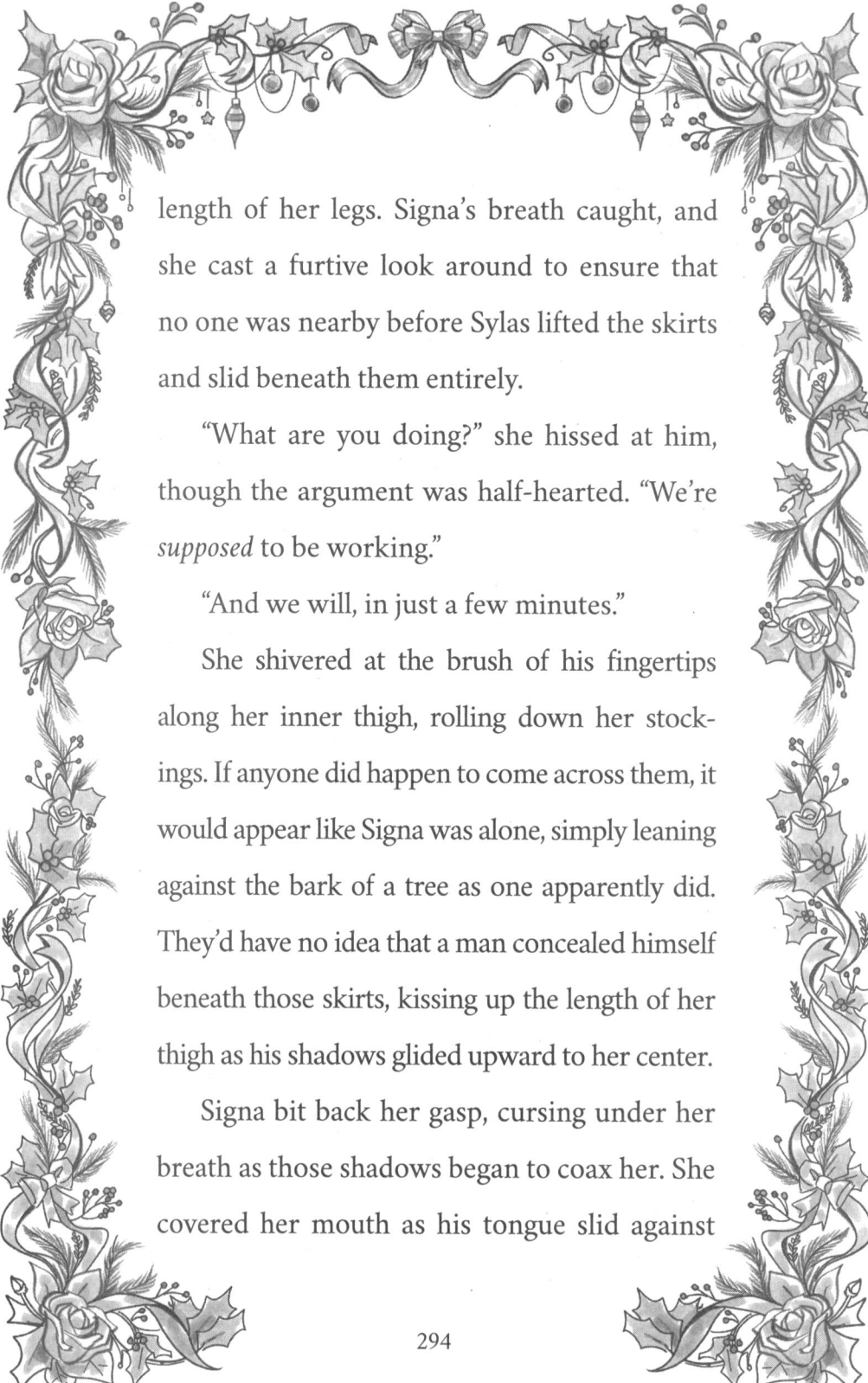

length of her legs. Signa's breath caught, and she cast a furtive look around to ensure that no one was nearby before Sylas lifted the skirts and slid beneath them entirely.

"What are you doing?" she hissed at him, though the argument was half-hearted. "We're *supposed* to be working."

"And we will, in just a few minutes."

She shivered at the brush of his fingertips along her inner thigh, rolling down her stockings. If anyone did happen to come across them, it would appear like Signa was alone, simply leaning against the bark of a tree as one apparently did. They'd have no idea that a man concealed himself beneath those skirts, kissing up the length of her thigh as his shadows glided upward to her center.

Signa bit back her gasp, cursing under her breath as those shadows began to coax her. She covered her mouth as his tongue slid against

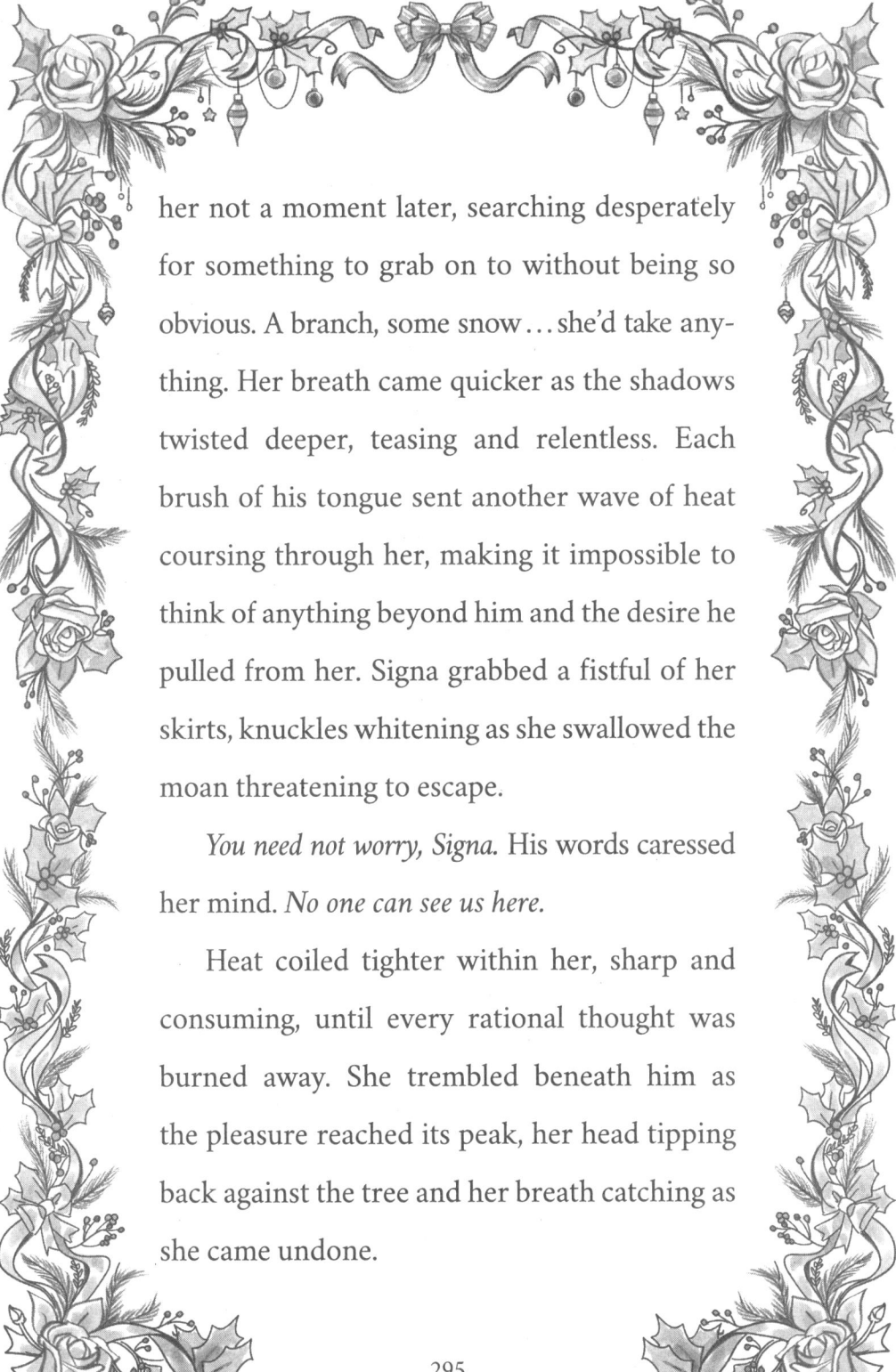

her not a moment later, searching desperately for something to grab on to without being so obvious. A branch, some snow... she'd take anything. Her breath came quicker as the shadows twisted deeper, teasing and relentless. Each brush of his tongue sent another wave of heat coursing through her, making it impossible to think of anything beyond him and the desire he pulled from her. Signa grabbed a fistful of her skirts, knuckles whitening as she swallowed the moan threatening to escape.

You need not worry, Signa. His words caressed her mind. *No one can see us here.*

Heat coiled tighter within her, sharp and consuming, until every rational thought was burned away. She trembled beneath him as the pleasure reached its peak, her head tipping back against the tree and her breath catching as she came undone.

Sylas lingered, taking his time with languid kisses against her skin. Slowly, he rolled her stockings back up.

"Is the coast clear?" he teased, to which Signa offered a breathy laugh.

"It's clear."

He slipped out from beneath her skirts a moment later, sporting a smug grin as his shadows traced the line of her thigh even then, as if to tell her that there was more to come later. Signa had to force herself to away from him so that *later* did not become *now*.

"I'm very much looking forward to our return to Foxglove," he mused, taking hold of her hand.

She was still adjusting herself, incredibly aware of how breathless she was and how flushed she must be. And heavens, was that a twig in her hair? She brushed it out quickly.

"No more distractions, Sylas. We've a mess to clean up."

"Of course," he agreed, still grinning. "You have my word—no more distractions."

While Elijah was out gathering an audience and Blythe and Aris were helping to prepare Wisteria for the ballet, Signa had a singular job. Unfortunately, she wasn't convinced she could accomplish it.

Sylas had transported them to a small cottage nestled in a clearing. It was a quaint and nondescript place, lacking even the barest hint of seasonal decor.

"You're sure this is the right house?" Signa asked. She stood upon the snowy stoop leading up to the door, hesitant to knock.

Sylas joined her there, far more confident as his eyes skimmed the terrain. "Positive. He should be just inside."

Signa nodded, smoothing out her dress as a means of a distraction. It was a high-collared wool gown in a shade of deep olive, covered by a coat several shades darker. She was dressed warmly enough that she could likely stand on this stoop all day. Unfortunately, they were pressed for time.

Signa's fingers curled tight in her kid gloves, and with a long sigh, she forced herself to knock on the wooden door.

She waited in silence for an excruciatingly long minute, then another, but still no one came to the door.

"You're certain he's inside?" she asked Sylas, who frowned at the cottage.

"He is, and he's alive and well."

She supposed she *did* hear some shuffling from the other side... Despite Signa's better judgment, she knocked again before shifting over to the window. She pushed up onto her toes, brushing the snow from the glass before pressing against it to take a look inside.

Jules was sitting alone by a small hearth, sipping from a glass of whiskey.

A bit early for that...

He'd pointedly ignored her knocking, profile turned to Signa as she sneaked a better view of his home. It was a simple place designed with warm wood furnishings and a stone floor. There was no decor, no proud tree or garlands strung, nor any warming scents of delicious meals wafting through the window.

It was Christmas Eve, and the man looked positively miserable.

"Jules!" Signa knocked again, this time on

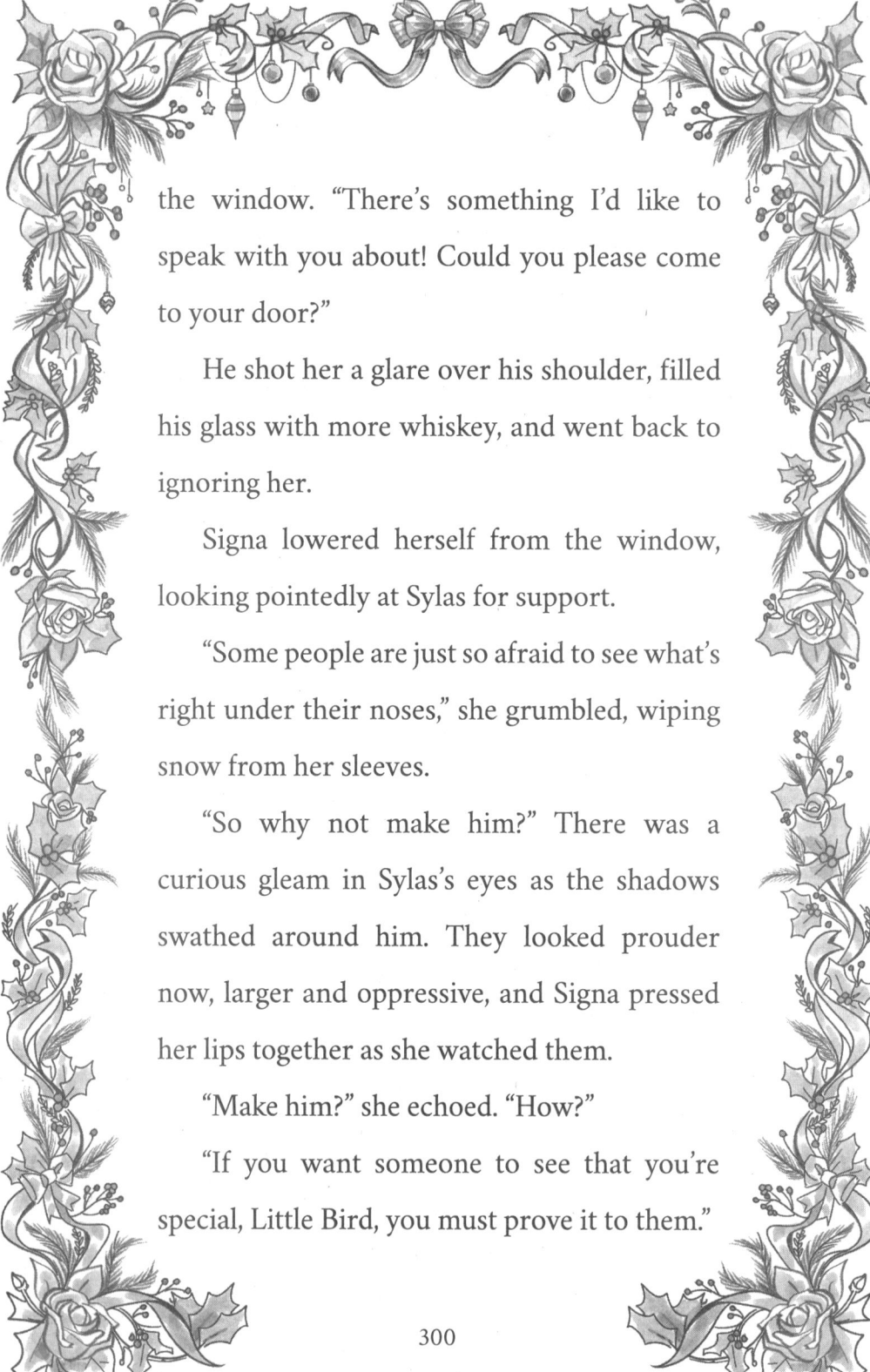

the window. "There's something I'd like to speak with you about! Could you please come to your door?"

He shot her a glare over his shoulder, filled his glass with more whiskey, and went back to ignoring her.

Signa lowered herself from the window, looking pointedly at Sylas for support.

"Some people are just so afraid to see what's right under their noses," she grumbled, wiping snow from her sleeves.

"So why not make him?" There was a curious gleam in Sylas's eyes as the shadows swathed around him. They looked prouder now, larger and oppressive, and Signa pressed her lips together as she watched them.

"Make him?" she echoed. "How?"

"If you want someone to see that you're special, Little Bird, you must prove it to them."

She looked again toward the window, and at the glow of the fire that shone through the frosted panels. "Very well, but I'm going to need your help."

Sylas smiled, and the next time Signa knocked, she did not wait for Jules to open the door. Instead, Sylas slipped through the walls and unlocked it from the inside.

Jules flew to his feet as Signa stormed through, likely looking every bit as terrifying as she felt with her windswept hair and skin chapped pink from the cold.

"How did you get in here?" Jules demanded, a question Signa ignored.

"I know you do not believe what I told you, but my words the other day were true." She took another step forward only for Jules to back into the wall. Signa, however, was only trying to get closer to the fire.

"There are spirits on the land where the theater once stood, and they cannot move on without your help," she told the man, figuring it wasn't the most menacing thing to be warming herself by the fire but hardly caring. "You told me that Odette was important to you. That you *loved* her. But that woman is now a spirit who will be stuck in her suffering forever if you do not trust me."

"You're a witch!" Jules spat, his eyes wide and terrified, glowing in the firelight.

"I really do hate that word." She gave a discreet nod to Sylas, and a second later a powerful burst of wind gusted through the room. Jules pressed himself farther against the wall, sputtering words that Signa didn't care to decipher.

It was all very dramatic and a show that Blythe would have relished. Signa could have used her own powers, certainly, though she didn't necessarily feel like dying today. Not to mention she wouldn't be able to speak with Jules in her reaper form. Having Sylas around made it easier, but he was having far too much fun with this. He'd made a chair of shadows for himself and was lounging in it as he gusted the wind at the hearth, grinning when it flared to life stronger than before. So strongly, in fact, that Jules fell to his knees while Signa brushed embers from her skirt.

Mind yourself, Sylas. We're trying to get him on our side, not give him a heart attack.

Apologies. I didn't care for the way he spoke to you, Sylas noted, silent for a long moment until he added, *You know, it* would *get him to believe you faster if he were dead...*

Signa made a note to get herself and Sylas

out of Foxglove more often. Their humor was growing far too dark for comfort.

She stood and crossed the floor, approaching the trembling Jules as though he were a frightened animal. Crouching beside him, Signa gently offered a hand. "I haven't come to hurt you, Jules. I want only for you to believe me. I am not a witch, though I do see spirits."

"They're really there?" He stared at her hand, not yet taking it. "All my friends... They're still stuck in that place?"

"I'm afraid they are. I believe we may be on the cusp of helping most of them pass on, but Odette... I fear that only you will be able to help her, and that we'll lose our chance to save her if you don't."

His jaw trembled as his eyes settled not on

Signa, but on the fire raging behind her. Voice weak, Jules whispered, "What do I have to do?"

If Signa could have crumpled in relief, she would have. But for now she set a hand on the man's shoulder and spoke the truth as she knew it. "This may sound ridiculous, but we're going to need you to dance."

NINETEEN

Signa

Everyone had made it back to Wisteria Gardens by late afternoon on Christmas Eve, Elijah assuring them that guests would surely arrive come evening. It made sense to have the most effervescent of them be the one to invite the townsfolk, though if no one decided to show, Aris promised to use whatever magic necessary to make them.

"I'll have to put a haze over their thoughts

anyway," he'd said. "It's not like we can invite the entire town to come and watch flying costumes and pretend that all is well and normal."

Signa sighed. This was far more complicated than she'd hoped. It was a wonder she and Aris had ever tried to figure this out on their own.

She paced circles in what was once the library of Wisteria. They'd fashioned the entire manor into a theater for the night, and the spirits around her practically buzzed with excitement. No longer did they bounce from wall to wall, reveling in their chaos. Having the theater around them seemed to have given the spirits a sense of place, mellowing them out. They whispered to one another, flitting to and fro while trying to peek beneath the curtains to catch glimpses of the audience. The ballet mistress snapped at them whenever they got too close.

"*Never allow the audience to see you before the show,*" she instructed. "*It ruins the mystique.*"

Blythe, however, followed no such rule. She came bounding through the stage door not long after, sporting a broad grin and looking immensely proud of herself. "People are arriving," she announced. "There are at least two dozen already seated, and they have fantastic taste. All are raving about the decor."

Somewhere behind them, Aris sighed. Each soul in the audience ultimately meant more work for him, though it also meant a greater chance that the spirits would be pleased with this performance and be able to pass on.

"What will they all believe they came here for tonight?" Blythe whispered, scooting closer to Aris.

"I'll make them believe we put on some abundantly festive performance. Perhaps it'll be about a beautiful princess named Blythe who tries to befriend the cute forest animals and get their help with delivering presents to the nearby orphanage. The villain will be a cackling witch named Signa Sorrow who does not believe in the spirit of Christmas. Blythe will be locked away in the highest floor of the tallest tower, only able to be saved by a dashing prince named Aris, who helps slay the witch and—"

Moss suddenly filled Aris's mouth, cutting off his words. "Blythe will save herself when she helps Signa see the joy of Christmas. For the witch was only lonely, and it pained her to see others happy when she was so misunderstood. But the two of them become friends, and together they save Christmas!"

"When in this story was Christmas ever in danger?" Sylas asked, appearing from the darkness and taking several long strides toward them, his boots making no sound.

Blythe frowned at him. "It doesn't matter if there are plot holes so long as the story is gripping."

Signa snorted, too distracted to participate in the conversation. She made a tiny gap in the curtains to peek through, uncertain whether it should relax or unnerve her to see that every seat was filling up. Only when the ballet mistress snapped at her did Signa withdraw.

"*Mystique,*" the woman snapped. "*We must maintain the illusion.*"

Signa slipped away, leaving the ballet mistress to her fretting. A few more hours, and this mess would finally be over. She just had to ensure that the spirits behaved, and that no one in the crowd was in danger.

"It'll be all right." Death had stepped up

behind her, thumb brushing the length of her wrist. It helped her breathe easier, though nothing would relax her until the show was over.

"I'm closing the doors," Elijah warned, poking his head backstage. "Consider this your five minutes to places."

Signa nodded, though she needn't say a word. The ballet mistress had been aptly listening, and the moment Elijah disappeared she swiveled and clapped her hands in the air, summoning the attention of every dancer. They quieted, as still as the earth and watching with hawklike eyes.

"This is the moment we've been training for, everyone. Five minutes to places!" She spoke in that thick accent of hers, looking over each performer. When her eyes landed on a very hopeful Odette, her thin lips pursed. *"Has anyone seen Ju—"*

"Jules is finishing getting dressed," Signa quickly told her. "I'll go and fetch him."

The woman's face pinched tight. *"Very well, but be quick about it."*

Signa tried not to let herself be irked by the woman's grating tone as she slipped out the back door of the makeshift stage to where Jules paced the length of Wisteria's hall. The older man had been outfitted in a costume of a silky gray with a high structured collar and silver embroidery around the neckline and cuffs. The buttons on his tunic were shaped like snowflakes, and his face had been painted with silver-leaf dust so that it would shimmer beneath the stage lights. His shoulders boasted wintry epaulets; he'd strike a heroic figure when he made his entrance.

"It's time," she told him, keeping her voice soft. "Are you ready?"

He grunted under his breath, fidgeting with his collar. "Do I have a choice?"

"Of course you do." Perhaps Aris would force the man's hand, but Signa would have no part of it. "I know you're afraid, but they've been waiting for you all this time. If not to give yourself the chance to finally say goodbye, then do this for them. You can gift them the peace that they deserve." She stepped forward, extending her hand.

For a moment Jules looked away, and panic tightened Signa's throat as she realized this might be too much for him. That he might turn and flee. Instead, he slowly took her hand.

"Take me to them," he whispered, and Signa pulled him inside.

It was a different world backstage, and one that Jules met with wide eyes. He gaped at the dozens of costumes that floated before him, stumbling back into Signa.

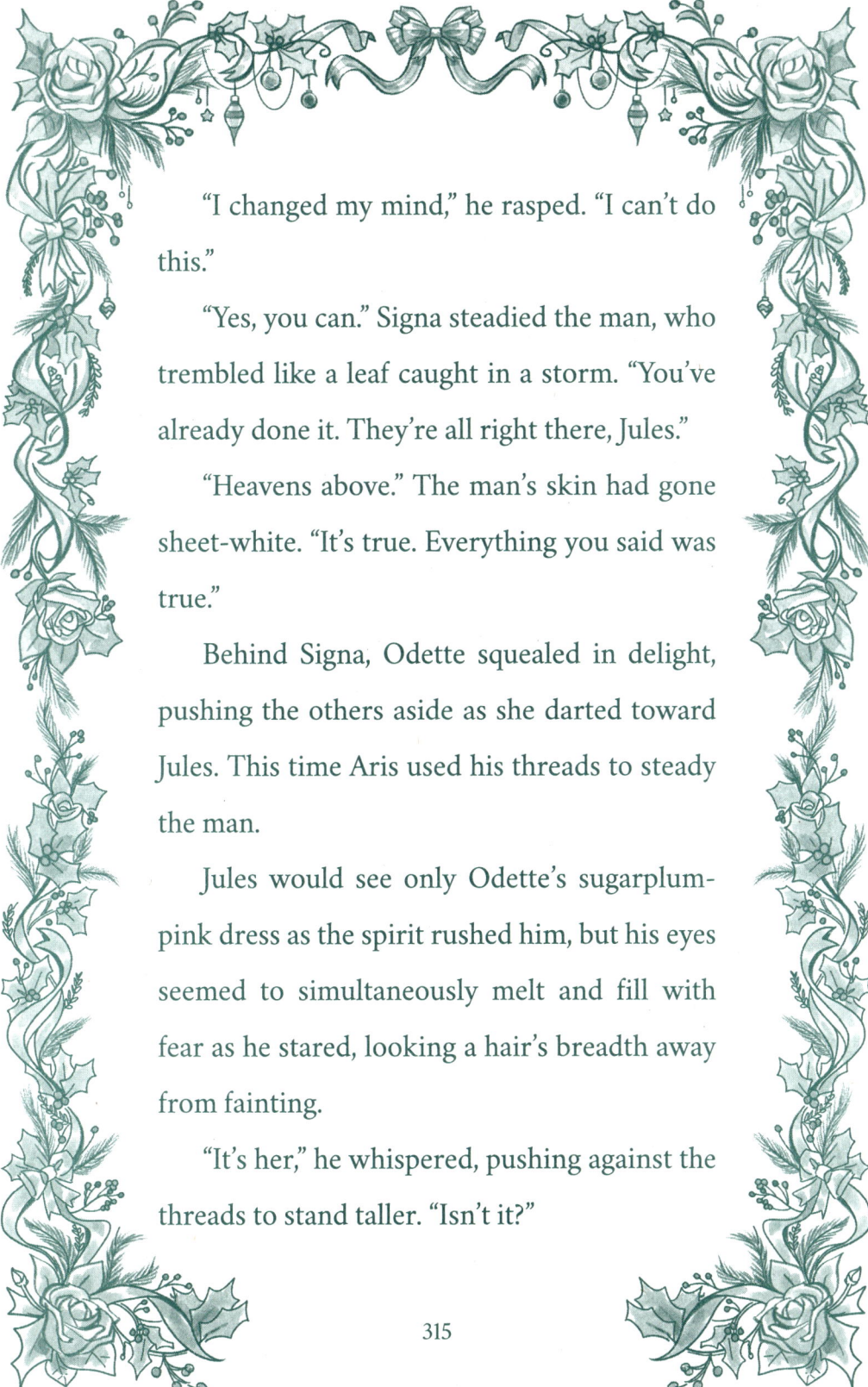

"I changed my mind," he rasped. "I can't do this."

"Yes, you can." Signa steadied the man, who trembled like a leaf caught in a storm. "You've already done it. They're all right there, Jules."

"Heavens above." The man's skin had gone sheet-white. "It's true. Everything you said was true."

Behind Signa, Odette squealed in delight, pushing the others aside as she darted toward Jules. This time Aris used his threads to steady the man.

Jules would see only Odette's sugarplum-pink dress as the spirit rushed him, but his eyes seemed to simultaneously melt and fill with fear as he stared, looking a hair's breadth away from fainting.

"It's her," he whispered, pushing against the threads to stand taller. "Isn't it?"

Odette, too, seemed curious about the man she approached, peering down in fascination as she floated before him. She bent close to inspect his face, and though her touch did not connect, Jules still sighed as if able to sense the way she smoothed her hands over his skin, peering deep into his eyes for a long moment before she smiled.

"*Jules,*" she whispered, and with that word Signa saw more clarity in the spirit's eyes than she had at any point in these past several days. "*You've come home.*"

"What's she saying?" Jules begged, his voice still tense as terror ate into him. "Is she angry with me? Does she want me to leave? Does she—" He lifted a hand to where Odette pressed a kiss against his forehead, mouth going slack as he was stilled by her phantom touch.

"She's glad you're back," Signa whispered.

"Odette is glad to have you home, Jules. They all are."

The spirits were peering over each other to observe the two, their wide grins making Signa's chest ache with happiness.

This was her favorite part of her powers. It was what made the thankless work she did so worth it. She may not have had a clear title like Death, Life, or Fate, and she may not ever fully understand how she came to exist. But one thing was certain—Signa was precisely where she was meant to be, and was doing the work that she was made to do.

"I'm sorry," Jules whispered, tears falling from his cheeks like glistening stars. "I never wanted to hurt any of you. I was going to ask you to marry me, Odette."

"I know," she whispered, Signa echoing the words aloud. *"And I was going to say yes."*

Aris had backed away, not at all built for such emotional turmoil. Blythe, on the other hand, was watching with a trembling bottom lip and tears streaming down her cheeks.

"Dance with me," Odette whispered, offering Jules a pale translucent hand. *"Be my partner one last time."*

He didn't need the translation. When Odette reached toward him, he wound his fingers around her sleeve and followed, his chin held high and his back straight, looking twenty years younger as they took to the stage.

"Places, everyone!" the ballet mistress called out, fretting about to ensure that everyone was ready when she saw that Jules and Odette were at the center. *"Places!"*

Odette lifted onto her toes as Jules took his position, seeming to remember the dance as though it'd been only days since he last practiced. He shut his eyes, lifted his chin, and the show began.

Velvet curtains parted with a soft rustle, revealing Blythe's magnificent stage, now dressed in an ethereal glow from the lights beaming down on the dancers. The audience, held under Aris's spell, leaned forward in their seats as the first notes of the orchestra swelled from the hidden pit.

Jules stood tall at center stage. He was an old man now, far from the youth who had been a part of this performance ages ago, and yet he moved nimbly on his feet, guided by Odette. She no longer floated but kept her pointed toes solidly on the ground, her movements so graceful that it seemed as though the air itself bent to her command. Every turn, every lift, was like a story woven by their bodies. Jules circled her, proud and regal.

The other spirits had floated from the shadows as the music continued to build. They moved around Jules and Odette like a winter breeze, their forms shimmering in shades of silver and ice. Their costumes billowed with each turn, glimmering in the light, while their silent feet glided over the floor in perfect synchrony. Signa watched from behind the curtains, her fingers clutching the fabric as she held her breath, unable to look away.

The audience might be seeing a performance, but she was watching a farewell.

Odette's face shone with a tenderness that Jules might not have been able to see, but Signa hoped with every fiber of her being that he could feel it.

Blythe, like the others, would only be able to see twirling costumes and pretty lights, and yet she watched with rapt attention as the pair moved through the final phases of the dance. Jules lifted Odette into his arms, and for a moment, the very world held its breath.

Odette's hands glided to Jules's chest, her body shimmering. The tears in her eyes were no longer bloodied as they fell. Her figure was blurring at the edges, and Jules tightened his grip as if he could sense it.

"Odette?" he whispered, loud enough that Signa heard his despair.

But Odette only shone that same soft, serene smile she'd worn since their reunion. She held on to Jules as he set her down, bending to press a tender kiss to his lips. And then, with a final graceful spin, she let go.

Her figure broke apart into thousands of tiny, wisping fragments, and her costume fell to the floor, her fading form no longer able to hold it up. Other spirits were beginning to

experience the same, each of them fading, one by one, as they gave their final performance.

Behind Signa, Sylas had begun to stir. It was time.

Jules stumbled forward, his hand still raised to where Odette had stood seconds before. His breath came in ragged bursts as he stared upon her fallen dress. He whispered words that Signa did not hear. Words that didn't belong to her, but that had Odette trembling. She turned to focus on Sylas, who stood waiting in the wings, and nodded to him softly.

The music swelled again, and at the final crescendo the reaper stepped out among the swaying spirits, who saw him with a new clarity, the fog lifted from their eyes. They turned to him, reaching out their hands, bodies vanishing from this world one after the other as Death guided them on to the next.

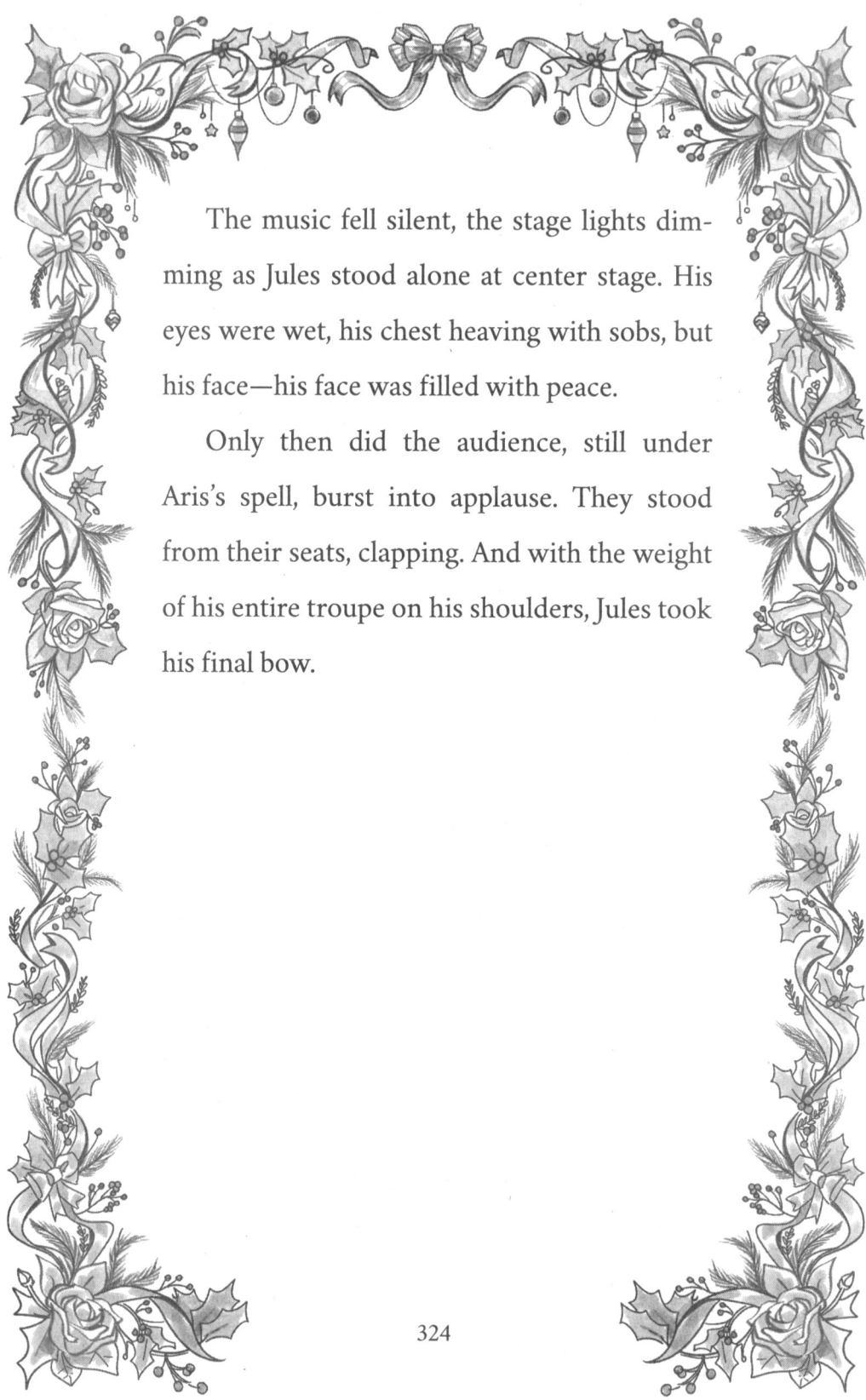

The music fell silent, the stage lights dimming as Jules stood alone at center stage. His eyes were wet, his chest heaving with sobs, but his face—his face was filled with peace.

Only then did the audience, still under Aris's spell, burst into applause. They stood from their seats, clapping. And with the weight of his entire troupe on his shoulders, Jules took his final bow.

TWENTY

DEATH

DEATH ENJOYED THE ACT OF FERRYING souls into the next life. He enjoyed being a silent spectator as they took their first steps upon his bridge of souls, all their fears and worries melting away and replaced by the endless possibilities of what awaited them.

Would they choose to reincarnate? Or would they venture to the afterlife to live among their loved ones? There were few things that relaxed him as much as watching the souls slip into their new lives, for in those few precious moment they no longer viewed Death as the enemy, but as their guide onward to limitless wonders.

Death could have stood beside that bridge for hours, watching each soul as it crossed over. But there was one soul in particular whom Death wanted to see above all others. One whom he had not spent nearly enough time with this holiday season.

Death returned to Wisteria late that evening, well past an hour when anyone should have been awake, to the room he and Signa were to share. It was his first time inside, and as such he examined her gingerbread door, tasting the clove and cinnamon that permeated the air, and then looked toward the plush bed that awaited him.

It was empty.

Death checked the attached sitting room and bathroom, but Signa was not in either. He could not sense her presence within the walls of Wisteria at all; the only sign that she'd ever been there was an open window draped with curtains that billowed in the wind, naked branches scraping like claws along the glass. Death moved to shut it, only to find that a plump belladonna berry sat atop the sill. He picked up the berry and rolled it between his fingers as he inspected the darkness ahead. There, far in the distance, was a flicker of lamplight.

Is that you, Little Bird? His eyes narrowed on the figure who plunged deeper into the night, as if beckoning him. He couldn't quite make out her form, but he felt Signa's amusement stir in the corner of his mind.

Why don't you come and find out? Her voice

was a balm to his soul, as welcome as rain in a drought, but it wasn't enough. He wanted to touch her. To curl into bed and rest beside her sleeping form.

Death slipped onto the windowsill and out into the night. He moved like the wind itself as he hunted her down. Like the very darkness that stretched across the forest floor, woven between ever branch.

He didn't need to hunt for long. Signa was waiting for him in a clearing, her head tipped back as her pale skin drank in the silver moonlight. It welcomed her, just as it always had welcomed him, shining its praise as the night cradled her in its embrace. Signa was a dream given shape, as lovely as he'd ever seen, with her hair unbound, the dark tresses dancing in the gentle breeze.

A smile graced her lips as she held her hand

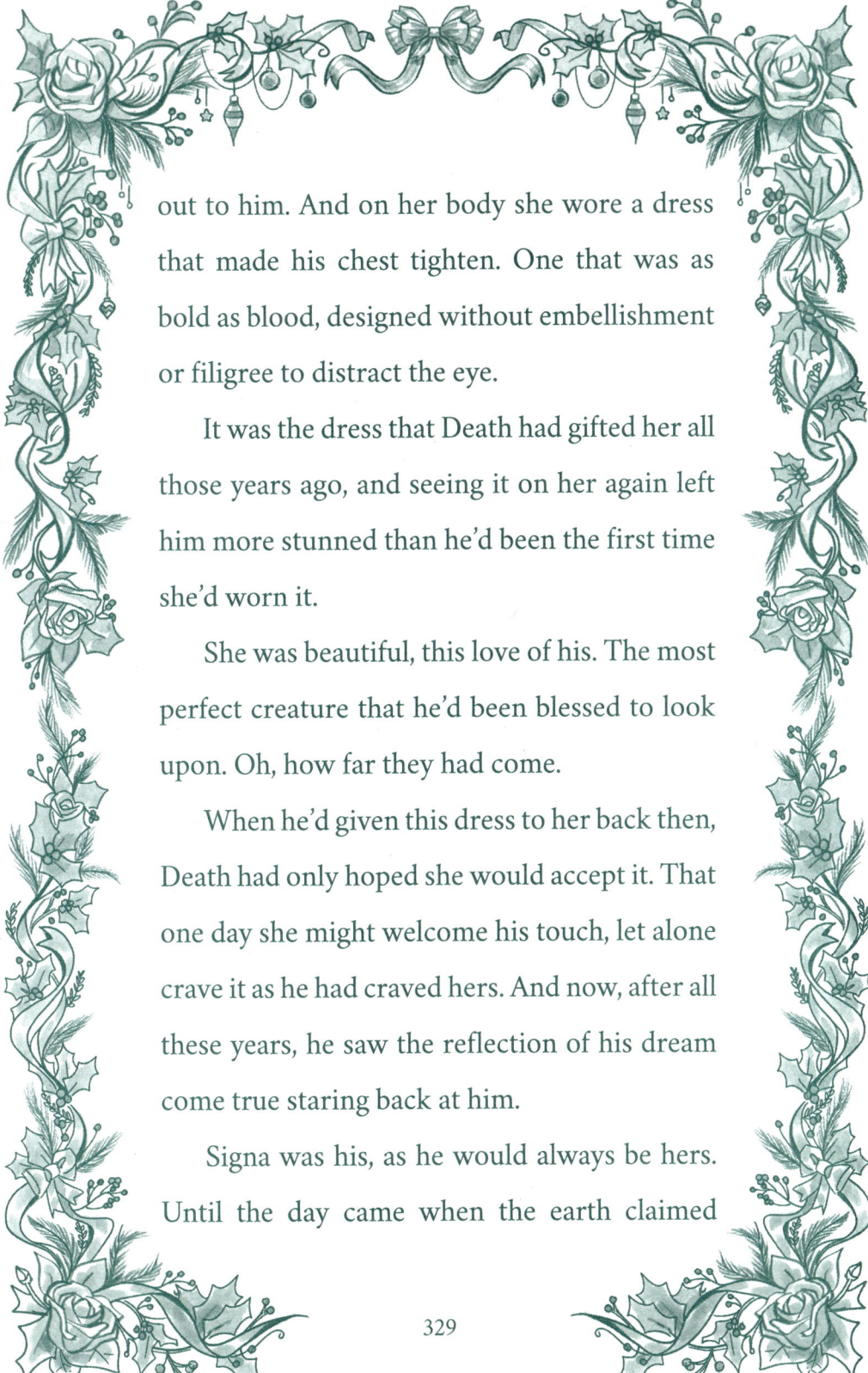

out to him. And on her body she wore a dress that made his chest tighten. One that was as bold as blood, designed without embellishment or filigree to distract the eye.

It was the dress that Death had gifted her all those years ago, and seeing it on her again left him more stunned than he'd been the first time she'd worn it.

She was beautiful, this love of his. The most perfect creature that he'd been blessed to look upon. Oh, how far they had come.

When he'd given this dress to her back then, Death had only hoped she would accept it. That one day she might welcome his touch, let alone crave it as he had craved hers. And now, after all these years, he saw the reflection of his dream come true staring back at him.

Signa was his, as he would always be hers. Until the day came when the earth claimed them and they were no longer of this world, Death would love her more than she could ever possibly understand.

All those years of being alone—of wishing for a single soul who might be able to understand him, let alone share his touch—and he wouldn't change any of it.

Signa stood in a clearing that was not blanketed with snow, but with wildflowers. With wolfsbane and marigolds. Foxglove and hellebore that brushed against the hem of her gown, a rainbow of colors. She wore the same masquerade mask that Blythe had gifted her the night of their first dance, and Death eased it off her as he stepped forward, smoothing his ungloved hand along her cheek. The bargain Blythe and Fate had made all those years ago was the best thing that could ever have happened to him. It was the only reason he could touch Signa without consequence, no longer stealing her life every time he wanted to kiss her. To hold her.

Now, he did both freely, cradling her warmth against himself as he pressed a kiss onto her perfect lips.

"The stars themselves should bow to you," he whispered against her skin, "for you are the most radiant creature to ever walk this earth."

Signa took her hand in his, sighing her contentedness. "Blythe helped me with the garden. I know it's not the same, but I suppose that having Aris back has made me nostalgic. For your gift this year, I wanted to re-create the night of our first dance."

"You mean the night you fell in love with me?" he teased, dropping his hand to her waist.

Signa leaned into his touch. "That's precisely what I mean." She was staring up at him

beneath long lashes, and if he had had the luxury of a heartbeat, Death was certain it would have given out then.

"We've had quite the journey, haven't we?" There was a dreamy tone to her voice as she dipped her head against his chest. "That night of our first dance... it feels like a lifetime ago. How quickly time passes."

Perhaps to Signa it did move quickly, but Death wanted to tell her that these years together had felt like minutes. That he was glad he was immortal, if only to ensure that every morning he could be there to watch as Signa roused from the bedroom in her robe and slippers. That he would forever be able to see her bickering with Foxglove's spirits and to hold her as they curled up by the hearth in the evenings.

It was a simple life, but that was all he had

ever wanted. And if the choice were his, it was one that Death would happily relive a million lifetimes more.

"I would not trade our life together for anything," he said, kissing the top of her head before he pulled her in for a dance. With each step, the shadows around Death darkened, his plain black shirt replaced by a suit of pure onyx. By gilded cuff links and a mask of shadows.

It was what he'd worn the first night he'd truly held Signa in his arms, and the mere act of donning it had him feeling all the more sentimental. They truly had come a long way—through murders and mysteries. Through deaths and heartache, and new beginnings.

"Do you ever wonder what's next for us?" Signa whispered, her voice a tickle against his chest.

Death needed no time to consider his

words. "I care not for what comes next, as you have given me more than I ever thought possible. You have given me a life beyond the shadows, Little Bird. And whatever happens from here, I know that we will face it together."

Signa lifted her head to meet his gaze. She pressed closer, and soon it felt to him as if the rest of the world was melting away.

"Together," she repeated softly, a smile playing at the corners of her lips. "Always."

He kissed her then. Kissed her like a man who had spent a multitude of lifetimes lost in the darkness and had finally found his way back to the light.

"Merry Christmas, Signa," he whispered between her lips.

She smiled, holding him close. "Merry Christmas, Sylas."

Atop the frost-coated flowers surrounded

by mounds of snow, Death and his bride danced. The night itself folded around them, promising that neither would ever be left to face the world alone again.

Promising that, no matter what, they would be together for all eternity.

TWENTY-ONE

Blythe

CHRISTMASES WITH HER FAMILY HAD never gone quite as Blythe intended, but she was beginning to believe that was part of their charm.

She awoke on Christmas morning to an empty bed and a house that smelled of cocoa and warm gingerbread. Blythe practically burst from her sheets, too eager to so much as run a brush through her knotted hair before she threw on a robe and followed the soft laughter and chattering of her family into the dining room. A feast lay before her—poached eggs and truffles, Christmas pudding, savory pies and roasted pheasant. Sun streamed in through a frosted windowpane behind the table, bathing a plate of orange-and-honey scones in an almost holy light.

Elijah sat at the head of the table, backlit by the sun. Aris sipped coffee to his right while Signa was to his left, adding a thick layer of clotted cream to her scone. Sylas was filling Elijah's teacup, and even though Blythe knew for a fact that her father found the presence of Death in his family a tad concerning, he did his best to make Sylas comfortable, even while the two of them couldn't communicate directly.

Sylas, for his part, made a concerted effort to communicate with Elijah by way of notes, as intent on impressing him as if he were Signa's own father. Even then he scribbled something onto a slip of paper and set it before Elijah, who read it quickly and shook his head.

"I'm quite well on food, thank you, Sylas."

Aris rolled his eyes. "Toady," he muttered under his breath, spluttering a second later when the coffee he'd been sipping spilled onto his lap, guided by a burst of shadows.

"I would be kind to me today, if I were you," Death told him as Aris glared murder at his brother. "I've gotten you the most wonderful present, and I could very easily send it back."

"I wish you would," Aris huffed, to which Blythe stepped forward and fully into the dining room.

"You most certainly do not," she told him as she moved to stand behind her husband's chair, a bundle of nerves when Sylas slid her a questioning glance. She nodded, heart racing as he flickered out of view a second later.

Aris, already having magicked himself new pants, leaned back in his chair as if he hoped it would suddenly save him from the present exchange by swallowing him whole. Signa continued eating without pause, though two curious lines etched between her brows as she explained what had just happened to Elijah, who appeared to be trying not to laugh.

Sylas returned several minutes later, grunting and with more tears in his shirt. He held a fat black cat out before him in gloved hands, the beast hissing and smacking at the shadows he had to use to control it. He'd tied a beautiful red bow around its neck, at which the cat clawed.

"This thing is your problem now," he said, letting the cat plop to the floor. It landed easily on its feet and shook itself off, growling low in its throat as its deep green eyes surveyed the room.

Aris bent to get a better look at the creature. "You brought me a *cat?*" He set his coffee aside, eyes tight. The cat glanced back, but something strange happened as it did. Its bristled fur began to lie flat, and while it had been rigid and growling seconds before, it now ever so slowly padded its way to Aris. The cat lingered several inches from his leg, sniffing, and then brushed up against Aris with a purr so loud that it sounded as though the table was shaking.

Aris's body seized, every muscle seeming to lock in place. His breath hitched in his chest, and with a shaking voice he asked Blythe, "Are we opening our home to strays, now?" The cat paused its purring to mew at Aris, who swallowed hard. His gaze never left it, and Blythe understood that he knew who he was seeing. Knew, but did not believe.

"This is no stray." She set her arm on his shoulder and squeezed tight. "You opened your home up to this beast long ago, Aris."

Never had Blythe seen Aris crack quite the same as he did in that moment. Her husband pushed from his chair with a clatter, startling the cat. He was down on the floor beside it before it could flee, capturing it in his arms.

"Beasty?" Aris whispered, cradling the suddenly placid cat against his chest as though it were a child. Blythe had gotten closer to Beasty after Aris's passing, though it had still always preferred Elijah and its original owner to her. Were she to cradle it as Aris was, Blythe was certain the cat would gouge out her eyes.

"It's her," Blythe promised him, a delightful warmth blooming through her chest. "Or at least a version of the fox you knew. It seems she's testing out being a cat in this life."

There were tears in Aris's eyes. Beautiful, glistening tears that made Blythe's throat squeeze. She reached for her husband, settling her palm against his arm as she stared down at Beasty's face. The cat was perfectly content there in Aris's arms, half-lidded eyes blinking slowly up at him.

"How?" He spoke as softly as the dawn, so fragile his voice threatened to crack. "How is she here? How did you find her?"

"It was your wife's doing," Death told him, and Blythe felt a flutter in her stomach as all eyes turned to her.

"I've been trying to find a way to identify and chase down souls ever since you left us," she admitted. "I'm not very good at it yet. I was never able to find you, but a few weeks ago I felt the stirrings of someone familiar. I couldn't pinpoint a precise location, but Sylas helped me narrow it down. I thought I might have finally figured it out, but I wasn't certain—"

The next words were knocked out of her with a gasp as Aris crushed Blythe against him in a hug. Smooshed between them, Beasty yowled and squirmed her way out of Aris's arms, moving instead to Elijah with a haughty twitch of her tail. Elijah happily obliged, stroking beneath the cat's chin as she hopped into his lap and curled herself into a cozy ball.

"Thank you," Aris whispered against Blythe's hair, still crushing her against him. "Thank you for bringing her back."

Blythe melted into his embrace, winding her arms around Aris and holding him close. He was stubborn, this husband of hers. Too stubborn and prideful to admit how deeply it hurt him to have lost Beasty without the chance to say goodbye. But now his armor had cracked, and she felt every bit of the pain and love that he'd been holding on to.

She held Aris until he pulled away, which was approximately ten seconds after Sylas threw his arms around them—careful to touch them with only the covered parts of his body—and thirty seconds after, Signa joined in. Elijah likely would have joined, if not for the cat that had claimed his lap.

Aris peeled away when he could no longer bear all the touching and emotion. He combed his fingers through his hair, blinking away what was left of his tears.

"Enough of that," he said quickly, clearing his throat as he crossed the floor and plucked Beasty from Elijah's lap. The cat gave no protest as Aris cradled her against his chest once more, turning to address the others. "Let's get on with the festivities, shall we?"

Aris and Beasty were inseparable for the rest of the day.

When Aris wasn't holding the cat, Beasty trailed behind him, swishing her tail about. The cat had watched from the back of the chaise as Blythe and her family set to work on finalizing the tree's decor. She'd pawed at the blown-glass ornaments they strung on the branches and sneezed her distaste at the ridiculous figurine of a reaper that Aris had sneaked onto the top of the tree. She'd also made a fast enemy of Gundry, who didn't know what to do with himself around Beasty. It was clear the hound was trying to be a good boy, but there was only

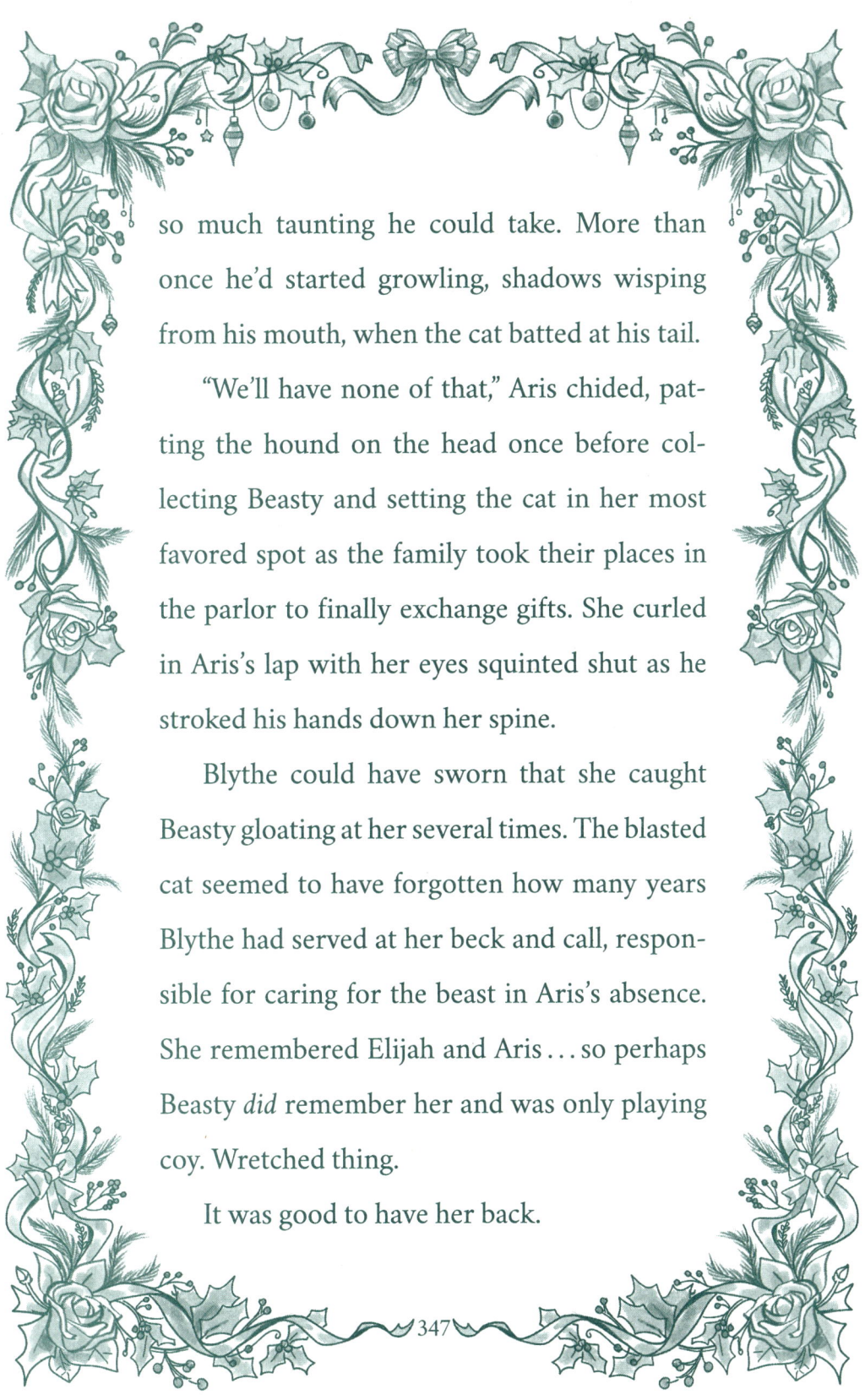

so much taunting he could take. More than once he'd started growling, shadows wisping from his mouth, when the cat batted at his tail.

"We'll have none of that," Aris chided, patting the hound on the head once before collecting Beasty and setting the cat in her most favored spot as the family took their places in the parlor to finally exchange gifts. She curled in Aris's lap with her eyes squinted shut as he stroked his hands down her spine.

Blythe could have sworn that she caught Beasty gloating at her several times. The blasted cat seemed to have forgotten how many years Blythe had served at her beck and call, responsible for caring for the beast in Aris's absence. She remembered Elijah and Aris...so perhaps Beasty *did* remember her and was only playing coy. Wretched thing.

It was good to have her back.

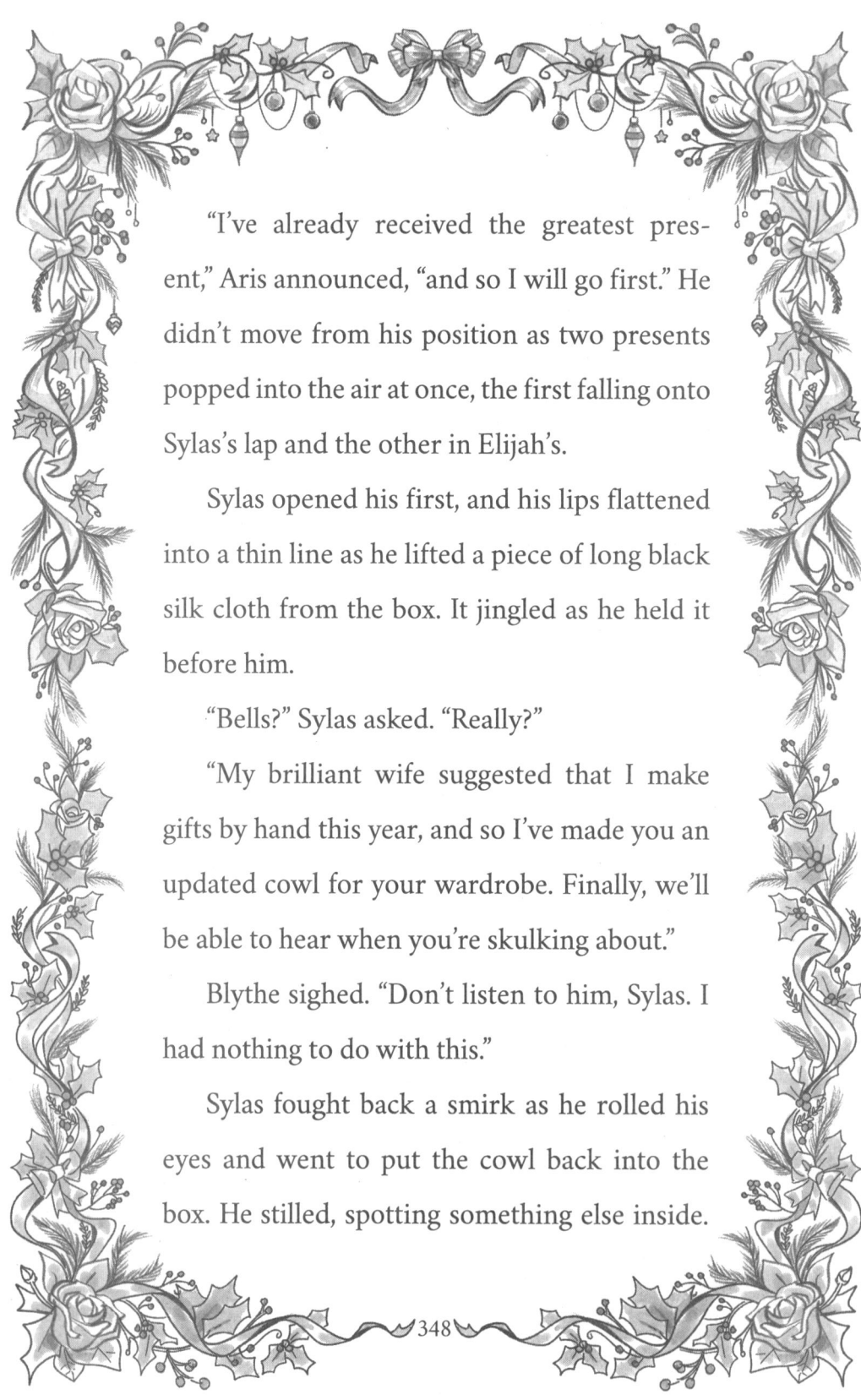

"I've already received the greatest present," Aris announced, "and so I will go first." He didn't move from his position as two presents popped into the air at once, the first falling onto Sylas's lap and the other in Elijah's.

Sylas opened his first, and his lips flattened into a thin line as he lifted a piece of long black silk cloth from the box. It jingled as he held it before him.

"Bells?" Sylas asked. "Really?"

"My brilliant wife suggested that I make gifts by hand this year, and so I've made you an updated cowl for your wardrobe. Finally, we'll be able to hear when you're skulking about."

Blythe sighed. "Don't listen to him, Sylas. I had nothing to do with this."

Sylas fought back a smirk as he rolled his eyes and went to put the cowl back into the box. He stilled, spotting something else inside.

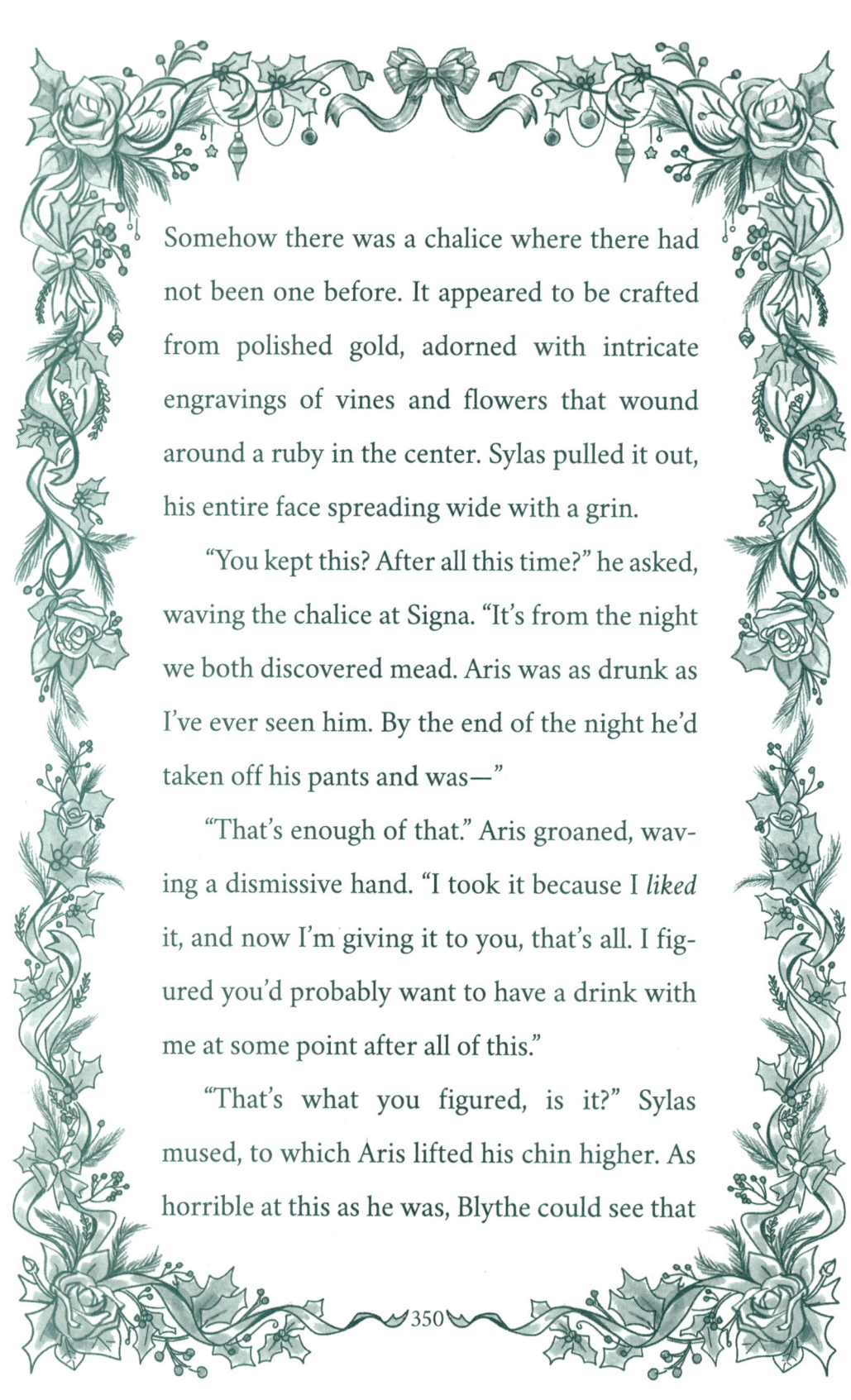

Somehow there was a chalice where there had not been one before. It appeared to be crafted from polished gold, adorned with intricate engravings of vines and flowers that wound around a ruby in the center. Sylas pulled it out, his entire face spreading wide with a grin.

"You kept this? After all this time?" he asked, waving the chalice at Signa. "It's from the night we both discovered mead. Aris was as drunk as I've ever seen him. By the end of the night he'd taken off his pants and was—"

"That's enough of that." Aris groaned, waving a dismissive hand. "I took it because I *liked* it, and now I'm giving it to you, that's all. I figured you'd probably want to have a drink with me at some point after all of this."

"That's what you figured, is it?" Sylas mused, to which Aris lifted his chin higher. As horrible at this as he was, Blythe could see that her husband was trying *so hard* to open himself up.

"I will provide you with a beverage of your choice," he told his brother with a sage nod.

"A *beverage*, you say?"

"Of the alcoholic variety, if you so choose. You may consider it a reward for returning Beasty to me."

Blythe's stomach twisted in her own embarrassment for this ridiculous man. But Sylas, to her dismay, was no better.

"And what if I don't want a reward?" he teased, shadows winding playfully around him. He'd found a dent in Aris's armor, and it appeared he was set to dig until he wore through it.

"Dammit, Sylas. Just have a drink with me—"

Finally having had enough, Blythe pressed

a hand over his mouth. "What my husband is trying to say is *thank you*. Isn't it, Aris?"

She dropped her hand, rolling her eyes as he chewed on the inside of his cheek even then, as though the words were a struggle to get out.

"... Yes," he admitted at last, making a face at the floor. "I suppose I would like to have a drink with you, as we used to. To thank you for Beasty... and for watching over Blythe while I was away." Aris paused for a moment, then added quietly, "Knowing that she had all of you made it easier for me to go."

The room itself was still. Even Sylas remained silent in his surprise for a beat too long, only thrust into a response when Signa elbowed him in the side.

"Of course," he agreed swiftly. "I would like that. Very much."

Oh, thank God. "There," Blythe said with relief. "Was that really so difficult?"

"Remarkably," Aris grumbled. "And I'd love to move on from it immediately. So, Elijah, if you wouldn't mind opening your gifts…"

He did so, first opening a dashing navy suit that Blythe was quite fond of, and an extravagant new tea set from Sylas and Signa. Only a small box remained beside him, and Blythe leaned in to catch a better glimpse as he undid the bow and tore open the delicate gilded wrapping.

Inside the box was a key. Elijah took it between his fingers, inspecting it curiously before he held it up to Aris with a questioning look. "What does it open?"

It seemed a rare day of emotion for Aris, as when he spoke, it was with a quiet tenderness. "I have so much to thank you for. You have

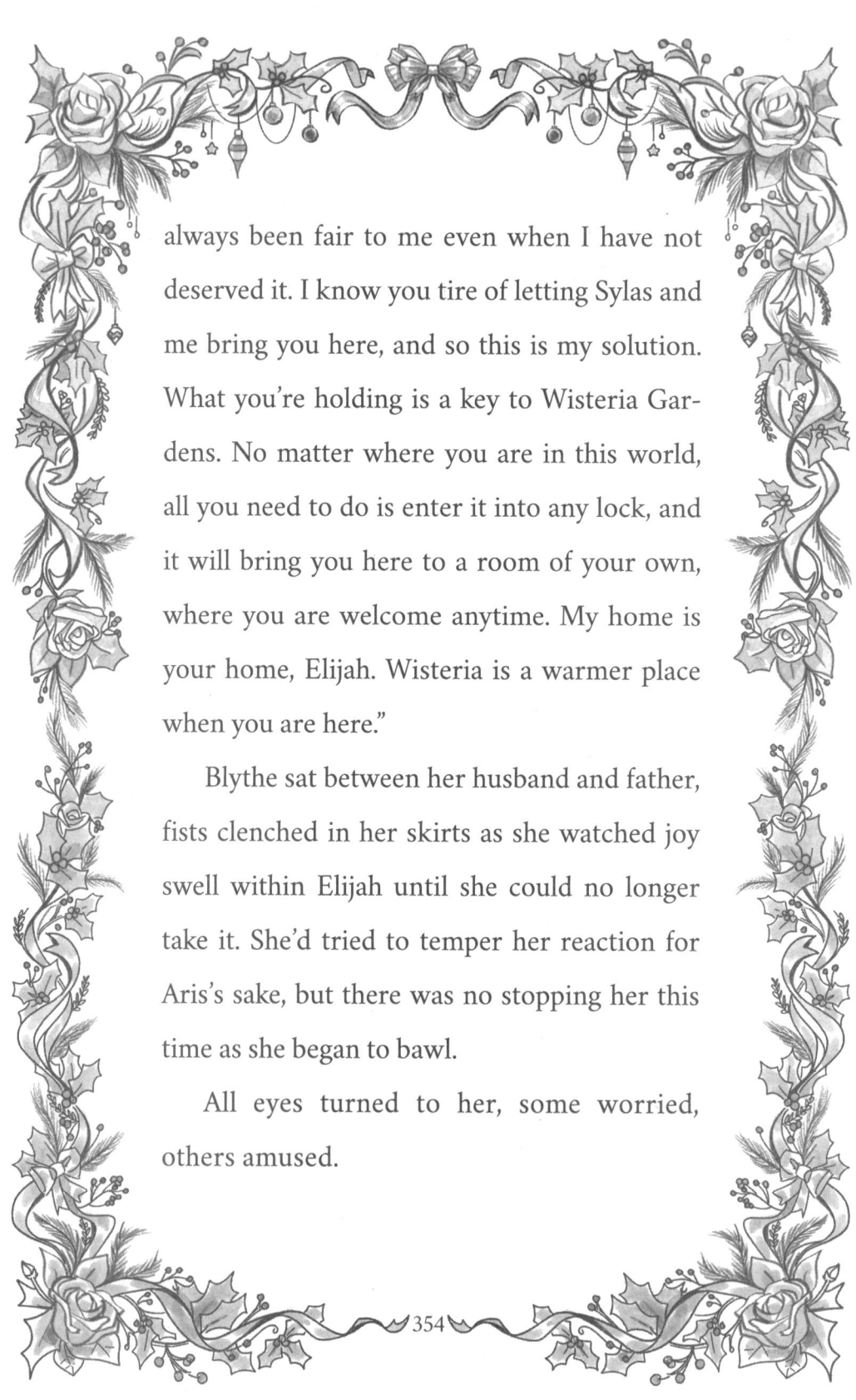

always been fair to me even when I have not deserved it. I know you tire of letting Sylas and me bring you here, and so this is my solution. What you're holding is a key to Wisteria Gardens. No matter where you are in this world, all you need to do is enter it into any lock, and it will bring you here to a room of your own, where you are welcome anytime. My home is your home, Elijah. Wisteria is a warmer place when you are here."

Blythe sat between her husband and father, fists clenched in her skirts as she watched joy swell within Elijah until she could no longer take it. She'd tried to temper her reaction for Aris's sake, but there was no stopping her this time as she began to bawl.

All eyes turned to her, some worried, others amused.

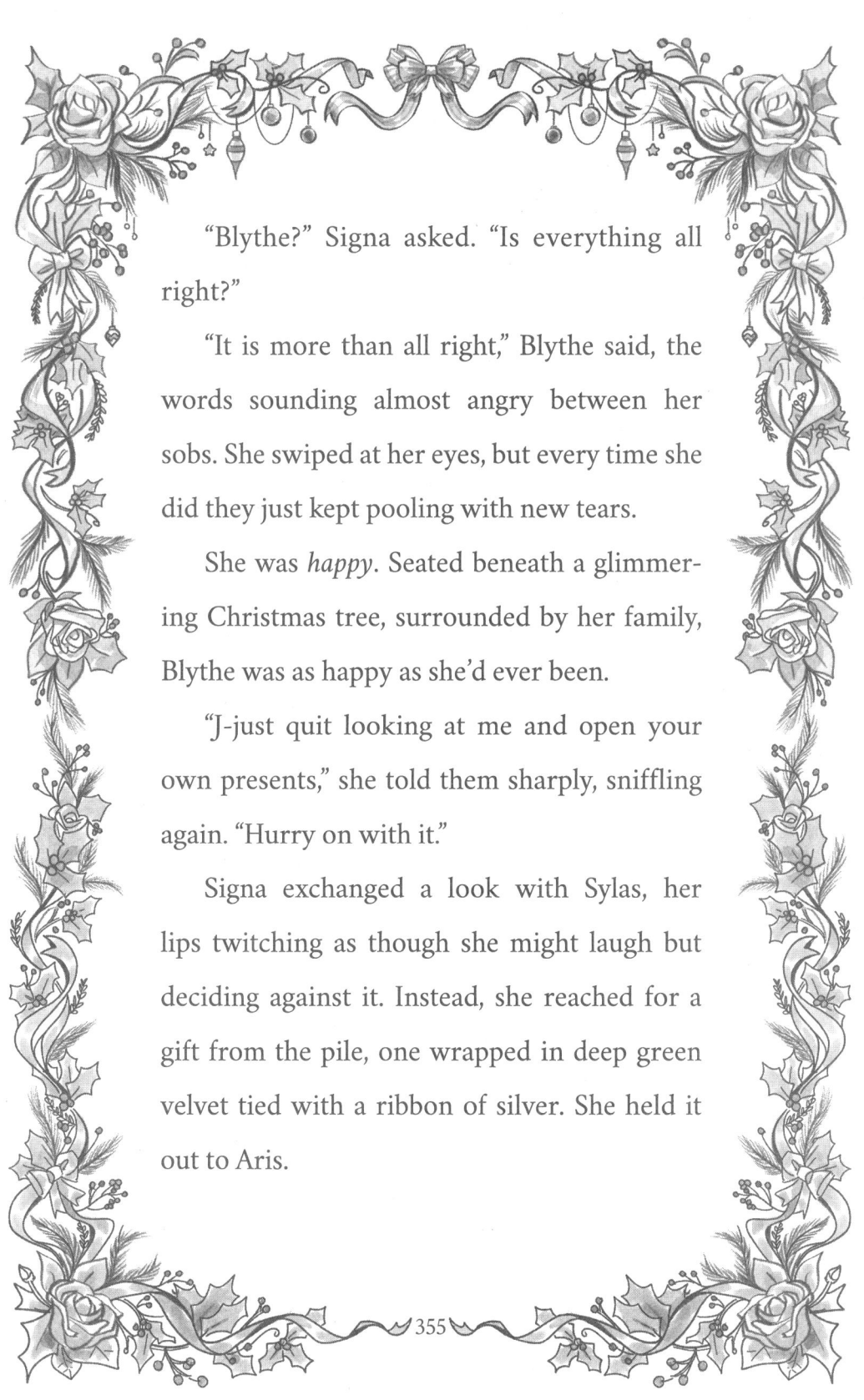

"Blythe?" Signa asked. "Is everything all right?"

"It is more than all right," Blythe said, the words sounding almost angry between her sobs. She swiped at her eyes, but every time she did they just kept pooling with new tears.

She was *happy*. Seated beneath a glimmering Christmas tree, surrounded by her family, Blythe was as happy as she'd ever been.

"J-just quit looking at me and open your own presents," she told them sharply, sniffling again. "Hurry on with it."

Signa exchanged a look with Sylas, her lips twitching as though she might laugh but deciding against it. Instead, she reached for a gift from the pile, one wrapped in deep green velvet tied with a ribbon of silver. She held it out to Aris.

"This is for you," she said.

Aris raised a brow, wary. "You didn't have to—"

"Must you always argue?" Signa pressed the parcel into his hands, and for once, Aris obeyed without further protest. Carefully, he untied the ribbon and peeled back the fabric to reveal a leather-bound sketch pad embossed with a golden needle.

"It's difficult to buy for a family who already has everything," Signa told him, "but I thought maybe you'd get some use out of this. Your dresses are gorgeous, as is everything you do with Wisteria. But since it's always changing, I thought that maybe more of your art could be immortalized here. Or that you could scribble away your notes or sketches or whatnot." Aris flipped through the thick, cream-colored pages, his expression softening as he laughed. Beasty, riled by the sound, stretched lazily in his lap, and he scratched beneath her chin.

"I'll be sure to put it to good use," he said. "You should open yours, Signa."

She did as he asked, eyes narrowed with curiosity as he did not hand her one package but three. The first was a leather-bound journal of simple black, and the second a beautiful quill with a glossy black feather.

"It's enchanted," he told her, materializing a matching journal of his own. "That quill can do many things. For one, it will never run out of ink. And, more importantly, whatever you write in that journal will immediately show up in this one."

He opened it to the first page, waiting for Signa to follow suit. Curious, she wrote a quick *hello* on the page, only for it to appear seconds later in his journal, which he soon handed to Blythe.

"If you ever need to get in touch with either of us, no matter where you are, you may do so through this journal."

Signa grinned, already thinking ahead to all the nights she'd spend by the fire, scribbling notes to Blythe. "This is brilliant, thank you."

"And are we not going to talk about the third gift?" Sylas mused, arching a brow as he held up Signa's gifted copy of *A Lady's Guide to Beauty and Etiquette.* Blythe recognized it as the same etiquette book Signa had with her when she first arrived at Thorn Grove all those years ago, taken from her mother's belongings. This one, however, looked new.

"Really, Aris?" Blythe nudged Aris in the arm before turning to her cousin. "I apologize on my husband's behalf for his poor sense of humor."

Aris, however, did not appear to be teasing.

"I expect that you'll find a good use for it," he told Signa, and Blythe might have thought to press him on it if she hadn't been distracted by the gift that arrived before her. Shadows slipped from it, revealing several long packages as well as a medium-sized box.

"This one's from me," Sylas told her, grinning as Blythe wasted no time tearing into the wrapping. When she saw what was inside, she immediately began to cackle.

"I know what we're playing tonight!" she said, holding up several croquet mallets. Beside her, Aris groaned.

"Dear God, not again..."

Blythe gifted Sylas a small pot of perfectly bloomed deadly nightshade trapped in a small glass container, where it would live forevermore. He seemed fascinated by it, keeping it protected upon his lap. Signa and Blythe continued their tradition of homemade charms to be added to their bracelets—a tiny teacup for Signa, and a golden sprig of wisteria for Blythe.

The room grew warmer, brighter, as the pile of gifts beneath the tree continued to dwindle, Elijah passing out his gifts while Signa helped Gundry unwrap a new leather collar and deer antlers, on which he began chewing right away. By the time the last present was unwrapped, they were all seated close, the glow of the fire mingling with the hazy lights of the tree.

Blythe looked around at her strange, chaotic family—at Signa and Sylas laughing, her father pouring tea from his new set, Aris cooing at his cat—and she smiled through the happy tears that welled in her eyes once more.

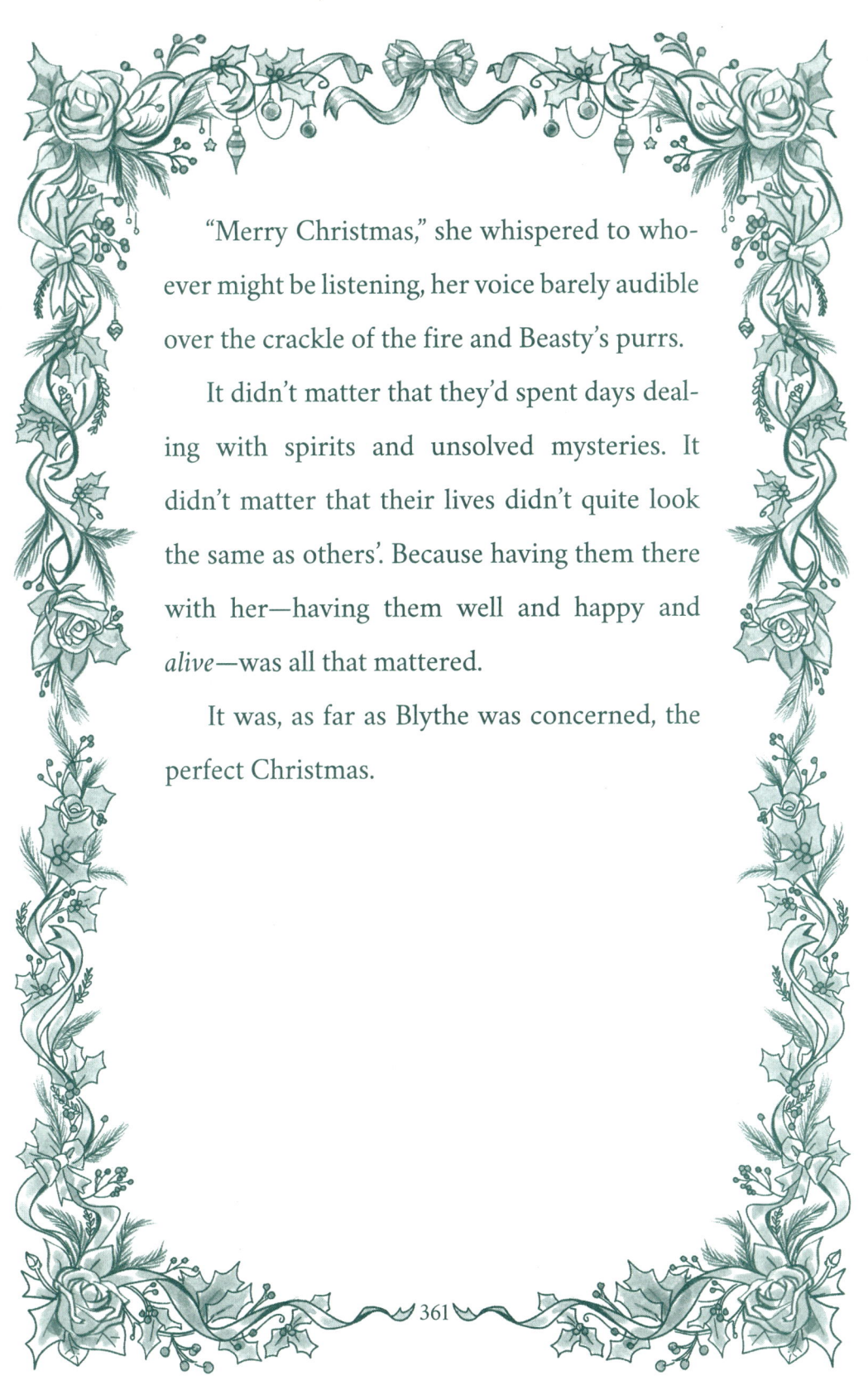

"Merry Christmas," she whispered to whoever might be listening, her voice barely audible over the crackle of the fire and Beasty's purrs.

It didn't matter that they'd spent days dealing with spirits and unsolved mysteries. It didn't matter that their lives didn't quite look the same as others'. Because having them there with her—having them well and happy and *alive*—was all that mattered.

It was, as far as Blythe was concerned, the perfect Christmas.

EPILOGUE

Signa

It was strange how fast a day could pass when a person had spent months anticipating it.

Christmas dinner had come and gone in a cozy haze. With everyone's belly full and spirits high, Blythe had been able to rope the family into several games. Charades had been Signa's favorite, given how deeply Aris despised it while still being determined to win. Cocoa was drunk and cookies eaten, and by the end of the night Elijah rested near the hearth with Blythe slumped beside him. She'd been stubbornly trying to keep herself awake, refusing to acknowledge that Christmas was coming to an end. But now, with only a few minutes left until midnight, she lay snoring beside her father, Beasty curled contentedly between them. Aris had left for his study about an hour prior, and Sylas, for his part, had managed to spend the majority of the day with his family before the souls had claimed him late in the evening. There'd been more of them than Signa cared to see given that it was a holiday, but he hadn't seemed surprised when he stood, gave Signa a kiss, and left to shepherd them on to their next journey.

His disappearance had left Signa alone near the fire, toes curled beneath her as she worked

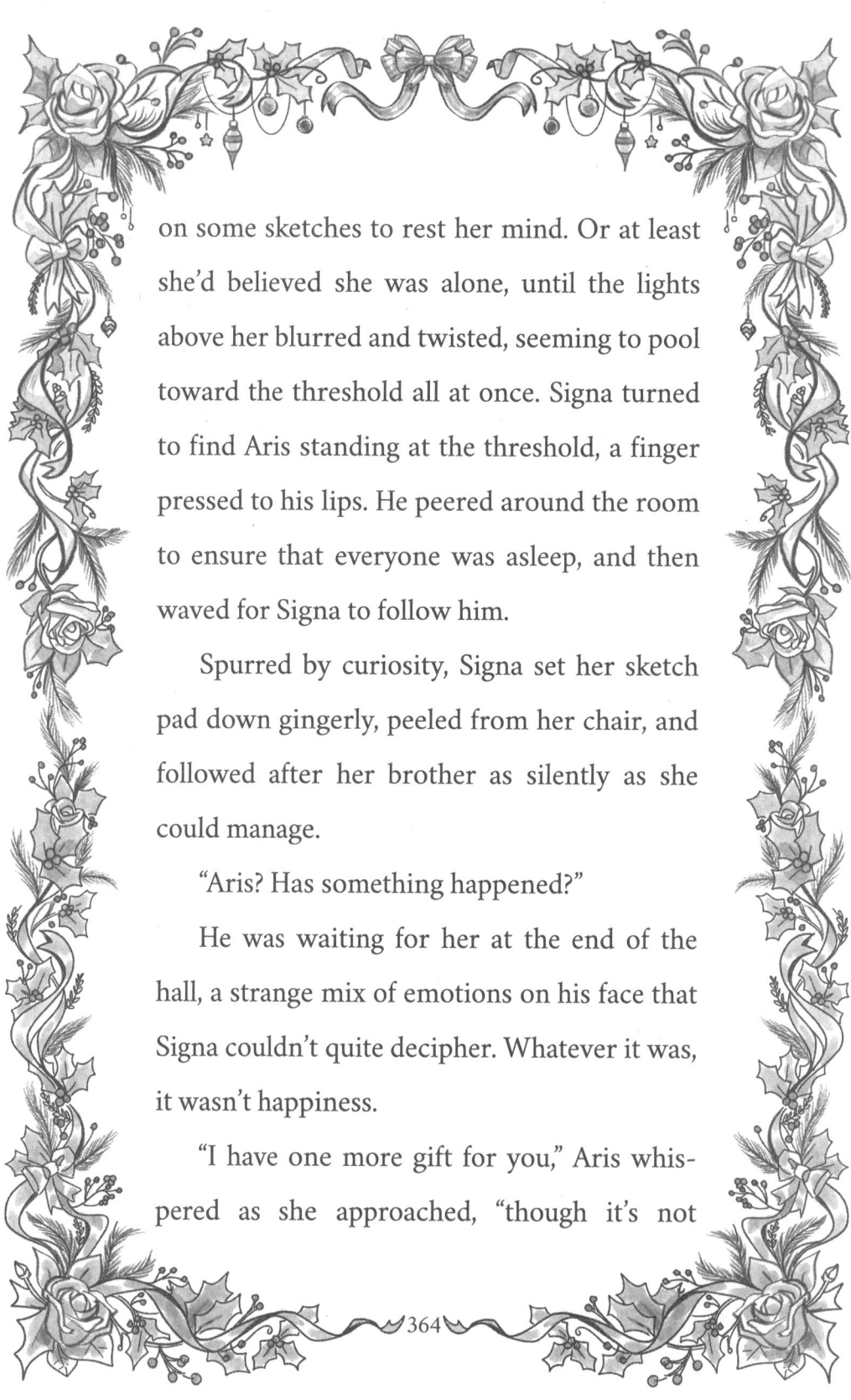

on some sketches to rest her mind. Or at least she'd believed she was alone, until the lights above her blurred and twisted, seeming to pool toward the threshold all at once. Signa turned to find Aris standing at the threshold, a finger pressed to his lips. He peered around the room to ensure that everyone was asleep, and then waved for Signa to follow him.

Spurred by curiosity, Signa set her sketch pad down gingerly, peeled from her chair, and followed after her brother as silently as she could manage.

"Aris? Has something happened?"

He was waiting for her at the end of the hall, a strange mix of emotions on his face that Signa couldn't quite decipher. Whatever it was, it wasn't happiness.

"I have one more gift for you," Aris whispered as she approached, "though it's not something I could give you in front of the others." There was a tension in his voice that captured Signa's attention, and the skin between her brows pinched. His foot kept tapping at the floor, and she couldn't for the life of her figure out why he was so anxious until she noticed that he was holding something small, which he carried with a tender touch.

"I came across this during my travels many centuries ago and have kept it ever since," he told her, thumbing nervously at the package. "I tried to use it back when Mila died, but I couldn't get it to work. Not for me. Still, I kept it, not believing in coincidence. And now... I believe I'm meant to give it to you."

He opened his hand to reveal a small stopwatch unlike any Signa had seen. Its glass face was smooth and faintly domed, with a warm amber tint that seemed to catch and hold the

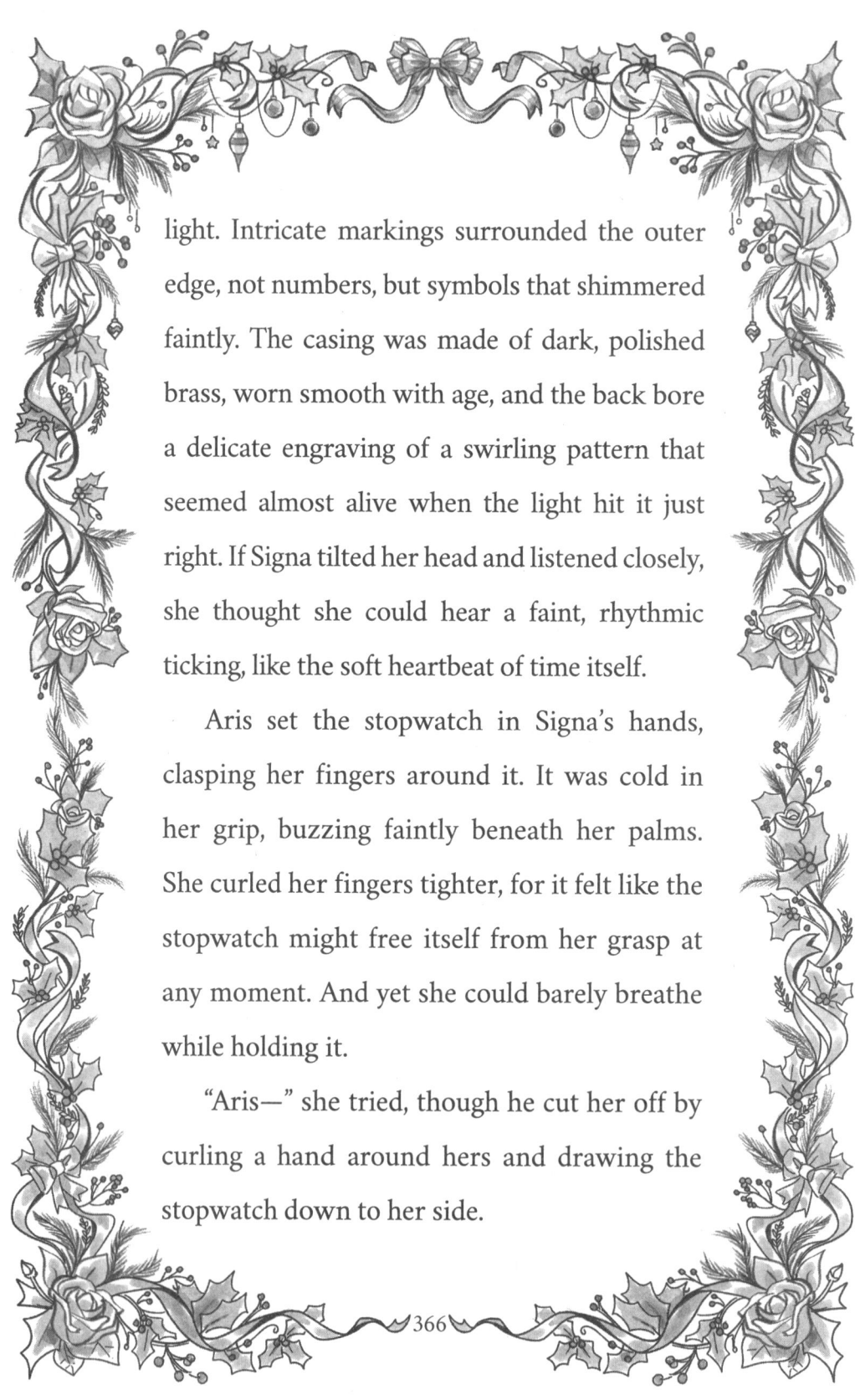

light. Intricate markings surrounded the outer edge, not numbers, but symbols that shimmered faintly. The casing was made of dark, polished brass, worn smooth with age, and the back bore a delicate engraving of a swirling pattern that seemed almost alive when the light hit it just right. If Signa tilted her head and listened closely, she thought she could hear a faint, rhythmic ticking, like the soft heartbeat of time itself.

Aris set the stopwatch in Signa's hands, clasping her fingers around it. It was cold in her grip, buzzing faintly beneath her palms. She curled her fingers tighter, for it felt like the stopwatch might free itself from her grasp at any moment. And yet she could barely breathe while holding it.

"Aris—" she tried, though he cut her off by curling a hand around hers and drawing the stopwatch down to her side.

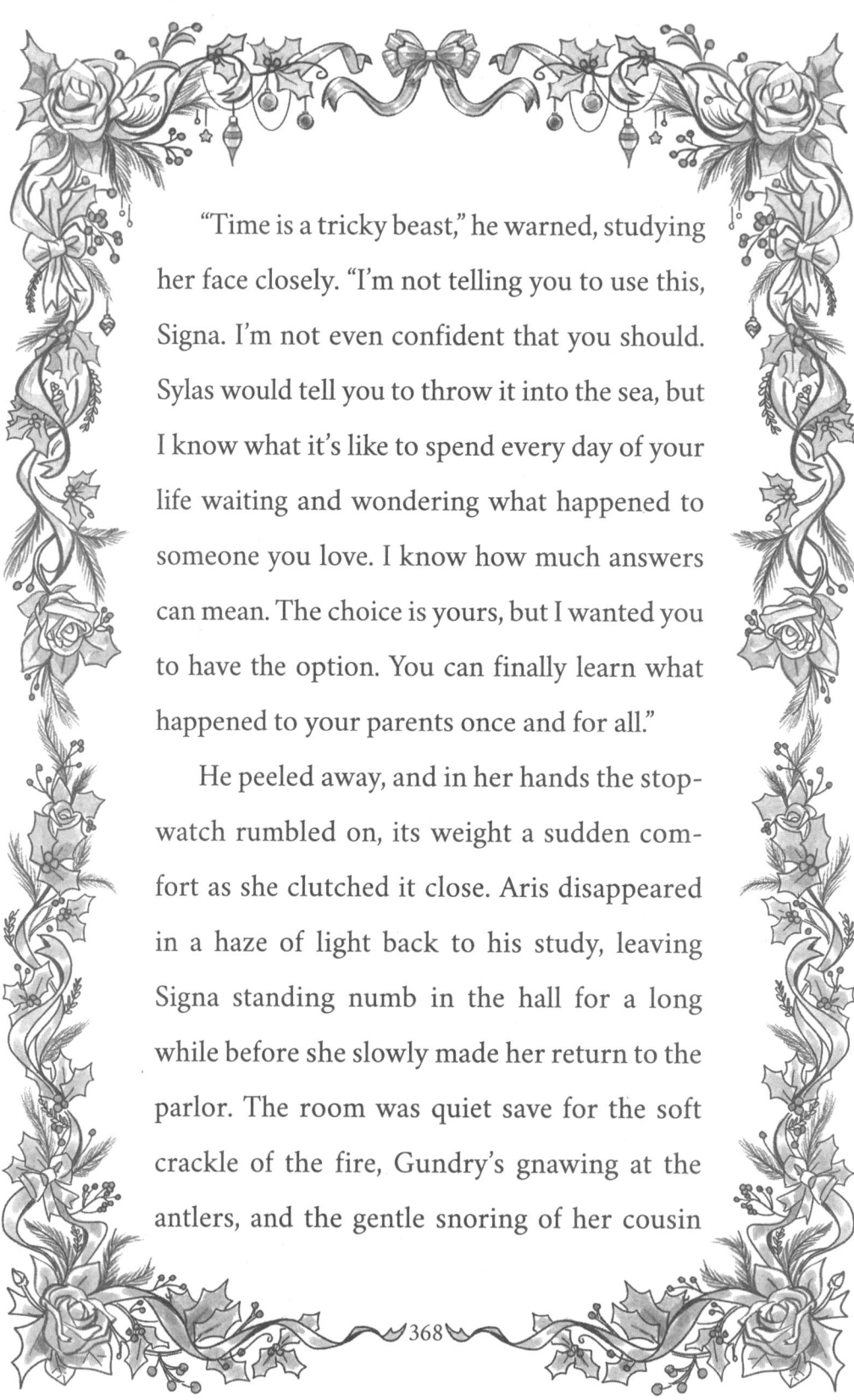

"Time is a tricky beast," he warned, studying her face closely. "I'm not telling you to use this, Signa. I'm not even confident that you should. Sylas would tell you to throw it into the sea, but I know what it's like to spend every day of your life waiting and wondering what happened to someone you love. I know how much answers can mean. The choice is yours, but I wanted you to have the option. You can finally learn what happened to your parents once and for all."

He peeled away, and in her hands the stopwatch rumbled on, its weight a sudden comfort as she clutched it close. Aris disappeared in a haze of light back to his study, leaving Signa standing numb in the hall for a long while before she slowly made her return to the parlor. The room was quiet save for the soft crackle of the fire, Gundry's gnawing at the antlers, and the gentle snoring of her cousin and the cat beside her. This moment, so still and perfect, was a rarity in their lives. And yet, as much as Signa cherished it, she'd long been hungering for more. For answers, and to understand what, exactly, had happened between her mother and Solanine—otherwise known as Chaos.

She glanced out the window, to where the first flakes of snow had begun to drift lazily from the sky, slowly blanketing the world in white. There was a shadow upon that whiteness, one that danced through Wisteria and onto the chaise with Signa, looping an arm comfortably around her.

She slipped the stopwatch into her pocket at Sylas's arrival, careful to keep it out of his reach—for now. She'd tell him about it eventually, once she'd decided what to do. Aris's warnings echoed in her mind, but so did the weight of her curiosity. Perhaps Time *had* refused him for a reason, and perhaps that reason had to do with her. Whatever truths lay hidden in its ticking heart, however, they would have to wait. Tonight was not for unraveling mysteries or chasing ghosts, but for spending the evening with those most precious to her.

The snowflakes continued to drift past the window, their silent fall like a gentle exhale from the world outside. In this moment, as the fire crackled and the scent of evergreen lingered, Wisteria felt whole once more, and so did she. For years Signa had longed to understand her place in this world, but now, surrounded by the family who had given her more love than she'd ever dreamed possible, that hunger softened into something she could bear.

When Sylas pressed a kiss to her cheek,

Signa curled into him, her heart full to the brim. Whatever mysteries tomorrow might bring, they would face them together. But for now, an hour of Christmas still remained, and Signa would not miss it for the world.

ACKNOWLEDGMENTS

In the acknowledgments of *Wisteria*, I told everyone that that was the final book in this series. Happily, I was proven wrong, and I have a lot of people to thank for that:

First and foremost, I want to give all my thanks to you. My being able to write *Holly* was a huge testament to *Belladonna*'s readership, and I'm so thankful to get to share this fun and fluffy story with all of you. This world is my comfort blanket, and I'm eternally grateful that you've continued to allow me to play in it.

Lydia Elaine (aka Lotusbubble), it has been my absolute joy to get to work with you. Your illustrations completely blow me away, and it was an honor to have my characters brought to life by your hand. You are such a talent, and

I'm thrilled that you agreed to help bring this book to life. You've created everything I hoped for and more.

Teagan White and Elena Masci, for the most gorgeous covers I could have asked for. I don't know how, but somehow they keep getting more and more stunning with each book.

Kristin Atherton, whose audiobook narration has continued to astound me. You are the perfect voice for this series, and magnificent at what you do.

To everyone at Hachette US and UK, for taking a chance on *Holly*. I know I have all sorts of ideas I throw at you, but I can't tell you how much it means to me to have a team who actually listens and helps bring them to life.

Deirdre Jones, for not only being a fabulous editor but also for being such a huge advocate. This series would not be the same without you.

Cheryl Lew, publicity director extraordinaire, I'm so grateful to get to work with you, and for everything you do.

Jenny Kimura, associate art director, for helping create the book of my dreams. You have continually made these books so much more beautiful than I ever could have imagined.

Bethan Morgan and the Orion team, for taking over this series as its new UK publisher. I couldn't feel better about having it in your hands, and I'm incredibly thankful for the opportunity to work with all of you.

The Little, Brown team—Savannah Kennelly, Jessica Levine, Stefanie Hoffman, Emilie Polster, Alvina Ling, Megan Tingley, Jackie Engel, Danielle Cantarella, Victoria Stapleton, Sasha Illingworth, Mary McCue, Marisa Finkelstein, JoAnna Kremer, Chandra Wohleber, Starr Baer, and Jody Corbett—for all your hard work bringing this book to life and getting it into the hands of readers, and for changing my life with this series.

Anissa and the Fairyloot team, for the stunning editions and for being such an amazing team of advocates. You're a huge reason this series has the UK audience it does.

All the foreign publishers for this series at the time I'm writing this (Urano, De Saxus, Eksmo, Artemis Milenyum, Corint, Ikar, Yoli, VR Editora, Rizzoli Libri, Foksal, Clube do Autor, Vivat, Ciela, Konyvmoly), for being wonderful partners and for giving my books a home in your beautiful countries.

At my agency, Park, Fine & Brower:

Peter Knapp, the greatest agent I could possibly ask

for. For being a brilliant second brain for all my schemes and for making my dreams come true. I couldn't imagine working with anyone else.

Kathryn Toolan, whose emails never fail to excite me and who has been an absolute powerhouse at selling these books throughout the world and helping them get translated into so many different languages.

Emily Sweet, Stuti Telidevara, Andrea Mai, and Danielle Barthel, for being brilliant strategists and the best partners. I got incredibly lucky when I landed with all of you.

Mysterious Galaxy, for being the greatest team of booksellers, and for the amazing work you've done handling preorders for this series. You all are such champions.

Rachel Griffin, for being one of the earliest readers for this series and letting me bounce ideas for everyone's Christmas presents off of you. I think it's time we had more soup.

Bri Renae, whom this book is dedicated to, for being the earliest believer that a Christmas book for this series would one day happen. We talked about it back in 2022, but you were far more convinced than I was.

Stephanie Garber, whose *Spectacular* paved the path

for me to do an illustrated Christmas story and for proving there's an audience for it. Also, I just think you're pretty great.

Josh, for being a wonderful and supportive partner and dog dad, and for your patience whenever I turn into a gremlin and disappear into my writing cave.

My parents, for continuing to be my biggest fans and support.

The street team, for sticking with me this long, for your invaluable feedback and excitement, and for keeping every behind-the-scenes secret I share with you all.

Every friend and family member who has supported me throughout my writing career and in my real life. Please know that I greatly appreciate and am so thankful for all of you.

Finally, thank you to God, bossam, Kaylie not Kay, badminton, my dogs, *Fields of Mistria*, and anime. This was the first book I wrote while simultaneously drafting another, and these were the MVPs that helped me get through the everyday life of it all.